A Row of Beans

An Allotment Murder
Mystery

Robert Irvine

New Generation Publishing

Dedicated to my wife, Barbara.

ROBERT IRVINE has had a variety of teaching and office jobs, including working for the Department of Trade and Industry until privatisation led him to join the commercial world, working for an audio-visual distributor called Steljes Ltd, from which he retired at the age of sixty-five. He has also held many voluntary posts in his local Anglican church, not least being a churchwarden.

He has travelled a lot, visiting unusual places as diverse as the remote parts of Iceland and Borneo, where he stayed in a longhouse only accessible by river. He has driven through Death Valley, climbed Ayers Rock in Australia, and driven alone to such disparate places as Nordkapp, the northernmost point of Europe, and Rome.

He has done a lot of hillwalking in Scotland and is a Fellow of the Royal Geographical Society.

He is Membership Secretary of the James Caird Society, which honours the memory of the explorer, Sir Ernest Shackleton.

He lives in Twickenham and has been married to Barbara for thirty-six years. They have two grown-up children, Peter, aged thirty-three and Amy, aged thirty-one.

This is Robert Irvine's first published work with New Generation Publishing for Phaedon Media

A ROW OF BEANS – CHAPTER LIST

CHAPTER 1

(Helen finds the victim)

Helen Archer opened the door of her dilapidated old shed and screamed. It was a loud, long piercing scream. Then she turned and ran past the row of beans, twined round their wigwam bamboo structures and strengthening in the August sun, down the side of her allotment, and the one beyond to the central path, where she turned right at the water tank and continued to the entrance gate. She was unaware of the resident of one of the three houses at the end of her allotment, who opened her window and stared out in alarm at her fleeing figure; she was also unaware of the three people who had been working on their allotments and who now stood staring with open mouths.

With the exception of the last hundred yards, which she was compelled to walk, having become so puffed by her unaccustomed speed, she had run all the quarter mile way home. She grabbed the phone and rang the police. At last there was someone on the line asking her what had happened. She reported the facts, still breathless after her running.

"The police will be with you very shortly," the voice said, with what Helen felt was a slightly disingenuous parting, "thank you for reporting it."

She immediately rang her husband at his office and again reported her horrifying experience to him. He kept saying, "How extraordinary!" and, "How amazing!" and, "I can't believe what I'm hearing." She in turn kept saying, "I will have to ring off the minute the police come."

Detective Sergeant Hughes arrived and surprised Helen by seeming so cheery, as if he was thinking, this is more like it, this is more interesting. However, he was businesslike. He introduced his colleague, Detective Constable Harrison, who seemed to undress her with his eyes, and then, patting the said Detective Constable Harrison on the back, turned to Helen and said, "Come with us and we'll go straight there, and you can show us everything and then I'll bore you silly with questions."

She got in the back of the car, still shaking a bit, and again unaware that neighbours on both sides of her little terraced house were looking at proceedings with interest. She was eager to show the police the horrifying scene, and frustrated by the slowness of West London's suburban traffic. When they arrived and parked, everything appeared as normal, though the entrance gate was still unlocked, and the three people who had been working on their allotments were now in a huddle of conversation on the central path. On seeing the police, they all three came up to join the party. One of them, who introduced himself as Charles, spoke out loud and clear, "I'm in charge here. I was wondering if we can help. We heard you scream; we've been looking around but can't find what the problem is."

"I'll want to speak to you later," said Hughes, adding, "just now, please leave this lady with me and my colleague for a few minutes."

Helen led Hughes down the central path to the water tank and then left past the first allotment and on to hers. "This is mine," she said as she marched on towards the dilapidated shed, which stood forlornly at the end, alongside a back garden fence. She pulled the door open, and like a triumphant conjuror, said, "There!"

Detective Sergeant Hughes peered through the open door of the shed and reeled back. "You never get used to this sort of thing. Oh, how awful!" he uttered. He appeared to brace himself for a second look, which he took within seconds.

The scene that lay before him was horrific. The blood that had seeped from the victim covered the floor of the shed. The several gaping wounds, which appeared to be stab wounds, had already attracted a number of flies, which added to the scene of carnage.

He gestured to Detective Constable Harrison to see for himself, reminding him not to touch or interfere with anything.

As Hughes radioed for back-up, Harrison too recoiled, saying, "Not nice, not nice at all", gagging at the pervasive, heavy stench of blood.

Helen looked at Hughes, feeling much more comfortable now that the police knew what she had seen. She was shaking a little less, and waited for him to speak; but he only said, "That's nasty, that is," and pulled out his notebook before adding, "we'll get to the bottom of this. I'm sure we will."

***

Mrs Martin, whose house overlooked Helen Archer's allotment and indeed whose end fence it was that stood alongside the dilapidated shed, had heard the scream too. She stood paralysed for a moment at her open window and then picked up the telephone receiver and made an emergency call to the police.

"I have absolutely no doubt it's some kind of an emergency," she stressed, aware that her voice was trembling. "It was the most horrifying, piercing scream that I have ever heard, and the woman was running away so fast. I feel certain it is a matter for the police."

Her emergency telephone call over, she sat down in her bedroom chair with her head in her hands, which were still shaking. She felt sure she had been right to phone. So many silly people, she thought, do nothing, and then it is too late. She would make some coffee. She had done her bit, and her address and phone number had been accurately registered.

When the knock on the door came, Mrs Martin just knew it was the police. Confidently she went down the hall and opened the front door.

Moments later, she was pointing out of her bedroom window, showing, as she thought, a rather handsome policeman the view she had and all she had seen. When she had run through her story at least three times and the policeman had checked her details at least three times as well, the policeman had invited her to accompany him to the allotment.

"I'll just take a photograph of the view from your window," he said. "Ah, as I thought, my colleagues are already down there. I suggest we go round and join them."

CHAPTER 2

(A year later)

A year later, Helen stood at her kitchen door and allowed herself to indulge in some deep thought about what she, her husband and many others had come to call 'the case'.

How those words of Detective Sergeant Hughes - "We'll get to the bottom of this" - still rang in her ears! But how unfulfilled they were.

Now, after twelve months, it seemed like the police had drawn a complete blank. The publicity had been over the top, with national papers publishing one false suggestion after another, and now those same papers were being threatened with libel charges by several people. There had even been days when there was a thinly disguised implication that she herself must have been the murderer, and one day when even her husband had beamed out from the front page of a tabloid with the heading, 'Why did she phone him?' The hullabaloo had been quite extraordinary, but now today there were other cases on people's minds and lips; the free newspapers that littered the Underground had new, and in their different ways, equally bizarre crimes to analyse from every angle.

For the first time it seemed to Helen that ever so gradually time was beginning to wash the case onto the shores of history. She thought of all the things that had happened since the crime. Her neighbour's baby had cut a first tooth; a child had been born across the road at Number 42; little Johnny at school had finally learnt his six times table; even a new planet had been discovered, and indeed a new astronaut in space had powered round the earth, which was itself ceaselessly turning.

When the phone rang interrupting her reflections, she broke the unwritten rule - which had surreptitiously arisen among the locals - of not talking about the subject. It was the victim's husband, Dennis Carr. She was always glad to hear from him. Originally she hadn't known much about Dennis, other than he was aged 47 and that he was a chartered surveyor, who seemed very preoccupied with his work, to the point that many in the parish had called him the invisible man. In her attempts to comfort him, she had got to know him better. He certainly looked now a lot older than Henrietta, when she had celebrated her 40th birthday so soon before tragedy struck.

"Do you know, Dennis," she said, "I'm beginning to think telepathy is so common it shouldn't really be regarded as paranormal – I really was just about to ring you. I wanted to discuss the case with you - they've really drawn a complete blank, haven't they?"

"Yes, they've as good as admitted it to me in so many words, Helen. That's exactly why I'm ringing. I'm going to tell you this straightaway and I know it must sound totally crazy, but I want you to know and understand. I've been seriously thinking of employing a private detective."

"Well, who can blame you, Dennis?" she cut in.

"But Helen, this one's a really private one, if you know what I mean. This guy is a friend, an old friend of mine, someone with a first-rate brain and someone I have a lot of confidence in. I'll tell you about him."

She settled back in a chair, stretching the telephone cord and letting her fingers play with it; it was a good moment for him to have rung. She had a bit of free time and a good old natter about the case was long overdue.

"Tell all, Dennis… By the way, you know everyone is so full of admiration for the way you've stood up to it all."

Dennis ignored this compliment and went straight to the point.

"This guy who I'm seriously thinking of employing – he's called Alistair MacTavish. I'll tell you about him. Where shall I begin? He's an incredibly enthusiastic private detective; he's so private he really just works on his own."

He would have liked her to say "Carry on", but when she did not he continued anyway.

"I met him yonks ago when I was on an airport bus in Washington going from the airport to a hotel. He had a collection of short detective stories in his hand, which I commented on, and he said he fancied himself as a sleuth.

"We kept in touch ever since, and he became a good friend of Henrietta and me. Whenever I reminded him how he had had that book of detective stories on him when we first met, he used to half-jokingly ask, 'Well, have you got any good mysteries for me to solve?' Do you know, the Christmas before she died" (somehow it helped not referring to his late wife by her first name and not to use words like 'killed' or 'murdered'), "we got a Christmas card from him and - you won't believe it - he actually put 'Got any mysteries for me to solve yet?'. It's so spooky; I showed it to the police and they said that's so weird they almost felt like checking him out."

"What made you think of him just now?" Helen asked, while Dennis allowed himself an unaccustomed laugh. She added, "Why are you telling me this right now? Surely the police wouldn't approve of this guy – bit too amateurish, isn't he, Dennis?"

"Well, I got this card from him a couple of days ago, and I've been chewing over it. You know, although he's a total amateur he has actually had one or

13

two successes in solving very much lesser crimes, and did actually get commended by the police on one occasion for assisting them in solving a somewhat more serious one. I have this very odd feeling that he just might be the chap to help at this point. I mean, I'll get a proper firm of private detectives on to it later on, but in this sort of gap after the great blank the police have drawn, I honestly feel it's not such a crazy thing to ask him to carry out a kind of private investigation. I mean there's nothing to lose by asking him, is there?"

"I know you're being serious Dennis," Helen began. "I can tell it in your voice, but -"

"Look, Helen," Dennis cut in, "I'm being serious, so let's meet up, eh? When can you come round? You see, there are things to tell you. I've already mooted the idea with the police, and the gaffer there said, 'Well, I don't blame you.' Yeah, they say they don't blame me, and that they'd try anything if they were in my shoes."

Helen did not need much persuading to pop over for a coffee and was soon on her way.

Although she was familiar with the vicarage, she had that usual initial thought on arrival, The clergy really do themselves quite well. If only Edwin and I had as much space. No more storage problems...

And wonderful to have so much space to park, she thought, as she walked across the large forecourt. She admired yet again the rather grand porch.

Dennis threw the front door open with great gusto and welcomed her with a slight bow.

Within a few minutes she was being made to feel at home in the large, comfortable drawing room, and was rather revelling in the change of routine and the unusual pleasure of being served hot coffee and biscuits. However, she still could not drown her envy of so much space compared with her own crowded house.

"Interregnums can last for ages at the best of times,

but this one is officially only just starting now," said Dennis earnestly, as if to show how serious he was about his new idea. "As you know, the bishop's been incredibly supportive, but he rang yesterday and said the normal procedure of selecting a new incumbent to replace Henrietta will start in earnest now. 'Dear old Bish', as Henrietta used to call him - he was very sympathetic as usual, but he was saying we need a very special type of person to take over in these circumstances."

He stared out of the window, and rather to Helen's surprise, his eyes began to water and his lip quivered.

"I know the bishop is a sincere man," Dennis began again, "but you know he used that exact phrase when Henrietta took over. I don't know … there had been some talk of the previous guy, Maurice, being such a hard act to follow. At the time it seemed like such a nice compliment to Henrietta, and meant so much to both of us; now I wonder whether he doesn't just say that to everybody."

He turned round sharply as if dismissing thoughts from his mind, "Anyway, it's there on the mantelpiece – that card from Toronto – that's from Alistair, read it."

Helen jumped up, took it down and admired for a few moments the city skyline, which it depicted. Then, turning it over and still standing by the mantelpiece, she asked, "May I?" Without waiting for a reply she began to read :

Hi Dennis,
Having a great holiday here – lovely city, been up the tower of course and awestruck by Niagara Falls. Yonge Street sure is the longest street in the world – it's just a very nice city with very friendly people. Writing this on an island in the lake – so peaceful. Got something I'd like to share with you – think it may be important. Any

chance of meeting up with you when in London en route home? Will give you a buzz on arrival, Yours Alistair.

P.S: You ain't going to believe this, but something to tell you re that bet we made in Liverpool.

Helen returned the card to the mantelpiece and propped the card up against the little ornament there.

"What's that about a bet in Liverpool?" she asked with genuine interest.

"Oh yes, I was startled to read that, but that's one thing that will never happen. He bet me he would never get married. I said, 'I bet you do,' but I didn't mean it. He's the eternal bachelor – just not the marrying kind."

"Oh well, you never can tell....."

"He's definitely taking his time. He's forty-six, I think."

She laughed, but then assumed a serious expression.

"You know, I've got to be honest with you, Dennis. When you first raised the subject of private detectives, I thought you meant a proper, official private detective, if you know what I mean." She laughed and added, "You know, some firm that at least advertises in the telephone directory."

Dennis laughed, "Yes, I know it must appear slightly ridiculous, and I'm aware it's a ridiculous thing to say, but the postcard arrived literally a couple of hours or so after the idea first came to me that really I ought to employ a private detective. Do you believe in that sort of thing? Coincidence, or rather *not* coincidence? Anyway, I rang the gaffer at the police and told him about my idea, and I've told you what the reaction was. Doesn't blame me, Helen."

She looked out of the window as if she was weighing the question up, while Dennis looked at her with eyes that betrayed an affection not entirely appropriate towards a married lady. He seemed to be thinking long and hard before changing tack. "I mean, by their own admission the police are getting nowhere. They went on and on about how there's no evidence against anyone; how there's no CCTV footage, no this, no that. They've actually told me, officially so to speak, that they have no breakthrough. Helen, I don't mind telling you, I cried when they told me that."

Helen sighed. "Well, I certainly agree that in a sense the more people who apply their minds to it the better, because frankly the danger is that everyone is stopping to apply their minds. But surely, Dennis, I would have thought you would want the very best sort of private detective firm with a great reputation and a proven track record."

Dennis continued to stare ahead in his now usual rather morose manner before saying, "Well, I'm glad to hear you say that you're at least in favour of a private detective in principle, and of course hiring an official professional firm will be my very next move after giving Alistair a chance to crack it. Oh Helen, I've been worrying that you'd think I'd taken leave of my senses! It means a lot to me that you approve – that you understand."

She knew he liked her a lot. She had told her husband that she could tell it by his eyes, and Edwin had gone into a storm of jealousy, which had taken days to abate. This had surprised her, not least because she thought she was beginning to lose her charms now in middle age.

"I mean, Dennis, this friend of yours," she began, trying to keep it businesslike, "he really does sound like a complete amateur. Would he have any idea about how to go about this? Would he know where to start?"

Dennis gazed into his coffee cup.

"As I said, he's had the odd success with helping the

police over the years, and on that one occasion received a really warm commendation from them for, as they put it, his invaluable help with the all important breakthrough."

He played with the coffee spoon a bit before looking up and saying, "I mean that's a pretty good recommendation, isn't it? The fact that the police commended him like that."

She nodded, but remained silent as she noticed his eyes had now changed to show slight initial signs of tearfulness again.

An angel is passing, she thought, aware that the silence had continued rather too long.

He looked up and said quite abruptly, "I'll reiterate, I just feel the police have got nowhere with what you might call the scientific approach, and maybe we need a kind of opposite sort of approach."

"Non-scientific, you mean?" Helen smiled at him sympathetically.

"Well, exactly. Someone with a good knowledge of human behaviour and someone going more on hunch, if you know what I mean. The police are experts at the scientific approach and we're still at square one."

She had thought for a moment that he was cheering up a bit, but again the tears came to his eyes before he continued. "I so want to get to the truth of what happened. It would help so much. I never really understood what people meant by closure but I see now how knowing the truth of what happened would be so helpful. I could never understand people saying that before my tragedy, but now I most certainly do."

"I think I can understand," replied Helen sympathetically, adding, "I've heard about and read about how once you have closure you can try and move on and rebuild your life more easily."

She wondered whether to say more or not, but

finally added, "I know it must be hard for you to accept, but is it any comfort that there are other people out there with similar terrible crosses to bear. The papers are full now of this poor mother looking for her missing child. We are not alone in our tribulation on this earth, Dennis."

'Tribulation' was a word her husband, Edwin, the churchwarden had used a lot recently, and it seemed appropriate.

Whether Dennis was registering her words or not, she wasn't sure, as he seemed lost in thought. Finally he looked up again and said, "You see the good thing is that this chap, Alistair, is not only highly intelligent and able and got this rather good track record, but he's had to take early retirement. He's got all the time in the world, and I know he wouldn't demand payment. I'm almost certain he hit the jackpot somehow – I don't know if it was the lottery, or maybe he's got some incredibly rich relative that he's never told me about - but anyway he appears to have got enough cash to do what he likes. He appears to be able to swan off travelling whenever he wants, and seems to be able to stay for as long as he likes in this little hotel which his brother runs over that way towards the airport. He told me once that his interest in detective work is simply a desire to get to the truth about things, and that's what I want, Helen – just the truth. That's all I'm asking for."

He put down his coffee cup, put his head in his hands and started to sob.

Helen knew from experience it was best not to react too much to this manifestation of grief. He hadn't been like this for some time, but the anniversary of the tragedy and the fleeting references to it in the newspapers, and particularly the local newspaper, had brought about a relapse in his efforts to cope. She waited a little bit, and then with her eye cocked inquired, "Is this Alistair MacTavish a church person?"

"No Helen, he isn't; that's one truth he hasn't got to the bottom of, eh?"

Helen played with the coffee spoon in silence.

"Yet," Dennis added, "you never know, he might learn a lot about the church if he took this particular mystery on; I suppose anything's possible – anything. Alistair, the born bachelor, could get married; Alistair the born sceptic could become a Christian."

"I suppose it doesn't matter having someone who is ignorant of church life investigating a vicar's murder," intervened Helen. "I had thought it might help him, but maybe paradoxically it's good to have a complete outsider, so to speak."

Dennis changed his wistful focus from straight in front to through the window. "Isn't it one of those cases," he continued, "where there is no harm in someone having a crack at it? You know, doing a bit of work on it. I mean, it's not going to interfere with the police. To be honest, I reckon they've put the whole thing on hold with a view to closing the case one day. This would be a real fresh start - someone with a completely fresh mind - and a very good mind, I might add. I don't think I've emphasised that enough to you."

"And if people know he's got your sanction to shuffle around making enquiries …" Helen put in.

"Yes, of course I'll have to make that clear to all concerned, and stress to them that the police do *not* disapprove, and that I have asked him to make some discreet enquiries with their permission."

He interrupted himself. "Yes, I feel he's got the time, the money and the energy - and quite honestly, the enthusiasm."

He interrupted himself again. "It's not like just employing any old Tom, Dick or Harry, is it?"

There was a silence while Helen wondered if actually it was just that, and Dennis got up and moved to the door.

"I know he'd investigate so carefully and thoroughly – very analytically - and yet, which I think is the important new approach required, he is a great one for hunches. Told me that himself." He ended with a shrug of the shoulders.

"We don't need to make a big thing of it," Helen called after him as he went off to the kitchen to find more coffee.

She got up and stood in the doorway and, raising her voice a bit, called out to him across the hall, "To be honest Dennis, I was a bit worried at first that you were employing any old Tom, Dick and Harry, but do you know, I think you've persuaded me! But do let those who need to know, realise that he has your approval. That is important, otherwise people just won't cooperate; and make sure they know that the police don't object. That's important too. I mean, I wouldn't cooperate if I didn't think the police approved."

Dennis returned with a tray of new plates, biscuits and coffee, which after years of being a vicar's husband he was more than proficient at handling.

"Yes," he said as he placed these refreshments carefully on the little coffee table. "You see, I keep coming back to the fact that what you might call the normal channels haven't achieved any kind of breakthrough."

"Quite agree," Helen nodded. "When you think about it, it's kind of a classic case of starting over – don't the Americans have that phrase?" She raised her coffee cup and added, "Here's to a completely different and fresh approach."

"I'm so glad to hear you say that, Helen," Dennis responded, with his eyes beginning to light up again, "because sometimes I think I'm going crazy myself. You know, to even contemplate such a remote chance – it's kind of clutching at straws, isn't it? I mean the police must be such experts, with all their experience – it's the British police, for goodness sake! We're not in some remote fly-blown corner of the world. How, how, how come they've drawn such a complete blank?"

"It is clutching at straws, but…" interjected Helen with a smile.

"But what?" Dennis pressed.

"…Well, you know what you said about hunches. Well, I kind of have a hunch that if this tragedy is solved, it's going to be solved by someone like this friend of yours - this Alistair. I wouldn't have said that throughout this whole year, but now after a year – a year in which we've got absolutely nowhere – oh, Dennis, go on, sign him up, and tell the old boy, as you call him, that he's got your approval to try and fathom out what happened. I'm longing to meet him."

"Right, I'll have to wait for him to make contact now – wait for his 'buzz', as he referred to it in his postcard. When was it written?" He got up and checked the date and the postmark on it before continuing, "It can't be long before he's back. I mean he's already gone to the top of the tower and been to Niagara Falls, and knowing him probably walked further up Yonge Street than anyone else in the history of modern Canada."

"He should be making contact any moment now, eh?"

"Well, you'll be the first to know when he does," said Dennis, giving her a lengthy smile, which as usual betrayed his feelings for her.

"Of course, he might very well not want to take it on, but then again I suppose he might," she said, feeling the usual need to bring Dennis back to earth.

"Oh, if I know Alistair, he won't be able to resist this," he replied. "He'll want to take it on, if he possibly can."

Then she gave him one of those smiles which she shouldn't, really, and it made him think her husband was a lucky man. It had the effect of making him ask, "How's Edwin?"

"Oh, he's fine. Said the other day he was back to being able to concentrate at the office and putting it all in perspective. I don't know if it helps, Dennis, but as you know, unlike me, Edwin's a great believer in prayer, and told me he prays for you every day. Well, actually he said every night!" she added with a laugh.

"Well, that means a lot to me," he responded, adding, "Edwin's a great fellow and you're both lucky people."

"Well, of course, I think so. If anything happened to him, I don't know how I could carry on; so I really, really, really feel for you Dennis."

Dennis gave a little bow and she got up to go.

She wondered whether he would kiss her. He did not always, but this had been a closer conversation than usual.

"Well, bye now, and good luck with engaging Alistair," were her parting words.

"Well, again, Helen, you'll be the first to know if he does agree to take it on," was his final comment. "And if he doesn't, I'll take your advice and get a proper firm of private detectives onto the job. Have a kiss before you go."

CHAPTER 3

(A romantic holiday for an unsuspecting private detective)

Some weeks prior to Dennis's conversation with Helen, the character he had referred to had set off on a much anticipated holiday of a lifetime. Alistair MacTavish was planning to celebrate his good fortune at both inheriting a handsome bequest from an enigmatic aunt, and an equally handsome lottery win, by spending a week in Chicago and then flying on to Toronto for "a further week plus some", as he phrased it.

For once there was nothing to worry about, and a feeling of contentment, such as he could hardly remember in his forty-six years of life on earth, came over him. The worst that could happen was that the plane would crash, and that was beyond his control. He sat back and relaxed even more; some cheery baggage handlers outside on the tarmac waved to him. He smiled, gave them a thumbs up sign, and leant even further back.

Yes, life had been very good to him. It was time to count his blessings.

Although it still hurt, the tangled complications of his first romance and unrequited love, which he realised had resulted in him becoming a caricature of a bachelor, seemed more distant than usual.

Now, without the old financial pressures, he could really regard himself as a gentleman of leisure, which was all the more sweet in view of his years of hard toil to earn his crust, first as a newspaper reporter and then as a clerk.

Added to all this, the horrors of the less fortunate, as portrayed in the newspapers being read around him, made him fully aware of his own blessings. He also, however, found himself rather curiously and ever so slightly embarking on a slow and relaxed questioning of what he should do with the rest of his life, or at any rate what sort of person he should be. In the absence of a nice juicy real life mystery to tax his amateur enthusiasm in that line, it was time to turn to that other kind of mystery, and seriously weigh the claims of the world's religions and philosophies – but perhaps that could wait till after this little holiday trip to Chicago and Toronto. He would have plenty of time then to apply his mind to such matters.

One thing was for sure, despite his good fortune on the financial front, he was determined to keep his old lifestyle. In fact, he would keep his new-found wealth a secret as much as possible; and when not on holiday, retain the deliberately modest way of life, which appealed to his sensibilities so much.

This was the life, he reflected … and then he saw her, struggling down the aisle with her suitcase and looking for her seat. There was something about her neat and trim appearance that he liked. She was forceful, but not too much so, and he could imagine her in that business suit addressing the directors of some company … No, it couldn't be – but it was – it was too good to be true – she stopped at his row and chucked her coat into the middle seat next to him and started to raise her hand luggage to the overhead cupboard.

Alistair surprised himself by overcoming his shyness. "Let me put it up for you," he ventured.

"No, I'm fine thanks," came the reply. But what a smile!

From where he was sitting, no man could avoid appreciating her fine, strong figure, and by the time she slumped down into the seat next to him, he had already felt his heart quicken a little. He would guess that she was about ten years younger than he was and in a while it would not be inappropriate to have a little chat with her.

He kept his silence; they had seven hours to go, and then the strangest of thoughts came to him that in the worst case scenario if she didn't want to speak, he would slip her one of his cards, which he had recently had printed, at the end of the journey.

A reassuring message came from the pilot – the weather was good – oh yes, it was a good day for flying – and the temperature at their destination in Chicago was apparently pleasantly acceptable.

The air hostesses demonstrated the safety rules, and to Alistair for once they were not so attractive as his neighbouring passenger. That's a first, he thought.

Shortly the taxiing was over.

"It's our turn next," came the pilot's calm, reassuring, almost friendly voice, reminding him of his enthusiasm for the early days of space travel.

Almost immediately he recognised that tremendous sensation of power, and within moments came the sudden realisation that they were already above the ground. For a fleeting moment he recognised an airport building and a church spire. Goodbye, England, he said to himself, and you too, my distant beloved Scotland.

It must have been somewhere over Greenland that it happened – he was in love.

Moments after this realisation the calm voice of the pilot came clearly over the intercom. "Passengers may be interested to know there is a fine view of the south coast of Greenland on the starboard side – the right-hand side to you." He heard a slight chuckle in the cockpit before the intercom cut out.

"Do you mind if I lean over?" she asked.

Did he mind? Alistair felt like saying "the more the better," but got out the word "Sure".

"Oh, you're from the States, are you?"

"Oh no, British."

"Oh, it was just the way you said 'sure'."

"I was a reporter for a year or so in the States."

The conversation started, and he picked up snippets of information, registering them keenly. She was flying to her brother Greg's wedding. She was from Exeter originally, but had been living near the suburb of Cookington, near West London, for some years. Now she was on a year's sabbatical leave from her university teaching and had let her house and would be staying with a friend, Elsa in Chelsea on her return. She hoped her brother Greg would be happy. His previous romance hadn't worked out. She had been quite close to her brother …

The wine poured.

"Nice to be going to a wedding," she said, seemingly keen to talk about it. Her brother had had quite a few romances. There was one girlfriend she wished he had married, but she supposed she wasn't his type – too good for her; they'd met at university; she had become a vicar in the end and married someone else.

"It's just possible you may have heard of her – Henrietta Carr. There was all that publicity in the papers – do you remember that terrible case?"

Alistair was stunned. He had heard of her alright, and so had every man, woman, child and their dog in the land. The story had dominated the news media for months; but not only that, the poor victim, Henrietta, in this sensational story had been the wife of his old friend, Dennis Carr. He made a split-second decision not to reveal that. It could spoil everything. No, he would explain later why he hadn't wanted to mention it. In a way he was annoyed that this sad case had, by a remarkable coincidence, impinged on his happy situation. It was like ink on a clean canvas.

"I think everyone has heard of that case," he commented. From then on, he tried, not always successfully, to put this amazing news out of his mind.

"Well, anyway, my dear brother Greg fell for Sonia," his neighbour continued, "she was, shall we say, not quite vicar material, and everything seemed fine; but as I say, now that's all water under the bridge, and I'm on my way to his wedding to girlfriend number umpteen. She's called Samantha."

It was almost impossible to describe Alistair's feelings as the plane reduced altitude. For the rest of his life he would wonder how you could board a plane as one person and disembark as another. The impossible had happened: he was in love. He kept saying to himself, she's such a nice person, she's so pretty, she's got such a wonderful figure … He was as surprised as any of his friends would be to find himself so in love. Now Zoe was his favourite name, and where she lived in Cookington must be the greatest place, and even Chicago, where she was going, must be a great city, which he was now even keener to learn about and visit.

The conversation had gone better than he could have dared hope. He would have loved to have learnt more about her situation, but she appeared a little cagey about that; he sensed she had a past, as he put it in his mind. By the time the pilot indicated that if ladies and gentleman were thinking of using the amenities, this would be a good time to go, as they would shortly be landing, he had a satisfying feeling that he had said everything he wanted to and given a good impression.

"Yes, I'll take him up on that suggestion," Zoe laughed as she got up and made her way down the aisle.

Yes, he would give her one of his cards; his one little bit of recent vanity was his printed visitor's cards.

It had all started a few months ago with the wrong spelling of his name. He pulled one out and slightly hurriedly scribbled the name, address and telephone number of the hotel that he hoped to stay at in Chicago. Momentarily he was in a dilemma whether to add a message such as 'Would love to hear from you', which he did.

In some ways Alistair was looking forward to the chance to be alone. He wanted to think things through and to think about this extraordinary coincidence of her knowing about Henrietta, but he had managed to put it out of his mind so as not to spoil his equilibrium. Yes, he would have a big think about that when on his own.

He chose the moment to give her his card just before she got up to get the hand luggage down, which he insisted on helping her with. "Please keep in touch," he said, trying to get the balance between sincerity and restraint, "it's been so nice to meet you."

"Oh, thanks," she replied, putting the card in her handbag.

He had wanted to add something a bit stronger than 'nice', but things would have to rest at that for the moment. Patience is a virtue that lovers must learn, I guess, he said to himself as they walked along the corridor and got separated by a guy organising different queues for different people. It was like a dagger in his heart.

He waved a distant goodbye to her at the luggage carousel. Her luggage had come first and she left for a taxi.

She knew he was smitten; a woman's intuition, or instinct as old as the hills, made her sure of that. She gave the address to the taxi driver and sat back, totally relaxed, and allowed her thoughts to wander. Oh well, another conquest ... but he's different, OK ... polite, intelligent. She looked keenly out of the window taking in the vivid images of a new arrival in a new city, but her thoughts returned to her recent fellow passenger. Actually, he's oddly interesting, she mused, maybe nine or ten years older …

For Alistair, a rather relaxing and pleasant feeling of the ball being not in his court was now coming over him. Thank goodness for visiting cards, he repeated over and over to himself. She'll either get in touch or she won't.

CHAPTER 4

(A nice surprise in Chicago)

For anyone arriving at O'Hare International Airport in Chicago it would be a place to keep your wits about you, but for Alistair smitten by Cupid's bow, it was like a dream world, where the main problem was that concentration proved well-nigh impossible.

The practical side of him made the very sensible suggestion to himself that he should sit down and collect his thoughts. Although keen to get to his hotel, he would allow time for an inaugural cup of good old American regular coffee.

"Is that the Sears Tower?" he asked an American lady, whose job seemed to be to clean a busy floor in a manner reminiscent of Sisyphus pushing a rock up a mountainside.

"That sure is, sir. Been to the very top of it with my grandchild only last spring."

One of the rewards of Alistair's rather friendly custom of engaging strangers in conversation was that he often picked up tips about a wide range of interesting matters, like where was best to have coffee and where was best to get a taxi, and much else besides. This encounter proved no exception, and soon, after a welcome refreshment, he found himself being driven at what he used to describe as a good rate of knots towards the city centre by a taxi driver who seemed to know more about English football than the average Englishman. He held his own quite ably, and with not a little wit, chided his new-found acquaintance for not having heard of his own rather obscure team of Brechin City.

He gave the man a generous tip on condition that

from now on he looked out for the fortunes of that noble team in the Scottish second division. He was full of joie de vivre, and besides it was good for Anglo - American relations, he thought to himself as he waved goodbye.

Alistair had chosen this hotel at random, for his guidebook had fallen open at the page. The impressively named Center Hotel had seemed to be in an advantageous situation and to be adequately comfortable. It was one of the great advantages of travelling alone and not having to be responsible for anyone else, that you could have the fun of just turning up out of the blue. However his first shock came when he found that, most unusually for an American hotel, the reception desk was unmanned.

He waited, a little overawed by the contrast between reality and what he had imagined; but on reflection, wasn't that always the way?

His wait continued as he stood there wondering what would happen next, and eventually ended when an obese gentleman waddled into view from the inner sanctums of the establishment.

"How are you this evening, sir?" asked this newcomer with a slight slur.

"I was hoping to book a single room for a week ..."

He was cut short by the gentleman. "Let me stop you there; you're not going to believe this, sir, but we're completely full up. There's a convention on across the road, and there's delegates from all over the country. Most times there wouldn't have been a problem. I guess there's nothing I can do about it."

"I'll take your advice," said Alistair politely, "if you know where I might ..."

He need not have finished his enquiry; for the gentleman had picked up the phone and was already asking some establishment if such accommodation was available. Within seconds he mentioned a number of dollars and raised an eyebrow to await Alistair's approval, which was immediately given.

"Name, please?" he asked and then repeated it down the phone.

The man wrote down the new address on a card and handed it over.

"You'll be alright there, sir. Nice hotel, is the Plaza. It's right along the road here. There's any number of taxis cruising around."

Alistair thanked his helper and had to call him back fairly sharply as he started to shuffle back to his inner sanctum.

"I say, I need your help about one more matter, please, if I can ask you?"

The man stopped in his track, turned with some difficulty and continued in his slurred tone, "Always try and help the Brits. My pop was at Omaha Beach. Told me, those Brits were as good as us. What's the problem, sir?"

Somewhat embarrassed and self-conscious, Alistair began, "I stupidly assumed that there would be accommodation here, and I gave this person this hotel as my address."

"Ah, we have a book here for forwarding addresses for mail."

"The only thing is, it might be a call."

"I don't understand; can't you call the person?"

Seldom had Alistair felt so stuck. There was nothing for it but to lay his cards honestly on the table. In what he knew must sound rather pathetic terms, he tried as best he could to explain how he hoped there might be an attempt to make contact by one fellow Brit by the name of Zoe.

"Oh, it's like that, is it, sir? You English are so romantic, but you know, you won't believe it. I had a girlfriend once, so I know where you're coming from. I'll make a note of it right here. She's called Zoe, is she, sir? I'll write that down here, alongside the note of where you're staying. Now sir, I'm only on duty nights, but I'll leave a message in the book here too, which might help. It sometimes works, and anyway I'll have a word with Hillary when she arrives in the morning to take over from me."

"I fear it may not be for some time, if at all," came Alistair's troubled response. "Also, of course, I'll need to confirm to you that I'm at this new hotel you've been kind enough to book for me."

In a way, Alistair regarded his new friend as a guardian angel, but the questions now became a little personal.

"What's she like, sir?" continued the guardian angel. By now they were standing together at the hotel entrance awaiting the taxi. "She cute, is she, sir?"

Fortunately the taxi arrived, and Alistair bade his helper goodbye with much politeness, not least because of the importance of him obliging with the arranged forwarding of any message.

Alistair, a little more distrait than usual, started up a second taxi driver conversation, relieved at least that football had been replaced by traffic as a subject for the agenda.

"I can't believe that London is as bad as here with cars," came his driver's seemingly honest view.

After paying this second taxi driver, including a no less generous tip, Alistair followed the bellboy and the luggage into a hotel foyer that seemed so grand that he was surprised that he could afford it. He took the key gratefully over the reception counter, and although unable to assimilate all the information about breakfast and much else, he set off for the lift and pressed the button for the seventh floor.

Once in his room, he sat down in the chair and spent a few minutes revelling in his new-found peace, before turning the television on quietly.

Very shortly he heard the rumble of what he rightly assumed was the 'El' rapid transport system.

Within minutes he was standing at the window.

His immediate attention was not surprisingly caught by a flashing cross on a Pentecostal church, opposite but far below.

He stood there for some time, drinking in the scene. For a moment he felt like an alien landed from another planet, or certainly an intruder, as for him everything was new and fascinating and crying out for close inspection; but he knew by the grime on the old buildings that they had stood for many a long year. Here, where he was peeping at for the first time, men and women and children had come and gone and lived their lives, wrestling with their problems, laughing and crying, working, trying to cope, managing and sometimes not, for decades. From his lofty vantage point he let his eyes follow an old hobo limping along what he knew the Americans called the sidewalk.

This is my favourite city, he thought, because Zoe is here. He knew of course that like all great cities there was much suffering within and, saddened at the television's reporting of police being involved in three shootings at some unknown spot called Bob's Bar, went over and turned the set off.

Having returned to the window and drunk his fill of the absorbing view, he retired to bed and slept well, woken once by some late guests returning to their nearby rooms. People are the same the world over, he thought, and turned over and slept.

It was the friendly rumble of the 'El' again that woke him first in the morning.

Another day was beginning. He had to look out of

the window, but was soon leaving the sanctuary of his room and on his way down to the dining room.

Breakfast was unexpectedly slow, and it turned out that the cause was a strike by some of the hotel kitchen workers.

Some French visitors amused him by taking all the menus and, having piled them up, hid them away.

He was impatient to get down to Lake Michigan. Apart from Zoe, that was what he wanted to see more than anything. He wanted to get his first view of one of the Great Lakes that he had so often looked at in his atlas since first hearing about them as a schoolboy.

Having returned to the haven of Room 799 for a brief moment after breakfast, he set out with as much expectation as an early explorer to go and gaze at this great expanse of water.

As he left the hotel, one of the kitchen staff on strike at the entrance handed him a leaflet. He engaged the fellow in conversation and was surprised to receive an apology for the inconvenience caused by the industrial action.

The mist was remarkably dense, and added to the wonder and mystery of his proposed exploration.

He could tell beyond doubt from the map that he was heading towards the water. It was not till he was really close that he quite suddenly saw it. Water! He stood enchanted by having reached a childhood goal.

He turned right and south at the water's edge, and walked down to Soldier Field. What an evocative name! A few joggers and walkers passed him, and one even wished him good morning.

He walked along the short promontory to the Adler Observatory. He felt oddly lonely. It would be nice to have Zoe with him, but that was probably just a pipe dream.

He turned and looked at the shining skyscrapers

beginning to make their presence more apparent through the receding fog. Somewhere in there in the heart of this great city was the girl he had been smitten by. It was up to her. He did not even have her address. He turned round with his back to the lake and revelled in the inspiring view.

The Adler Observatory was just what he felt like. After a snack that hit the spot exactly, he bought a ticket for 'the Night Sky Experience'. When the lights dimmed and the intelligent and enthusiastic young astronomer began his entertaining commentary, shining beams at different parts of the roof where the constellations were displayed, Alistair found it took his thoughts away from himself and his feelings and made him wonder at the greatness of the universe, and concentrated his mind on how tiny and seemingly insignificant he and his thoughts really were in the scheme of things. Yes, he thought to himself, I'm forty-six now. It's time I really took stock and worked out what I believe and what I don't.

After the event was over, he wandered back down the promontory. You walk further than you think, he thought, and sat down on a fortuitous bench. For several minutes he sat there, entertained by the perseverance of some young anglers catching a large fish, which they hauled out of the water with some difficulty. He decided that his foot-weariness demanded a little rest back in the sanctum of Room 799, and then he would make his way along to where he had his aborted attempt to check in last night. He would see if the kind man with the father who had been at Omaha Beach, and to whom he had entrusted the important task of taking any message from Zoe, was there again tonight. 'My guardian angel', he called him in his thoughts, not knowing the man's real name.

When he arrived at that first hotel in the early

evening, following his rest, he found a very different person on duty, someone who was as fast and nimble as his guardian angel had been slow and plodding.

"John's ill, sir. Went to hospital last night," was the answer to his enquiry.

Momentarily stunned, Alistair stood there, stroking his chin.

"Are you the person he was talking about? There was an important message for an Englishman. It wasn't you, was it, sir?

For a further moment, Alistair's speechlessness continued.

"He went on about it some," continued this new night duty receptionist. "I wasn't here myself, but they told me about it. When he collapsed and they'd called 911 and were waiting for the ambulance, they told me they kept saying, 'don't you worry about anything but taking care of yourself and getting better.' But he kept saying, 'make sure you give that Englishman the message from his gal.' Told us his dad had been at Omaha and had told him to always help the Brits. I heard it was the last thing he said, when they were carrying him out of here to the ambulance."

Alistair now regained the ability to speak. "That was me, OK. How kind of him. I'm obviously more concerned about John, and I'll ask you about the message later. How is he?"

"Last I heard, wasn't too good news. Hillary told me, when I took over from her, that some said he won't make it."

"He did me very well; I'd like to pay him a visit."

"Yeah, well, they're saying not at the moment."

There was a moment's pause while Alistair, feeling genuinely concerned tapped his fingers on the desk.

"Yeah," continued the new man at the desk, "we wondered what he was talking about, and then in the morning Hillary found the message in the book. Told me she had immediately called the Plaza and left it for you there. She'll be in, in the morning."

The news of John's collapse and the report of a message for him combined to result in Alistair walking back to the Plaza Hotel both at a swift pace and also in a trance.

On arrival, he went to the reception desk and asked for a message he had been assured was given last night.

"Room 799? Here it is. Sorry, sir, hadn't realised it was important."

He was irritated by the inefficiency, but the smile that came with the apology resulted in him taking it without comment. He would wait till he got to his room before reading it. He opened the door of Room 799, which already felt curiously homely to him.

He sat down in the chair and opened the message, reading its brief content.

How are you finding Chicago? Give us a ring on this number at the City Hotel where I'm staying.

He was ecstatic and immediately felt an overpowering desire to get a message of thanks to the stricken John, as he could now call him, though still thinking of him as a guardian angel. He did one of his idiosyncratic thumpings on the table and decided, yes, before anything he must somehow get his gratitude to John.

He would go in the morning when Hillary was on duty and ring Zoe afterwards.

He was overtired and needed rest.

***

Next morning, early, found him back at the Center

Hotel.

He guessed the smart, cute little girl behind the counter must be Hillary.

"I've come to ask how John is," he began.

"You know John?" she asked, looking up at him with some surprise.

Alistair nodded.

"He's dead," she said, solemnly.

Even more stunned than when there yesterday, Alistair managed, "I'm so very sorry to hear that. He did me very well, finding me alternative accommodation as you were fully booked, and looking after messages for me."

"You the guy he was going on about giving the message to? When they told me about that I found it in the book and rang the Plaza."

Alistair held out his hand, which she involuntarily took, and he squeezed it gently, which made her say rather coquettishly, "She your girlfriend, then? Good luck!"

"Goodbye, and thanks," he said and left, walking slowly and contemplatively to the lakeside.

What a mystery life is, he thought as he sat on the bench, reliving the vivid experiences of his arrival at the first hotel only a couple of nights ago.

That evening he called Zoe on the number written in the message. It seemed unreal to be talking to her.

They met up for a meal in a restaurant which she recommended.

Their conversation ranged over a wide number of subjects, but was mostly about the city, where they were.

Alistair revelled in the joy of her company. For a moment his recent experience at the Adler Observatory came into his mind, and he found himself thinking how you could travel for millions of light years through space, and what would you find but him and Zoe chatting, and that lady over there putting down a saucer of milk for what must be the restaurant's cat.

He was careful to keep the conversation normal and natural, and tried not to talk about himself, and certainly not about anything too private for her.

At one point she seemed to want to say something about herself. She hinted there was a lot to sort out in her life. He shuddered slightly, but was gratified that his intuition had proved right, for he had guessed she had a past. Was that good or bad? However, they agreed to meet up for a little sightseeing, and on the next day they visited the top of the Sears Tower.

He pointed at the Hancock Tower and half jokingly said, "Let's do that one tomorrow," and was surprised when she seemed keen.

The day after that second 'summit', as he jokingly called it, was conquered, he suggested she might like to see where he had been at the Adler Observatory in the afternoon.

It seemed to Alistair like God was giving him an overflow of blessings, for the following day they travelled together out to Oakland, where she had expressed an interest in seeing and visiting houses designed by the eminent architect, Frank Lloyd Wright. It was a happy excursion, and they had both laughed at how long the freight train beside them had seemed.

As the train trundled back towards the centre of the big city it was curiously like coming home. When it arrived, he found he was already familiar with the station and the streets leading away from it.

Familiar landmarks seemed to welcome him as he recognised them. No wonder American cities had songs written about them; he might even try and write one himself, he thought.

It was in the evening that he laid bare his heart. An

unlikely place, if ever there was. It was a bar called the Jazzman's Bar.

Normally a slow and cautious mover by nature, he felt he just had to give words to his feelings, because she was going to Washington the next day and he no longer had time to play with.

"Zoe," he said, rather too formally for his liking, "I've just got to tell you something."

She knew what it was. She had wondered how he would say it and had not expected it to be so formal. She could tell it in his eyes; but had hoped that this conversation would not take place, at any rate not just yet, for she had so much to work out in her personal life, and in so many ways it was too complicated for her to explain. She did not want him thinking that she had some major defect of character, having been let down now by two boyfriends. She wanted to be so sure next time.

She sat at the table in the rather opaque green light with the distant rhythm of the jazz in the background, trying not to reveal the slight tension she felt.

Alistair did feel it, however, for he put his arm across the table and took her hand, but immediately sensed a reticence.

He had to say something, but already felt the need to moderate it.

"It's just that I'm going to miss you so much," he said brushing a crumb away as if it was not really such a serious thought. Worried that he might have given an impression of not being so serious, he looked up at her and said shyly, "I know it's stupid, but I've kind of fallen for you."

If only she would speak, he thought, but she sat there silently for a moment before withdrawing her hand.

"Oh, it's too complicated to explain," she said in a

near-normal voice, "I've got things in my life to sort out, think through. One way and another my personal life has got a little complicated. Possibly, I'll be able to explain to you later."

There was quite a lengthy silence between them as some more not unharmonious music drifted towards them from the distant stage, which they had sought to sit as far away from as possible.

Alistair felt awkward, but knew he would be happier if he made his feelings clear.

It seemed so clumsy to his own ears when he said it, but he managed, "if your affairs don't sort themselves out, would I have a chance of being with you?"

Now she did look at him rather lovingly and gave what was almost, but not quite, a nod.

The distant band changed the tempo, and with the sound of much faster traditional jazz - no doubt for the benefit of some British tourists - their tone changed too.

"I'll come with you to the airport tomorrow," said Alistair cheerfully, thinking, this is absurd at my age, but I can remember my mother saying, "Girls like their boyfriends to be cheerful."

"There's no need to, Alistair. Going by plane isn't quite like the old ship disappearing over the horizon, is it?"

"But I'll be able to help with the luggage, and besides it'll be good to familiarise myself with the way for when I go on to Toronto the day after."

They agreed to meet in the foyer of her hotel on the morrow, where she would be waiting with her luggage. Shortly they walked back to her hotel, and he said goodnight on the steps with a peck on the cheek.

When he arrived the next morning, they stood together at the counter as she handed her key in and checked out.

A young couple arrived and checked in. Alistair

found himself wondering if he would ever be able to do that with her.

He would travel out tomorrow to the airport on the train when it was his time to go, but she understandably did the normal thing and ordered a taxi.

They chatted, exchanging sweet nothings until the airport came into sight.

"I'll hope to see you in England," they said, almost together, which made them laugh.

She seemed quiet when they were walking to the terminal, and Alistair thought it best not to fill that gap with banal remarks. After a bit, she turned to him and said, "Alistair, I'll hope to get in touch with you when I get back to England, but I really do need to sort things out … yes, man trouble. I'll be in Washington for a bit and then back here for a bit. I'd like to hear from you when you arrive in Toronto, but when you go back to England, I need a bit of space, so please leave it to me to make contact. I'll drop you a line whatever happens."

He nodded sagely and his looks must have betrayed the slight concern he now felt, because she said, "Cheer up! I didn't say I didn't want to see you again."

He tried to laugh, but in a moment it was her turn in the queue and he sensed the time for goodbye was practically there. He stayed with her while she checked in, impressed by her efficiency in all that needed to be done.

He was wondering how they were going to say goodbye; but in the end it turned out so matter-of-fact.

When they reached the entrance to the security control area, she turned to him and smiled. "Your turn for all this fun and games tomorrow. Goodbye and good luck in Toronto. Give us a ring from Toronto, though, when you've settled in to your new hotel."

He referred to their journey from Heathrow, and

made some rather awkward joke about hoping she wasn't going to sit next to too chatty a passenger on this flight.

"It couldn't happen twice running," she joked, and gave him a kiss on the cheek.

He felt the kiss on his cheek for a long time as he walked away, and a curious mixture of happiness and loneliness came over him as he journeyed back to the city centre. In many ways things had gone well and were indeed propitious, but she was not there. How strange love was, that it could make you feel so high and so low in such a short space of time.

.However, he only had one day more to wait in Chicago, and was impatient now to get to the second city of his holiday. As he travelled back to the city centre, he vowed he would be the most busy and earnest of sightseers, and then get back to England and hope that Zoe made contact. One way or another, when settled back home, things would pan out, and at any rate life would be easier to organise.

He was roused from his thoughts by a traveller asking him how to get to Oakland. He could more than answer that question, but soon it had reminded him of his trip there with Zoe and his wistfulness returned.

***

Back at the Plaza, he passed a night of mixed emotions and was glad to be woken early by the friendly rumble of the 'El' below. He looked through the window. The weather had turned, but the flashing cross was still visible through the murk.

Although his loneliness continued during breakfast, he was soon cheered by a friendly waiter, who befriended him with talk of his visit to London. "If I couldn't live in Chicago, I'd live in London," he said amiably.

"And vice versa," replied Alistair, adding, "that's if we're not bringing Edinburgh into the equation."

"Oh, you recommend I go to see Edinburgh too, do you?" came the earnest response.

To the amusement of his new acquaintance, Alistair found himself replying, "Aye."

Soon he had checked out, and pulling his suitcase behind him, set off for the station. It was markedly colder, and indeed flurries of snow blew forcefully across, inches from his face, as he struggled to the station. He found pulling his luggage increasingly difficult. Twice some helpful citizens of Chicago asked him if he needed help. How kind Americans can be, he thought. An old newspaper blew irritatingly across his face, with its glaring headline about the police being involved in those three shootings. It reminded him of how he had heard about it on his arrival that first evening and felt wistful. Guess every city has good and bad, his mind told him.

Once safely ensconced in the train, he leant back and enjoyed its steady trundle towards the airport and adventures new. Since childhood, he had always found it fun going by train. "Whats wrong with the train?" he answered when someone suggested he should have got a taxi.

Despite a slight hitch, when he stupidly left his totally unnecessary Edinburgh flat key in his pocket, he got through Security in plenty of time to relax in the departure lounge before the flight.

There were no problems on the flight, and he laughed to find that this time the seat next to him was occupied by a very different member of the human race from his companion on the flight from Heathrow. He thought of the story of the ugly duckling, but it was the other way round, for here was a man whose size and weight made Alistair wonder if the plane could get off the ground.

However, he made pleasant small talk, got his reward for being sociable with some good tips on where to go in Toronto, and settled back for this new experience in a new city.

Once again, he thought, the ball is in her court, but I'll give her a ring from Toronto.

Soon the plane began its descent, and Alistair leaned forward to catch a glimpse of Canada beneath. A bit of sightseeing, he thought, and then a bit of my favourite custom of mooching around and resting, writing the odd postcard … mustn't forget my landlady in Edinburgh, nor my brother running that superb little establishment of his, the one and only Concord Hotel in West London. Nor indeed must I forget to send a postcard to my old friend Dennis Carr in Cookington, continued his thoughts. And after that back to good old Blighty – a nice prospect …

An air hostess worked her way past his chair with her trolley, caught his dreaming eye, smiled and said, "Have a nice day, sir."

CHAPTER 5

(Alistair arrives back in the U.K.)

As is often the case, expected things happen when not being impatiently thought of. All that afternoon and evening after Dennis's morning coffee and chat with Helen passed by with no contact from Alistair. There were other "buzzes" aplenty, but not that one.

Caller one rang, but Dennis was quite satisfied with his present electricity supplier.

Caller two rang, but no, Dennis did not have time to answer a short questionnaire on consumer items.

Caller three rang, but he had already donated to that particular charity.

Caller four wasn't Alistair either, just a Liberal Democrat council candidate indulging in a little telephone canvassing. He would just have to be patient and await the great man's return over the pond. He would come when he would come.

It was actually three days after his conversation with Helen that the long awaited call came. Dennis was in the garden. At first he thought it was next door's phone, but then he knew unmistakeably it was his own. He went swiftly in through the French windows, thinking it was probably the insurance company which he had just rung.

The receiver boomed in his ear, "Dennis?"

"Yes, who's that?"

"Alistair."

"Alistair, where are you?"

"Heathrow."

"What's yer plans? When are you going to Scotland?"

"Tomorrow evening, I thought; so I'm going to

book myself into my brother's wee hotel near here – you know, the dear old Concord - just for the night like I always do. I'll cough up with the usual token payment to cover the costs; but anyway I thought I'd keep the tradition and give you a ring straightaway, Dennis, as I always do when passing through the great metropolis, and I would indeed like to arrange meeting up - as time is short."

Dennis cut in, "Why don't you stay here at the vicarage?"

Like many people who have a windfall, Alistair MacTavish liked the principle of saving money. His usual "Are you sure?" when people invited him to stay was never very convincing, and Dennis sensed it coming.

"Actually, Alistair, I've just remembered … oh, I wish I could say forget about your brother's hotel and that I could put you up for the night, but I've got quite a lot going on … I've just remembered it might be a little tricky tonight."

"That's OK, Dennis, I'll stay here as usual – it's good to put in an appearance at my brother's hotel every now and again. Gets him used to the idea that I might pop in unexpectedly any time, which is useful. But look, I'll pop over your way, say in a couple of hours or so, just to say hallo."

"I'd have come and met you," continued Dennis enthusiastically, but Alistair cut in with, "Och, it's OK. I'll get the old Tube and bus. All news when we meet, Dennis, but there's something I'm longing to tell you – I'll keep it till then."

What was this 'something' that was pressing enough for Alistair to mention on the phone, even when he was shortly to arrive? mused Dennis as he replaced the receiver. No, I can't believe that …

Alistair made two further phonecalls, firstly to the

Concord Hotel, which his rich brother ran a few miles from this great travel centre of the world.

"Good thing it wasn't last week, Alistair," laughed his brother over the phone. "We had a double booking and had to use the family room. Anyway, it's yours for as long as you want it, as usual. I may be out when you arrive, but Donna will look after you; see yah soon."

Alistair heaved a sigh of relief that he had at least a definite roof over his head for the night.

Next he made the final phone call to Mrs Davidson, the landlady of his digs in Edinburgh. It was a kind of unwritten rule that he kept her informed of his comings and goings, and in return she provided him not only with a roof over his head but many a fine meal too. He gave her a good synopsis of his American holiday, and most importantly of all asked her to keep an eye out for and inform him of any letter from America.

He played it down when, as expected, her interest was roused; but that was what he wanted more than anything – a letter from Zoe. He fended the landlady's questions. She knew him so well that she could tease him.

"Have you fallen in love at last, Alistair?" He did not reply. "Oh, you're an old sweetie, Alistair, and you'd make a jolly good husband. I just love the way you're such a nice old-fashioned guy, who believes that falling for a girl will lead to love."

For some reason he felt a bit hurt, and despite a feeling of compulsion to speak of his new-found love, he made a decision from now on not to mention these too precious feelings to anyone, and on second thoughts not even to Dennis. Yes, he would wait till he received that letter, if it ever came, and a long time more before telling Dennis of his feelings for Zoe.

That call marked the end of Alistair's holiday, and as he left the telephone kiosk at Heathrow he recalled the wonderful time he had had since last being in the airport, thinking back to his happy outward flight. He allowed his mind to revisit and savour it all while he sat back and indulged in one final cup of coffee. As he stirred it in the little airport café, he leant back, relaxed and indulged in one of his favourite occupations, namely people watching, as an old actor friend had once described it to him. His actor friend had told him that people watching was the way to learn to be a good actor, but for him with his passion for detective stories, it was a kind of detective game, trying to work out what was going on in their lives.

Yes – what is going on in their lives? And that makes me think of Zoe, he mused. And what is going on in her life? He had rung her at her hotel in Washington on his arrival at Toronto. She had been pleasant and friendly, but had reminded him of what she had said about leaving her to get in touch.

However she had given him her phone number, referring to it jokingly as an emergency number if she became too dilatory in tying things up. I'll ring to say I'm safely back, Alistair pondered, but after that I must be patient and wait for this promised letter, however long it takes to come, he concluded, as he stacked his cup and saucer and plate and got up from the table.

Soon he was on his way.

Funny old life, he thought, as the Tube train hurried him in the direction of the hotel. Everything is in the future. I'm waiting to tell Zoe about knowing her brother, Greg's former lover, Henrietta, and I'm waiting to tell Dennis how I've fallen for Zoe; but both matters have got to go on hold big style! Waiting is the name of the game for me at the moment.

He got easily to the main road where his brother's familiar little hotel stood, rather gamely keeping up appearances in an otherwise rather down-at-heel area.

As his brother had said, Donna was at the reception desk. He greeted her politely, even warmly, and promised to tell her all about his transatlantic holiday. She took the hint that he had somewhere to go on to and curtailed her natural conviviality, pulling out a crossword for alternative entertainment. It was only minutes before he was up in the little top-floor room, which his brother always kept available for friends, family and emergencies.

After a refreshing shower and a short rest, he was, by some good synchronisation of bus and Tube, within a surprisingly short time arriving at the vicarage of his old friend, Dennis. He had to get the social visit over with, because one night was not a long time to be staying, and he did not plan on being down this way again for a bit. Alistair had been a good friend of Dennis and Henrietta for many years, meeting up with them a lot, usually when he was passing through the capital and sometimes when they were on holiday in Scotland, which was where he had met them. He had seen them dancing at a Burns Night party. Something in the way Henrietta had twirled in time with the music 'just got him' as he put it. In one way he felt he knew them very well; but they had never had what he termed a real, in depth conversation. Of course, they were as ignorant of his secrets as he was no doubt of their's. As usual he concluded this reflection with the thought that he was lucky to have had such loyal friends and didn't deserve them. He recognised the old nameplate from when Dennis and Henrietta had invited him to dinner some little time before the tragedy, but noticed it had been changed from Dennis and Henrietta to Dennis's name only.

Dennis came to the door promptly, and after the usual warmly expressed civil greetings and hanging up of the coats, ushered him into the pleasant living room and disappeared into the kitchen to produce refreshments.

He's looking a bit older, thought Alistair, he's a year older than me – only 47 – not surprisingly after all he's been through plus all the hard work he's taken on in his job of chartered surveyor – anyway quite a bit older than his poor wife had looked at her 40th birthday just before the tragedy.

Although Alistair had expected to feel a bit tense about keeping the secret of the woman whom he already privately thought of as his new-found girlfriend, curiously a great sense of peace came over him. Leaning back in the comfy chair and stretching his legs, he noticed the Bibles and course books dotted around the furniture. So this was where God's work was done in Cookington, he thought. The dignified clock ticked pleasantly and the window seemed the best advertisement he knew for double glazing, as the traffic appeared to glide silently by outside.

While his old friend Dennis was in the kitchen, Alistair allowed himself to relax as if he was in his own home. How peaceful and contrasting this was to the noisy bustle of planes and airports, with their checking-in and their wearing security procedures.

Soon enough, Dennis appeared with that greatest of all drinks – tea.

"You know, that's the only thing I've got against Americans," joked Alistair, "they don't drink tea."

"Always coffee, isn't it?" responded Dennis, sitting down opposite.

"It's why they don't play cricket – I mean, taking tea is an important part of the strategy of the game."

"You and your cricket, Alistair; nobody would ever think you were a Scotsman!"

On the trivial conversation went, and a lot of ground was covered over those particular cups of tea. Chicago and Toronto were described by Alistair in glowing terms.

Although pressed by Dennis to reveal what it was he had to tell him, Alistair kept to his new decision to keep the affairs of his heart a secret until such time as things were clearer. God willing, he thought, there would be time enough to tell his old friend the bombshell of his falling in love with Zoe. It would of course all depend on Zoe's letter, whenever and if ever that came. How Dennis would guffaw, but how he would sober up when indeed he introduce him to her; for Dennis, he knew, appreciated the fairer sex.

"Sorry, Dennis, even for you I've decided now it's got to wait," he said defensively. "It'll be a surprise when I tell you, but please be patient. It may all come to nothing."

The use of his own phrase, 'come to nothing' gave him an unpleasant shudder. That would be unthinkable, he told himself.

"Alistair ... No, I won't say anything," uttered Dennis, putting his hands up to his face and smiling behind his fingers.

Then he moved - slightly uncomfortably, the observant Alistair thought - like a politician when asked an awkward question, and said, "Well now, Alistair, to turn to other things ... "

Dennis left nothing out in his account of what had been happening both in Cookington and nationally while Alistair had been away. Inevitably the conversation moved more and more towards the sad subject of the unsolved crime.

Alistair looked at his watch and made as if to get up. It struck him again momentarily that Dennis looked just a bit nervous, as if he had something on his mind.

"Now, Alistair, before you go. I want to put something to you. I don't know how you're going to react, but before I spit it out, I want to say that obviously it's totally up to you. Just say 'No' if that's your feeling, or possibly you may want to chew over it. I obviously hope you say 'Yes', otherwise I wouldn't be asking you."

Surprised and intrigued, Alistair interrupted him, "What on earth's all this about Dennis? Spit it out, man!"

"Right, now, I've been discussing this with Helen. She, as you probably remember from all the press coverage last year, is the wife of dear Edwin, one of our churchwardens here at St Peter's, and I've been confiding in her a lot since that dreadful day she found poor Henrietta's body in that shed – her shed. We've actually become quite close."

Alistair managed to control a smile. He had long suspected that Dennis had a soft spot for Edwin's wife.

"Well, as we were saying," resumed Dennis, "the police have drawn a complete blank – an absolute blank – after a thorough investigation lasting over a year. So we still have this complete mystery on our hands." He paused and added, "And the terrible thing is people have started to move on and to stop wondering about it. I, of course will never give up, never, never, never, until I get to the bottom of this, and I've been seriously thinking of employing a private detective. I had actually got as far as looking in directories, taking advice and doing a bit of research on them, when I found myself thinking, how can they possibly do more than the police with all their professionalism and expertise? And so it suddenly came to me – and I told Helen, and she totally supported me in this – that I would go one better than that and ask someone, absolutely privately, to carry out a very private investigation; perhaps taking a completely different approach to the police, and going more on ..." he paused again and appeared to be groping around for the mot juste … "psychology, hunch for want of a better word. Do you get my drift, Alistair?"

Alistair looked more shocked than Dennis could remember, so to ease his own embarrassment Dennis continued, "Do you remember, Alistair, how you used to tell me you really fancied yourself as a detective, and would love to have a real mystery to solve one day? I can actually remember your exact words, because you made me laugh when you said once you'd gladly investigate some crime for no fee. Then when you saw me laughing, you said you'd probably *pay* to do it! I was drinking tea at the time, and you made it start coming down my nose. I remember you said to Henrietta, 'Oh Gawd, Dennis is doing the nose and throat trick.' After that, she started and I had to leave the room."

Alistair, who had been somewhat taken aback by Dennis's change of tone from the gravity of the unsolved crime to the amused recollection of past friendly conversations, had recovered himself a bit. "Oh, golly yes, I remember that conversation. Those were happy days, weren't they? Gosh, Dennis, I never in my wildest dreams imagined it would be the mystery of poor Henrietta's murder." There was a pause and he added, "Oh, how awful! Life can be like a sick joke sometimes."

"There was more than one occasion when you spoke to me in that vein," continued Dennis. "Once it was when you had just finished reading a really good whodunit, but there was another time when we were walking in the country and having a rather serious discussion about things we would really like to try our hand at in life, and, whether or not you remember it, you came out, oh so seriously, at the time with how you'd love to have a crack at solving a mystery as a private detective."

"Yes, yes, yes, I remember it well, Dennis. Gee, we little knew, eh? It's just awful. The irony of it – I can hardly cope with the irony and the awfulness of it. Your poor, poor Henrietta …"

Alistair's head was literally racing with different thoughts. His gut reaction was that this offer did appeal to him. He even found himself momentarily having the strange notion that maybe he was meant to take this on, as he had by an extraordinary coincidence this information from Zoe about Henrietta's former love life and affair with her brother, Greg. More than ever he would keep quiet about all that – more than ever, he repeated to himself.

As Dennis continued, reminding Alistair of one or two past successes when he had assisted the police and received their thanks and compliments, and pressing his suggestion or indeed invitation, Alistair found himself thinking that from many points of view it was the ideal time to take on such a mission, or 'assignment' as he later called it. He had a good few weeks free, which he had ever so vaguely been planning to spend on one of his favourite occupations of hillwalking in Scotland; but just for one year he could forfeit or at anyrate defer that pleasure and take this on. There would surely never again be such an extraordinary opportunity to adopt a role that he had so often fancied himself in.

From a logistical point of view, it would be the easiest thing in the world to stay on at his brother's little hotel, he realised.

"Look, Dennis, this is the last thing in the world I was expecting you to come up with! It really, really is. I'm gobsmacked, I think the word is, at the moment. However, I've got to say my gut reaction is that you've chosen a good time to ask me this, because at the moment I was going to go back to Edinburgh, where

I'm just staying on in my digs; and as long as I pay the rent promptly, my dear landlady, Mrs Davidson, will be happy to let me keep the rooms on there while I'm down here at my brother's hotel. My brother couldn't have been more welcoming, as usual, and I know I can stay in his little hotel down here for as long as I want; and I mean, if I'm not getting anywhere I'll know after a few weeks, I presume, and just pack it in. You wouldn't think bad of me if I just got nowhere, and it came to absolute nothing?"

"Of course not," answered Dennis promptly. "I'd probably then engage an official firm of private detectives; but you know I'm really keen on you having a crack at it first, if you know what I mean. Helen Archer, who found poor Henrietta, and as I've just said is the wife of our dear churchwarden, Edwin, is the only person I've discussed this idea with, I admit. However she totally understood me and supported me in asking you. Oddly enough, she's the person I've found most helpful throughout this whole nightmarish ordeal. I don't know why, because she more or less withdrew from the congregation when Henrietta took over; but she is. It was Helen I phoned the other day, on the anniversary, when I thought of you taking this on."

Alistair was staring at the ground, seemingly in a trance.

"But what on earth would all the other people in the parish and all the other people connected think? They'd laugh their heads off, wouldn't they? I mean they probably wouldn't want to cooperate with me, would they?"

"Well, Helen was strong on that point, saying I would have to let it be known loud and clear, and officially, like, that you had my total support."

"But I mean, Dennis old chap, aren't people going to say, 'He's just an old codger poking his amateur nose into our tragedy?'"

"When I said I would let it be known loud and clear that you had my total approval and support, I meant *loud and clear*."

Dennis had raised his voice towards the end of this last remark in such a way that Alistair appeared convinced and nodded his head.

"I need to think about this, Dennis. I need time. It's one hell of a bombshell to chuck at someone."

"Don't backtrack now, Alistair, I saw your nod. I realise you'll want to think it through, but is there a chance you'd consider it? What's your gut answer to that?"

"I'll think about it. I'll actually possibly extend my little stay at my brother's hotel for a day or two while I think."

"Right, that's understandable. That's great. As far as I'm concerned Alistair, as soon as you say yes – well, you're on!"

Dennis gave Alistair a handshake, making such a theatrical gesture of it that the poor man was yet again rather taken aback.

"Well, please think about it seriously, Alistair," said Dennis, reentering the room with Alistair's coat, adding, "you've always been a great friend, and if you can crack this one I will be so indebted to you. My life has so totally fallen apart. I feel kind of desperate. They say drowning men clutch at straws, don't they? Well, that's how it feels like, Alistair. I feel I really must ask you to help. You used to go on so much about wanting to be a sleuth, and you used to get so annoyed when we laughed, because you used to say you were so deadly serious about it. Henrietta once said to me you'd missed your vocation, and for once she wasn't using that word in connection with the priesthood. Oh, Alistair, it's a kind of crie de coeur."

He stopped rather suddenly and put his arm round his friend's shoulder and they both stood there in silence for a moment.

Eventually, Dennis continued. "As I say, if it turns out to be a non-starter, then I'll more than likely get round soon enough to hiring what Helen calls an official private detective firm. But you know, in this kind of hiatus after such a thorough police investigation, it came to me, why not try this? You know Henrietta always said you were a canny so-and-so and could do anything you put your mind to. She wasn't always right, but she used to say you'd never get married."

Alistair bit his lip while Dennis added, "No one would have you with your weird lifestyle and eccentricities!"

How Alistair longed to say, "You can never be sure," and to tell his old friend about Zoe and his magical flight to America and their time in Chicago, for love makes us want to tell people of it; but for now he must bite his tongue and be patient, particularly so now, as he knew already about Greg, a seemingly unknown lover of the victim.

Alistair was very quiet as he stood by now in the hall. A realisation of just how much time and actual work would be involved was beginning to dawn on him.

"Look, Alistair," said a somewhat cheered Dennis, going back into the room and fumbling in the bottom right-hand drawer of a rather grand desk, "if you do agree to take this on, we'll discuss how and when you're going to begin; but in case you decide, as I hope you will, to take it on, for starters I'll give you a parish directory – one of our very fine St Peter's, Cookington, parish directories. That will be the first thing you'll need. Let's get one now."

The fumbling in the bottom drawer continued as did his chat. "Henrietta used to keep dozens down here for use with various campaigns and goings on. Ah, look, here's one - that looks a smart one – you take that, and if you do take this assignment on you'll need it. And then, as they say, the best of British."

Alistair, who had re-entered the drawing room, took the slim paper booklet and they both sat down on the edge of their chairs to show their intention not to stay longer than a moment. Dennis beamed over to his old friend, who gave a cursory flip through the pages and placed it carefully in his inside jacket pocket.

"That's pretty up to date," added Dennis pointing at Alistair's inside jacket pocket, where he had now carefully ensconced it, "there's not been many changes since that edition was printed about a couple of months before the tragedy."

Sensing that Dennis was cheering up slightly, Alistair allowed himself a smile.

"Seems like I'm being inveigled into taking this on, then," he said with a certain deliberation, adding, "it's such a big thing, though, Dennis, I can't quite get myself to formally agree to it – though obviously, from many points of view, as you well know, detective work of this nature does very much appeal to me."

Dennis got up to stretch his legs and said, " actually, we don't really need another discussion. If you do decide to take it on, I'm going to say from now on, Alistair, you're on your own; that's the whole point, isn't it? No red herrings from me. No distraction; you bring a completely fresh mind to it. A different approach to the police, and we'll hope for the best. Do you agree that's the point?

"Righty-ho, Dennis. I haven't committed myself yet, partly I think because I can hardly believe you're asking me this – it's so totally unexpected. I'm not dreaming, am I?"

Alistair paused and again noticed the relentless but silent traffic. He wanted more time to contemplate the offer; but he did not want to lose the opportunity of a lifetime.

"One thing, if you were me, where would you start – assuming I do take it on?"

"No, I'm not even going to say that," said Dennis with a kind of resolution. But after thinking for a moment in silence he added, "Oh, alright then, I suppose with the churchwardens – they're meant to know everything that's going on. You'll like Florence, everybody does, you and she have the same kind of humour, I often think. "

He paused smiling at Alistair. "Does that help?"

Alistair gave a loud laugh.

"How do you know I wasn't tricking you, Dennis, my old pal, by asking that question? Maybe it's the first question of my investigation. Maybe, I'd already started!"

He winked and stood up and picked his hat up, throwing it up into the air and catching it. "If I take this on, I'm going to start with you, my old friend, but it's going to have to be a fairly formal kind of an interview, isn't it? It'll involve some pretty personal questions too. You realise that, of course, I'm sure. You tell me when is convenient. Not today; I need a bit of quiet and a whisky."

"Gee, Alistair, that is kind of spooky, you saying you might have started already! You're a bit of a wizard. I have a lot of faith in you. Good luck. Of course I realise you'll have to ask me all sorts of highly embarrassing and awkward questions; I've obviously thought about that. But I've decided it's worth it. For Henrietta's sake I've got to allow myself to be humiliated, if necessary. I won't keep any secrets from you. I only suggested starting with the churchwardens because they are meant to know everything about what goes on in the parish. I think Florence does, and Edwin thinks he does, but I'm not sure he does."

"No, Dennis, it would be good to get the questions to you over and done with at the very beginning, wouldn't it? Even though we're such good friends, and you're asking me to carry out this investigation, I can still be objective, and if you agree to it ask you the sort of questions any police investigation would involve, can't I?"

"I suppose so."

"Look, as I say, it'll have to be pretty formal, and it obviously doesn't seem quite right to launch into it straight away; but what say you I come round tomorrow and we just go through what any investigator would ask, just for me to get the feel of it? And then I'll put the clappers on speaking to all the others, because we don't want this experiment of me fulfilling my aspirations to drag out too long, do we?"

"You'll find the fuzz grilled them all pretty thoroughly. Many of them had some highly suspicious things to explain, but it seems their alibis and explanations were OK, and everyone managed to convince the police of their innocence."

"Hearing you say that, I can't wait to get my teeth into this, Dennis. So when can I come round and start the ball rolling with an in-depth interview with you? When shall we do that?"

"Tomorrow teatime – that will appeal to you old chap – you always loved your tea. It's just possible that I'll have to put it off till the morning after, or you might want to. Let's keep arrangements mutually convenient, eh?"

"OK, let's play it by ear. I'll give you a buzz," assented Alistair.

"One of your famous buzzes," joked Dennis.

"Yes – and during the day tomorrow I'll mooch around and about St Peter's, Cookington, and try and get the feel of the place. Gosh, I've got my work cut out for me, haven't I? It'll have to start with a call to Mrs Davidson in Edinburgh, looks like she's going to have to wait a little longer before welcoming me back. Cheerio for now."

"Look," said Dennis rather abruptly at the front door, "I might as well just pop across the lawn here and show you the inside of St Peter's Church, not that it'll be much help in your investigation, but you should know what it looks like inside. Here, let me get the keys, and we'll have a ten-minute whizz round."

Together they walked across the patch of grass between the vicarage and the church, turned the corner and came to the big west door.

Dennis opened it with a loud clanging noise. "We're very proud of our West Door, it's genuinely 150 years old. You'll have to study all the carvings another time, but come in and stand at the back here to get a general view."

They both stood in silence for about four minutes before Dennis said, "Just to brief you on the basic geography of it, up there at the front on the left is what we call the sacristy, and on the other side, there on the right, is the choir vestry. They are linked behind the altar by what we rather pompously call the ambulatory, which has a door out to the car park too. Basic layout of your average church, really, and the door to the tower is here to our left in the narthex."

"As you say, very straightforward. I'll really enjoy studying the windows and carvings and statues etc. next time," said Alistair, picking up a copy of the latest newsletter from a little welcome table.

They stood quietly for another two minutes, looking

round with a kind of wonder, like tourists arriving at that other St Peter's in Rome.

Eventually Dennis broke the silence. "I used to find it too distressing to come in here after the crime, but I'm over that now. I had so many memories, even though we really weren't here very long at all. Of course, nothing has changed, everything is exactly as when Henrietta ran the place. The police even gave us back our visitors' book. Henrietta always made visitors sign the book. We had quite a few round about the time of the crime, which apparently gave the police a lot of work tracking them all down and eliminating them from their inquiries."

"I'll just take the quickest of looks at that," said Alistair in businesslike tone. He took advantage of Dennis replacing a light bulb over the bookstall to scribble down some names.

"There's so much history here," Dennis commented, returning to him and turning the narthex light off. "We'll have to go round properly next time, Alistair, but I'd better lock it all up again carefully now."

"I'll hold you to that," replied Alistair, once they were out again in the bright Cookington sunshine. He turned to make a farewell handshake.

"Hey, Alistair, before you go. Please tell me what it was that you were going to tell . What is it?"

"Sorry to tantalise you – that's got to wait for the moment," replied Alistair, "I'll tell you by and by if it all works out." Then he added with a theatrical bow, "But you ain't going to believe it!"

"You're not in love, are you, old chap?" Dennis asked with the biggest beam of the afternoon.

"Who, me? You know me, Dennis – give over!"

"Well, you know, it can happen to anyone, as Henrietta always used to say whenever she said you'd never marry!" Dennis laughed, seemingly more cheerful now.

"Yes, I remember she used to say that, didn't she? But as you say, she was also stronger on betting I'd never get married – nobody would have me, she used to say!"

"She was only joking, but she also said once if ever she got to heaven she'd try and arrange it."

"Yes, I remember her saying that." Alistair replied sympathetically lest these recollections upset Dennis, but could not help saying, "and heaven is where she is."

***

Alistair walked thoughtfully down to the station with enough ideas whizzing around in his brain to keep him preoccupied for days to come, never mind all the way back to his hotel. *If ever she got to heaven, she'd try and arrange it.* How ironic! Now she was in heaven, if it existed, which he could not help being doubtful of; but wouldn't it be wonderful if she could arrange it? He must be tired to be having such stupid thoughts, but in an inexplicable way it seemed to confirm him in his decision to take on this utterly extraordinary and unexpected assignment.

As the final Tube station approached, he summarised his thoughts. What a good friend Dennis is, and how incredibly flattering that he should ask me to help investigate this appalling tragedy of his life in the absence of any headway by the police. I don't deserve friends like him.

Yet, as sometimes before, he had that feeling that Dennis was keeping something to himself. Why should he think this about his friend? But he did. However, he could shelve that till he started the investigation in earnest; however, he reflected how perhaps everybody held back some information. He himself certainly did.

How very remarkable that he should have met a lady on a plane, who had referred to her brother being a former lover of Henrietta, and how utterly more remarkable that he, Alistair MacTavish, the born bachelor, should have been so besotted by that very same girl on the plane …

Back at the hotel, he took a shower and then sat at the bar of the little saloon and indulged once again in that favourite pastime of people watching. There were the usual comings and goings of groups of guests, asking the usual questions about taxis, Tube stations, times and distances. Tomorrow he would have this little 'mooch' around the parish and get the feel of the place. Yes, one needed to get the feel of a place. That was essential. Perhaps that's what potential new incumbents and church ministers did prior to signing along the dotted line. He would take it as it came tomorrow - following his nose, as he used to say - and have no prearranged route. His approach must be different to that of the police if he was to have any success. They had drawn a blank, and there was no point in doing a similar and inferior investigation down the same track. No, he must go down a different track. It probably wouldn't work, but it just might.

He had another drink. Yes, it just might work, if Zoe could help down here and Henrietta could help up there. I should not have had that last drink, he said to himself, and went upstairs to bed, where he slept the sleep of the just.

***

At the vicarage Dennis hadn't waited more than a couple of minutes after Alistair's departure before getting on the phone to Helen. "He's practically agreed to take the assignment on," he exaggerated enthusiastically. "He's the only man in England who'd agree to a thing like this, just like that. Mark you, I put the pressure on big style, I'll tell you. It's not absolutely definite; he hasn't exactly signed on the dotted line, but -"

"Only man in *Britain,*" corrected Helen. "You mustn't say England; he's a Scot, Dennis! He only lives down the road from where my parents used to live in the New Town up in Edinburgh."

"You're absolutely right, he's a Scot, but a Scot who likes cricket and tea. He'll go down well in Cookington. Maybe I'm absolutely stark staring crazy and bonkers to have set this up, and I'll be the first to get a proper firm of private detectives if it proves to be a nonsense. Oh, Helen, what have I done?"

"Have faith," answered Helen. "Remember what you told me Henrietta used to say about Alistair – he's a canny old so and so."

"Yeah, she used to say that, and he certainly is," replied Dennis. He put the phone down and for the first time in many years proceeded to go one further than Alistair and get badly drunk in his own living room.

CHAPTER 6

(A mooch around the parish)

When Alistair woke up the next morning, he had to still metaphorically pinch himself to be sure that yesterday's discussion with Dennis and possible arrangement had been for real. Yes, it was, and there as if to prove it on the little bedside table next to Sparky, his alarm clock, was the little parish directory which Dennis had given to him. He would take it down to breakfast and have another cursory look at it after the usual perusal of his breakfast newspaper. He would keep an open mind today about whether to commit himself to this enterprise, and make a decision by evening.

Breakfast went as normal in what was for him after so many years his familiar hotel, and the newspaper seemed to indicate that the world was much the same as ever.

He then turned to the little directory, which no doubt would be invaluable to his new found task and forthcoming inquiries. It was typical of Alistair that he should wait until he had finished both his breakfast and his newspaper before turning to it. It was not his style to sit down deliberately at a desk to study such a document, or indeed such a case. The directory was indeed what it purported to be on its impressive green front cover, a clear list of the congregation, with their addresses and telephone numbers, and in strict alphabetical order. Even Henrietta herself and the churchwardens took their place strictly alphabetically. At every page there were reminders to use the directory with discretion and to be mindful of people's privacy.

He was amused to see that Dennis appeared, presumably inadvertently, to have fished out Henrietta's own copy of the directory, because there at the front on the first page she had scribbled her now familiar signature with a date which was indeed only a couple of months before the murder. His preliminary dekko was nearly over when he suddenly noticed that on the back blank pages headed "Use these pages for New Members, Notes etc.' Henrietta had scribbled rather a lot of illegible handwriting.

Along with several miscellaneous names and addresses of people and firms as diverse as printers, cleaners, gardeners, tree surgeons, an insurance company and an undertaker, there, staring him in the face, were the names and addresses of other individuals living locally and elsewhere in Britain, including his beloved Edinburgh, and even, he noticed, one in America too. Who were these people? he wondered. Presumably the police had checked them all out – or had they? A sense of the enormity, difficulty and probable impossibility of the task, which he hadn't quite agreed yet to take on, began to dawn on him. His eye was caught by one name in particular. Who on earth was this guy Buzz, who lived so close to his modest digs in Edinburgh, for example? And who was this couple in America? There were also strange combinations of letters - presumably initials, he concluded, but he was not so sure. Maybe they were just random doodlings, such as you might pen while listening to someone on the phone; but some were mysterious, and some had what could be a date of day and month alongside. 'GF' was one that cropped up three times in these back note pages, and once with a date, 5 November, alongside. Like having solved a crossword clue, Alistair looked up with a sense of achievement; if nothing else, he had worked that one out.

"You look like you've got something on your mind today," said the friendly waitress, Cissie, whom he had known for years, as she cleared his plates away after breakfast.

"Yes, I have, and by and by I'll let you and Donna know what it's all about, Cissie," he replied.

Soon, as agreed yesterday with Dennis, he was on his way the short distance back to Cookington, to get 'the feel of the place', as he termed it in his mind. By this evening, he thought, I'll know if I can't resist taking this on. It's certainly the chance of a lifetime; but surely a Herculean task by any stretch of the imagination.

The sun shone pleasantly down, and Alistair had to remind himself that actually all was not right with the world. There was a dastardly crime to be solved, and he had been given the chance of having it entrusted to him by a dear friend in a last desperate effort to solve it and find some kind of closure and way of resuming some form of normal existence. Do I owe it to Dennis, as a long-standing friend, to give it a whirl? It'll be a serious whirl, he said almost out loud.

He spent all morning walking around the parish, engaged in precisely that task of getting to know the feel of the place - the ambience of St Peter's, to coin a phrase he was later to use a lot.

He did indeed take advantage of no one knowing him yet to have a good nose round. People said hallo and he responded warmly, all ready to make out that he was a tourist if necessary.

He decided he would not try and gain entry yet into the church for a second look; that could be done later and in some detail if he accepted the assignment. Yes, he thought, this was just a nose around, and that could indeed wait, but to walk around the vicinity of the church and indeed the parish would be a useful preliminary.

When he had completed this to his own satisfaction,

he determined to climb the nearby hill that had rather intrigued him and which overlooked the seemingly ordinary outer suburb of London, and admire the view.

He was glad he had made the effort; how compact the parish looked from this hillside viewpoint! It was the stillness which struck him and oddly the silence too; for up here, although there was a distant hum of traffic, there was none of the noise of below – no hoots, no exhausts, no voices, perhaps the occasional bird - and yes, oddly, you could hear the bell of St Peter's tower – only just, but unmistakeable.

"It's a good view, isn't it sir?" Broke in a stranger's voice behind him and then continued, "It's so strange how you can get down there so quickly; and when you're down there you wonder how it ever looked so peaceful, don't you?"

The mischievous streak in Alistair came to the fore; he shocked himself by his own deviousness in acting dumb. "Which tower is that? That one down there - you can just make it out."

"Oh, that'll be St P's, or St Peter's to give it its proper name. I should know, I used to attend there, long time ago, before the Flood."

"Really?" Alistair continued to be shocked by his own acting. "What sort of congregation was it?"

"Oh, your typical C of E in those days; I've heard it's quite High Church now – that's the church whose vicar was found in a shed nearby. A right case that is, or I should say *was*. The papers have tired of it now … police drew a complete blank, despite there being so many names in the papers."

"Oh yes, I remember now. It caused quite a stir, didn't it?" Alistair bluffed.

"I shouldn't say this – this is me talking crazy now - but I always had a theory about that, you know," said the stranger, sounding a trifle lonely.

"Oh, go on, tell me. Actually, I was just going to have a pint in that pub over there. I see it's called the Antelope, isn't it? Come on, let me get you one. Do you know, I love a good yarn."

The one thing this new-found fellow human being could not resist was the offer of a free drink.

"I'm going to order a ploughman's as well," said Alistair rubbing his hands as they entered the welcoming establishment. "No, this is on me – it was my idea. I invited you in, and I'm the visitor. I'm the tourist."

"See, this vicar that got murdered, she was from Olchester. Knew it well, used to live on the outskirts – a village nearby. I had a colleague at work there, yonks ago it was, my old mate Buzz, who lived only about a couple of miles from me."

Alistair's new-found companion seemed to check himself. He stopped and said, "No, you don't want to hear all this – let's talk about the cricket."

"Later," interrupted Alistair, who for a Scotsman knew a surprising amount about the game, and in other circumstances would have so welcomed the topic.

His companion now turned uncharacteristically silent.

Alistair prompted him, "You were saying about your colleague at work … I like a good yarn, you know."

"Oh well, alright then, I know this sounds crazy," the stranger continued, "this vicar what's been murdered. I don't know if Buzz would want me to tell you all this, but she was only his girlfriend, wasn't she?"

Alistair looked as surprised as he felt.

"Honest, I'm not making this up," continued his new companion. "It was ridiculous, really. He was hell's young at the time and she was older by a good

73

few years."

"As I say, I like a good yarn," muttered Alistair, trying to hide his excitement and adding, "other people's lives are so interesting, aren't they?"

"Well, I can tell you all about it if you want me to. I mean all that hype in the papers last year – it brought those distant times back to me – quite vividly, actually. She – the vicar what got done in down there in Cookington - was a lot more serious minded than dear old Buzz. I mean it was absurd, it was never going to work, not in a million years. He was quite young for his age and she was quite old for hers. Mark you, he was well stuck on her, despite the big age gap, I remember. I used to tease him and say that's what turned him on, but I remember he got quite cross when I took that line. He would say 'No I'm not going to talk about us.'"

The stranger paused to sip his beer before continuing.

"That made me think it was quite serious. I mean, I was such a good mate of his, and this was so special to him that he didn't want to talk about it – even to me, his old mate."

Alistair wished he had a pipe. He turned his glass on the mat, nibbled at a crisp, and felt his pulse quicken once more.

Again there was a rather long pause and Alistair mumbled, "Go on," trying to hide his impatience.

"This is good beer," came the response, to Alistair's frustration.

"So you're saying this romance didn't last very long then," Alistair prompted again.

"It was over before it began; but old Buzz, he never got over it."

"So she left him."

"Yes, she just told him one day, 'Buzz, marriage is not for us' - and when he went to see her, she told him she was getting married and was very happy. He put on an act of taking it like a man, but he hurt real deep inside, I know. Anyway, he's never seen her since."

Alistair was trying to hide his intense interest in all this. He turned in his chair towards the bar, gesturing with his arms that his companion might want another drink, and repeated rather inanely his phrase about loving a good yarn.

For a moment he was in a dilemma how to continue, for he felt strongly that, absurd though the situation was, this might be an interesting line of inquiry to pursue. After a little he said, "You don't mind telling me all this, do you?" and repeated, "I find other people's lives so interesting."

He opened a packet of crisps and pushed another packet towards his new companion saying sotto voce but audibly, "Takes your mind off your own affairs, doesn't it?"

"There's not much more to say, really. I mean, like I say, Buzz never saw her again. I know that. He was curiously rather insistent that he shouldn't. I asked him why not once, and he simply said it would be too complicated."

Alistair glanced at the pictures on the pub's wall; he did not want his questions to sound too interested or indeed too investigative. He deliberately made a joke to the barmaid about a dog that had come to join them with a hopeful expression. He patted the dog long and slowly.

At length he leant back. "If you're not in a hurry I'd like to ask one or two things. I'm not joking, but I really do find these situations so interesting."

"I really can't tell you any more."

Alistair ignored the reply.

"You say he never got over it, but I mean this was yonks ago, as you say; is he happily married now?"

"More or less lost touch with him. But no, he moved up to Edinburgh shortly after that. I asked him once before he went up there if he had got a new girlfriend, and he said rather sadly that no, there would never be anyone else."

"And you really lost touch with him after that..."

"We swop Christmas cards – that's all. He did once put 'You're my only contact with the old days.' Course, I was shocked stupid when I read about the murder in the paper, and I tried to contact him out of sheer curiosity. I sent a letter, but got no reply – assumed he had moved - couldn't track him down. Didn't get even a Christmas card for the first time last year."

Alistair leant back on the pub bench, thinking. If it was his rival that he had stabbed that would make more sense, he mused.

"Well, look at me, chatting away as if I'd got all the time in the world. Talk too much – that's my problem; but I've really enjoyed that. No, it's a funny old world – don't mind meeting up again sometime – perhaps you've got a good tale to tell me – anyway the name's Eric – Eric Watson. I'm up around these haunts quite a lot. The evening staff know me here in the Antelope quite well."

Alistair stood up to shake hands and fumbled in his wallet for one of his cards. He scribbled his phone number down on the back.

"Thanks," responded the jovial Eric, tucking it safely into his wallet. "I'm afraid I haven't got one for you - don't do cards."

"Oh, you should – very convenient for sliding to some girl who takes your fancy – you can always scribble a few words on them before you hand them over." Alistair, the born bachelor, could hardly believe that he was saying such things. What an effect Zoe has had on me, he mused.

"That sounds like a good idea; might get round to having a few printed one day. Anyway, as I say, the name's Eric and you'll find me most days in and around, either here at the Antelope, or further afield beyond Cookington at the Queen Dowager." He pointed vaguely towards Central London and disappeared out of the door.

Alistair waited a few minutes and then got up to go. As he carried the glasses to the bar, he threw out a nonchalant inquiry to the barmaid. "You ever been to a church round here?" He must be more careful; the beer was making him a little freer in expression than he used to be. He was almost glad when she replied that she had never darkened the door of a church since being forced to Sunday school by her well-meaning father. He picked up his hat, smiled and unfortunately said, "God bless."

Well that's someone with a motive, he thought – someone called Buzz, last heard of in Edinburgh. It just has to be the Buzz scribbled at the back of Henrietta's directory. Wasn't that a well-known attitude in horror stories? *If I can't have her, nobody can.* He shuddered at the thought of it. This terrible possibility had to be considered. To what extent was all this known about and investigated by the police?

Well, that's one person to suss out already, he thought as he strolled down the hill back towards the parish of St Peter's, Cookington, and I've hardly officially started.

For a moment the beauty of the bright sunshine, the blue sky and pleasant grass of Cookington Hill took his thoughts away, and he contemplated how nice it would be to get this all over and revert to a carefree life. Him and Zoe, living in a place like this without a care in the world. It's amazing how a glass or two of beer can make you feel so good, he reflected.

Now he must turn his thoughts back to his old friend, Dennis. Dennis in a way would be the most interesting person of all to chat to. It would soon be teatime in the vicarage, but he was rather full of beer, so that could wait till tomorrow, as they had agreed if it proved necessary. He would give Dennis the half-expected phone call to defer. This evening he would go to the local cinema. He felt the need of a film, but it must have no murder in it, for he was beginning to think that he was going to be involved with murder rather a lot in the coming weeks. How could he resist Dennis's offer, now that there were two things about which he seemed to be the only person in the know?

CHAPTER 7

(An interview with a murder victim's widower)

It was a strange situation, thought Alistair as he rang the vicarage bell the following afternoon. Here he was about to have what they had both agreed should be a formal interview between himself and one of his oldest and best friends. However, as Dennis had said, once he had agreed to ask Alistair to investigate this mystery, he had to agree to what he called a kind of official, formal interview, of the sort that any investigator would want.

Dennis opened the front door promptly, and within a couple of minutes the usual pleasantries and small talk were completed and both men seemed to acknowledge a kind of change of gear. They leant forward with a businesslike demeanour on the comfy armchairs that faced each other.

"I'm going to take this on, Dennis. In a way, it's quite crazy, but I'm never going to have a real life mystery of this proportion to deal with. Of course, given my inclination to this sort of thing, it appeals to me greatly. I won't let it drag on: a couple of months, or maybe three at the most. I think I'd probably go mad after that. It's OK with big brother for me to stay at his hotel for that long. Mrs Davidson in Edinburgh doesn't seem to mind me keeping my rooms on up there, as long as she gets her rent."

Dennis, who had appeared the slightest bit nervous, now seemed to relax considerably. He beamed across at Alistair and said, "Oh I'm so relieved, Alistair. I've really got a lot of faith in you."

Alistair's response was to say briskly, "I'm going to be different from the old me for a bit now, Dennis.

Afterwards we'll go back to being the good friends that we are. Now, as a rough plan of campaign, Dennis, let's start with any problems in this parish, and then after going through the allotment holders, and also the neighbours who overlook the allotment and who seem rather an interesting bunch, work backwards from this parish, through your – sorry, Henrietta's - past parish, and go right back to early life. I mean, that's how I see it, Dennis. Those are the groupings of people to be considered."

Dennis nodded, keeping quiet to show that he was in favour of this businesslike style.

"As regards the parish, Henrietta didn't have any serious trouble or problems with any of the parishioners, did she?"

"No, really she didn't. There were disagreements, but I gather that's normal and expected in any parish."

"I suppose, again naturally, she liked some of them more than others. I mean, who did she like best, and who least?" Alistair asked, introducing a slight laugh into his voice, as he felt the tone was perhaps a trifle too formal.

"Well, she liked the two churchwardens very much – I'd say the best. Found them both very nice people, and very good and helpful in their different ways. Said they were very different. Florence, she said, was very efficient, practical, and to call a spade a spade, useful. Edwin, she said, was very supportive and encouraging, good for morale, and very willing to oblige. He was good at making the parish gel - or 'swing', as she used to jokingly say – but casual as they come. I doubt right now if he could find the key quickly."

"Well, that's great!" Alistair laughed. "But now, what about the ones she had difficulty with?"

"Ah, now, Fred was awkward she said. That's Fred Goodman. Funny fellow – quite sincere in his own way, but you know, one of those chaps who had been churchwarden for years and years – something like fourteen - and thought he still should be. She used to say he was obstructive; she felt sometimes he tried to block ideas and suggestions almost for the sake of it, she told me. One evening she came back from a PCC meeting – it was the only time it happened, but she was in tears. Turned out that Fred had put the dampers on both the purchase of a piano and the temporary hiring of an organ, while we were waiting for the big one to be repaired. She was absolutely furious. I rang Fred up myself and arranged for him to come round and talk it over with us personally the next day. I didn't want to interfere, but I thought it was my husbandly duty to support my wife when she had been made so upset. He was quite rude on the phone – said he didn't think I cared, or something like that – didn't think I was interested. I found him quite pompous. He said he would have to look in his diary and phone back on the morrow. I started getting annoyed with him myself."

"So, Dennis, I take it you don't like him."

"I'm trying to. Isn't that what it's all about? Trying to follow the way."

Alistair smiled and answered, "I mustn't get sidetracked by philosophical questions; mark you, I'm interested in getting to grips with all that shortly. Taking stock, really, now that I'm forty-six. Right, back to business."

"Promise not to digress any more," responded Dennis, putting his finger to his mouth.

"Would you say that was the biggest row in the parish, or were there others of similar magnitude on the Richter scale?" asked Alistair, half jokingly, and again trying to ease what he still felt was the rather formal way things were proceeding.

"Well, of course there was the great bell-ringing

dispute. This guy over by the allotments cut up real rough about that. I expect you'll meet the man in your inquiries."

"Can you tell me in a nutshell about that one?"

"Basically this guy, Aaron MacQuarrie or some such name … funnily enough, he had a house backing onto the allotments, I believe … anyway he objected to the church bells, said they woke him up or something. Henrietta made a joke about the bells not helping his hangover. I can't remember the details, but anyway there was one hell of a row. Henrietta said he seemed like a violent man – said she was scared of him. No doubt you'll check him out. I know the police certainly did."

"Anything else like that?" asked Alistair.

"Well, there was quite a bit of argument between certain members of the congregation about the church car park rules etc."

"What was all that about?"

"Some people thought we were charging too much on match days, and some not enough. Some thought it wasn't right anyway to take advantage of being so near the stadium; some thought it wasn't right on Sundays … Oh golly, it drove poor Henrietta mad! She said once, 'How the hell can I run a parish where everybody disagrees so much?'"

"Presumably, she was in favour of this method of raising money for the church, though?" checked Alistair.

"Oh, very much so," replied Dennis.

"These all seem terribly trivial matters to me as an outsider, Dennis. Was there ever anything a bit more meaty?"

"Not really, but definitely a few what you might call theological disagreements – or I should say disagreements about style, about churchmanship, I

82

suppose I should say," replied Dennis, adding, "surprisingly heated for Christians, when you consider what they were talking about, if you know what I mean."

"Well, of course people got burnt at the stake only a few hundred years ago over things like that, didn't they?" commented Alistair, in a last attempt to make Dennis ease up a bit and relax.

Dennis ran through the main personalities of the parish throwing out his personal opinions about their various characters. Alistair scribbled notes as fast as he could while this continued, and tried for the moment to shut out his thoughts of how all very unchristian it sounded.

Before long the subject of their talk had moved on to the allotment holders.

"OK. Now, as regards the allotment holders, I gather you just didn't know them. You never met them. Is that correct?"

"No, I never did – why should I?"

That sounded a bit on the defensive, thought Alistair, before continuing.

"I know you say you're always at the office or here, but come off it, Dennis, you've always told me you like to take an evening walk. Do you remember, I've always said they sound very civilised? I remember once Henrietta butted in and said 'Well, Dennis *is* very civilised.'"

"Yes, I remember her saying that," he said quietly, and he seemed to fight back a tear. "Funny how you never forget a compliment."

"Where do you go on these evening walks?" asked Alistair pleasantly, trying to pre-empt any breakdown into tears.

"Oh, just round and about. Always have done – wherever we've been. I like the different light and just the calming effect it has on one, especially after a fraught day at the office. Henrietta used to say it made me sleep better. Wherever I am I've always gone for evening strolls, and funnily enough, Alistair, I particularly like strolling in the evening in your great city of Edinburgh with its long lingering twilight – amazing how being just that little bit further north has that effect! I must say here the traffic can be a pain, though, so I like to get away from at least the main roads. I prefer the side roads, and particularly the little parks near here."

"Did Henrietta accompany you on these strolls?"

"Only on holiday; not here. I think that unfortunately and unnecessarily she thought the vicar shouldn't be seen strolling around the place as if she had nothing to do, so yes, I got into the habit of going on my own."

"Did you ever go to the allotments?"

"No, truly I didn't. You can imagine the police pressed me on that one – but no I never went. I had no reason to."

Dennis seemed to change tack rather deliberately.

"Henrietta told me about them once and how she'd found some poor guy stoned out of his mind there. I remember she said it was the guy in charge – someone called Charles, I think. She had a bash at a little bit of evangelising there, which was unusual, because it wasn't really her style. I gather he told her to piss off."

Alistair stifled a smile, but sensing that Dennis had noticed it, said, "Oh dear, my trouble has always been, I can't help seeing the funny side. Tragedy and comedy go together so often. So, Dennis, you didn't know any of the other allotment holders?"

"Never got to know them – they weren't church people – rather the opposite, from what I heard."

"What do you mean by 'rather the opposite'?" asked

Alistair, looking up abruptly.

"Oh, just that Henrietta told me some of them – well, more than one of them - had had some bad experience with the church, and I don't know, they seemed to think they could commune spiritually rather better on the soil than with the irritations of parish life. I think they may have a point there."

Alistair looked thoughtful for a moment, for such a line of thought was relevant too to his own musings at the time, before continuing, "Now, I gather from these old press cuttings that the police were understandably quite interested in the people whose houses looked over the allotments – people living in that road which runs parallel with the west side of the allotments - Lime Grove, it's called, isn't it?"

"Well, the only one I got to hear about before the crime was that chap I mentioned who complained about the church bells. Phew … take a Rottweiler with you when you go and see him, which I suppose you must if you're going to do this thoroughly, as I know you will."

"I'll be brave … You get bad vibes from that guy, do you?" asked Alistair seriously.

"I'll say," said Dennis, jokingly loosening his collar as if to cool himself and exhaling air through bulging cheeks.

"You see, I'm a great believer in being able to tell a lot from vibes," stressed Alistair.

"I know you are, Alistair; that's one of the reasons I asked you to take this on."

Alistair was already on to the next question, "And you didn't know the other house owners alongside the allotment?"

"No."

"So you never heard about any rows between those people and the allotment holders?"

"Oh, I think there was some kind of blaming each

other for rats. Yes, I seem to remember that our dear churchwarden, Edwin and his wife Helen had a bit of bother with one of them - one of those house owners – I have a vague memory of hearing about that."

"Let me just jot that down. Now, Dennis, old chap, this is where it gets a tad embarrassing, but we've got to go through with it, if my investigation is to be thorough. We've got to move on to -"

"You're going to say Henrietta's previous boyfriends," interrupted Dennis with a shy smile, adding, "I realised we would have to go through all that when we agreed this little game, Alistair, so don't worry – fire ahead."

"Well, yes … also, Dennis, old chap, I'll have to ask about your own former relationships etc. Funnily enough, although we're such great friends, you've never really told me anything about that over the years we've known each other, have you? I suppose it's normal not to have done so."

"Well, I don't recall you telling me much about your private life, either, Alistair."

"Funny how one can be such good friends and yet not really know the secrets of each other's hearts," added Alistair, thinking of Zoe.

"How true that is; but to the point, it's fair enough that you should ask, and it won't take very long."

"Shall we do it that way round, then? Talk about your exes first - and then have a break before tackling Henrietta's exes?"

Alistair's hope for another cup of coffee was turning into a need.

"Good idea, and I can say I've nothing to hide and am only too happy to tell all, which is exactly what I told the police; they were kind enough to rule out me having any motives for a crime of passion. I had a couple of fairly serious relationships, to use your word, before I met Henrietta. First was a girl I met at university called Samantha, but it didn't last more than a few months when we left; and the next thing I knew she had married one of the lecturers, who I didn't like and was several years her senior. I must admit it was a bit of a shock, but I'd say now more a bit of a giggle."

"Everyone has a past, eh? I wonder you never told me that one, though, over the years, Dennis," said Alistair, laughing.

"Didn't think you'd be interested, old chap! However, the next one was a bit more serious, but we never got engaged or anything. I mean to say, not like my darling Henrietta; she had actually been engaged to a guy called Rhys. It doesn't bother me. I was the lucky one who got her in the end."

"Before we get on to her past lovers, tell me more about this second, more serious as you say, girlfriend that you had. I remember you telling me once how you nearly married someone else, and how different life would have been. You never told me about her, though."

Dennis put on an expression of some surprise, as if not recalling what Alistair had said.

"You told me," persisted Alistair, "when I was giving you and Henrietta dinner, and next minute you said Henrietta had kicked you under the table. And we all had a good laugh, remember."

"Yes, yes, yes … oh, she was a girl called Frances, who was working in the office when I first started … went on for a couple of years. Henrietta used to joke that the lucky girl had a narrow escape. She married the sales manager in the end. As with Samantha, the police checked both of them out, poor things, *and* their husbands – all incredibly embarrassing for me, though curiously in my bereavement it did not upset me at the time, though now I do feel a bit embarrassed. The police told me they were both happily married."

"Did Henrietta ever meet these people?" asked Alistair with interest.

"No, she didn't seem to want to, and actually I never suggested it. I think there may have been one time when I wondered aloud to her whether or not it would be a good idea, because Frances still sent a Christmas card; but she didn't seem to think it would be. I remember, like you, she said we've all got a past."

Alistair would have requested more coffee, but mercifully Dennis suggested it and there was a pleasant hiatus while he was in the kitchen and Alistair again had a chance to lean back and stretch his legs. He looked around the smart room and admired some old prints of Cookington on the walls. Did Cookington ever really look like that? he wondered. I suppose it must have. He enjoyed looking at old prints at the best of times, and this was no exception.

When Dennis returned with the refills, he had to make quite an effort to get down to business again.

"OK, right. Now, about Henrietta. You say she had actually been engaged to this guy called Rhys. It's funny, I never knew that. When you mentioned Rhys just now, I had to hide my surprise, because I never heard either of you ever mention him. Anyway, how did all that end?"

"I think we never mentioned it to you, because it was more serious; she broke it off. He didn't seem too bothered, actually. I met him at a party about that time and of course I was a trifle embarrassed in case he felt I was nicking his girl, but he came up to me and said, 'Good luck, mate.' Yes, I remember, I was pretty relieved at the time, because I was worried he would think I was at fault, which I wasn't – never did anything he could complain about. Actually, he sent me rather a nice letter later; Henrietta made me laugh by telling me it was rather out of character. She joked that if she'd known he could write such a nice letter, she might have thought again. She loved winding me up."

Dennis put on a faint smile, went over to a desk and started to rummage in a desk drawer. He found an already rather faded photograph, which he took out and handed over for inspection.

"Time is relentless," commented Alistair. "You two look so young there! So that's Rhys, is it? He looks a bit cocky."

"Cocky is the word; he was, a bit. To be serious, Henrietta said he could never have been a vicar's husband."

"You were more suitable, were you?" asked Alistair, a little too abruptly for Dennis's liking.

"Well, not so cocky, anyway," he answered defensively.

"There weren't any other former boyfriends of hers?" asked Alistair again rather abruptly,

"No, I'm pretty sure of that," came Dennis's quiet response.

Dennis looked out of the window, and Alistair felt he was deciding whether to say something or not. His silence had the desired effect.

"A kid had had a crush on her absolutely yonks ago," he blurted out, "but as she once said, that was a non-starter."

This must be the enigmatic Buzz I heard about yesterday, thought Alistair, keeping his recently acquired information secret, as Dennis momentarily appeared a bit awkward and started fiddling with his teaspoon.

Aware of Dennis's unease, and sensing that he had something awkward to say, Alistair waited for him to speak.

"To be honest, Alistair, I never told you this – here

we go - I knew we would get to know each other better through all this, so I'll tell you. Yeah, it used to irk me a bit. Whenever we had a slight row about something, she'd sooner or later bring up this young guy's name – he was called 'Buzz' for some extraordinary reason – I think it was a name he got at school; anyway she'd get a bit wistful. She used to say 'I wonder what he's doing now, and where he is' - things like that."

"How did you feel about that?" asked Alistair sympathetically, once again hiding his surprise.

"Normally pretty indifferent, but sometimes I was aware of being a bit ruffled by it. I used to think it odd that she spoke of him more than of Rhys, the guy she had been more or less engaged to, for goodness sake. It didn't make sense. I mean, she'd dismissed Buzz as a kid."

"Did you ever comment on that to her?" asked Alistair, allowing a slight look of puzzlement to cross his brow.

"Yes, I did once," answered Dennis promptly, "and I remember she said, 'Well, you see, I got to know Rhys too well.'"

"Was there ever any contact after you two got married with either of these good people?" asked Alistair, more like a policeman than ever.

"With Buzz, no – absolutely not, he seemed to completely disappear. With Rhys – well, we used to get Christmas cards from them – from Rhys and the new lady in his life, Sheila – a rather attractive lady, I thought. Anyway, as Henrietta used to say, paradoxically vicars don't do Christmas cards – they reckon they're too busy and that anyway it could all get a bit invidious – you know, people saying 'He got one, but I didn't' sort of thing. I told her once you ought to send Rhys and Sheila one back, but she said she wasn't going to break her rule, and joked about letting sleeping dogs lie."

Alistair was finding it hard to concentrate on all this talk about Rhys, whom he had yet to meet. His mind was still racing with the talk of Buzz and his conversation with the stranger yesterday. Also the fact that Dennis had just said that Buzz had seemed to completely disappear; yet if he was not mistaken the address was clearly written in Henrietta's hand at the back of the parish directory; indeed her handwriting of his name was particularly neat for once. Did Dennis really not know this?

Alistair chewed the end of his pen. He had only been on the case five minutes, but he already thought he was on to something.

"As far as you're concerned, you feel sure there just couldn't be any connection between this terrible event and all these good people?" Alistair asked after a pause, looking at Dennis straight in the eye.

"Absolutely not!" came the prompt reply, with an equally straight look.

"I'm glad you said 'absolutely', because I've got to be absolutely sure you feel that; if I'm going to make progress. Please tell me if there was any other boyfriend in her life, Dennis, as I'll obviously just have to get all that straight and cleared up before I start. I think everyone knows that, alas, in this fallen world the evil of murder can sometimes be linked to the passion of love."

"No, there weren't any others - not that she ever told me of – perhaps an occasional allusion to things she'd done in her youth. I think she did once say, kind of jokingly, things like 'You know, I've had my admirers in the past.' Yes, she said that once, and it made me very jealous, I don't mind admitting it." Dennis stopped and looked at Alistair, adding, "Stupid, isn't it?"

Was that an allusion by Henrietta to Zoe's brother, Greg? wondered Alistair immediately. Why had Dennis not mentioned Greg? Was he really in the dark about it? In case that were so, he must keep quiet about it, and also about the further extraordinary and possibly significant coincidence of his meeting Zoe on his holiday flight. It was difficult, because a part of him was dying to tell his old friend about his having fallen in love with Zoe.

"You spare yourself a lot of trouble being a bachelor, Alistair," came Dennis's voice, stirring him from his thoughts. "I'm sure there's a lot to be said for it."

Yes, how in love I am, thought Alistair, as this remark hung in the air; how more painful than ever were such jibes as that – but I must not tell, he reminded himself, for Zoe's brother could conceivably be crucial to the mystery.

"How true that saying is, that grief is the price we pay for love," continued Dennis wistfully.

A part of Alistair wanted to change the subject and allow himself time to think things through later, but he knew he must pursue the matter.

Dennis brought him back with a jolt. "A penny for your thoughts, Alistair. What were you thinking just then? You looked miles away."

"Just thinking things through," responded Alistair skilfully. "Now, I was asking you about whether there were any other boyfriends in the past."

"And I said no. No, I really can't recall her ever having mentioned anyone else. I assumed she'd been out over the years with a few guys other than this young lad, Buzz, and this Rhys chappie before we met, but she never mentioned any names. You know, if someone's good-looking, you assume they have had a few relationships – Gawd, how I hate that word –

people use it like they're getting in and out of cars. I've gone off the modern world more than ever these days, since the crime, Alistair."

"OK, well, no doubt we'll get back to those vague allusions as time goes by, but let me ask you on a different tack, were you just being polite to me when you said you like strolling in Edinburgh, or have you been up there a lot?"

"We used to go a lot because Henrietta really loved the city. We would sometimes spend a week or so, just 'chilling out', as the modern phrase has it. I've never liked the hills like you, Alistair, but I went up on Arthur's Seat a few times. Once in the summer I even went up one of the Pentland Hills, Carnethy – really beautiful." He paused as if he was trying to remember something. "Oh yes, I climbed North Berwick Law too. I saw it from the train once, and Henrietta said, 'I bet you never climb that' – so I did – about forty-eight hours later."

Alistair laughed. There had always been a fun side of Dennis, which he supposed was no doubt a factor in why Henrietta had married him. He just managed to stop himself saying, 'There you are; marriage is good for you.'

Dennis laughed too. "Do you know, I don't remember laughing like that since the crime. I've quite shocked myself by finding myself laughing. I think you're being very therapeutic in a way."

"Did Henrietta ever go with you up these hills? I seem to remember her telling me I was quite mad to climb them so often."

"No, never on those occasions," replied Dennis, continuing, "she usually opted to visit an art gallery or a museum or something. Most of all she liked visiting the city's churches round and about – there's enough of them. To be honest I can have too much of that, so yes,

I used to toddle off on my own, and yes, she likewise."

"And apart from visiting me, of course – I have some happy memories of your visits - you and she never ever visited any friends up there in Edinburgh … not that there would be any living there, but any former lovers there or whatever?" He tried to make it sound like a joke.

"Good heavens, no. Absolutely not. I don't mean it in a bad way, but we liked to get away from it all up there. That's one of the reasons we liked to go because, as Henrietta used to say, a vicar needs to get away from people occasionally as she spends so much time helping them. She was good at visiting people down here."

Alistair kept thinking of the Edinburgh address, which he had seen written neatly in Henrietta's own hand in the back of the parish directory, yet Dennis had said they never visited anyone. Again, the burning question came to him. Does Dennis not know about this? he wondered. Or is he concealing it?

A funny thought came to Alistair's mind as Dennis popped out to replenish the biscuits. The fact that he had seemingly inadvertently given him a parish directory with Buzz's address in suggested he was not trying to deceive. Surely he would have been too careful to do that if he was a villain.

Or had Dennis given him that particular directory on purpose? Alistair's thoughts raced as he leant forward to the newly arrived plate that his friend had put down on the coffee table.

"I'll just allow myself one of those biscuits, Dennis, and then I'll leave you in peace. I'll take your advice and start properly with a visit to the churchwardens."

"Yes, I would if I were you, so as to speak. I mean, obviously you'll want to speak to Sylvia, our dear curate, whom the bishop has banished down to the

94

country; and then of course dear Barnaby, our esteemed lay reader. But no, Florence is the one who really knows what's going on. You'll hear all you need to know about parish life, and a great deal more, from her."

"Well, I'm going to try my damndest for you, Dennis, that I promise," said Alistair emphatically, allowing his notebook to snap shut rather expertly.

"Well, also for Henrietta, I'm sure," added Dennis. "I owe her a never ending determination to get justice. I loved her so much, you know, Alistair. We were more than husband and wife – I know it sounds like a cliché, but we were best friends too – soulmates. She used to tell me she never kept a secret from me. She didn't mind that I wasn't quite so active as regards the church – she said it had its advantages. She said the bishop had told her that. You know, we had a kind of understanding about all that."

"Well, of course, it's because you were such soulmates that you are probably the most important person for me to address questions to," commented Alistair, looking as if to get up.

"I've not kept anything back. Absolutely nothing. I mean, I wanted to show that I'm so in earnest about asking you to investigate. Now that she's gone, for the sake of truth I would tell you her innermost secrets if I felt it would bring her justice."

Alistair drew the conversation to a conclusion. He had enough material to chew over for now. He stood up, admired an indoor plant and talked a little about the prints on the wall and other such matters.

They shook hands again at the front door.

Alistair turned on the porch and pointed up at the robust church tower standing so magnificently, with its fine flag of St George gently fluttering against the blue sky.

Dennis saw him admiring its stately grandeur and commented, "She used to say that if she ever really needed absolute peace and quiet to communicate with God, she would go up there for a while. Used to tell me how Our Lord went up mountains to pray and get strength for work when he came down. She told me once that she was very impressed by something a former Bishop of London had said – something to the effect that churches were great places *to go out from*. It was one Robert Stopford. She'd come across it in an article and cut it out and kept it in her Bible."

"That's the sort of really interesting thing I should learn. I mean, to get the feel for the situation and everything. Anything else like that?" asked Alistair, putting his arm round his old friend's shoulder; something he would never normally do, but which seemed so natural in the circumstances.

"No, that's the only thing that comes to mind – the tower. Used to say it was somewhere nobody ever went to. Ironically, she used to say that over by the allotments was also away from the bustle, but I think it was the tower she liked best. Yes," Dennis chuckled audibly now, "She used to call it her sanctuary, and she used to say playfully to me that if ever she wanted to hide something, she'd hide it at the top of that tower. No-one would ever find it in a million years. There you are, I've started telling you her innermost secrets already."

Alistair made a mental note that a little adventure climbing this great tower was called for, but kept his counsel.

"It's difficult this, isn't it? I mean, taking this role on really involves pretty intrusive enquiring regarding rather personal and even intimate matters, doesn't it? The more I think about it all, the more I'm realising that; but I keep reminding myself that you yourself did ask me to take it all on. I mean it was your idea, eh Dennis? You engaged me, didn't you?"

"I did indeed, and I want to keep nothing back from you. I mean, really nothing. Look, you can have her diaries," Dennis said excitedly, going back into the hall and removing two bags from the bottom drawer of a chest of drawers.

"The police went through them with a toothpick," he continued, "and I've no doubt they've taken copies galore, which actually for some reason does hurt a bit. It is so intrusive – such a ghastly invasion of privacy on top of everything else, and I handed them over for the sake of justice; but you're a friend Alistair. I really want you to pursue every angle, so I don't mind you having them. For Henrietta's sake, I really do want you to see them."

"Are you sure about the diaries, Dennis? I can understand they could help me in this."

"Yes, you take the diaries. There's not much in them. They are mostly work engagements, with one or two family things here and there; but look, I want you to take these little pocket ones which she kept too. They only came to light the other day. They're silly little paper notebooks that I used to put in her stocking every Christmas. They're not so easy to read, what with her secret funny habit of using letters for words. She usually just puts down the first letters of each word."

"Eh, you'd better explain that to me more clearly, Dennis; deciphering codes is not my forte."

"It really is simple – look - letters just stand for words. I remember when we first got married I came across a bit of paper stuck on the wall by the back door with the letters RTLD on. I asked her what it meant and she said 'remember to lock door,' and then added 'stupid.' I said, 'How could I possibly have worked that out?'"

Dennis seemed a little emotional at this recollection and sighed.

"I'm sorry but I can remember it so well – just like yesterday. It's so evil, what happened..."

"Yes, I'm sorry, Dennis. You've just got to remember it's only because you seemed so keen on all this probing that we're here right now talking like this, isn't it?"

Dennis then seemed to cheer up a bit.

"Here, look," he said opening one of the diaries, "here's another example. 'LC' means 'Light candles'. She put that in a little procedure, which she gave to one of the servers. I can remember the server rang up one day to enquire, and I answered the phone. I hadn't a clue what it meant. Henrietta had a good laugh about it, then rang the server back and said it means, 'light candles, stupid.' You get used to it, but it can be difficult if you don't know the context or what's going on. I mean, look here," he continued, opening one at random, "I happen to know that particular one, because I remember what it was about you see – 'AB' – you'd never guess that one, but I know it means 'Ask Bill' - but there's lots I can't work out."

"Oh golly," muttered Alistair, "as I say, it's not my forte. I bet the police had fun and games with this."

"Yeah, that's exactly what they said to me, and I'm not surprised. Course they only had her bigger, official, main diaries, where she really just has appointments and main events. They're quite full, though, and in them she only used that funny technique of hers much less frequently, but you're right, it took 'em a little while. I asked her once where she got that odd little habit from and all she said was, 'Well, I'm a very private person really, I suppose.' She also said 'There's nothing sinister about that little habit – they're just private reminders usually. Sometimes if I think there's something I really wouldn't want anyone to read, I deliberately use the last letter for one of the words instead of the first.'"

"Gosh, Dennis, that's too difficult! That would really make it beyond me. It's interesting, though. I mean, we've all got little habits – idiosyncrasies, foibles - haven't we?" said Alistair politely.

"Well, anyway, best of luck with it. Obviously the police have their experts in these fields and apparently they pored over the big main diaries for many a long hour. How much they managed to decipher, I don't know, but as you know the whole horrid mystery remains as deep as ever it was."

"I'll apply the old brainbox to them; but I'm not sure any lucky break is going to be found there. We'll see. Anyway, thanks for entrusting them and these little ones to me, Dennis. I'll take care of them and ensure you get them all safely back."

"Oh, you'll have fun with her little game of using letters. Look at this one," continued Dennis, opening one of the diaries again at random. "You see they are normally the correct way round. 'TLG' means 'Take Lent Group'. 'TE' is 'Take Evensong'. That looks a tricky one 'BC-MAS' - but I know it means 'Bishop coming – meet at station'. To be honest, I think she really only used the *last* letters of words when it was something really private, you know – like she wouldn't want someone knowing something. I mean, she didn't want people knowing she was talking to the bishop about Ben and she put 'EOP re N', which meant 'Spoke to bishop about Ben'. I suppose you could call it one of her absurd, but to me very endearing, idiosyncrasies."

"As you say, I'll have fun with them. Then maybe not," joked Alistair. "I mean where does it stop? You could go on for ever, couldn't you? Using penultimate letters of words, I suppose.... Oh dear, oh dear."

"Oh no, she told me – just first letters, or if very secret, last letters. Of course as you will see you can't always work out what the hell the letters mean. There's one entry at the crucial time of the crime, which is a complete mystery. I'll leave you to find it – just four letters – 'TATT'. Haven't a clue what that meant – not an inkling!"

"You're a clever so-and-so, Dennis, inveigling me into taking this assignment on. You know I simply love trying to crack mysteries like that – beats my other passion of crosswords any day of the week."

Considering the two men were friends of some years, their parting in the vicarage porch was quite formal.

"I'm entering on this assignment really seriously and energetically, Dennis. I'll give it my best efforts," said Alistair deliberately and almost solemnly. "I would love to give you the help and peace of mind that closure of it all would bring. My efforts may come to nothing, but I've got faith we just might get that lucky break that the Old Bill couldn't get."

"Well, I've got faith in you, Alistair. I asked you, because of all the chaps I know I reckon you're the most percipient when it comes to studying human nature."

"Well, thanks, that's a compliment."

"You and your people watching!" said Dennis in a jollier tone, patting him on the shoulder. "Do you remember when you said to me that people watching is for actors and detectives? Well, you see I remembered that. I remember your words of wisdom, Alistair."

Sensing that Dennis was about to show some emotion, Alistair stepped down to the lower step of the porch and held out his hand. Dennis took it and gave it a hearty shake. Alistair's prescience proved right, and he noticed tears welling up in the bereaved man's eyes as he managed, "Here, it's starting to rain. Take Henrietta's umbrella."

Alistair walked away from the vicarage. Oh God, he said to himself, almost out loud, I don't know if I believe in you, but if you're there and it's all true about prayer and all that, then please for Dennis's sake, help me to solve this mystery and give him the peace that would come with closure. Not for me, but for Dennis, please hear my prayer.

The rain increased as he walked to the station. He had surprised himself that he had found himself praying, and at one point he was not sure whether it was the rain or a tear on his cheek.

CHAPTER 8

(The first of two interviews with a churchwarden)

When he woke next morning, Alistair decided to shelve a perusal of the diaries till another time; they would probably make more sense when he was more familiar with the personalities and the set-up at St Peter's. He would lock them carefully away in the little wall safe marked 'Air tickets, Passports and Travel Documents', which he regarded as one of his brother's better gimmicks. Yes, he would get to know more of the set-up at St Peter's, Cookington, and a few of its key personalities and collect his thoughts before tackling anything intriguing in the diaries.

Now for a lot of characters and personalities that I don't know, he thought. In a way, that's easier than being formal with a friend like Dennis, who I know so well. He would take Dennis's advice and indeed start with Florence, the churchwarden.

As he knew Dennis so well and did not know Florence from Adam, so to speak, he would regard this as his first real interview.

He liked what he had heard of Florence so far. Dennis had told him how she had said that the church bell had summoned her to church. It reminded him of some distant English literature lesson in which he had read how Saint Joan of Arc had felt bells telling her something – but wasn't that to attack the English? He chuckled to himself and could not shake off the image of a gallant warrior. Will I be disappointed? he wondered.

What else do I know about her? he pondered further, as he made his way on the now familiar route to

Cookington. Not much, his mind answered, apart from the fact that this church-going and change of lifestyle had annoyed her husband, who had apparently said like many other people that he could strangle the vicar!

Was it normal for so many people to have used that phrase about their vicar? he wondered as he turned into the aptly named Apostles Way. This was the street where Florence lived, and it led down to the stately portal of St Peter's.

Before long he was at her house, which stood rather smartly at the foot of the road, and was indeed the last house before the church. That's as close as a parishioner could be, he thought to himself. He rang the bell with not a little excitement. This was really going to be the start of it all; a first interview with someone he had not met before. He could almost rub his hands with enjoyment as for someone with a passion for amateur detective work, this was as good as it gets …

"Come right in," welcomed Florence, poking her head out from behind the opening door.

Alistair made one of his usual apologies for disturbing her, something he was aware he would probably become very practised at.

"No, no, no, that's quite alright. Dennis said you would be coming. He phoned to say stand by for probably being the first person to be interviewed. Am I the first?"

"It's not really an interview," said Alistair, hanging his hat up on the hook in the hall. He smiled. "Well, I suppose it is in a way; it's a chat, really, but Dennis and I seemed to agree that the churchwardens were a pretty good place to start."

"Eliminate us from enquiries," joked Florence, ushering him in to the living room with an engaging smile that put him instantly at ease.

He immediately became aware of a smart and

almost opulent room, but one well lived in, with many letters and documents around and about.

"I know enough about the Church of England to know that churchwardens are the key members of the parish," he replied, warming to the slight hint of a fellow countrywoman's dialect.

"Well, we certainly deal with a hell of a lot of admin," agreed Florence, adding rather humorously, "sorry, I'm trying to stop myself using phrases like that since being a churchwarden."

At his request she ran through a summary of the duties which she was now so familiar with. She explained how she was the star warden, as only one of the two could be sent all the endless paperwork emanating from various church bodies. It struck Alistair that she was a business-like woman if ever there was.

"Him upstairs," she said cocking her eye toward the door, "brings in the post in the morning and always says 'More church rubbish!' It used to annoy me - his attitude - but as time has gone by, I've realised more clearly than ever that this church-going isn't everything, and he's probably far more spiritually at peace than me when I get back from the morning service, absolutely fuming over something annoying that someone has said to me."

"He's Anglican too, is he?" enquired Alistair.

"Ah, now that's the point, you see; he tells me he can't possibly go as he's Presbyterian." She laughed quite heartily, adding, "Well, I was too until we moved in here, right next to this church, and after ignoring it for some time, the bells started getting to me and I felt kind of like being called." She laughed out loudly again, but Alistair felt there was a sore subject here.

"He doesn't mind you being the churchwarden, though, does he?" he asked in sympathetic tone.

"Roy gets annoyed sometimes with one or two interruptions – you know, the phone going at mealtimes and the odd event interfering with family arrangements - that sort of thing. Once when the phone rang, he said, 'It's that bloody vicar again!' I admit he had made the dinner that evening so I can see it was annoying for him. Anyway, we had an argument and he was very morose for about a week, but since then everything has been back to normal."

She sat silently for a moment with a rather cross expression on her face while Alistair bit his lip to stop himself asking if her husband had ever suggested strangling the vicar.

"The other day," she resumed, "I said to him, 'Carry on like that, and people will think it was you who murdered the vicar. You didn't, did you?' He went white, until I told him it was a joke."

Alistair looked like he felt – slightly taken aback.

"He's perked up a bit lately," continued Florence, "because some time ago I put him on the waiting list for an allotment. I'd got the idea from Edwin's wife, Helen. I felt they had a lot in common. After all, Helen has stopped going to church, and I know her husband Edwin has hinted to me that he himself often feels more solace and spiritually tuned in on Helen's allotment than here at St Peter's." She nodded in the direction of the tower outside, before continuing, "Anyway, Roy has warmed to the idea and now he's due to take over one of the allotments next week. You see a lot of people on the waiting list pulled out after the crime. Understandably, in a way, they felt they wouldn't be at ease there."

Alistair waited till he felt she was really finished with talking about her husband.

"Now, Florence, it's difficult to know where to start, but let me ask you if you have any kind of hunch or feeling that the police may have missed something, or not taken something into account as much as they should … or really anything you feel strongly about in this whole wretched business."

"For months it was such a bombshell that I really couldn't get my head round any sort of thinking at all. In a word …" she hesitated, gazing out of the window, and then continued … "to put it bluntly, there were a lot of tensions around the parish after Henrietta arrived. People find change difficult. Having a lady vicar was a surprise for nearly everybody, and of course having such a High Church lady too - that was unusual. People who didn't like the change of churchmanship started having a go at her because she was a woman. I know for a fact she was once or twice reduced to tears."

She noticed Alistair's look of slight surprise. "Oh yes, she came round here once or twice and had a bit of a cry."

"About people's attitude to her?"

"Well, yes, she used to say people were ganging up against her. Also, round at the vicarage at least twice I took on the role of agony aunt trying to cheer her up when she was crying. Once she really got it off her chest about Dennis being difficult for her as a vicar to be married to. Seemed to cheer her up a lot when I told her about Roy's attitude. She was a well-balanced person, but I remember that time I did wonder, because she started giggling when I said Dennis couldn't be as bad as Roy."

"Life's so strange, isn't it?" mused Alistair. "I mean there are so many people around who would, from the point of view of belief and church-going, be far more suitable to be married to each other, wouldn't you agree?"

"Ah, you never know," came Florence's quick reply. "Maybe there's a plan to it all. Our former vicar,

Maurice, he used to say God's ways are so beyond our understanding that we might as well not even start trying to answer questions like that."

"Murder can't be part of his plan, though, can it?" put in Alistair, quite sharply.

"I agree – and of course you can't judge anyone, because you don't know everything; but yes, sometimes everything is just totally incomprehensible."

"Totally," agreed Alistair, unnecessarily stirring his tea, which Florence had carefully prepared. To him it seemed to have appeared miraculously.

"Tell me more about her arrival here, and please be really frank with me Florence. This whole horrid business may have absolutely nothing to do with the congregation here, but I've got to get to grips with this part of the investigation."

"Where shall I start?" Florence asked herself gazing out of the window. "We, that is the PCC – you know what that is, don't you, the parochial church council, no less – we were asked to elect a couple of people to visit the suggested appointee of the bishop. If we strongly objected we could say so. Well, the PCC in their wisdom, or lack of it, elected Ben, who was one of our lay readers and myself. In short, though surprised to find it was a woman, which I suppose we shouldn't have been, we liked her, and you may laugh at this but we prayed about it and we fairly quickly felt there were no grounds for objection, and had faith that it must therefore be God's will for her to come here. I mean, there wasn't any other name being banded about, just hers. We had to consider if that was because it was God's will."

"How did you let everyone else know about the suggestion that it might be her?" asked Alistair with interest.

"We announced it at the PCC. I had told Edwin, out

of courtesy as my fellow churchwarden, and he had actually raised an eyebrow and quickly commented on the fact that he knew of that church where she was coming from and that it was kind of 'High'. His wife used to work near there and he had seen the parish magazine when it had been delivered to his wife's office, and he had noticed how the clergy were called 'Father' and 'Mother', and how the Holy Communion service was called 'Mass'. To be fair to him, he came out with all that straight away, but he stressed that if that was not a problem to everyone then he personally would welcome her warmly with the faith that it must be God's will. There had been a lot of prayer, and the bishop had stressed how much he had prayed over this particular appointment. Of course, poor Edwin didn't know then how his dear wife, Helen, was going to react, and how it was going to raise her Protestant hackles."

Alistair took a biscuit and kept his thoughts to himself as to how all this prayer and so on squared up with God allowing such a terrible crime to take place. He asked, "So Edwin accepted the appointee straight away, although commenting on her High Church origins?"

"Yes … and oh, it was quite funny when I told him, because I said of course she had to get permission from her 'father', meaning her vicar; but Edwin thought I meant her dad, and I'll never forget how I got the giggles, because he asked incredulously, 'How old is she?'"

"Yeah, that is funny," responded Alistair, laughing genuinely and pulling out a little notebook and jotting down some words.

"Well, Edwin actually turned out to be the first of many who didn't really like her being called 'Mother' and all that terminology, and said they only had one mum. I mean, to be fair, he said he felt the same about calling a priest a 'father'. We never called Maurice 'Father'. I mean Edwin is not against women priests."

"Well, of course, going back to my childhood, I was a Presbyterian too in origin, so I kind of sympathise," commented Alistair in a serious tone.

"You don't go to church these days?" asked Florence, also rather earnestly, and as Alistair shook his head, she added rather hastily, "of course it isn't everything. I think I've come to agree with Edwin that being good is the main thing. He told me that his dad had said that to him once when he had asked his dad if he thought it was OK to go to a football match on Good Friday. It's an old chestnut, that one, about can you be a Christian and not go to church, isn't it?"

"What do you think, Florence?"

"I would say yes you can, but not a mature one – sorry that's terribly rude of me. I didn't mean -"

Alistair interrupted her. "No, don't worry, it doesn't apply to me because I'm afraid, to be honest, I lost any faith I had a long time ago."

He kept to himself the fact that he was actually quite seriously considering all these great matters. As he joked to himself, it's the other even bigger mystery I am trying to solve.

Florence seemed a little taken aback by his utterance, before commenting, "It must make it all rather difficult for you, working on this particular case, then, I imagine. I mean, trying to understand us church people."

"Oh no, I actually think it may help. I certainly find that side of it very interesting – I mean, learning about people's views and how they work for the church and the community etc."

He fiddled with his biro as a slight pause ensued, and then continued, "So how did the PCC respond to this announcement that Henrietta was going to be their new vicar? Any objections?"

"Nobody was critical. I think they were a bit stunned, to tell you the truth. It was funny because old Fred Goodwin, he was pretty slow to realise it was a woman. He's a bit deaf and he thought the name was Henry. You should have seen his face, when later at the meeting, he realised it was Henrietta! I think they were all surprised, mighty surprised at first, but then rather intrigued - and to be honest, they none of them made any adverse comments."

"Can you take me, as it were, to the first signs you got that there was dissension in the air?"

"Well, that's easy enough. The induction went trouble-free, but at the very first Sunday morning service Edwin let me know that someone had been critical of the bell that was rung at the start of the service. We had never done that before. Ironically, it was someone called Mr Bellman who objected, and I think he came a few more Sundays but soon stopped attending; of course by that time a few more bells had been introduced.

"I can understand how poor Helen, Edwin's wife, thought it had all become too Roman Catholic," said Alistair.

Florence laughed and said, "Well, to get back to dear old Mr Bellman, I was told by a Mrs Brown that the real reason old Mr Bellman stopped coming was because he had heard Edwin cracking one of his jokes and referring to him as 'Mr Nobellman'."

Florence laughed quite heartily before continuing, "When I heard that, I just had to laugh. I could just imagine Edwin saying that - it's so typical of him - such a strange mixture of seriousness and cheeky humour."

Alistair scribbled something in his notebook and,

not wanting to be sidetracked, looked up, waiting for Florence to continue, which she did.

"It was quite early on, one of those first Sundays that a member of the congregation, a certain Mrs Tapp, collared me in what we call the narthex, the kind of porch at the entrance to the church. She was in high dudgeon about Henrietta calling herself 'Mother'. I had all this 'I've only got one mum' business. Others took this line too as time went by. Funny, that never bothered me. As I say, I think it bothered dear Edwin; but from an early stage he was having the problem that his wife, Helen, who had been brought up as a Presbyterian, was finding so many other things too much."

"What other things?"

"Oh, I think Helen didn't like Holy Communion being called 'Mass', she didn't like the 'mother' bit, and some of the new kissing the Bible carry-on, and shall we say, increased bowing and bobbing. It was awkward for her – well, for both of them - what with him being the churchwarden. I think what really made her stop coming was when we came into church one Sunday and there was a statue of the Virgin Mary. As Edwin said, the Reformation went further in Scotland than anywhere, and poor Helen found it too much; and yes, she stopped coming. Edwin told me his wife found herself far more in tune with the Almighty on her allotment. I was a bit taken aback when he added that he wasn't sure if he didn't too; but then Edwin's always coming out with things like that. I used to think he partly did it to shock me; but you know, I like old Edwin. Deep down he's a sincere old chap, I think. Him upstairs can't stand him – doesn't think he's sincere at all - but I always say to Roy, 'That's because you don't know him.'"

Florence stopped and looked rather pained, gazing

at her necklace as she played with it, curiously reminding Alistair of a nun with a rosary.

"Well, you lot - I mean, sorry, you church-goers - are only human like the rest of the world," he offered in an attempt to get Florence restarted; but she stayed silent for what he thought was rather a long time before going out to get more biscuits.

As she returned, he began the conversation again.

"You say Henrietta came here once or twice about personal matters, and you said she'd also spoken to you about them at the vicarage. Please tell me, Florence, did she ever get onto matters of the heart - separate from her husband, if you know what I mean?"

He noticed her expression turned slightly disapproving so he added, "I need to ask these questions; after all, we have an unsolved murder on our hands. Though I'm enjoying it immensely, I'm not really here for a pleasant cup of tea and chat, am I?

She remained sitting with a distant but slightly disapproving look.

He tried prompting her. "Obviously, murders are often caused by deeply personal matters, and although I don't like asking these sorts of questions, well as I'm sure you understand, I have to."

She continued to wear a rather stern countenance and maintain her silence, so he persisted.

"You see, Florence, if the cause of this ghastly crime was something very personal – shall we say, completely unrelated to church life here at Cookington - then there aren't all that many people who could help with information, and I just have this feeling that you would be the sort of person, if anybody, that Henrietta might have confided in."

Still Florence remained quiet, so he made one last attempt to encourage her.

"Henrietta would know that, as a fellow deeply

112

committed Christian, she could rely on your integrity."

"That's exactly the problem," Florence blurted out, before pausing and then continuing. "You see, she did tell me things, but they were things in complete confidence."

Alistair leant back. He wondered, but only for a moment, if Florence had known things that she had kept from the police. After a bit he said quietly, "I totally trust your judgement, and please only tell me things that you think might just possibly be relevant to the terrible crime."

"It was just about Dennis, really," began Florence, "How it was difficult being a vicar with a husband like Dennis, because he really didn't like joining in, basically. He went to the Sunday service very regularly, and I give him credit for that – it's a lot more than him upstairs - but not much else. He hardly came to any social events. I tried to tell Henrietta that that could be helpful – you know, not having a husband in the way; but she wouldn't be comforted. Said she'd had it up to here with his attitude."

Florence raised her hand to her neck, before continuing, "They'd had a working arrangement, but she said it had been straining a bit. Yes, she felt the strain. Apparently, that day she came to see me about it, he had said the wrong thing to the bishop. Henrietta said, 'Like most clergy, we're not very concerned with what in the old days was called preferment, but we like to feel it could happen - and how could it, after what Dennis said to the bishop?'"

"That's interesting, isn't it? As they say, things are never what they seem. Can I ask what this terrible thing was that Dennis said to the bishop?" said Alistair.

"Oh, it was just something about Henrietta's private political views; but as she said that day, it was the straw that broke the camel's back."

"Did she ever tell you anything about her pre-Dennis life?"

"Do you know, in the circumstances of murder, I think I ought to tell you; and surely she would want me to try and help you get to the truth. I never mentioned all this to the police, because we swore to each other that we were talking in confidence, and it's been on my conscience a bit. After all this time, and in view of the seeming total lack of progress, I feel I ought to tell you now. What with the police drawing a blank, it's kind of new circumstances now, isn't it?"

Alistair nodded but said nothing, not wanting to divert her flow.

"She told me she had no regrets about splitting up with a guy called Rhys, who she had actually got engaged to, but was wistful about what might have been if she'd accepted the advances of a young lad she met ages ago; I'll never forget laughing when she told me his name was Buzz! That was it – same as the astronaut chap. Nickname, of course – I never found out what his real name was. It was while she was telling me about this fellow Buzz that the tears came to her eyes. I remember saying to her, 'Now, Henrietta you're tired and overwrought, and not in a fit state to chat. How about we meet up sometime and thrash this all out?' She said that Dennis was going to be away that next weekend so why didn't I come round to the vicarage and she would give me dinner. To cut a long story short, I did go round, and she told me that this kid – this Buzz - had fancied the pants off her … Sorry, I'll rephrase that."

"Probably quite an accurate description," commented Alistair with a wry smile, having detected that this Florence, for all her conventional uprightness, seemed to have a naughty side to her.

"Well, anyway, that's really it," added Florence,

wiping the smile off her face. "In a nutshell, she was saying that this lad Buzz would have been a lot more of a suitable husband than poor Dennis. I remember she added, 'A more suitable husband for a priest.' I can't really tell you any more than that. We spent a lot of time chatting – you know, commiserating about what a funny old world it was and how strange life was - that sort of thing. I tried to cheer her up. I told her about my early days before I met him upstairs. We had quite a good laugh in the end; but I'm afraid she did get a bit drunk. She said her excuse was that other people were always telling her about their problems and nobody understood hers. When I left she asked me to help her up the stairs, and I remember her cracking that old chestnut, 'Don't drop me I'm going to be a bishop' - which I thought was rather funny at the time."

"You say you never told the police of this conversation, or did you?"

"I withheld it; Henrietta had made me swear to secrecy about those two chats of ours, the one at my house and the one at hers. Also, of course I didn't want to mar her much esteemed reputation, and of course, as you can understand, it had made us very close; it was like a kind of secret bond that I didn't want to spoil. But what with the police drawing such a complete blank, and the whole thing being so horrific, well, I'm glad I've told you now. I often thought I should have told the police in the circumstances. Anyway, Dennis explained to me on the phone all about you having a completely different type of approach to the mystery. We're over a year on, and one has to adjust one's decisions in this stormy life, don't you think?"

Alistair gave a silent nod and wrote a little in his notebook before continuing, "Well, as you say, the whole idea of Dennis asking me to do this was to see if approaching the mystery from a completely different angle might lead somewhere. Poor Dennis, he told me he realised that I'd probably hear an awful lot of 'stuff', as he called it, some of which he admitted would probably be very embarrassing for him. Was there any other, shall we say, matter of the heart that Henrietta ever mentioned to you?"

There was a good half-minute's pause.

"Any other past boyfriends?" he asked keenly, using the word 'boyfriend' rather than 'lover', deliberately, thinking it might make it easier for Florence to reveal any such knowledge.

"No, absolutely nothing more, other than what I've told you. Now, I'm going to make you swear to keep all that secret. I never told you all this, OK?"

"Of course, Florence – that goes without saying. Now I think I'll get round to checking all that out; but first I'm going to have a wee word with the allotment holders, and the people in the houses nearby which overlook the crime scene. Those houses are in Lime Grove, aren't they?"

Florence nodded without speaking, as if she felt she had spoken too much.

Alistair continued, "And of course I'll also visit your fellow churchwarden, Edwin, plus this rather intriguing guy called Fred, who I gather from something Dennis joked about, thinks he ought still to be churchwarden."

Florence seemed to cheer up a bit at the mention of Fred Goodman's name.

"Oh yes, old Fred," she said with gusto. "You're right, he never got over it. When the previous vicar, Maurice, asked him to give way to a younger chap, old Fred actually stopped coming to church for three weeks. That was unheard of – Fred being absent for three weeks."

"Really?" Alistair laughed. "We've got to be

allowed to laugh during an investigation, haven't we?"

As she answered, "Oh, heavens yes, especially after all this time," he continued, "Anyway, that's my rough plan of attack in the way of interviewing in the immediate future."

He got up and zipped his little briefcase. He stood thinking for a minute before sighing and saying, "By the time you add in a good miscellany of parishioners, I can see I could be busy round here till Christmas. Let's hope my brother doesn't get impatient with my stay at his hotel."

"Good luck," said Florence rather pessimistically.

"You know, Florence, amateur detective work has been a passion of mine all my life; but now, I've hardly been on this case five minutes and I'm already vowing I wouldn't touch another with a barge pole! I really ought to learn to keep my mouth shut and not get myself landed with onerous and indeed Herculean tasks by my friends."

Florence saw him to the door, muttering, "Yes, it's a funny situation for you, alright. Why do you think Dennis didn't call in a professional firm of detectives?"

"Oh, he's going to if I draw a blank – I can assure you of that. Yes, he would do that immediately."

Florence opened the front door, stood for a moment admiring and commenting on the blue sky, shook hands and then returned to her little living room, where she sat down and cried.

She said out loud in the empty room, "Sorry, Henrietta, I only told him because we've got to get to the truth of this terrible business."

"Why are you crying, dearest?" came her husband's voice from just outside in the hall.

"Oh, Roy, we may disagree about religion but we're never, ever going to split up or let it effect our happiness!" she sobbed.

He embraced her, and that evening they chatted till two in the morning. She always remembered it afterwards as the time they made love in the living room.

CHAPTER 9

(An interview with a curate)

It seemed utterly impossible to Alistair, as he journeyed back to his hotel, that Florence could in any way be a suspect. The very thought of it made him laugh to himself. Of course it would appear Florence had been very close to the victim, and anyone that close must be considered; but no, his thoughts continued, no, she couldn't be a murderer. There was no motive, unless she had divulged some great secret to Henrietta and regretted it, but that was too far-fetched to contemplate.

Possibly because he had found his meeting with Florence curiously rather more intense than he'd anticipated, his whole inclination already was to give himself a break, as it were, from the environment and congregation of St Peter's, and to interview the allotment holders; but a sense of duty made him feel that such a welcome respite must wait until one or two of the rather important members of the dramatis personae were ticked off. The first of these must obviously be the curate.

He had learnt from Dennis that the curate, Rev. Sylvia Patterson, had been moved to the country by the bishop shortly after the tragedy. He also knew that she herself had asked for this, apparently suffering from nightmares, according to Dennis. The implication of Dennis's comments had been that he might not find her as easy and helpful and obliging as one might expect a curate to be.

However, presumably a curate would know, as well as anybody, anything that might be useful in throwing light onto this terrible situation, Alistair mused. In a second, the thought came to him that he could combine getting his break and getting on with the job by making a little visit to her in the country. The more he thought about the matter, it rather surprised him that Dennis had not suggested starting with her; but perhaps that was just because she was now away in the country, seemingly hoping to regain her equanimity.

Luck was with him when he phoned to make an appointment, for she was in. He would have hoped that she might have given him a more encouraging welcome, but she was civil enough, and the arrangement was made for him to travel down that day, which fitted in so well with his desire to see the country that he found himself singing a few bars from *Oklahoma* to the effect that everything was going his way. Within a short space of time, he was giving his usual "Cheerio" to Donna, who was the official receptionist at the Concord Hotel, and had left for his day's sojourn in the country.

Once in the High Street, which lay a stone's throw from his hotel, he hired a car as easily as if it was an everyday occurrence.

He sat in the little car hire office waiting for the clerk to get the keys, while occupied with the crossword, which he always excused on the grounds that it kept his brain in working order. The early morning sun shone in. A feeling of contentment came over him as he stretched his legs. It would be a nice day in the country, if nothing else.

The journey lived up to his expectations, with the traffic flowing easily and the sunlight streaming down on the fleeting fields. He even managed a few more bars of 'Oh, what a beautiful morning!'

It seemed almost a shame when he left the main road and pulled in to a convenient lay-by to study the map and refresh his memory of the short remaining part of the journey.

What an adorable village, he enthused to himself.

The village of Stoneriver was indeed quintessentially English, with a charming cricket field as its central focus, but surrounded by pleasant houses and one shop bearing rather grandly the title 'The Shop'. A rather picturesque and genuinely old inn stood boldly at one corner of the field, and through the nearby trees he could see an old church steeple pointing to the heavens. I mustn't forget about that other mystery, he told himself, Does that steeple point to the truth?

His ultimate destination, Cherry Cottage, was not difficult to find, and the new experience of being able to park easily all added to his feeling of well-being.

The Reverend Sylvia Patterson appeared at the door. His first impression was of a confident, and to his surprise, rather cheerful person.

He was given the briefest of tours of the little garden, and it being so near lunchtime he was offered sherry, which was just what he felt like.

"Do you prefer to be outside or in?" came his host's polite inquiry.

He reminded himself that under his own terms of reference he was on business, and on the whole, business was done more efficiently indoors.

They sat down in some comfortable armchairs. The little table between them had some neatly prepared crisps in a bowl, and the former curate of St Peter's had obviously gone to some care, as there was even a bowl of olives too, which she pushed gracefully towards him.

Alistair sat back, entering into the homely atmosphere, and relaxed even more.

"As I said on the phone, you can understand Dennis would want me to make a visit to you a priority," he said diplomatically if not truthfully, and added, "I mean, it's obvious, isn't it, that a curate would be able to give tremendous insight into a parish's affairs?"

"Well, I'll help all I can, but I didn't seem to have

been able to help the police much; and actually I'm also worried you're going to ask me a lot of questions about people and think I'm a terrible gossip," she replied politely enough.

"No, no, no," Alistair assured her. "As I say, I knew the curate would be the person who could throw most light on a congregation – indeed, on the whole parish …"

She interrupted him. "Well, of course, I hadn't been there very long when this terrible business blew up in my face. Sorry, that probably doesn't sound quite right, does it? But that's how it felt like to me. I just wanted to do my stint as a curate and carry on with getting my own parish somewhere as soon as possible. I mean, I just wanted things to go smoothly. You see, I'd come to ordination rather late, and of course I wanted to help all those good people at St Peter's and all that; but really I wanted things to just go smoothly, and for me to be able to move on."

She paused, held her hands up to her face in what Alistair thought was rather a theatrical gesture, and said, "Next thing I know is, the police are round asking me questions like they suspected me of murder, no less."

"Oh, I'm sure they didn't really, Sylvia," he responded, rather aware that he had not sounded very sincere, and adding, "I am allowed to call you Sylvia, am I?"

"Of course you can; but no, really, you've no idea how horrible it was. Honestly, it felt like I was a suspect."

Alistair put on one of his simulated laughs of which he had become quite an expert at.

"I know they can appear a bit high-handed sometimes when they come round. They're just being businesslike; I'm sure you would be the very last person they would think that of," he said consolingly.

"Well, it jolly well felt like it," she emphasised. "Questions galore! Where was I? When did I go? What time was that? Did I have any witnesses? I promise you I felt like they suspected me. I'm not joking. I had a cry about it, which was one thing I had vowed never to allow a parish matter to make me do. Of course, when I made that vow I hadn't envisaged coming up against a murder - and murder of the vicar - that's a little out of the ordinary, isn't it? I really felt a little sorry for myself about that."

Alistair leaned back and sipped the sherry, thinking, I wonder why she felt the police were accusing her, or is it just a conventional way of saying there were a lot of questions?

Hiding his thoughts, he responded, "Well, quite; and of course, like me, the police had to probe everyone remotely connected and try and get information. I can understand them thinking you might be the one who could help them most. You see, that's why they had to be so businesslike, I expect."

This seemed to be the necessary prompt that got her commenting on all and sundry.

As their conversation continued, Alistair became aware that there was hardly a member of the congregation who she didn't have a question mark against.

He was quite taken aback when she referred to Dennis's marriage as 'an odd set-up'. She had said, "Of course, I'm not married, but I'd never expect a marriage to be like that."

"How do you mean?" he asked tentatively, reminding himself of Florence's allusions to it yesterday.

"Well, he was never there, was he?" Sylvia retorted, putting her hands over her mouth as if she had said something she ought not to have, but repeating it. "He never, well, hardly ever came to parish events - I mean even quite important ones."

"I suppose, to be fair, he had his own job to give priority to ..." Alistair replied, sticking up for his old friend.

He was somewhat taken aback when she interrupted abruptly, "Of course, no offence, but I think it's all a bit odd him getting a friend of his to take on this further investigation. I mean, I've got to say this, he was a suspect at one time, for goodness sake; you realise that, don't you?"

Ignoring her last salvo, Alistair said good-naturedly, "I can understand you feeling that, but you know he's not got the closure he sought and hoped for with the police investigation drawing a blank, so I think it's fair enough. Unless I achieve a miraculous breakthrough, he'll be employing a private detective agency soon enough, I assure you. I'm just an interim stopgap; but to get back to what I was saying, in fairness Dennis had his own job to give priority to."

"Yes, but I mean, even the annual meeting...."

After further critical comments about Dennis, on she went, making her way through the various members of the congregation, in what he noted was a kind of descending hierarchical order.

After Dennis, who as the vicar's husband seemed to top the bill, she had moved on to Barnaby Hatch, the senior reader, who came in for a fair share of digs. "Very self-important chap," she said sagely, "thinks because he's been there a long time that he can rule the roost. Could be very irritating. She, Henrietta, found him irritating, that's for sure."

"Really?" Alistair cocked an eyebrow.

"Oh yes, I'll say; but I think the congregation had a certain affection for him. I mean he's been there for years – since the year dot. After Ben left, for want of a better word, people started to call Barnaby the good reader – as opposed to Ben the Bad Reader or 'Wicked Reader', as I heard him called once."

"Ah, I want to get on to Ben, but first tell me more about Barnaby," said Alistair, unable to resist the temptation to learn more.

"No need to, really, he'll tell you all about himself. That's the thing about Barnaby. Although he's actually quite popular with all the old stalwarts, and everyone's always saying how loyal he is etc., etc., you know if you work with him … well, how shall I put it? Very full of his own importance … to be honest, a bit of a Dogberry. Of course he has been there since the Flood, and we did always have to listen to what he said, but to be honest it was usually pretty good garbage. His sermons used to drive me mad. You should hear him trying to explain the mystery of the Trinity. He's long-winded too – can never just say 'the world', but has to list all the countries of the world that he can think of."

Alistair threw his head back and laughed out loud.

She smiled back, pleased with what she thought was her own humour.

"Of course, Edwin's quite right; as he says, if the speaker and the listener are both sincere, God can make good come from it," she remarked, sounding more like a priest.

"I look forward to meeting him; as you can understand I thought a word with you first was a good idea," responded Alistair politely.

"Poor old Barnaby," continued the former curate of St Peter's, "bit too full of himself. It could be very funny. He always liked to do the readings whenever possible, and there were lots of occasions when he misread things. I think he may have been a bit dyslexic; a lot of people thought that, though he never admitted it. There was the famous occasion when he read out very solemnly, 'Thou shalt commit adultery.' We all had to put our handkerchiefs in our mouths that day."

While Alistair wiped the tears of merriment from his eyes, she continued, "Oh golly, his nose was put out of joint when I arrived and he had to hand over to me to read the Gospel, because Henrietta said it was part of my job! Do you know, for the first time in history he missed two Sundays after that. Put him in a right sulk, it did."

"I'm not going to take notes," said Alistair with a smile, "I don't think I'd be able to keep up with all this. I'll just sit back and take in as much as I can."

Sylvia moved on to the person whom she too called "the Bad Reader", and told him all about Ben, and his sudden departure from the scene after the split with his wife, Faye. Alistair was amused that on one occasion she ratcheted up the criticism and referred to him as "the Wicked Reader".

"Oh, you've stepped it up a notch calling him 'wicked' now. I thought he was just the Bad Reader."

"Well, really – preaching to us all one day and then going off with a girl at the office like that the next!" Sylvia protested.

Of course, he had learnt about all this from Dennis and Florence, and although he had much to ask, he did not want to interrupt the flow of Sylvia's talk yet, and allowed her to move on to the next person.

She had not a single good word to say for one Fred Goodman, who she continually referred to as having strange movements, patrolling around the premises.

"Thinks because he mows the grass there, it gives him a right to patrol the premises. Jolly irritating! Asked me once what I was doing when I'd just popped into the vestry to get my cardigan."

Alistair fumbled again for his notebook.

"He always seemed to try and obstruct everything that we were trying to get the PCC to approve of or pass," she said with a hint of irritation in her voice.

"Yes, I've heard he was a bit like that," answered Alistair.

"Henrietta used to call him 'the obstructionist'," continued the curate in full flow, adding, "Edwin used to say every parish needs its Fred, but I remember Henrietta saying, 'It's not funny, Edwin.' Of course, typical Edwin said, 'Oh, yes it is.'"

This memory of a mild ticking-off for Edwin moved her conversation on to that interesting fellow himself, of whom she was not a little critical. She even went so far as to cast aspersions on his lifestyle, and described him as living loosely to his religion. Alistair mused to himself that surely there was something in Holy Scripture about not judging other people …

"I should really mention Florence before Edwin," continued the Rev. Sylvia Patterson, "because she is what we call the star warden or the most senior one."

Here she was more complimentary, but even Florence was accused of being a busybody, and had "driven her mad" on more than one occasion. "Churchwardens like to exert their authority every now and again," she stressed, adding, "pride, that's what it is."

She talked about one member of the congregation, an old soldier called Len, who had killed so many people in the war that probably one more wouldn't be too difficult for him. "I remember walking to church with him one morning, and he was rambling on about his war experiences up and down the wretched Italian peninsula, and I couldn't believe it because one moment he was telling me the best way to kill Germans, and the next he was on his knees in church looking like St Thomas à Kempis."

Alistair could hardly restrain a smile when she referred to the insurance officer – one Bill Thompson - as a debauched character.

"I don't know why a man like that goes to church – talk about Jekyll and Hyde!"

"But he goes to church every Sunday, for goodness sake! Isn't that a little to his credit?" put in Alistair, like a defending barrister.

"I'm afraid I've come to learn that doesn't necessarily mean anything – although it can mean a guilty conscience," she added.

"I'm finding this all very entertaining, but there are an awful lot of good people there, surely, aren't there?" he suggested helpfully.

She laughed and then said, "Who?"

He liked her joke and laughed out loud, but pursued the matter seriously.

"Well one assumes there are some good people in every congregation. Of course, I know the dear old C of E is going through its difficulties, but I'm sure there is a strong core of good people. What about Emma Duncan? Dennis told me she did the flower arranging practically single-handed all through the year ... I remember him mentioning her, because he said people like her should get the M.B.E. or something."

"Yes, I know, there are people like her who are really good and live the faith, but I'm beginning to think they are the exception." She laughed and added, "Maybe she's got some dark secret that none of us know about." Then, pausing as if wondering whether to say something or not, she added,

"I shouldn't really tell you this – you know people tell us things in confidence, and I couldn't possibly say anything said in the confessional, but outside the confessional it's up to my discretion – and even Emma told me she was only a church person because she

128

wanted to be reunited in heaven with her husband, who went down with his ship in the war. Seems like all she's interested in is whether she'll meet this great love of her life in heaven."

As she continued with some joke about how Emma Duncan would get a surprise at the pearly gates if her husband wasn't there, Alistair found himself thinking how extraordinary it was that he too now was wondering the same thing about Zoe, and that was even with her still being alive.

On and on Sylvia went, giving her views of various personalities in what was now her former parish. Sometimes she was complimentary, but more often she was critical, and he could not help but reflect to himself how it was just as difficult for Christians to live up to the teaching as for non-believers.

He certainly felt that he was getting a good overall view of the parish, but he felt growing frustration that this was really all it was. How could anything useful to his investigation come of all this amusing chit-chat – entertaining and humorous though it was?

He decided to change tack, asking abruptly if Henrietta had ever mentioned anything to her that she had ever connected in her mind with the crime.

"She never said anything about her personal life; but funnily enough I remember once I asked her for help about something – something in my personal life – and she was very helpful, let me say. But I always remember, she said, 'You'd be surprised how we all -' and then she corrected herself – 'a lot of us have problems in this area.' You know how you sometimes remember things people say for some reason? Well, I remember her saying those exact words. I did recall them when the crime happened."

"This was when you say you were asking for advice or help about a personal matter."

129

"Yes, and I'm not going to go into that."

"I quite understand, but am I allowed to ask whether it was something …?"

She interrupted him swiftly. "No, I'm not saying anything about all that."

After a moment's rather stunned silence, he gave her a kind of nod, and said, "Well, let's go on down this sort of invisible list of congregation members."

On they went, with a few words about everyone.

Eventually Alistair stood up, put away his pen, which in the event he had not used very much, and stretching his arms said, "No, that's fine. I think we can call a halt to the business side of today. I feel you've increased my insight into the St Peter's set-up quite a bit. Thank you."

A pleasant late lunch took place in the conservatory, and after a second walk round the garden appreciating flowers and plants and meeting the cat, Alistair made his goodbyes.

"Who are you going to see next?" Sylvia asked in a slightly patronising manner.

"Well, who would you recommend?" he responded with a laugh, feeling pleased that soon he would be journeying home.

"I know who I'd go to if I wanted to know anything about St Peter's: old Fred Goodwin every time. You know there ought to be a title for someone like him instead of ex-churchwarden. But no, I suppose that might put a few backs up if word got around that you'd gone to him so soon; perhaps it ought to be our beloved reader, Barnaby Hatch, first. As I've told you he's a funny fellow. Very self-important, even a bit vain, and not the brightest of characters, but I'll say something for him. He has a strong faith, and there were times when I found him quite helpful. Yes, I'd go to him first, if I was you. You should find it easy enough to arrange.

He gives priority to anything to do with St Peter's; I'll give him that. I commented on that once to him, and he said it might be God's will for him to attend to it immediately."

"I shall take your advice," said Alistair very deliberately. He nodded his head and added, "I'll ring him this evening when I get home, or rather back to my little hotel, which is nearly home, but not quite."

"Goodbye and good luck," Sylvia responded waving her hand as he walked down the short garden path. Alistair wondered for a moment if she was giving him a blessing.

Although less full of the joys of spring than in the morning, he nonetheless had a trouble-free journey home. It seemed as if he had just beaten the traffic.

He had managed for safety's sake to avoid thinking about his day's work while driving; but now back in his room at the little hotel, he pondered possibilities. Did this curate, with her rather unexpected character, have some great disagreement with the vicar? A disagreement, which, to use the cliché, might just have made her flip? She certainly must have worked very closely with the vicar, closer even than the churchwardens or than anyone else in the parish, presumably. Oddly, she had rather implied the opposite, playing down her role and putting suspicion the way of many members of the congregation. It seemed a curiously unexpected line for a curate to take.

Anyway, it was indeed time to ring the amusingly named Good Reader, Barnaby Hatch.

As predicted by the Reverend Sylvia Patterson, Barnaby sounded quite willing to be helpful. Life in the parish of St Peter's did indeed seem like his only world, and he was more than ready to oblige.

"Ah yes, Sylvia called me a little while ago and told me you'd be ringing. I gather you had a nice day in the country with our former curate, eh? Tomorrow would be ideal, looking forward to it already," said the "good" lay reader in a sprightly manner.

"Well, see you tomorrow, then, and thank you in advance," replied Alistair. He knew it was wise to keep this central figure in the life of the parish onside, as it were. He would show him the respect that Barnaby felt he deserved and hold judgement till afterwards on whether it was warranted in reality.

CHAPTER 10

(An interview with a good lay reader)

Alistair slept soundly that night, and woke raring to get on with his mission.

Cissie, the waitress, noted a certain expedition in the way he ate his breakfast, but kept her thoughts to herself, knowing when he was not in the mood for a chat.

Soon he was on his way back to Cookington, and then he followed the little street map of the parish with a touch of the explorer about him.

Ex-soldier, ex-policeman, lay reader, Barnaby Hatch lived with his wife and children on the very edge of the parish.

"So this is where you are," pronounced Alistair with bonhomie as the door opened.

"Bit of a trek, isn't it?" offered Barnaby, as, not uncivilly, he ushered his visitor in. Before closing the door, he pointed down the street towards a fence on the far side of a rather busier looking road, which crossed his street.

"Look – see that fence? That's the parish border," he announced enthusiastically.

"Oh, that's interesting," replied Alistair, peering over Barnaby's shoulder. "So you're just in it by a whisker, eh?"

"Yes. Do you know that every year – on Rogation Sunday - we beat the bounds of the parish?"

"That sounds a bit like the common riding up in the village where my grandparents came from," enthused Alistair. "What happens, do you have a party or something?"

"Just walk round the parish border, stopping every now and again to say prayers; but yes, we have a cream tea in the hall afterwards."

Alistair was ushered further into the house.

"Now meet my wife, Brenda … and that couple of members of the human race, sitting down in the corner playing snakes and ladders – they're our grandchildren, John, aged seven and Holly, aged five. We do a lot of babysitting for our son and daughter. My son works on a train – he's probably chuffing along the line somewhere right now." Barnaby looked very deliberately at his wristwatch as if to add credence to his remark.

"And my daughter is a dinner lady at the school near here," he continued, "very convenient, but just outside the parish."

Oh yes, he's very parish-conscious, and he certainly has a nice friendly family, thought Alistair as he was ushered still further from the pleasant living room into a room that immediately screamed "study" at him. As Brenda backed away shyly, Barnaby beamed at him with the words, "Brenda doesn't come in here much. It's not that I keep her out, it's just that -"

Brenda interrupted him, "I don't like to disturb his studying and all his church work and preparations for sermons and all that sort of thing. I mean, you need peace and quiet to study the Bible and all that. I mean, he's in there for hours sometimes."

Barnaby beamed again and shook his head, while Alistair smiled to himself with the thought that Barnaby was obviously regarded as the intellectual of the family.

The door was closed and Barnaby gestured towards a comfortable armchair, which stood beside his desk, facing his own swivel chair.

"Well, Barnaby, you know why I'm here," said Alistair, sitting down. "I know you helped the police a lot. Is there anything you can tell me that might help me? Anything possibly that you thought the police didn't seem to be too thorough about, or to take as seriously as they should?"

Barnaby appeared keen to start. He hit the palm of his hand with his fist and said, "Of course, it was the second big shock I'd had at the church. I mean I was just getting over the shock of my fellow reader, Ben, walking out on his wife. 'What's going to happen next?' Brenda asked me. Well, the answer was murder, wasn't it? Thought I'd finished with that when I left the police. Oh yes, I'd come across murder in the Met, but the cases I was involved in, well, we always solved 'em. This is an absolute mystery."

"Yes, it certainly is," intervened Alistair, to encourage him, "and of course that's why Dennis thought having a guy like me, who he knew and could trust, come and nose around and get hunches like some kind of a private detective could just possibly find the missing link."

"I think most people think it's nothing to do with the church," continued Barnaby. "People think it's got to be an outsider. I reckon it's a maniac. We, that is, the Met - keep thinking of myself as still in the Met - we had a tremendous reputation for securing convictions, but there were one or two exceptional cases over the years that remain a mystery. It's not totally unknown to have inexplicable crimes remaining unsolved for decades. When I think back to my days in the Force…"

"That really is what you think, is it? An outsider, a maniac?" Alistair cut in, leaning forward earnestly as if seeking confirmation. "I'm interested in what people think can explain the mystery."

"Well, yes I do, because I mean Henrietta was a happily married wife and to be honest not the sort of lady who some besotted Italian waiter met on holiday is going to shoot himself over. Yes, I think it's a maniac. I mean, it's got to be, hasn't it?"

135

Barnaby gave Alistair one of those staring grins as if he had just solved the problem of the universe.

"You've never ever thought it might be in any way connected with parish life, or goings-on here at St Peter's?" probed Alistair.

"Good heavens, no! I mean, we're not saints in the conventional meaning of the word – we're all sinners, but I mean not murderers."

"Out of interest, what do you mean by the conventional meaning?"

"Ah, well, you see, theologically speaking … " Barnaby paused, and appearing pleased to have been asked such a question, seemed to think this was a suitable moment to put on his spectacles. "We church people, we're all saints. That's why, on All Saints' Day, I always preach about how we're saints too, and how the martyrs and people like that were just better at it than us, but we're all in it together."

Alistair nodded and continued, "You do so much for the church; I find myself wondering whether you ever felt called to ordination yourself."

"A lot of people ask me that," replied Barnaby, with a friendly smile. He gazed out of the window at the bright sunshine beaming down onto the patio plants. Again, he looked as if he was glad to have been asked the question.

"Well, I have thought about it obviously, but … " he began, before hesitating and starting again. "It's very difficult to explain or to put my feelings into words."

"Try, I'm interested; I'm trying to learn what church people think and feel, while I'm carrying out this investigation … what makes them tick," urged Alistair, returning the friendly smile with one of his own.

"Well, people don't seem to understand this, but I feel my calling is to this particular parish, St Peter's, where the Good Lord landed me. I don't think I could ever leave the town. Brenda and I have been here since the year dot, and …"

"That's interesting," replied Alistair, and continued, "that rather appeals to me. I find it rather refreshing in a way. So many people seem so concerned with their careers and all that."

"Yeah, well, maybe I'm different. I like this place. Don't know why. Just do. Always have done, ever since I went into St Peter's one day after a narrow escape when I was in the Met. I'd been sent to a brawl, but it turned out to be a little more than a brawl, and a guy with a knife took a lunge at me, which I managed to deflect. Only time it ever happened, but it was a ghastly thing all the same. I had nightmares for ages after that incident, and Brenda tried to get me to leave the Force. Anyway, they offered me a lift back home that evening, but I declined it – said I wanted to walk. They said, 'are you sure?' But something made me say, 'Yes, I want to walk home today.'

"I passed St Peter's Church on the way up from the station coming back home, and I don't know why, but after that day's experience something made me go inside. I'd never been in before, though of course I'd walked past it many a time, hadn't been in many churches before, to tell you the truth. Anyway, for the first time in my life I got down on me knees and said a little prayer of thanks that I'd survived, and I asked for protection too; and anyway, to my surprise and to be honest with you a bit to my annoyance, along comes the vicar, a mad fellow he was in those days, guy called Featherstone, Maurice Featherstone; anyway he come up to me and asks, 'Would you like to come to church on Sunday?' Well, I was still pretty emotional after the narrow escape and I replied, 'Why not?' I remember he said, 'I can't answer that,' and he kind of gave me a blessing. For a moment that freaked me out, but then I

137

felt it somehow gave me a kind of protection, and I felt very at peace and serene as I went on home. Felt like I wouldn't be lunged at by any passing crook with a knife! Anyway, that's how I come to be at St Peter's."

Barnaby Hatch screwed up a bit of paper and threw it rather skilfully into a waste-paper basket and gave Alistair a look as if to say, "That's it."

"It's an interesting and actually rather wonderful story," said Alistair with genuine enthusiasm.

"Well, next thing I know, this Featherstone guy, he says to me after that next Sunday's service, 'We need people like you in the church.' I said to him, 'You wouldn't say that if you knew me.' At first I thought he didn't seem to see the joke and then he said, 'No, we need people with a bit of experience – people who've seen life a bit.' And he says, 'How would you like to go on a course and learn how to be what we call a reader, and then you'll be taking a big part in the services, and even preaching.'"

Barnaby stretched back and held up his hands like a conjuror finishing a trick before continuing. "It had never entered my head before, but anyway isn't it wonderful how things happen to one in life?"

"Do you know, I really find that interesting," said Alistair with sincerity, but went on to ask, "How come he should ask you so soon, without knowing you?"

"Well, funnily enough, I asked him that, but he said he had a strong feeling it was God's will, and started telling me how Our Lord had called unexpected people rather suddenly to just start." Barnaby put his finger to his mouth and said, "I'm talking too much, but well, I've come to learn it was all part of God's plan for me."

Alistair kept silent to be sure that Barnaby had finished, which wasn't quite the case, for he added, "Anyway, to cut a long story short, I've been doing it for years, and when Henrietta arrived she was keen I should continue. Think I helped her settle in. I got on well with her...."

"I wanted to ask you, how did you get on with the new vicar?" Alistair asked.

"We never had a cross word. I was as surprised as anyone when we found we had got a woman priest, but you soon get used to that. I know she brought in a lot of changes, and I had a bit of a job smoothing things over with certain people here. I mean, some left. Oh yes, some left OK. One guy said to me, 'This is more papist than the Vatican.' Stupidly, I told Henrietta, thinking she would take it as a joke, but she only burst into tears, didn't she? My wife, Brenda, said that's why some people think women shouldn't be priests, because they can burst into tears so easily."

He seemed genuinely amused by the recollection of this particular incident and continued, "I said to Henrietta, 'Don't take it so much to heart.' She said, 'This is the only form of service I know.' Well, as I say, one or two – well more than that actually - did vote with their feet, and upped and left."

"Do you agree with me, Barnaby, that OK, there may have been a lot of disagreement in the parish about this ratcheting up, for want of a better word, of the service, and OK some people were mighty annoyed about it, but they'd never in a million years end up blinking murdering the vicar, would they?"

"Well, I know, but when my former employers – the Met - came and cross-examined me and I put that to them, just like you did, they said, 'Oh, you'd be surprised, Barney.' I remember the inspector said to me he came across a chap who murdered someone because they beat him in a game of snooker in front of his girlfriend."

"Ah, well, of course as soon as you introduce things like girlfriends and boyfriends and sex and love and all that – well then, maybe anything is possible," suggested Alistair, hoping to get the reader to speak more uninhibitedly.

"Yeah, I think you're right there," was Barnaby's only response.

"But as far as you know, Henrietta was a happily married lady, and there was nothing untoward going on in her life?" persisted Alistair.

Barnaby seemed to be rather silenced by this question, so Alistair added, "I mean, that's the $64,000 question, isn't it?"

Barnaby, who had been stroking his beard with an air of new-found seriousness, looked out of the window and said, "I don't know if I should tell you this."

There was another long pause, which Alistair eventually could not restrain himself from interrupting.

"I'd be grateful if you could tell me as much as you feel you can."

"I never told anyone this," declared Barnaby very solemnly.

"You never told the police?"

"No."

"Well, you see, I think Dennis wants me to pick up on things that for whatever reason may have passed the police by."

"Do you know, I'd rather not. I can keep a confidence. I don't think it's relevant anyway."

Alistair sat back disappointed.

"You see, Barnaby, that's what makes my job so hard," he said at length. "I feel people probably do know useful things that they keep to themselves, and then wonder why no progress is ever made."

"I think if the bishop was to tell me it was OK to speak to you about it, then it would be OK."

Although irritated, Alistair did not want to lose the confidence and help of this seemingly rather key personality in the life of the parish so he reluctantly assented to this unsatisfactory suggestion.

"OK," he said, trying to hide his annoyance but with a certain sarcasm, "I await His Lordship's gracious permission to you to enlighten me further in this matter, then."

Becoming aware that Barnaby may not have realised he was joking, and seeing a rather confused and disapproving look come over the reader's face, Alistair commented, "You see, some of us in Scotland don't go along with bishops, but don't take me too seriously, I was only joking – I'll wait till you feel ready to tell me anything you think might help. I hope you don't mind my Presbyterian origins, with their views on bishops etc."

"I know; we did that on my refresher course," said Barnaby with not a little pride.

"Oh well, needs must; I'll stand by to hear from you, then. How long will it be, do you think? Can I ask if it's something someone confessed officially in the confessional - if one can use that phrase in the Anglican Church?"

"Well, not officially. I mean, I'm not a priest, so I can't officially hear confession, but it's kind of a bit like that," replied Barnaby, rather enigmatically.

"And how long would you say will I have to wait?"

"You never know with the dear old C of E," commented Barnaby.

"Guess I'll just have to be patient on that one, then. You call it the dear old C of E, but you go along with it all, and are indeed a stalwart pillar of the organisation." Alistair had already ascertained that Barnaby responded well to a little praise.

"Yes, I shouldn't use that phrase, 'dear old C of E' - I picked it up from our beloved churchwarden, Edwin. I think he's the one I first heard use it. I'll blame him."

After a fairly quick run-through of various personalities in the congregation, about whom one or two suspicious matters were raised, Barnaby nonetheless reaffirmed that he had no suspicions about any of them having anything to do with the crime.

Brenda and the grandchildren seemed to have vanished as they finally shuffled out into the hall and said their goodbyes.

They shook hands, and Barnaby asked, "You got a list of people to see, then? Doing the rounds, are you?" It was by way of a final remark, but was spoken with a certain interest.

"Well, working my way through the main protagonists here – your junior, this chap Ben, will be interesting if he'll agree to meet. I suppose he might refuse now that he's cut his ties here."

"Well, actually, I can probably help try and arrange that for you. In fact, might be a good idea if I do. I'm about the only person from St Peter's he'll speak to at the moment. I'll try and get some dates for you that he can manage. I'll give you a ring tonight and let you know how I got on."

"Well, that's absolutely splendid of you, Barnaby," replied a pleased Alistair. "I had thought he might be a difficult one to get to agree to a chat. Burnt his boats with the place, I gather; but probably got one or two interesting things to say, no doubt."

"You'll find him difficult – hard to explain, but yes, difficult," nodded Barnaby.

"Really?" responded Alistair, turning in the hall.

"Well, it was quite something, really, him going off like that after all that time taking services, preaching and everything. Made a lot of people start talking about how the devil was stirring it up over here. Of course it was bad timing. There were a lot of bad jokes about him having done poor Henrietta in – real tittle-tattle,

142

there was – what with the coincidence of the two things happening so close … him going off like that, and her arriving … Heard said it could be poor Faye, his wife or wife that was, I should say. I even heard a rumour that people were saying they had done her in together; but I happen to know that Ben and his wife weren't even speaking to each other at the time of the crime." Barnaby gave a little laugh as if to say, "Funny old world."

They shook hands at the front door. Alistair noticed that Barnaby, who had appeared quite talkative, was now surprisingly rather silent, almost as if praying.

"Thanks again for all your help. Goodbye," said Alistair, conscious that Barnaby's farewell wave, not unlike the Reverend Sylvia Patterson's, was rather similar to a blessing.

Alistair took his by now familiar route home. What a mixed bunch of characters, they are here, he mused. True, old Barnaby is not the brightest of people, he thought; but he was prepared to give him the benefit of the doubt, and felt he might have detected a certain dedication, and even sincerity, which demanded respect.

He certainly seemed an impossible candidate for murderer. True, he was the most long-standing of all the dramatis personae, and he was certainly opinionated and here and there had his nose put out of joint by the late Reverend Henrietta Carr, Alistair reflected, 'But no, no, no – a thousand times no – he could not be a murderer.

Later that evening, just when he had begun to put all thoughts of the investigation out of his mind, the phone rang, and a slightly more animated Barnaby told him that he had not been able to raise Ben. He had used the phrase that Ben was in "one hell of a sulk". However, perhaps just as usefully he had managed to contact

Ben's wife, or as Barnaby corrected himself, former wife, Faye. "She could manage tomorrow morning," Barnaby said, adding, "and you'd better take it, because she's off on holiday the day after tomorrow for a few weeks – and if it's with a new-found boyfriend, I don't want to know just now!"

"That's absolutely excellent!" declared Alistair down the telephone. "It's kind of her in all the circumstances to agree to speak to me."

Alistair put the receiver down and thumped his fist into the palm of his hand. It had been a useful day. Another interview tomorrow had been arranged, and now he really could give himself an evening off and rest his mind with some reading from one of his favourite books. Occasionally the case drifted back into his consciousness. What on earth was it that Barnaby could only tell him once he had got it cleared with the bishop? It had to be some kind of secret. Whatever it was, he ought to find out, because any breakthrough would only come from some kind of new material. Yes, he must chase that one up all the time...

However the book was a good one, and although Alistair didn't often fall asleep in his chair, he did that night.

CHAPTER 11

(An interview with the wife of a bad lay reader)

The morrow dawned as brightly as the day before, but as Alistair strolled along, he somehow anticipated a less cheery ambience.

The house, when he tracked it down, did indeed seem not only to be dark, but to radiate an almost tangible gloom. Maybe it was just the contrast with the lightness of Barnaby's house yesterday, or maybe it was because Alistair knew there had been much unhappiness within this stark exterior. Faye opened the door, with what he took to be a forced smile on her face.

He got the usual pleasantries out of the way more quickly than was his custom. He felt he wanted to get this particular appointment over with.

"I know you've been through the wars. I think it's very good of you to offer to help in the circumstances," he murmured politely, as she ushered him into her front room.

"Yes, I have been through the wars, as you put it," she replied rather tensely. "But I'm through now – *through* is the operative word. No, I can cope now. Anyway, I've got a new man, Cyril, with me now." She threw her head back and laughed rather loudly, possibly from embarrassment, thought Alistair.

"I've heard a lot of people admire you for being so brave about it all," lied Alistair, as she sat down on a sofa opposite him. Aware that she seemed keen to talk about the new man in her life, he added, "I'm glad to hear things are picking up for you."

"It was rather romantic; we met in a museum," she announced.

"Oh really, which one?" asked Alistair, who as a

lover of museums himself was genuinely interested.

"The British Museum," Faye replied with some glee.

Alistair gave one of his silent nods.

"I was looking at some old Roman coins and bits and pieces," she continued, "and I saw him taking notes there, so I asked him some question about one of the exhibits. The answer proved rather long, and anyway we ended up in the cafeteria there."

"How tremendous," enthused Alistair, wondering how anyone could feel about her as he did about Zoe. "How romantic," he managed, "but look, sorry, I've got to get back to the crime, though, and life at St Peter's; and if you feel up to talking about it, because I realise it must be very difficult for you, in particular I'd like to ask about Ben and how it all ended, and so on."

"Yes, sorry, it was my fault we went off at a tangent. I'm quite happy to talk to you. Barnaby told me all about you and your investigation, and as I said to him, I'm only too happy to try and help. I did check with Helen Archer first, after he rang, because she's the only one I trust round here about all these matters. We've both had such traumas - Helen finding that murdered corpse, and Ben walking out on me. We've kind of got to know each other so much better. "

She sat back and folded her hands, waiting for him to fire a first question.

It took a moment for him to get over his surprise at her seemingly callous terminology, before he asked, "Am I right in thinking you don't actually have much dealings with St Peter's these days?"

"Well yes, I mean I never really did anyway, but of course Ben did. And yes, I mean, I said to Ben one day, 'You really can't go on preaching to that congregation – telling them how to behave and behaving the opposite.' I told him he just had to resign from his post of reader there. Anyway, to my surprise he kind of agreed about that, though of course I didn't really trust him to … "

"Do you mean trust him to resign or to …?" Alistair began.

"I didn't trust Ben to tell the vicar about the situation, so we composed a sort of joint letter and I delivered it personally. First and last time I went to that bloody vicarage! She wasn't in, of course. Probably out gallivanting and enjoying herself."

She checked herself, "no, sorry, that's probably unfair; but I expected some kind of response – you know, some kind of communication by way of reply."

"What? She never got back to you?"

"Do you know? She rang me up about three days later and asked me if I knew if Ben wanted certain robes he had left in the vestry."

"What, just like that?"

"Yes, just like that." Faye echoed his words, fighting back a tear.

"That surprises me. That's terrible! I suppose she didn't know what to say, but then she should have been trained how to behave correctly … No, that's terrible," said Alistair, with some feeling.

"It was the giddy limit," agreed Faye. "I'm afraid I put the phone down. I did it before I said anything I might regret."

Faye gave a girlish shriek, which Alistair had by now learnt to definitely attribute to her nervousness at this rather awkward interview.

It suddenly struck him that here was a situation that could have led to her losing control. He looked at her intently. No, he established almost immediately to his own satisfaction, she does not have the eyes of a murderer.

He felt a strong sympathy for what she had been

through.

"I'm not surprised you aren't exactly pro church," he said, under his breath but audibly.

He paused, then added, "I'm right in saying that, am I? You're not pro church?"

"You're absolutely right, I'm an agnostic," Faye said with some feeling. "Yes, I've had a good think about it all, and I'm happy with that. That's my position. I'm not an atheist – no, I considered atheism quite seriously, if you know what I mean; but no I am happy with agnosticism."

She shrugged her shoulders and said, "Can't really put it clearer than that. Don't want to get too deep, but I do sometimes think there must be something deeper to human existence than its face value, if you see what I mean; but Christianity … no I can't buy it. You see, the way I think, no earthly father could allow a son to suffer a crucifixion … sorry, another time maybe … As I say, agnostic. I can't really put it clearer than that."

Again there was a type of laugh, which this time Alistair thought was really to cover her embarrassment.

"About sums up my position too," he responded, trying to put her at ease and finding her word 'position' rather a convenient one to copy in expressing his own thoughts.

"I'm thinking about religion a lot these days," he commented, "but so far, at least, I'm not finding anything at St Peter's to lead me on in that direction."

He nearly smiled, but stopped himself. This lady has had more than her fair share of aggravation recently, he thought, as she nodded, saying, "No? Well, I'm not surprised; not surprised at all. I never found anything at St Peter's to lead me to religion."

"Is your new man, as you call him – Cyril - a churchman?" he asked rather too abruptly for his own liking, but wanting her to calm down a little.

"No, he's not," replied Faye with some emphasis and then rather paradoxically added, "thank God!"

Alistair was genuinely amused by her emphasis. "I think it's wonderful that you've met Cyril," he said in a kindly manner.

"We've just agreed that there's all the time in the world – we'll get round to getting married one day, I expect, but no rush," she added, as if pre-empting a question about marriage, which actually Alistair had not intended to ask.

"Well, look, as you know, I've been asked by Dennis to have a crack at the mystery; looking at things from a different angle … different perspective." He let the word hang in the air before asking, "You don't have any theories yourself about this crime, then?" He then stretched back and gestured with his hand for her to speak.

"Not really. I hope they do solve it; we all need a kind of closure on the goings-on here over the last several months. It seems a real mystery. I had a wild thought when it first happened that it was her husband, Dennis. I recognised a sort of tension there. You know, other way round to me and Ben. He didn't go along with it. You could see her irritation with him sometimes, and then you could see his back going up every now and again when she seemed to force him to do things. Surprised me somewhat; I mean, even Ben and I had a sort of system worked out – a way of coping with our great differences - especially in public."

"But I mean this was just your hunch, wasn't it? You didn't have any real evidence to back such a thought up with, did you?" asked Alistair.

"Well now, I found this in what used to be Ben's drawer." She got up to go and get something, stopped, turned and said to Alistair, "You see, Ben used to keep a diary. Well, of course he took all his diaries with him when he cleared out. Sometimes he was too busy to do his diary entry – or thought he was; anyway, he used to write little bits of paper headed 'Notes for diary' and stuff them into his diary, and then when he had more time he would copy them out into the diary later. Well, I found one of these blessed little bits of paper, which must have dropped out – here it is. It's dated two days before the crime. Here you are."

She opened a book and pulled out a scruffy bit of paper.

"Look what it says," she said as she handed it over and stood watching him with her arms folded.

Alistair read it carefully twice.

There was the date OK, neatly written in what he assumed to be Ben's unique handwriting style and the words 'Notes for diary'; but underneath in a scrawl were the words: *Went to vicarage as arranged after work. H was late, but had surprise when she came. Had been crying. Said she had troubles of her own, but wouldn't elaborate. Felt irritated by the anticlimax. Found her no help at all. Will just act on my own judgement – am through with getting advice now.*

Alistair laid the piece of paper down on the table in silence and seemed deep in thought for a moment.

Faye broke the silence by saying, "You should have seen his face when I told him I'd found that! Went ashen white, because you see at that time he hadn't told me he had gone to her for advice. He said, 'Don't you ever read anything private like that again.' I said, 'I'm your wife, Ben, for goodness sake!' I let him know I wasn't too happy about him getting marital advice and counselling from her, either."

"And this is definitely Ben's writing?" Alistair checked.

"Oh   yes,"   she   nodded   her   head   sagely, "unmistakeable."

"Did Ben ever elaborate about this?"

"No, he never referred to it again - and well, of course, I wasn't allowed to read his diary. I reckon that particular bit of paper must have slipped out of it. It had happened before a few times that I've found these ruddy little 'Notes for diary', as he calls them.

On using the phrase "Notes for diary", she had made a little gesture of quote signs with her hands in the air.

After a pause she continued, "Of course, as I say, he took all his diaries with him when he left – made damn sure of that. He became so secretive. Do you know, his diaries actually had keys? He knew somewhere where you could get them. They were kind of specially made. I challenged him once and asked him what was so bloody private that it needed to be locked up. He replied in such a childish way, 'Ah, that would be telling, wouldn't it?' I said, 'I am your ruddy wife, for Pete's sake,' and you won't believe what he said. He said, 'At the moment.' That's what he said, 'at the moment'. I couldn't fucking believe it! Sorry, I don't usually swear."

She started sobbing quite loudly.

Alistair felt genuinely sorry for her, and though not attracted by her, found it quite difficult to resist the urge to put his arm round her.

She sat sobbing for what seemed like at least two minutes.

"We can stop talking about it if you want," managed Alistair sympathetically.

"Oh no, I want to tell all; get it off my chest, if you know what I mean," she rejoined. Composing herself, she continued, "Helen advised me to be absolutely frank with you. Anyway, to get back to the diaries, in earlier times, he used to leave his diary hanging about a bit, but of course as soon as he started going with that bitch – I won't even mention her name – that bloody girl at his office – well, the diaries were under lock and key after that. Of course, when I came across that particular bit of paper, I recognised his style and knew it was from his diary – knew it must have slipped out. I know he called Henrietta 'H' - said he got the habit of using letters for words – a kind of shorthand from Henrietta herself. He didn't use it as much as Henrietta, who I gather used it all the time, according to Ben. I've seen notes from Henrietta to him about the arrangements and parish business that were definitely the same style. Funnily enough, I found one of these silly little notes in cryptic letters from her just before he walked out when we were having our final argument. I said to him 'How do I know you're not having an affair with the bloody vicar?' I remember he said, 'Right, that's it, our marriage is over' – just like that - and walked out."

Alistair did not want more time taken up with sobbing, and said in a businesslike manner, "Right, but you didn't find any other intriguing 'Notes for diary' bits of paper hanging around, did you?"

"That's the only one of interest. There were one or two others, but I threw them away. They were just ridiculously trivial ones – you know, 'went to get milk' – that sort of thing."

"Did any have that style, which Henrietta used, of using letters instead of words?"

"Only one I saw like that was, 'AS for M'- which I worked out meant 'Arthur's Store for milk'. He told me once that Henrietta had given him the idea of doing notes like that," she said, looking out of the window.

Alistair detected the imminence of tears yet again, and thinking there was not much more to be gained, started to make movements as if he was ready to go.

Faye did however start throwing a few insults at some of her erstwhile husband's fellow church members.

"I was glad to find I was seeing you first before Ben, because from what I'd heard you are very much the injured party," Alistair said eventually with some feeling, as he moved towards her front door.

The tears having now manifested themselves, he added rather rapidly, "But I suppose I'd better do likewise with Ben, and pay him a visit. I'll be very discreet, I assure you. You don't have any objection to me arranging an interview with him some time soon, do you? I don't like doing things behind people's backs, but I think Dennis would expect me to be as thorough as I can be and not leave someone like Ben out."

"No, of course I don't object – not at all. Ben's nothing to do with me at all now."

"I'll try my luck at arranging a meeting with him tomorrow, then."

"I mean it's up to you, but I warn you he will go ballistic if you bring up his diary notes. For some reason it seemed to make him get extremely annoyed on the few occasions that I found those damned notes for the diary."

"Oh, I'll play it close to my chest, alright, don't you worry."

"Wait, before you go, there was another one I found. Must have got stuck at the end of his drawer when he cleared out. I'll get it."

"It all helps," said Alistair, as she went back into the front room. She was saying, "Some bit of nonsense which I can't make head or tail of, but I kept it. I'll hand these bits of scruffy paper over to you now."

Soon she returned with another scruffy-looking scrap of paper. She handed it to him and said, "That's a funny one, isn't it?"

Alistair read the now familiar heading 'Notes for diary', and then the scrawl underneath, which went as follows : *Went to vicarage for further counselling. H sympathetic, but distracted. Wrote 'TATT' in her diary while she was speaking to me. Thought it was something to do with me, but she said, "No, it's nothing." Noticed she looked a bit flustered. Not herself today.*

Alistair put it into his wallet, saying, "That'll keep me out of trouble for a bit, trying to solve that one." He wondered, however, if it would not do just the opposite. He thanked Faye again for her civility and help, and on reaching the porch, shook hands, rather too formally, he felt.

What a world, he thought as he strolled down the road at the start of his journey back to the homely hotel. So much trouble and tension around. How could two people, who fall in love and get married, end up like that? It could never happen to me and Zoe.

When he phoned Ben that evening to make an appointment, he immediately felt the lack of welcome in the tone, which he had expected.

"These days I'm too busy for all this tittle-tattle, but I've had a call from Barnaby, and he's persuaded me that Dennis is really keen on this, so you're lucky; by chance I can spare you a little time tomorrow morning, if you like. I'm doing it for Dennis's sake."

Alistair accepted the suggestion with alacrity.

Tomorrow should be interesting, if nothing else, he thought as he went into the little saloon bar.

This church-going business – what was it all about? he asked himself as he waited for his drink. He did not blame Faye for having nothing to do with it. Who could blame her, after that experience?'

He was about to allow himself to completely relax and to 'switch off' as he termed it, but as so often his thoughts persisted. Faye obviously held it against the church from way back, not least because it took up so much of Ben's time and he was so preoccupied with the church, and again who could blame her for that. No doubt Ben's new bit of crumpet wouldn't have that particular problem ... Alistair found himself wondering if on the arrival of this new vicar, who was unexpectedly a woman, Faye had thought or even unexpectedly found out that Ben was receiving advice to ditch her. That could drive anyone to go berserk.

He paused in his thoughts to think twice about that one.

In Faye's mind, they didn't like her at the church, because she had always kept her distance and seemingly not supported her husband. However Faye herself felt unsupported.

His thoughts were interrupted by a guest asking him where the dining room was. It momentarily irritated him, and then he found himself thinking, if I can be annoyed by something so trivial, did Faye's annoyance with something a million times bigger reach a point where she just flipped?

"Yes, I will have another," he said in answer to the young university student, earning a few bob as a barman, who had raised an eyebrow and pointed at his glass. With that, the line from Holy Scripture - 'Sufficient unto the day is the evil thereof' - came to him, and he allowed his mind to stop thinking of the matter for the day.

CHAPTER 12

(An interview with a bad lay reader)

When he woke the next morning, Alistair felt pleased to be able to keep the momentum of his investigation going. He knew there would be times of frustration and no doubt plenty of hold-ups ahead, but for the moment things were on a roll. With the help of his road atlas, he quite easily tracked down the new address, which Ben had given Barnaby permission to inform him of. It was not as far away as everyone, including himself, had seemed to think.

The house seemed nondescript and soulless. The door was opened promptly and the conventional greetings took place. Maybe it was subjective, but there seemed that same air of melancholy about the place as he had found at Faye's, thought Alistair.

Ben was icily polite, or as Alistair afterwards was to say, had "no warmth"; but to give the devil his due, not quite the monster Alistair had half expected.

"You explained why you were coming," said Ben rather abruptly, "and I want to go along with what Dennis wants, because I feel sorry for him. So just go ahead with questions if you want to."

Taken aback by the suddenness of this invitation to cut the ceremony and get started, while they were still standing up, Alistair remained silent for a moment.

"I'll answer anything you fire at me," continued Ben with the flicker of an unpleasant smile. He now ushered Alistair to a rather uncomfortable chair, adding, "Barnaby explained to me how Dennis was keen for you to carry out this private investigation. I had a great respect for Dennis, who I think has been through more than any man deserves, and as I say I'll answer anything you fire at me."

Coffee was produced, which Alistair found to be tepid, and he was almost expecting it when he found the biscuit tasteless too.

Ben sat back and cocked his ear as if to prompt a first question, before saying, "Well, let's get started."

"OK. If you want to do it that way, let's go straight to it. How did you find Henrietta yourself?" Alistair asked equally baldly.

Ben shrugged his shoulders.

"Henrietta," repeated Ben as if deep in thought and considering her character for the first time. "Didn't really get to know her," he eventually replied with a hint of another of those smiles, before continuing, "I mean, I'd spoken a lot about my situation to her predecessor, the retiring vicar, Maurice, and indeed to Clarissa, another fairly local priest, who used to come and help out a lot during the interregnum; but you know that was embarrassing enough, and I realised it was probably best to pull out before Henrietta got started."

"I quite understand, but you did meet Henrietta when she arrived, I suppose?"

"Well, I decided to pull out of all church activity before her arrival – her induction, as it's called. You know, I didn't attend the church or do any preaching, obviously, or any leading of services etc., but I did meet her privately a few times for a couple of weeks or so, to discuss my situation."

"Did you find her sympathetic?"

"Not really. She said it was ultimately up to me and my conscience. I suppose she had been trained to say that sort of thing in such circumstances. I suppose it was better than the criticism I was expecting. She said the commandments are all there for us to obey. I suppose to be honest I didn't quite get the attitude or advice I wanted; but seemed a bit cold and, well, just plain unhelpful."

For a moment Alistair was taken aback that someone he was already finding cold could find somebody else cold. But he needed to remember that despite his initial impression, Ben was a human being too, with feelings the same as the rest of humanity.

"I understand you decided to leave the parish, and indeed have set up in a new house here."

"I made that decision. I'm sure you can appreciate it wasn't easy."

Alistair resisted the temptation to add, "for your wife". Instead he looked Ben straight in the face and said, "Do you mind me asking how, when the time came, you went about letting people in the parish know about your decision?"

"How do you mean?" asked Ben, defensively.

"Well, it can't have been a very easy thing to set about informing the parish. I mean, you were a reader; though as you've told me, you had stopped preaching and being involved in the services for some time, I understand."

"Yes, I was aware people were beginning to ask questions. My spies told me there was much talk of me having lost my faith, which actually I hadn't. Also to my surprise I heard there was a rumour going round that I had become a Roman Catholic."

"Well, it seems like you'd have been OK at St Peter's if that had happened," intervened Alistair, trying to lighten things with a little joke.

Ben made no response.

"Sorry, that's a bad joke," continued Alistair. "It's just that I've heard Henrietta had ratcheted it up somewhat to being so very High Church that there have been jokes about it becoming Roman Catholic at St Peter's. One wag even refers to it as St Peter's Basilica."

"Oh yes, that made me chuckle. I didn't mind people thinking that," responded Ben, loosening up a bit and shifting a little less uneasily in his seat, before adding, "I mean, I've always thought England used to have a Catholic faith in centuries gone by."

"It's quite extraordinary the difference between the different wings of Anglican thinking. I mean, to someone like me, meeting the Anglican Church for the first time as it were, it seems remarkable that both wings are in the same Church. Has nobody ever thought of having two distinct Churches, or perhaps even three, for people who are kind of in the middle?" asked Alistair, not entirely unseriously.

"Well, anyway, I'm having a break from it all just now," answered Ben with a slightly bored expression. "I know, and confess I was at fault in preaching what I wasn't practising. Mark you, I'm not the only one guilty of such lapses in that lot, I'll tell you," he continued. "But it's over, I've said sorry - I mean truly confessed - and now I'm having a complete break from it all."

"Really, that's interesting. So you don't go to church at all now?" checked Alistair, a little bit better disposed to his interlocutor.

"No – I've decided to stop for a time," confirmed Ben.

"Really?" said Alistair automatically.

"Yes, really. I pray – that may surprise you - but I don't go to church."

Myriads of questions came into Alistair's mind, and they were not all confined to this particular mystery, but he determined to get back to business.

"But to return to my question," he continued, "how did you go about getting the parish informed of your decision? I suppose you realised it would be a bit of a bombshell."

"I asked Florence to announce it at a PCC meeting and at one or two other meetings, like the finance and fabric team meeting and the ministry leadership team meeting. Oh, and the pastoral care team meeting too. Yes, I used to be a member of that, till I found I was the one who needed the pastoral care." Ben's smile became unpleasant.

Alistair had to suppress his reaction to the irony of this, as his sympathies were increasing very much with poor Faye, the deserted wife.

"Also, I went round and visited Barnaby," continued Ben. "I mean, he was the senior reader as regards length of service; so kind of above me in the pecking order."

Alistair nodded, somewhat deep in thought.

"Of course, Barnaby positively beamed - loved becoming the 'good reader'. He looked so pleased he nearly purred," said Ben, with not a little hostility in his voice.

"No, I'm sure he was sympathetic … " suggested Alistair.

"Not sympathetic, but he's been helpful, I'll grant him that. He's my kind of contact now, or shall we say liaison officer, for anything to do with my old life at St Peter's. I guess you probably had to get my new address from him, did you?"

Alistair nodded silently.

"I'd be very grateful if you would keep that confidential."

He gave Alistair a very long hard look, adding, "You know how irritating do-gooders can be. I got a note via Barnaby from Emma Duncan, which irritated me. Someone like that just can't understand my predicament. Trying to help, but making things worse. Anyway, please keep my address confidential. "

"On my honour," said Alistair to break the silence

that followed, during which he contemplated that for all Ben's sins and unpleasantness it would appear that there had been some agonising.

"And I told Fred Goodman. I kind of felt I had to. That's about it," said Ben, starting up again.

"What was Fred's reaction?"

"Well, I think Barnaby, Florence and Fred all knew I'd got personal problems. I'd more than hinted at that for some time, and I'd even told them that I was speaking to both Maurice and this kind of interregnum priest, Clarissa, who had been helping out a lot during the changeover. Maurice, who I actually had found to be the most helpful, had actually suggested I tell Florence, as senior churchwarden, about having personal problems.

"You never told Edwin, the other churchwarden?"

"Good heavens, no! I didn't. To be honest, I didn't like him. Didn't like him at all. Don't know why, just didn't. Actually, I think I do know why. Just a bit too slick for me – always had an answer for everything, always an excuse for not joining in things, getting out of things. Thought he was a bit of a fraud, really."

Alistair could just imagine his own mum repeating her favourite phrase about the pot calling the kettle black.

"But as I say, I told old Fred Goodman. I mean, although he wasn't churchwarden any longer, we all still *thought* of him as the churchwarden. Yes, I went round to see him too. Curiously, he was more sympathetic than the others. Florence pretended to be very shocked, Maurice just kept saying he would pray about it, and Barnaby seemed more interested in the administrative side of things. Yes, Fred was the sympathetic one alright."

Alistair restrained himself from asking, "To whom, Faye or you?"

There was a pause while Ben, sitting with a raised eyebrow, appeared to anticipate a further question from Alistair, but the latter had decided to remain silent.

"Yes, dear old Fred," continued Ben, "said nothing surprised him anymore; cheered me up a bit. He was complimentary about my ministry there. He was kind enough to say that I'd done a lot of good work for the parish over the years."

Another silence fell before Ben added, "Well, I hope I did, anyway – I like to think it wasn't all meaningless. What Fred said helped a bit. I mean, I'd been a reader there for many years, it had been kind of part of my life, you know, and he thanked me."

"Well, whatever the rights and wrongs of these sad situations, one always feels sorry for the people involved," said Alistair, by way of winding things up.

He tried to sound friendly and had indeed come with an open mind, conscious that even the guilty have their own kind of suffering in such situations.

"Getting away from you, have you any theories about the crime? What on earth could be behind it all?" Alistair asked quite suddenly, aware from Ben's frequent glance at his wristwatch that his time was limited.

"None whatsoever. Mark you, I'd say Henrietta seemed to have a way of putting people's backs up, from what my spies told me after I left," came Ben's reply.

"Really?" queried Alistair, genuinely interested, and also wondering who Ben meant by his "spies".

"Yes, I gather things have changed a bit there now, haven't they? Oh well, you probably know more than me now," said Ben in lighter tone.

"Who are your spies?" asked Alistair, wondering if perhaps he should have kept a discreet silence about that.

162

"Now that would be telling, wouldn't it?" came Ben's irritating reply.

"Well, I suppose you don't have to tell me," said Alistair in a resigned tone.

"No, I don't; but you'd be surprised. Things ain't always what they seem. You must know that too, better than me; I mean you're a blinking private detective, aren't you?"

Alistair was becoming irritated by Ben's style and replied, "Well, certainly it turned out not to be the peaceful parish church it looks as you drive by on the main road. Of course, for me it's irritating the way people keep things back – talk of their spies, and all that sort of thing, doesn't help; but no it ain't all as pretty as it looks when you drive by."

"No," agreed Ben in a tone that was almost spooky.

"There's a lot of sadness in there, isn't there?" pressed Alistair, in one more attempt to gather any further snippet of information.

Ben nodded, and they went on to cover a few of the personalities.

Alistair, having seen Ben slapping the arms of his chair as if to call it a day, determined to ask one final time, "You really don't have any thoughts or theories about how such a crime occurred?"

"No, I really don't. Haven't a clue. Complete mystery," replied Ben and then added, "anyway, mate, it wasn't me!"

"It's caused an awful lot of sadness," repeated Alistair, mildly irritated by the man's response.

"There's no shortage of that wherever you go," repeated the melancholy Ben.

He looked down at the floor with a sad and even glazed expression, and then looked rather deliberately at his wristwatch. He got up and manoeuvred himself nearer the front door, opened it and put out his hand for

Alistair to shake.

Alistair had by now decided that beyond doubt he did not like this Ben character. To think he had been a lay reader! Can the devil quote scripture? he mused to himself with a chuckle. Thank goodness I never had to listen to one of his sermons!

He stood at the front door and turned, "One last question, Ben. I don't want to hurt you, but I'd like to ask you."

Ben looked up with his characteristic, slightly surprised movement of the eyebrow.

"Are you happy now with the decision you made?"

"Of course I am," he answered, throwing his head back with a rather false effort of a laugh and continued, "I wouldn't have made it otherwise, would I? A lot of people could have tried a bit harder, I think, to stop me, but they chose not to when perhaps they should have. Maurice and Clarissa did try a bit; Henrietta didn't try at all. She just kept saying it was none of her business, and then as I've told you, saying that line about we have the commandments to guide us."

Alistair looked at him intently. Although critical of Ben, he felt very conscious at that moment that the human lot was in so many ways a sad one for everyone, be they saint or sinner.

"But no, I wouldn't have made the decision if I hadn't wanted to," repeated Ben glumly, uncomfortable with the way Alistair was looking at him and staring down at the floor again.

"I mean, you've no regrets about it all now?" asked Alistair, shuffling even nearer the front door, in what he was sure would be his last words of this unhappy conversation.

"That's my business, isn't it?" came the terse, but by now almost predictable tone of reply.

With that, Ben rather rudely moved his arm as if to

show Alistair the way out.

That was the last straw; Alistair decided yet again that he quite definitely did not like this person.

Rather too soon to be polite, the door was closed behind him. By the time he got down the little front garden path to the gate, Alistair had muttered the word, "Bastard!"

He walked on, lost in thought. "Well, Cyril's got to be a nicer companion for Faye than that so and so," he murmured to himself.

*****

Back at his base camp, as he had come to call his hotel, Alistair relived the interview in his thoughts, sitting at the bare table in his room.

If we were dealing with a poisoning I'd suspect him, he thought, but a crime of passion and going berserk – hard to imagine; mark you, that glazed look at the end was pretty spooky, and what was all that about how people could have done more to stop him? "Henrietta hadn't done anything." Perhaps he thought she should have done. Perhaps she unwittingly tipped him over to his course of action, by not urging him to stay with Faye. Had this driven him mad, and had he gone berserk and murdered her?

He went downstairs and ordered a drink at the little saloon bar.

No, he told himself, I'm tired, my imagination is running riot. You don't murder someone because they didn't stop you leaving your wife. And yet in a way the more he thought about it, the more he could imagine it.

He took a long sip of his drink.

Imagination, his thoughts continued, isn't that just what Dennis said was needed if the crime was ever to be solved? Isn't that just what Dennis rather unfairly accused the police of lacking?

"I'll leave you in peace, Mr MacTavish," said Cissie, who was normally only seen in the mornings, blowing him a cheeky kiss as she unexpectedly passed by.

Alistair was surprised to find his mind would not let go of his train of thought. Ben's life had been so caught up in the church, and now that was all gone up in smoke, presumably in his passion for the new girl. Alistair had worked in an office. He knew how passionate office infatuations could be. Could a murdered vicar be the result of a combination of church life going up in smoke and an obsessive passion for the opposite sex?

He needed a little break from thinking, and in the immediate future it was sleep he needed more than anything.

CHAPTER 13

(An interview with one of three allotment holders)

It seemed to Alistair when he woke the next morning that he was getting nowhere fast - or rather, slowly, as he corrected himself. It had seemed such an interesting and exciting, once in a lifetime opportunity when Dennis had first asked him to take on this investigation. Now these few days later, the enormity of the task and the sheer improbability of success in what he had taken on began to dawn on him. Had Dennis been losing a sense of reality in assigning him this task, and had he made himself a laughing stock by being a naive fool in accepting it? he wondered.

Unlike Florence, Sylvia and Barnaby, there did seem to be some sort of possible motive for Faye and her erring departed husband, Ben; nonetheless, having met them, Alistair found his imagination could just not make such a leap.

The difficulty in contacting and arranging appointments combined with a feeling that he already needed a break from the church people made him determine to interview the allotment holders. Perhaps he would have more luck there with managing to meet up with people, and it would make a welcome change of a sort, for it had all been rather intense yesterday, he thought, as he pulled out his map and began to work out his route.

Dennis had told him about Roger, who worked the allotment next to Helen's, and that seemed a pretty good place to start; not least because, as Dennis had further revealed, he and Roger had met through evening class, and apparently Tuesday afternoon was a good time to catch him there, demonstrating his green-fingered abilities.

Alistair decided that he would take this opportunity of killing two very important birds with one stone and visit the crime scene, which he had deliberately delayed doing, for the simple reason that he wanted his investigation to be of a totally different kind to that of the police.

"Oh yes, I'm not surprised you want a word. I mean, I've not just got the next door allotment to Helen's, where the victim was found, but the victim's husband and I were in the same evening class," said Roger almost proudly when Alistair, having arranged it telephonically in the morning, tracked him down at the main gate to the allotments in the afternoon.

Alistair shot him an interested glance as they walked down the central path from the road towards Roger's patch.

"Oh yes, I mean, it's well known," Roger reiterated. "It was in the papers. Her husband and I were in the same evening class. Resulted in a hell of a lot of awful publicity, when they found that out."

"Did he ever leave early from that class?" Alistair asked quite suddenly, as they turned left from the central path towards Roger's allotment.

"It's interesting that you should ask that; I don't recall the police ever asked me that. I don't think so; maybe he did once, I really can't remember. I used to walk home with him sometimes; not always, but sometimes. Of course he would be going back to the vicarage. Yes, that reminds me, there was an occasion when he told me he was going on somewhere else."

"Can you remember where that was?"

Roger appeared to be quite genuinely thinking hard.

"No," he replied, adding, "sorry, I wasn't expecting you to ask me such a question."

"Did you ever talk to him about the allotments?" Alistair asked, equally abruptly.

"I think I told him I had one; yes, I did, because I remember he said that it must be nice … 'therapeutic' was the word he used, which I'd never heard used about an allotment before, and I rather liked it. Yes, I remember now he was the first to use that word – therapeutic - about the allotments. He said he found strolling therapeutic, felt like getting away from it all sometimes himself."

"He didn't say from what, did he?"

"I suppose he meant his work, or maybe life at the vicarage, I suppose. I just don't know."

"And he never mentioned that again?" Alistair cocked an eyebrow.

"Well, no, not really. Perhaps he did occasionally rather suggest that evening class was a nice break for him. Yes, I think he once said it was good to be doing something that wasn't either work or home. That's right, I remember now – 'a third world', he called it."

"Did he ever ask about or mention your allotment to you?" pressed Alistair.

"I asked him in the tea interval at one of our evening lessons if he wanted any beans, but he didn't seem interested."

"Did he talk about his wife and her role locally in the parish?"

"No, I don't think so, except possibly, as I said, only to say he liked evening class because it got him away from things a bit."

"That sounds a bit sad, doesn't it? Though perhaps not. We all like a break from things, don't we?"

Alistair had pulled out his notebook during this comment and started writing.

Roger stood there in the pleasant afternoon sunlight, studying the earnest countenance of his newly acquainted inquisitor. It struck him that it was a not ignoble countenance, showing a good mixture of alertness, intelligence, humour and humanity.

Alistair was then subjected to a rather detailed account of what Roger was growing - or more accurately, trying to grow - on his allotment. He listened politely and posed questions such as a visiting dignitary might have asked.

There was a longish pause while Alistair appeared engrossed in the mechanism of his biro. Then he looked up quite sharply.

"You see, Roger, as you know, the odd situation you find yourself in is that you had an allotment absolutely next door to the murder site – literally bang horizontal," he added in emphasis, before continuing, "and however coincidentally and indirectly on top of that, you were also an acquaintance -"

"I'd like to think a friend," interrupted Roger, nodding.

"Indeed, as you say, a friend of the victim's husband. It is a coincidence, isn't it? I'm not suggesting it's anything more." Alistair tried to laugh. "But you see what I'm getting at; embarrassingly, you're kind of in the midst of this mystery, aren't you, old chap?"

Roger stood staring at the earth, again seemingly deep in thought.

"I mean, whether you like it or not, aren't you?" emphasised Alistair again.

"Yes, I'm still a bit amazed about it all when I think about it," replied Roger, calming the tone.

"And of course, the annoying thing from an investigator's point of view is that you can't help at all!" Alistair laughed, leaning forward and patting Roger on the shoulder.

"Well honestly, I've racked my brains to try and remember anything suspicious – gone round in circles chatting to my wife about it - but honestly I can't come up with anything to help at all."

They went carefully through all the matters relating to where he had been standing when Helen had screamed and run away to report her horrific discovery.

"Would you have expected her to come and tell you first? I mean you were standing relatively near. Did she look at you at all?"

"Well, my wife and I discussed that one. I suppose at the time she didn't know me as well as all that. Of course, now we've all got to know each other quite well; but one forgets, then it was more the odd comment about the weather or slugs or something like that. No, my wife said she felt it was quite natural that Helen would want to run and tell her husband first. Funny, that – I'm not sure I actually agree with my wife about that. I mean, her husband was at the bloody office, wasn't he?"

"Can I ask you to show me round, as it were? This is my first time here at the crime scene."

"'Scene of crime', they called it," corrected Roger as he ushered Alistair over to where the dilapidated shed still stood, like a rather macabre memorial of the crime.

"Of course, they took everything out – absolutely everything - and pored over the old shed inside and out afterwards; but oddly they've left it standing. I don't know why," said Roger, adding, "like a lot of old sheds round here, there's a kind of Heath Robinson method of opening and closing the door. This one of Helen's is a particular joke – look at this, the door is kept up against the main frame of the shed by these two paving stones down the bottom, and these two poles wedged between the door and this old brick storage structure opposite. Of course, for a long time during the police investigation, nobody was allowed anywhere near it,

171

but in the end they've left it just like it always was. Yes, dirty great tent they put up round it. And yes, it was really annoying; nobody was allowed anywhere near the allotments for ages. The police had the whole area taped off."

By this time, Roger, having proudly removed the door, gestured towards the interior of the small, dilapidated old structure going by the proud name of a shed, saying, "There you are."

Alistair poked his head in. He felt inexplicably uncomfortable, and for the first time experienced a feeling that he was an intruder into someone else's tragedy. Inside were lots of mostly broken plant pots, old buckets and gardening trays, a gardening fork, a spade, a rake, a hoe and an old hose and a wheelbarrow. Despite the antiseptic smell, some airborne insects hovered menacingly, and there were a large number of spiders' webs.

"Odd place to hide a body," offered Roger eventually, trying to rid himself of the nasty sensation he had felt on seeing for the first time where the victim had been found.

"An even odder one to murder someone at," came Alistair's response.

"Yes, I know. The police were fairly adamant when they spoke to me that their experts were confident the murder had occurred right there."

They walked round it together and examined it closely. Alistair pulled out a little packet of photographs of the crime scene that Dennis had obtained from the police liaison officer for the private investigation.

He identified the exact spot where the body had been found lying on the shed floor and checked where the victim's left foot had almost protruded from the makeshift door. He hated looking at the photographs,

172

which all too clearly depicted the vicious knife attack that had occurred within the small confines of this unlikely and dilapidated crime scene.

"This is the bit I knew I'd hate," he said, turning round to Roger and adding, "But needs must that I study this carefully – please bear with me for a few minutes."

He compared the photographs of the bloodstained walls and floor with the present scrubbed and bleached condition, smelling of disinfectant.

"They've certainly done a good job of getting it back to normal – it's a wonder it's still standing."

"I heard the police were in favour of leaving it up for a bit," said Roger.

Alistair seemed lost in thought and muttered, "Well I never."

"One bloody great mystery," declared Roger eventually, very deliberately and almost solemnly, before asking, "do you reckon you're likely to have a kind of breakthrough? I know Dennis has got a lot of faith in you, a lot of people are saying that."

"I just don't know. I've got to keep optimistic and positive, but I agree it's going to be difficult. My main hope is if someone, just someone – someone like you for all I know - tells me something they may have been holding back."

Roger appeared to nod slightly, but kept his silence for a while, eventually repeating himself. "Word has spread that Dennis thinks you're his best bet – everyone round here is saying it."

Alistair made it fairly clear that he thought he'd want to speak to Roger again on many matters, but soon they were on to other things, and shortly they had said their goodbyes and gone their separate ways.

For Alistair, it was to meet up with Charles, the supervisor of the allotments, whom Roger had pointed out hard at work on an allotment in the distance; for Roger, it was back home to Dolly, his wife.

"How did it go?" asked Dolly, for all the world as if he had just had a job interview."

"Oh, as expected. It's like with the police; I feel so helpless not being able to say anything useful. Nice guy, though. I liked him. He's got an honest face. Felt he knew what he was doing – in an odd sort of way. Not at all what I expected. Educated. Scottish."

For all his energy on the allotment and with his evening classes, when at home Roger liked to slump in his favourite chair in the living room, and that's exactly what he did on his return.

Distractedly, he turned the pages of a local free newspaper, which had been delivered and somehow avoided the usual immediate placement in a bin.

Every now and again he looked up and offered a few words to his patient wife, who hovered in the doorway with all the appearance of someone who was about to put the kettle on.

"This Alistair guy is a nice chap," he reiterated, for it was his custom to repeat himself. "Such a pity I can't help at all in this ghastly case. One feels so helpless and useless. It's that same old frustrated feeling, dear; I just can't throw any light at all on it. He gave me all that usual stuff about not being able to help, even though I know the victim's husband and know the murder site – you know the line people used to say to us when everyone was talking about nothing else last year."

He became aware that his wife was in a kind of daze as he continued in the account of his meeting with Alistair. Not for the first time she asked him to try and rack his brains and see if he could remember anything however trivial, that might in any way be worth reporting to an investigator.

"This is probably the last chance to get to a solution

to the horrid business," she muttered.

He hardly bothered to respond to what was now such a hackneyed suggestion.

He was about to throw the paper away when his eye caught a small story heading on an inside page of the freebee.

POSSIBLE OLD CLAY PIPE CLUE TO ALLOTMENT MURDER MYSTERY

"Bloody hell," came one of his usual phrases, which he often jokingly used to his wife when genuinely surprised. "They're still going on about it in the local newspaper. Look at this!"

For over a year the local papers had had a field day with this mystery. Recently, at readers' requests, the story had been put on the back-burner.

As the editor had stated recently:
Not to put too fine a point on it, we have explored every avenue relating to our local whodunit. The police have thanked us for our every assistance and have told us that many a memory has been jogged by our refusal to let sleeping dogs lie. However, at the request of our readers, we have now agreed to only report developments if we have some reason to feel they may be significant.
"Not another red herring," moaned Roger's wife, changing her tune as she finally went to put the kettle on. She called out, "Read it out, then - quickly though, because some of us are ready for a cuppa."

Roger began to read out loudly so that his slightly stuttering and uneducated voice would carry to the kitchen.

"A local resident whose hobby is to collect old discarded clay pipes has told the *Cookington and Renshaw Weekly Times* that he broke into the

175

allotments by means of the break in the fence by the river one day before the murder victim was found. He was looking for broken stems of old clay pipes, and if he was lucky a broken pipe bowl to add to his collection. Over the years he has acquired large numbers of these items from the earth, particularly where he reckons old inns used to be. The allotments near St Peter's seem to be a particularly rich picking ground for these items, which are of great interest to some who are collectors, but of no interest to most of us."

"Are you hearing this dear?" he checked.

"Yes," she replied from the kitchen, "Read on. Sounds like it could be a new tack."

"He always goes after rain," he continued to read, raising his voice slightly, "which helps bring the old relics to the surface."

Roger's wife returned to the living room as his voice droned on, "The resident, who has asked for his name to be withheld, says that he did not report this to the police at the time in order to avoid misunderstandings and because it seemed to him at the time not to be relevant. He feared he would be accused of stealing fruit and vegetables rather than collecting old pieces of discarded clay pipes, which nobody wants, and for which he has often ridiculed. He now realises that he should have reported his trespass to the police, and has asked us to act as mediator to avoid him getting into trouble with the law for withholding information. Significantly, he says that he did see two people acting suspiciously and has given us the details. We are not at this stage providing our readers with those details of this new intelligence, but feel it right to report that this has happened. We hope to be able to quench your curiosity, which we have no doubt aroused, at some time in the future, and assure our readers that they will be the first to know if this lead proves as significant as we think it might."

Roger put the paper down and stared across the room at his wife, who had by now tiptoed right up to him and was staring at the paper with a fascinated expression.

"That's all it says. Blimey, sounds like a 'development', to use their own word, dear," said Roger.

"Interesting," replied his wife, "very interesting; wouldn't it be wonderful if there was a sudden breakthrough!"

Then she seemed to caution herself. "But, of course, you know, you do get this sort of aftermath with a crime, I imagine. You know, people imagining this and that, perhaps even wanting to be involved - that sort of thing. Perhaps they just want to be on television."

"I presume Alistair knows about this, or will do very soon one way or another. Funny, he didn't mention it this afternoon, even though he covered quite a lot of matters. Do you think he knows?"

"The police will, dear; that's the main thing."

"But you know, dear, you don't seem to have fully taken on board that this bloke Alistair, he's been officially asked to investigate the crime by Dennis, the vicar's husband. It's a serious investigation – a serious assignment. Dennis is regarding it as a very serious investigation indeed. The police are aware of Dennis having called Alistair in aid, and are not opposed."

"Well, as you've just been talking to him and he didn't mention it, perhaps you should give him a ring, then. I personally think poor Dennis is losing it, hiring a person like that. A crime like that should be left to the police; but go on, dear, give him a ring."

"Oh no, I've had enough of it. Give us a break, dear, it's time for tea."

"No, dear – go on, get it over and done with, and then we'll have an early supper, and afterwards we can relax and have a telly gawp evening."

"Or Scrabble," he added.

Roger knew when not to argue with his wife, and when she was about to cook him a meal was a case in point. He reached for the phone and got through straight away to the mobile number that Alistair had given him.

Alistair's clear voice sounded interested.

"No, I haven't seen that or heard about it yet. I'd have picked it up OK, I'm sure, but thanks, Roger – that's great. I'll get on to them tomorrow when they open up. Dennis has said if anyone digs their heels in and refuses to cooperate I'm to get him to speak to them. So one way or another we'll find out what all that's all about tomorrow. I wouldn't have thought they could refuse to speak to Dennis - you never know – sounds like it could be quite interesting. But on the other hand, I know what newspapers are like. Maybe they just need a boost in their circulation."

"Hope I was as helpful as I could be this afternoon. Sorry I can't throw any light on this maddening mystery. It must be so frustrating for you," Roger said in a sincere tone.

"No, you were very helpful – thanks. But, er, Roger, there was one thing I wanted to check up with you about. Since you're on the phone perhaps I could just do that right now. I was going to wait until tomorrow. Dennis says you did once -"

The phone cut out.

"That was just getting interesting and he was just about to ask me something, and the line's gone phut!" spluttered Roger, before telling his wife how Alistair had responded.

"I wonder what he was going to ask you. You'd

178

better ring him up again."

Roger was about to do just that when the phone rang and it was Alistair. "Hi there, Roger, we lost each other. I think it was your end that went wrong. Nothing wrong with my mobile. I just wanted to check with your memory. Dennis told me you and he had actually one day... He'd forgotten, what with time passing and so much else on his mind. You'd gone to the pub after your evening class. Do you recall that?"

"Eh, which pub was that?"

"The one near your evening classes, the Griffin."

Roger's wife stood expectantly watching, but realised the line had been cut again.

"Oh Gawd, what's wrong with this line? It's gone dead again," complained Roger, looking genuinely frustrated.

"We'll have to get it checked out. I think it must be our end. Well, try ringing him back, dear. Come on, you've got time before dinner."

Roger tried ringing back but got the engaged tone.

"I expect he's trying to ring me – let's wait a minute," he suggested.

Sure enough, just as he got back to his armchair, the phone rang - rather shrilly and persistently, he thought.

"Roger, old chap, we keep getting cut off. What the deuce is going on, I wonder? Anyway, I was just saying I wanted to check that out with you. The Griffin. Sounds rather nice; rather wish I was there at the moment having a pint, but, er ... Dennis was saying you did once have a drink there together after evening class. I'm not surprised you forgot but can you recall it now?"

"No, I don't recall being in the Griffin with Dennis ever."

"Is it one of your haunts?"

"I've been there in my time, but prefer the Turk's Head."

"No worries, Roger, but let me know if it comes back to you. Maybe Dennis has got his wires crossed, or rather his pubs mixed up. Between you and me, he's been getting one or two things wrong and muddled lately. Bye for now."

At his end, Alistair switched off the mobile and found himself deep in contemplation. Curious, he thought to himself. Roger seems such a straight kind harmless sort of a guy, yet he says he didn't recall that, and why did the phone keep getting cut off just at the point of my questions? And why was he ringing up about this just now? I only saw him a few hours ago. I hope he's not one of those freaks who suddenly changes behaviour. No, no, no, definitely not, his thoughts continued.

Meanwhile, back in Lime Grove the husband-and-wife conversation resumed.

"That's interesting," commented Roger to his wife, who was by now in the kitchen preparing the evening meal.

"What?" she asked as she chopped the cucumber.

"Alistair says that Dennis has been getting things wrong lately and is muddled."

"Well, you can't blame him, can you? I mean after all what he's been through. I mean, it's a wonder he hasn't had a stroke after all he's been through," she replied.

"Yeah, but come on, Dolly, you remember how you used to say he might have flipped and bumped her off himself. You know, you didn't like him from the first time you heard about him."

"Oh, that was just chit-chat. I said I didn't like what I'd heard about him. No, poor man, I think now he's shown a bit of dignity, really I do, the way he's carried on and dealt with everything and coped. Why are you bringing that up now?"

"Well, I'm just telling you that this private detective chappie – this Alistair MacTavish - says Dennis is getting things wrong and muddled. I didn't say it was suspicious."

But Dolly was still thinking of the previous remark. She said, "Besides, you didn't like Dennis either, Roger, didn't like him yourself; that night after...."

"Which night?"

"That night you came home from evening class late. The night I was worried to death what had happened to you. You know, the night you said you'd gone to the Griffin with him."

"Oh, that was when we went to the Turk's Head..."

"Well, I could have sworn it was the Griffin. Anyway, you came home and said you agreed with me there was something about him you didn't like. Got bad vibes from him, you said. I remember because I had a call that day from old Mrs Hepplethwaite, and she'd said much the same thing."

Such was the distance in time since the crime that soon Roger and his wife were distracted from further consideration of matters relating to the crime by such mundane events as a salesman at the door, and even the television.

Back at the allotment, poor Alistair had had a frustrating time. On saying goodbye to Roger he had hoped to have a meeting with Charles, the allotment holder in charge, but had found him in his shed too busy to speak to him. However, as amicably as possible, he had managed to get this rather loud and irascible officer in charge to agree to meet up on some future occasion.

He would have liked also to have kept the momentum of his inquiries with the allotment holders going by having a word with Sid, the allotment holder on the other side of Helen's patch. However, he had

181

been advised by Roger that unless he was lucky enough to track him down by chance, he would most likely only be able to get contact details from Charles. So here too he was frustrated in making the further progress that he would have wished.

Anyway, at least I've made my acquaintance with Roger, he thought as he set off back home, feeling somewhat frustrated.

It was as he was thus weighing the good points and the bad points of his day's work that his mobile had rung with the call from Roger about the local newspaper article.

Having stopped at a nearby bench to take Roger's disjointed call, he now strolled on, immersed in thought.

The more he thought about it, the more intriguing Roger's information concerning this local newspaper's story seemed. He needed to read it as soon as possible, and laughed to himself to think that having enjoyed the change of visiting an allotment holder, he would now experience an even bigger switch of scene to a newspaper office to check out this latest development. He looked forward to the prospect with relish, but he knew that the newspaper might prove somewhat proprietorial about their scoop, and that he would most likely have to call Dennis in aid to get admitted to the stately portals of the *Cookington and Renshaw Weekly Times.*

Alistair had succeeded in avoiding troubling Dennis up till now, but having read the article, felt justified that evening in telephoning him to suggest that he pave the way for a visit to the editor by assuring him of his approval of himself as a quasi-investigator.

As he knew he would, Dennis readily agreed.

"Sounds like you're on to something," he said cheerily.

"More like the newspaper is," replied Alistair modestly.

"Anyway, how are you getting on, old boy?" asked Dennis.

"Well, I won't say anything just yet. I'll give you a progress report in a couple of weeks or so. Isn't that more or less what we agreed, Dennis? However, this could be an interesting one if you can get the editor to agree to meet me."

Later that evening, Dennis rang Alistair back. The editor was happy to hold an interview as early as tomorrow morning, but on condition that total confidentiality was agreed.

"Seems to think he's got something pretty significant," added Dennis with some enthusiasm, before continuing, "like all newspaper editors, wanted to keep the possible scoop to himself, but he owed me a few from last year's goings-on with the press, and anyway because of that I've managed to get him to agree to see you. If possible, we're going to try and get this chappie they're on to, who I think is called Gary, to be there with you. Fingers crossed on that. Apparently, he's a bit of a simple guy, and his mum's a bit protective and kept stuff back at the time."

"Cheers, Dennis. Sorry, that doesn't sound right. I know how deep the hurt is, and I want to achieve closure for you so much by getting the truth all parcelled up. Believe me, Dennis, for you I'm trying my damnedest."

"I know, Alistair. I knew you would; that's why I asked you to take it on. There's nobody else I'd ask, apart from an official and professional firm of private detectives."

Alistair slept fitfully that night, with a strong feeling of much unfinished business ahead.

CHAPTER 14

(An interesting morning in the local newspaper office)

The next morning dawned fair and saw Alistair arriving promptly at the offices of the local newspaper, confident of a welcome in the light of Dennis's preparation.

The editor, a robust-looking man with the traditional braces and eyeshade, had welcomed him civilly enough and with a certain amount of joie de vivre. He now leant back in his editor's chair behind his desk, stretching his legs in a relaxed manner and said, "It's a funny old life. We had got word that you were about and doing this private investigation, and we were just about to track you down and do a story on you, when Dennis rang last night and pleaded with us to hold on that. He'd done us so many favours over all this that I agreed to hold our horses. Anyway, he was mighty keen that you should see us as regards this latest development in our current edition." His voice rose excitedly. "Well, we got it from this simple guy, who goes by the name of Gary, and the facts are all as published in this week's edition … and it's quite a turn-up, eh?"

Alistair pulled out his notebook and retrieved his pen from the depths of his inside pocket.

"The more we think about it, it's remarkable that the cache of old bits of clay pipes is all wrapped up in an edition of our paper dated at the time of the crime," said the editor importantly, looking Alistair straight in the eye as if to say, 'How do you explain that one?'

"They were found near the break in the fence," he added, as if that was final proof of the importance of his newspaper.

"Yes, it's quite a development in a way, isn't it?" agreed Alistair. "I'm looking forward to meeting this Gary character. What's he like?"

"Well, you're about to find out, because Dennis arranged it all last night and we've got him all ready here waiting to meet you. To be honest," continued the editor, a little embarrassed by his own lack of political correctness, "I reckon he's as simple as they come."

"Still, could be very useful, I'm sure," replied Alistair eagerly.

"Well, you're telling me. But oh boy! He's not the sharpest knife in the box. I hate to say it, but in the old days we used to say mentally retarded. Anyway, wait till you hear what he has to say. Don't think he would be capable of making it all up – that's the point - and it's quite a little story he has to tell. Look, take a seat alongside my desk here, and I'll get the chappie called in. See what you make of it all. I think it sounds mighty interesting."

Alistair sunk into the comfortable chair. I've tasted better tea, he thought.

The editor returned, and turning like a showman to the door behind him, announced, "Here he comes - here he is – here's our friend."

Gary entered the room showing signs of excruciating nervousness, not least by twisting his hands in a way that was almost painful to watch and stopping after every forward pace.

Alistair immediately tried to put the young man at his ease by jumping up with outstretched hand and a friendly pat on the back.

"Hallo, and congratulations and well done, Gary. Take a seat and make yourself comfortable. I'm a kind of private detective, who has been officially asked by the widower of the victim to try and help with the investigation, as the police have got a bit stuck, shall we say."

Gary seemed to warm to his new acquaintance, with his demeanour changing surprisingly quickly from one of fear to one of ease.

"I've been terribly worried and nervous about all this," he commented, still twisting his hands to some extent.

"Who can blame you, Gary? Don't worry about anything. Just feel free to tell me anything you'd like to get off your chest," replied Alistair, trying to sound as friendly as possible.

"First I was worried I'd get into trouble if I did, and then I thought I'd get into trouble if I didn't. You don't look like the sort of person who would want me hanged, so I'll tell you anything you ask me as honestly as I can."

"Well, there are lots of things I'd like to ask you about, Gary, like where you were and the timing of your sighting and all that sort of thing, which may be possibly very significant. But to start with, I'm interested that you decided not to tell the police. Can I ask you first about that?"

"To be honest with yer, I didn't tell the fuzz, sorry, I mean the police, because you see I thought I might get well in trouble for trespassing, and I thought they might think I was nicking vegetables and fruit and that, like. I thought they wouldn't understand why anyone should want to collect bits of old broken clay pipes on them allotments. Then I was going to tell them, but I had this nightmare that they came round and arrested me and I got hung for a crime I didn't commit. I woke up bloody screaming, I did, so I decided never to speak a word about it; but the other night I had another dream that they came and arrested me, because I hadn't reported what I'd seen, and a guy in a wig said it was treason

186

and I got hung. So when I got up I went to this newspaper and told them everything."

"What did this newspaper say about it?"

"They said I could make a lot of money out of this."

"Sorry," interrupted the editor, "we newspaper people are quite as bad as everyone thinks – probably worse."

"Anyway, I bet that pleased you, Gary," said Alistair, trying to get back to the momentum.

"I said I don't want no money; I just don't want to get hung."

"OK, well, I've got that straight about you being reluctant to speak to the police, but now tell me what you saw – what you, Gary, actually saw. Now take your time – tell it to me in your own way, and take as long as you like, Gary."

"What I saw?" repeated Garry.

"Yes, please tell me as simply as you can in the way you would tell your best friend or your mum."

"I did tell my mum at the time, and she said, 'Don't go telling the police nothing, because I don't want you in no trouble and you could get into terrible trouble.' Anyway, I saw these two people on the allotments. They was talking a lot. I thought I'll wait where I was and when they've moved on, I'll go and search for my bits of pipe; but they bloody stayed talking for hours. In the end I left rather hurriedly as they seemed to be coming towards me, and I couldn't even get the little pile of broken stems of clay pipes, which I collect and which I'd left by the apple tree. I just scarpered."

Alistair had determined not to speak himself and to allow Gary to wax forth, but he soon realised that his tendency to suddenly stop speaking necessitated a bit of prompting all the way along.

"Tell me how they appeared to you."

"What's that mean?"

He sure is simple, thought Alistair, but aware of the importance of what he might report, he was only too happy to prompt him further.

"I mean, really, tell me what you saw and what you thought they were up to or doing."

Gary still looked blank, so Alistair tried yet again.

"What they looked like and who you thought they were – that sort of thing."

"Well, they stopped a lot as if they were in rather deep and earnest conversation. I obviously couldn't hear what they were saying but I heard voices. So distant, but if I had to guess I'd say they were both ladies … but the funny thing was they didn't look very ladylike, if you know what I mean."

"I suppose women working on an allotment don't put on their most ladylike clothes, do they?" suggested Alistair, still trying to put Gary at his ease.

Gary remained silent and gave Alistair one of his usual confused looks, which Alistair had already learnt meant "I don't quite follow you", so he continued in his efforts to try and help Gary describe his recollection.

"How did they walk?"

"That's the funny thing. I remember it as if it was yesterday. One of them walked like this."

Gary got up and demonstrated a rather slow, limping walk.

"And the other one?"

"Only thing I remember about her was she crossed herself like she was in church."

Alistair gulped. He was aware of his heartbeat quickening. He tried not to show his excitement. He also tried to ignore the rather crass gesture of the editor, who gave him a schoolboyish thumbs up.

"And do you know what time of day this was, roughly? Morning, afternoon or evening perhaps?" he asked as calmly as he could.

"Oh yes, I know that OK. I heard the church bell chime six o'clock."

"One of our reporters has ascertained that St Peter's always rings the Angelus at six o'clock in the evening – bit unusual for an Anglican church, in my day at any rate," put in the editor with a smile, "but I gather they go in for that sort of thing at St Peter's."

"Just a couple more things, Gary, before you go. How do you know it was the date of the crime?" Alistair asked.

Gary fidgeted uneasily.

"Like I say, my mum," he began, "she said to me the next day after what the police say happened there yesterday, 'You'll be in dead trouble if you open your mouth. You shouldn't have been in them allotments last night. They'll think you was stealing food.' She said a lady in one of them houses along there had reported people stealing vegetables. I says to mum, 'But I never stole no vegetable in my life. Only bits of old clay pipes, which nobody want anyway.' But that's what she said to me, and she made me promise not to open my mouth. She said, 'You don't want to spend the rest of your days in prison, do you?'"

"She kept saying, 'Don't get involved with it,' but I didn't know what that meant. I didn't know what getting involved meant. She said it means just keep yer big mouth shut. So I did."

A relatively lengthy pause followed, then Alistair sighed. "Well, the last thing for the moment is, Gary, how did you get into the allotment? I mean they're locked to keep the public out, aren't they?"

After more fidgeting, Gary embarked on an even longer speech, possibly the longest he had ever been known to utter. "See, there's this place, where the fence between the allotments and the little river is broken a bit. Yer still have to do a bit of a jump to get over it, but it's possible. One time there was a man there saw me do it. He said to me, 'I wish I could jump like that.' I said, 'Why would you want to get in here?' He said, 'Because I like to collect old bits of clay pipes, and I've heard there's a lot in there.' I said, 'You're same as me, then.' He says, 'Can you make this fence a bit easier for me to get in, then?' I said, 'Blimey, governor, I thought I'd seen you looking after the church and mowing the grass there,' and he says to me, 'That don't mean I don't collect bits of old pipes.' Anyway, I couldn't believe it, 'cause he says, 'Here, can you break down this bit of fence, 'cause it's pretty well broken down already.' So I did, and in he comes looking for the bits of pipe, same as me."

Gary seemed to suddenly realise that he had been talking unusually lengthily and proceeded to stop abruptly and finally.

"Well, you're being very helpful and useful, and I shall ensure you're properly rewarded in time. For the moment that's enough. This must be a difficult business for you. Thank you very much," said Alistair in conclusion, trying not to sound too condescending.

After the editor had ushered Gary out of the room, and indeed the office, he returned to Alistair, and closing the door securely behind him, walked back to his chair.

"Well," he said with a beam bordering on pride, "quite interesting, eh?"

Alistair was writing hurriedly in his notebook.

He looked up and said, "It was really helpful and useful. This is the kind of thing that could well lead to a breakthrough – but please be patient, I beg you. I'm going to have to do a lot of thinking and investigating."

He looked up again and added in a sincere tone, "If it comes to something, I promise you that you will have the scoop."

"Well, well, well," said the editor, very slowly and deliberately, "I've always regretted not working for a big national newspaper, but this would certainly make up for it. In the normal way I'd put every reporter I had back on to this story, but we've been inundated by our readers telling us to ease off it."

He tossed a letter which had been lying on his desk over to Alistair, who could read clearly the large handwriting entreating the editor to "stop going on about the bloody allotment murder mystery". Well, bloody it was, thought Alistair, and I must help my friend Dennis get some closure.

The editor's voice roused him from his thoughts. "And Dennis was quite adamant that it would be better for you to take over, as it were, and to hold my reporters back."

"Let me work on this a little while first, at any rate, please," responded Alistair, still seemingly deep in thought.

Soon they were shaking hands and assuring each other of keeping in touch.

"It's interesting new material, isn't it?" beamed the editor.

"As I say, give me a little time to think it all through," reiterated Alistair.

Alistair returned to the hotel and remained deep in thought. Not entirely to his surprise, Dennis rang later that evening.

"How did it go, old chap?"

"I think it's the sort of thing that may well prove significant, Dennis, but let's keep to our agreement of not giving you a running commentary. I promise to report if and when I reach a stage of any significant breakthrough. It's early days, and my job is to try and keep positive and optimistic at the moment. I've certainly got a lot to think through."

"I'm with you," mumbled Dennis in a less sprightly tone.

Alistair sat in his room that evening with his head in his hands and a big piece of paper in front of him on his little table. His pen lay ready, but at the moment it was his brain only that was at work.

CHAPTER 15

(An interview with the head of the allotments)

It proved very difficult to arrange a meeting with Charles Burton, the unofficial officer in charge, as it were, of the St Peter's Allotments.

"We've been through all this a hundred times; what the hell's the point of you suddenly getting involved?" came the gruff voice over the phone.

However, Alistair could be very persuasive when he wanted to be, and eventually it was agreed that he could turn up at Charles's shed on the morrow at eleven a.m.

Charles was a large man with a loud voice and one of those countenances that makes it clear beyond doubt that he is one of the world's boozers.

"So you're in charge of this whole batch of allotments are you?" asked Alistair, imitating Charles's confident style on arrival as that ruffian's smart shed door swung open and he popped out, as much like a cuckoo in a cuckoo clock as anything else.

"That's my role in life," confirmed Charles, with much coughing and spluttering.

He was interrupted by Alistair continuing, "I imagine there's quite a little bit of admin to do, what with there being quite a few allotment holders."

"Yeah, there is a bit; but, you know, main thing I have to do is keep an eye on things, patrol around a bit. I'm strict about enforcing the rules regarding keys and locking the gate on arrival and departure – main thing is to keep people out. Don't want 'em nicking all our hard won produce when we've done all the work, eh? Oh yes, I keep an eye on things alright; people may not realise just how much I do in that way – I mean I don't like doing it when people are there, but oh yes I keep an eye on things alright. Don't mind admitting it, I come along here sometimes when it's quite late and see what they've all been up to. Some of 'em wouldn't like to know that, but someone's got to check the rules aren't being broken. Found someone lighting a bonfire in the morning the other day; had to tell them it's not allowed till an hour before sunset. Claimed they never knew it, but I'd told them myself before, *and* put a notice up about it in our little noticeboard. Anything the council send to me like that, I just bang it up on the noticeboard, and it's up to people to stop and take note. People think I'm nosey, but the way I see it, it's part of my job, and you see we have such long waiting lists. People wait years for allotments. They're ever so popular these days. I reckon people think they'll beat the credit crunch, and all the prices going up, by growing their own. Actually, there's a rumour that the council are going to put the rent up and force people to take half an allotment rather than a whole one. Only heard about it the other day. My God, I'd fight that one! Thought I might call a meeting about it and stir it up a bit – they're a timid lot, these people – thought I might goad them into action a bit. They need shaking up a bit, some of them."

Normally happy to let people ramble on in the hope of picking up snippets of information, this morning Alistair was determined to get down to business.

"Have you ever seen anything suspicious going on here on your walkabouts or patrols, as you call them?" he cut in.

Charles looked somewhat taken aback by this sudden change of gear and remained silent.

"Anything that you ever thought could just possibly tie up with the crime?" persisted Alistair.

"Well as I told the fuzz, I wracked my brains to try and recall anything odd back last year when it happened. I honestly couldn't say I ever did, you know. I wanted so much to help them. You know, the way I see it is, I'm the guy in charge of the bloody murder scene. Wanted to really be the hero of solving the mystery, but no, I just couldn't think of anything helpful or useful to say to them – just couldn't. Wife kept saying you must have seen some suspicious things over the years; but I mean, you know there's suspicious things and there's murder – not quite the same, I told her. Often felt like making things up to earn a bob or two from the papers, but you know you can't do that – not when a woman's life has been taken."

"You're not a church person, are you?"

"Me? Fuck no!"

"No," confirmed Alistair with a smile.

In his experience, such plain-speaking people were often more honest and straightforward than they were given credit for.

"I mean," said Alistair, changing tack, "I'm obviously spending an awful lot of time on questions in the parish and indeed further afield, but this is the crime scene here at St Peter's Allotments, and you're in charge of it …"

"Well, I know," cut in Charles with some irritation, adding, "that's why I say I feel I ought to be able to help. But you can't make things up, can you?"

"Absolutely not, but anyone can be helped to remember things. Have their memory jogged; that sort of thing."

"Look, mate," said Charles in almost a threatening sort of way, "you don't think the police didn't pursue that line with me more times than you've had hot dinners! I tell you I wanted to help. Wanted to earn a bob or two from those ruddy reporters down here, but you can't make things up – not when there's a human being found lying over there in that shed across the path. I may be a rogue, but I'm not so bad to go trying to make money out of telling fairy stories about something like that, am I?"

"There's been a possible new lead, Charles, and I wanted to ask you if you ever saw a young man – a rather simple guy – a chap who collects bits of clay pipes. Did you ever find him on the allotments."

"Clay pipes, now let me see, there are quite a few of those old bits in the earth round here. People find them all the time and usually just chuck them to one side, but I know some people collect them. Helen's husband, Edwin – he puts 'em in his pocket when he sees 'em, I know that. Saw him nick one from my flower bed once, but let it go. He was lucky, I was in a good mood that morning. Also, there's an old geezer from the church, Fred I believe he was called, or something like that; caught him at it once, and he doesn't even have an allotment here. We had one hell of an argument, because I asked him how he got in, and he wouldn't tell me. Anyway, I frogmarched him out. Bloody cheek of it, while I was escorting him off the premises, he had the audacity to tell me I ought to go to church!"

Charles, having just missed Alistair's smile, paused and beamed. "Funny how time heals; don't feel so cross about it now. I never connected it with this crime – slightly different league, isn't it?"

"This was some time after the crime, then, was it?" Asked Alistair with interest.

"Oh yes, I would say so."

"You never saw a younger guy up to the same sort of thing, did you?"

Charles stood leaning on a rake, with his great beard rubbing the top of its handle, and thought long and hard.

"Do you know, I bloody did, now you come to mention it! I haven't thought about it for years, but yeah, I do remember, because that was the day I found two people walking down the central path here. I said, 'Where the hell do you think you're going?' And one of these ladies said, 'We're just going for a walk.' I said, 'Going for a walk? I'll say you're going for a walk,' and I frogmarched them both up to the gate and put them out. One was a right tomboy and put up a bit of resistance, but I got 'em out. Told 'em it's either me or the police helping you out – that did it. They scampered away like mice."

"When was that?"

"I can answer that, because it was just towards the end of everything being peaceful and quiet here. Yeah, must have been a few weeks after that, there was the crime – yeah, not long after that we had all the bloody media frenzy all over the place. I suppose that's why I've forgotten all about it. Funny that, you mentioning about the clay pipes – it brought it back. Funny thing, memory, isn't it?"

CHAPTER 16

(An interview with another allotment holder)

At breakfast the next morning, Alistair flicked through his notebook.

"You keep me so much in the dark about what you're doing here," Cissie rebuked him.

"I've promised you and Donna a meal out explaining it all, when it's all over," replied Alistair with a teasing grin. He liked Cissie, not least because on the whole she was very discreet and left him to get on with things in peace.

He turned back to the notebook. That was two of the three allotment holders ticked off his interview list. All three had been there when Helen had found poor Henrietta murdered.

Roger, who had this added intriguing connection through attending the same evening class as her husband Dennis, had the allotment on the near or road side of Helen's; and Charles, although having an allotment some distance from where Helen made the discovery, had nonetheless been present, and most importantly was in charge.

There remained only Sidney Walsh MBE, who had the allotment alongside Helen's, but on the farther side. This was easily arranged, as Charles had told him that you could more or less bank on Sid being there on a Saturday morning, and had also offered to let the said Sidney Walsh MBE know that Alistair would be calling.

So Saturday morning it was. He found Sid, as arranged, sitting in his little shed reading the morning newspaper.

The shed was a complete contrast to Helen's

dilapidated old shack that poor Henrietta's corpse had been found in. It looked new and clean; inside everything was orderly and there was room for the rather comfortable-looking chair in which Alistair found the expectant Sid sitting.

He liked Sid from the word go. He was courteous, pleasant and welcoming, and also seemed the kind of chap who couldn't tell a lie if he tried.

"This blinking crossword gets harder and harder every week," announced Sid with a wry smile, as Alistair lowered his head and peered in.

"Hallo Sid, nice of you to agree to see me. I gather Charles explained why I'm here. Well, I'm trying to solve a bit of a puzzle too – different sort of clues to what you're struggling with!"

Sid laughed out loud, came out of the hut and said, "There's not room for two people in there, I'm afraid."

After a little general conversation relating to the case, Alistair adopted his technique of asking rather suddenly and directly whether there was anything that he could think of that was worth commenting on.

"Yes, it was about that time of the tragedy, a week or so before it. I complained to Charles that my little ladder had been moved. Of course I presumed someone had borrowed it, and I just wish they'd put it back where they found it. Same with the hose; I mean you don't mind people borrowing things, but surely to goodness they can put it back where they got it from! There's a lot of new people with no sense of allotment etiquette. I reported it to Charles."

"What did Charles do about it? What was his reaction?" beamed Alistair.

Sid began to launch into a fairly prolonged criticism of Charles, the main thrust of which appeared to be that he never did much about anything, but was quite nosey.

Alistair was happy to let him go on for a bit. In one

way he felt these were just absurd ramblings - sweet nothings - yet, he kept reminding himself, Roger, Charles and Sid were all people who knew the murder scene well, quite apart from being present when the victim was found. He needed to keep his antennae sharp.

They left the environs of the neat, homely little hut and strolled around as Sid's words flowed.

"Sorry, Sid, I was miles away. What did you say was Charles's reaction?"

"Well, as I was saying, that's the annoying thing about Charles – he didn't seem to react very much - not very much at all. Says he's in charge, but doesn't really help in a situation like that. Just seems to like going around poking his nose into our allotments. Oh yes, I've caught him doing that. The trouble is," Sid paused to struggle with his conscience before launching further into criticism, "I don't like having a go at him, but the thing about Charles is, he loves his vino. Used to get a bit tight of a summer evening when he's working down here. I suppose it was really funny; once after the AGM he got well whistled and a little too flirtatious with one of our younger allotment holders – a lady I called Miss Portugal, only because she went there for a holiday one year. She complained to me about it."

"Bit high on the booze was he? Well, that I can imagine," put in Alistair.

"We have our little AGM in the Rusty Nail pub over there." Sid nodded in the direction of a distant edifice with a flag of St George fluttering grandly against the blue sky in the breeze. "But the proprietor has told me that after last year's little performance by Charles, we've got to have it in a marquee in their garden. Charles doesn't seem to have clicked that it's due to his behaviour. I didn't dare explain it to him when he actually said to me that as long as it was close enough to the bar to order some liquid refreshment, he didn't mind!"

"Liquid refreshment! Quite a character, isn't he? Where did he get that phrase from?" wondered Alistair to jolly the conversation along.

"There used to be an Australian guy in there, who used to say, 'pass the liquid' - just for fun, I think. I personally count Australian wines as amongst my favourites. But to get back to Charles. To be honest I have in my time found Charles almost incapacitated. One day ... no, I won't start," continued Sid, "I guess he must be sad or unhappy about something. Anyway, I remember one day I found him flat out, just over there on that patch. I got him up on his feet and generally sobered him up a bit. Strange, his main concern seemed to be that I didn't tell a soul about how I found him. I reckon he's got a supply of the good stuff in his shed. To be honest, just once I thought I'd break my rule, and I went to have a dekko. There was a curtain, would you believe, across the window. Not even I have that! Anyway, it was well locked. Looked like Fort Knox. I'm digressing – sorry. It wouldn't be so bad if he was more likable, but he's pretty gruff, to be honest. You know, if he was the sort of bloke who invited you in for a wee snifter – well, that would be OK. But he just swigs the stuff himself without much grace, if you know what I mean. I've heard he's quite sociable in the pub, but here on the allotment when he pulls the cork of a summer evening, you won't get a tipple from him. Funny, that, isn't it?

"Anyway, someone has to be kind of OC St Peter's Allotments, which is our official title for this little patch of land, although we've got no connection with the church. Seems like in the old days they just acquired the name on account of being so close. Anyway, to get back to Charles, he's kind of assumed the role on account of his long time here. Someone has to receive all the bumph from the council – you know, he's the one the council send notices to and kind of liaise with about anything to do with their blessed regulations and all that."

Alistair decided to fire another of his sudden surprise questions again. "When you heard about the tragedy, you never in your mind, even in your wildest thoughts, thought that it could be Charles who was responsible, did you?

Sidney seemed less taken aback than Alistair had expected.

"Do you know, my wife and I, we sat up all night. We couldn't think of anyone we knew who could commit such a crime, but funnily enough we did keep saying, 'It couldn't be Charles.' I remember, as if it was yesterday, my wife laying the spoon down in the kitchen and saying, 'No, he couldn't have done it.' She must have been thinking deeply about the crime and wondering about Charles. I agreed. I said Charles may be a gruff old bastard with one hell of a temper if anybody crossed his path, but no I had to agree it just couldn't be him. He seems to have a certain basic human decency way down in him somewhere."

"He didn't really know Henrietta, did he? Knew *of* her, but that's different," put in Alistair.

"Oh, he knew of her alright; heard him give her a compliment once when there was some row going on here between one of the allotment holders and one of the residents in that road that runs alongside, Lime Grove. Somehow the church was involved in it somewhere."

"A compliment! What, you mean he fancied her?" Alistair bit his tongue, wishing he hadn't gone so far.

Sid did not bat an eyelid. "He fancies anyone in a skirt … Sorry, I wouldn't put it past him to have tried it

202

on with that poor vicar; but no, he might swig her glass of plonk when she wasn't looking, but he'd never murder her – never."

"No, I'm sure you're right," said Alistair, thinking his words must sound somewhat inane.

"I mean, I know he was a bit of a Hitler here on the allotments," continued Sidney, "but, as I say, away from here he was nicer – more generous; to be fair, a lot of people have said that, and apparently he's been known to go up to perfect strangers in the pub, pat them on the back and even buy them a drink occasionally. I think he feels when he's on the allotments he has to be like a sergeant major in charge, and he kind of changes his personality a bit and becomes all possessive and full of being in charge. Don't they say that? Give a fellow a bit of authority and it can go to their head – used to know a parking attendant like that. Charming fellow, till someone tried parking where they shouldn't ought to have! But no, I'll never be persuaded he could do a crime like that. Charles a murderer? Not in a million years."

"A million years? Well, that is rather a long time," joked Alistair. "Thanks Sid, it all helps to get the picture and to learn how others see people. I tell you something, I think I'd trust your judgement about people a lot."

"Well, thank you, that's a compliment," Sid replied shyly.

"Well thanks again, I'm glad to have had this little chat with you. Every detail helps. I'm glad I've now met all three of you allotment holders who were present on that unforgettable morning. You were all here when Helen Archer found the victim, eh?"

"I'll never forget that scream as long as I live. It was really ghastly. I thought Helen was being attacked. I was paralysed for a moment while she was sprinting down there, down the side of her allotment towards the central path. I didn't think I was a brave person, but I found myself going over towards her shed half expecting to meet a dragon."

"But you didn't look inside, did you?"

"No, I was expecting some kind of animal or snake or large insect, or something that had given her a fright. Never entered my head it was something actually *in* the shed. I couldn't find anything, of course, and when I looked round she was gone and down the road. Of course, I met up with Roger and of course Charles came over to find out what was going on, and we started chatting. Next thing we knew the police were here. Tapes going up everywhere, and we were asked to leave the allotments. That put Charles's back up, I'll tell you, but I guess the police have dealt with more difficult characters than Charles, and they kind of escorted him off the premises. He was effing and blinding; it would have been really quite funny, if it wasn't such a tragedy. Only thing I heard Charles saying to the police was, 'I'm effing in charge!' Anyway, the police said, "No you're not, mate; *we're* in charge.'"

CHAPTER 17

(An interview with the other churchwarden)

Interesting and entertaining though it had been to give himself the refreshing diversion of meeting and talking to the allotment holders, nonetheless Alistair felt that duty required a return to the parishioners, and a chat with the other churchwarden, Edwin Archer, was somewhat overdue. He hoped that the slight delay in contacting him would not be thought rude.

However, arranging an interview with Edwin had proved no more easy than it had with Charles. Time seemed precious to Edwin. Fair enough thought Alistair, he is in full-time employment and has a family all living at home with him. Eventually it was established that Monday evening seemed most convenient and so found Alistair knocking on the front door, as requested by the notice stuck with Sellotape to the outer glass porch door.

The door was opened by Helen. Alistair took off his hat and beamed in at a very domestic scene as the black cat shot upstairs.

Over Helen's shoulder appeared Edwin, tea towel draped over his shoulder and wearing a genial smile. A warm introductory conversation took place in the hall, during which Alistair admired the photographs in the hall of their two children on graduation day. This seems a happy family, he thought, as he was ushered into the front living room, which he noticed they referred to as the drawing room.

"Goodness, what a lot of history books," he commented as he entered, "you've got almost as many as me!"

Further introductory conversation took place, mostly

referring to the pictures of Scottish mountains, Edinburgh and London that adorned the walls. By what seemed like a near miraculous sleight of hand to both Alistair and Edwin, Helen, who had actually been working hard in the kitchen preparing refreshments, appeared with a tray offering, amongst other things, his favourite coffee.

Skilfully, Alistair steered the conversation round to the case and to Edwin's role in the parish. At length he determined to stop talking and give Edwin free rein.

"I feel a bit guilty sometimes because Florence does all the work," Edwin began modestly. "Of course," he continued, "she is actually what they call the star warden, which means that all the bumph emanating from Church HQ comes to her rather than me. When Maurice, the previous vicar, asked me to take it on, he said he admitted there wasn't exactly a long queue, but it seemed an honour, and I'm very fond of the building, which I stupidly let slip to him; and so that was me on the Finance and Fabric Team too."

Alistair maintained his deliberate silence, as this sort of insight into the set-up was exactly what he wanted. Edwin was indeed painting a vivid picture of life at St Peter's and Alistair was registering every nuance.

"Oh it's not so bad," Edwin went on. "Anyway, I'm doing it. The Bishop of London asked me after the induction service, which all churchwardens were invited to, at St Paul's Cathedral, if it was my first time. I nearly said, 'Blimey, I didn't know people did it twice!'"

"I think perhaps he meant were you just starting. Was it your first year?" put in Helen helpfully.

"I think you're right, because when I said yes, he said 'See if you can do it for three years.' I rather liked that, coming from the Bishop of London, no less; so that's the challenge I've accepted."

"It takes up quite a bit of his time," offered Helen, "but it keeps him out of trouble. It's about four meetings a month I'd say, darling, what with your pastoral care meetings thrown in too."

"That's right: PCC, Ministry Leadership Team - we call that 'MLT' - and then there's the Finance and Fabric Team, which we just call 'F and F', and lastly there's the Pastoral Care Team, which I don't think has any initials for short. I'd say on average I go to about four meetings a month. It's manageable," concluded Edwin, with a look to the corner of the ceiling as if trying to convince himself.

Edwin seemed to dry up rather suddenly so Alistair prompted him. "Where do these meetings take place?"

"We have the PCC meetings in the hall," replied Edwin, "but the others are in each other's houses mostly, round and about."

"You've had them here, then?"

"Many a time and oft," replied Edwin.

"Well, I'd say you sound like a committed Christian Edwin. What brought you to St Peter's?"

"Maurice, the former vicar here, impressed me. He apologised for all the trouble the Church had caused me with what he called my frustrated vocation – we won't go into that; but no, him apologising … that impressed me. Also, I think, it was the church on my local patch, if you know what I mean. After so many years of going to churches involving journeys, it was nice to be able to just stroll round – you know, go to one's local patch. I felt the need to go to church. I don't know why, quite; I suppose it's kind of making a public statement, isn't it? Nailing one's colours to the mast and all that. My wife, Helen, she doesn't feel the need to go. Takes that old chestnut line that you don't have to go to church to be a christian, and in many ways I agree with her. Of course, I keep coming back to Our Lord saying, 'Do this in remembrance of me.' Helen always says, 'But He didn't add "in a church building"'. I've got to admit that when I'm in church of a Sunday, irritated by some member of the congregation or something, I often think of Helen on her allotment, and I'm sure she's a million times more attuned spiritually than me."

He took off his spectacles and looked through them at arm's length as if there was some speck to be removed, before continuing. "I remember asking my dad once when I was a lad whether it was OK to go and watch a football match on Good Friday, and I remember he took absolutely ages before answering as if he was really thinking about it deeply, which rather impressed me; then he said, 'Yes I think it is OK, because the important thing is to be good.' I often recall that, and think he was right too – you know the line, 'Whatsoever things are of good report, cleave unto them.'"

Alistair sat there in a bit of a daze. He had been thinking about such questions a lot himself lately, but was here strictly on business relating to his assignment. There was a lot to assimilate, relating both to his investigation and also to his own life's pilgrimage and search after truth. One thing he felt sure of – this guy Edwin was not the murderer. You might as well suggest the Queen or the Archbishop of Canterbury.

"Nothing to do with the case, but out of sheer curiosity," asked Alistair, allowing himself to be sidetracked, "have you always been a Christian?"

"Yes – no sudden dramatic Damascene conversion – just a seed planted in childhood, I suppose, which has grown. It's stood me well with all the buffets in life. Who else should we turn to? As Saint Peter said."

"Very interesting. I'd like to talk further about all that sometime," said Alistair sincerely, "because I think I'm on a kind of journey of inquiry or discovery or something like that; but back to murder," he added with a laugh, before continuing, "It must have been quite incredible for you when Helen first rang you at your office and reported this crime. It must have seemed unreal. I mean, did you think she was making a bad joke? What was your reaction?"

"It certainly took some time before it all sank in. I remember I kept asking her to repeat herself. About the fourth time she repeated it, I realised we had a situation on our hands."

"You said we had a 'situation', did you?" asked Alistair.

"Well, yes. I mean she had asked me to come back straight away and emphasised that the scene of the crime was our shed. I remember, however bizarre it might sound, checking that she meant our allotment shed and not our garden shed back at the house here. I suppose that's because I'm so much more familiar with our garden shed, where we store all our overflow, than I was with that dilapidated old thing on the allotment." Edwin pointed in the direction of the back of the house.

"I remember her stressing repeatedly – can you believe? – it was our broken-down, half-ruined old shed. I suppose I was in shock, though oddly I remember saying things seem to happen to us, and kind of bracketing it with all sorts of ups and downs that we've had to face – us and the family – which are too numerous to mention. However, I must admit that of course this was in a class of its own, though I felt oddly detached from it, even though it took place in Helen's blinking allotment shed."

"You, of course, are quite familiar with Helen's allotment shed?" Alistair checked.

"Indeed yes, because I go with her to help occasionally – well, quite a lot actually. I join in the picking and I often do the watering. I like doing that;

it's very therapeutic, especially now that we've got such a good hose and don't have to go up and down the path filling the watering can with water from the tank. Also, in summer I like to go there and read sometimes – get away from it all – no blinking telephone. Sometimes I just like to contemplate there, though you can feel a bit guilty if people around you are working. You begin to worry that they're thinking, lazy old git, lets his wife do all the work!"

"And you like looking for your smelly old bits of clay pipes there, don't you?" commented Helen, adding with a glance at Alistair, "we have got millions of those blessed old bits, and a hell of a lot are from my allotment."

"Oh, you're another of those are you?" Alistair smiled at Edwin, before turning to Helen. Changing tack, he commented, "I notice you say 'my' allotment, not 'our'."

"That's right, it is my allotment. I do all the work; at least I didn't want other members of the family feeling that I was inveigling them into a lot of work when I took on the allotment – it was my kind of recreation."

"Is Helen always with you, Edwin, when you're there, or do you sometimes go on your own?"

"Yes, but of course, when she's away, I go on my own to do the watering - or sometimes with one of the kids, usually my daughter."

"How often is that?"

"Well, Helen goes up to Glasgow every couple of months to keep an eye on her poor mum, who is not too good, and lives all on her own up there now since her husband died. She's not quite ready for a care home. It's a bit more often now, actually; I'd say she goes every six or seven weeks."

"And you've never seen anything you felt significant to this case when you've been there on the allotment, I gather …"

"That's right."

"That's a shame – it's frustrating," said Alistair, laughing.

"Well, I'm sorry. I wish I could say I saw a guy wandering around the place with an axe dripping with blood," put in Edwin, hoping for a laugh, "but honestly I never thought of crime in relation to the allotment until this heinous incident."

"And you too of course, Helen," added Alistair, "I must have read your original statement to the police more times than I've had hot dinners."

Helen agreed that she really could not improve on the statement she had made to the police in the early days of their investigation, stressing that she really couldn't add anything new.

"You can imagine how the police asked me over and over again if I could recall anything else. I just had to keep telling them that I truly couldn't. It was all written down by me on that piece of paper they gave me that day."

Alistair could see she wanted to speak more, so he leant back and gestured with his hand for her to speak.

"It was weeks before the penny suddenly dropped that because I'd found the body people might think *I* had something to do with the crime. It didn't help – the fact that I'd more or less stopped going to the church when the new vicar arrived. It was nothing to do with her being a woman, which I gather from Edwin is what Henrietta thought and actually told people. It was that I just suddenly found my Presbyterian roots, and then kind of felt most at peace there on my allotment. I can't get back to that feeling of serenity which I had before the crime. I've just put all religious thoughts to the back of my mind and kind of get on with life, if you know what I mean. I've found it almost impossible to feel serene there now; I've tried telling myself that God made the allotments so beautifully, and man's inhumanity to man can't spoil that; a bit like the sea still looking so beautiful in the background, despite all the horrid fighting in the Lebanon. Sorry."

Helen stopped quite abruptly and, looking rather unhappy, put her hands across her mouth.

Alistair made no response to these comments, other than giving a sympathetic nod. Sensing that Helen needed time to regain her composure, he turned to her husband.

"Right. Now, Edwin, please tell me as churchwarden about any tensions in the parish."

"There just weren't and aren't any that could lead to murder – really, there just could not be any," Edwin began earnestly. "I mean they were so trivial – differences of style, taste – OK, differences of churchmanship. Not a few people raised their eyebrows when they found that Henrietta was coming from such a High – let's call a spade a spade – from an Anglo-Catholic church. I mean myself included; I'd said to everybody when her appointment was announced that whilst I welcomed her wholeheartedly, there would be disapproval from some quarters. I mean, when I looked up the church which she was coming from on the Internet, the first thing I noticed was that she was called 'Mother' and that all the services at her then church were called 'Mass' – you know, not Holy Communion. But as you know, the dear old PCC – that's the parochial church council – well, they had elected a couple of people to vet the new appointment, but they'd gone ahead and agreed to it."

"Too embarrassed to query it, I suppose, but anyway it was too much for me," intervened a now composed Helen, "too Roman Catholic. I'd found Maurice, the previous guy, a bit too High for my Presbyterian

212

origins, but this was something different. I'd hoped the new vicar would ratchet it down a bit, not up!"

Alistair nodded sympathetically and asked, "So, as you said, you stopped going more or less straightaway, did you?"

"I kept on for just a little bit, because what with Edwin being churchwarden it was all a little awkward. However, one day they had incense, and that was it – I just started going to my lovely allotment on Sunday mornings instead. Oh, the air smelt so fresh that first Sunday morning!"

"Yeah, and although it's sad for me not to have Helen sitting alongside anymore, I completely understand her attitude," continued Edwin. "When we're up in Scotland visiting Helen's mother in Glasgow, we go to a Presbyterian church there, and would you believe they pray for the preservation of our Protestant Church! We went up for Easter once, and I told the minister there that we had a 5 a.m. service on Easter day back in Cookington, and he seemed quite shocked. He replied that his was at 11 a.m.. Told his congregation the next day in his sermon that they were lucky they didn't live in Cookington, because they would have to go to church at 5 a.m.! Some of them came and asked me about it afterwards, and I had to point out to them that was only on Easter Day. Actually the minister there had quite a serious chat with me later, basically saying that they don't go in for all this re-enactment carry on, which of course Henrietta went in for big style. The minister said it was maybe something the Church of Scotland ought to think about."

Alistair laughed out loud before continuing, "I don't think 5 a.m would catch on in the New Town, where I hang out. Of course I was brought up Presbyterian as a lad, before I lapsed, and I'm thinking about it all again now at this later stage of life; but this discussion is for

213

another time. To get back to here – the parish of St Peter's, Cookington - and this ghastly murder of its vicar. Tell me more about some of these tensions here; tell me more about the criticisms you heard."

"Well … where shall I begin?" sighed Edwin, "A lot of people objected to calling her 'Mother'. 'Only got one mum,' I heard people say, and I must say I agree with them." He looked quizzically up at a corner of the ceiling, as if he was genuinely lost for choice in examples.

"Another thing that springs to mind would be, say, how at her very first service she introduced a bell. 'What's that for?' said this guy sitting next to me. I told him it was a call to order to stop people like me talking and remind us what we're about to do. Never saw the guy again. You did though, didn't you, Helen?"

"Yes, I met him downtown and he told me he had switched to St Mary's."

"You make it sound like a transfer from Arsenal to Chelsea," joked Alistair dusting his trousers down and nearly spilling his coffee.

"And what about the statue?" Helen put in with some feeling.

"Oh yeah – that caused a stir. Mark you, I must be honest, I personally don't have a problem with that. I've always believed that Saint Bernadette saw the Virgin Mary at Lourdes. To me, the story just has a ring of truth about it. I had more difficulty with Henrietta's idea of the Holy Communion service. I was always brought up to believe in the outward and visible sign of an inward and spiritual grace. To be honest I think she really believed in the Real Presence."

"You didn't like this statue, I take it, Helen?" asked Alistair, turning to her with one of his penetrating glances.

"No I didn't. I often quote the Ten Commandments

to Edwin about that. Shall I tell him or you, Edwin?" she asked, looking lovingly at her husband.

Edwin, conscious that he had been talking a lot, nodded to her.

"Right," Helen began. "Well, Henrietta got given this statue by her previous church as a leaving present. At first she had it in her study at the vicarage. I remember Edwin telling me about it, after one of his meetings. Well one day we went to church and, blow me down, she had moved it into the narthex. Even Florence was upset about it, saying her mother would have had forty fits. Anyway, next thing was she moved it into the back of the church, and I'm not joking it, started being moved surreptitiously up the side aisle."

Alistair tried to hide his smile.

Edwin took over. "And when we got back from Glasgow after Easter, we heard from Florence that all sorts of bowing and bobbing had gone on in front of it during the Easter service!"

Edwin looked very deep in thought before continuing. "Yes, she changed things a lot - changed the way we did things. No kind of gradual leadership or discussion; just wham from the word go. This is how we're going to do things from now on. Yes, it put people's backs up; I received a lot of comments from a wide range of parishioners about it. I remember wondering, 'Aren't they trained to introduce change gradually, and after discussion etc.?"

Alistair leant forward earnestly and said, "But for goodness sake, these are meant to be holy people talking about holy things."

"I quite agree, one wouldn't, *couldn't* possibly link these little comments with murder, with such a horrific murder; I mean, it's ridiculous to suggest that because someone felt strongly about this and that, they would then go out and butcher someone who disagreed with them. I mean, there wouldn't be a politician left in the country would there?" added Edwin rhetorically. He concluded by saying, "Helen and I discussed all this over and over again."

"I think it's just got to be something personal, nothing to do with church, purely personal," put in Helen. "Just how and why it came to be in my allotment shed is just a mind-bogglingly impossible question."

She looked as if she was fighting back tears. "My dear lovely shed, which I loved so much, on my lovely allotment, where I got away from all these horrid irritations … I mean it's too ironic for words. It's just so horrible!"

A tear came down her cheek, adding to her beauty, thought Alistair.

After a pause she seemed to cheer up a bit.

"I suppose it could just be that my shed was one of the obviously unlocked ones," she managed, "with the door kind of held in place leaning against the shed doorway, with a pole and a couple of pieces of old crazy paving propping it up at the bottom."

Alistair looked sagely at her and said, "I agree with you about all these differences of view as regards churchmanship being not the stuff of murder, but of course people do have incredibly strong feelings about these church matters, and we know from history they can't always see the wood for the trees. How blind our ancestors were, burning their fellow man at the stake and thinking they were doing God's will! It can't be totally ruled out as the cause of such a tragedy, because, I mean, it's not unheard of that people do flip their lid, don't they? But no, I agree with you – this is the twenty-first century – it seems absurd that such differences could lead to a grisly murder. So therefore tell me, Edwin, do you know of anything remarkable in

Henrietta's personal life? Did she ever mention anything about her personal life to you? Or did her husband, Dennis?"

Edwin seemed to think hard before replying. Alistair took advantage of his pause to press the inquiry.

"I mean, churchwardens are meant to be pretty close to vicars, aren't they? They are the ones in the know, I gather. Aren't they?"

Edwin looked as if he was about to comment but then said, "You know, our role is very much as an administrative support to the vicar, rather than a pastoral care kind of role. I don't think if she'd got personal problems or difficulties that she would have come to me about them. In fact I'm sure she wouldn't. Probably more likely to go to Florence. You know, I mean lady to lady. I think Florence did once say she was getting to know Henrietta and beginning to feel quite close. In a way that surprised me, but I realised it was probably a good thing. You're right, vicars and churchwardens should be close buddies, in my view."

"It's funny, a moment ago when I first asked you, before I stupidly interrupted your train of thought, you paused – you know, before you came out with all that - as if you were going to say something else."

Edwin laughed. "Not really, but oddly I've often felt like she was wanting to say something to me, but couldn't quite spit it out. It was like she was holding something back, but maybe not – perhaps it was all in my mind."

"Yes, you said that once or twice to me, didn't you, Edwin?" added Helen, sounding serious and nodding. For the only time that morning, she took her husband's hand and squeezed it.

Alistair was deep in thought, for he too had always felt that about his friend, Dennis. He was his oldest and most loyal friend, but always seemed to avoid totally baring his soul in the various heart-to-heart chats they'd had over the years.

There was silence for a moment, with everyone thinking. Alistair himself was musing that maybe this tied in with what Barnaby was getting permission from the bishop to divulge.

After a while, Alistair said, "Oh well, it's interesting that you should say that; even so-called close friends may sometimes keep secrets, and therefore aren't really as close as perhaps we think."

Edwin and Helen remained in silence, as if weighing his comments seriously.

"That's what's good about marriage – we don't have any secrets, do we, Helen?" beamed Edwin, breaking the silence eventually.

"I suppose we've all got a past, haven't we?" Alistair continued, not wanting to be distracted from his train of thought. He added, "I expect there were a few interesting little goings-on in hers. I mean she wasn't bad looking, was she, Edwin?"

"I suppose not," replied Edwin with a smile.

"When Edwin first met her, before I did, I asked him if she was good-looking," put in Helen rather cheekily, staring at her husband, "and he said 'half-and-half.' So I said, 'Come on, Edwin, would you kick her off the sofa?' That's a horrid phrase Edwin uses about girls on television. And you said with the silly smile, 'Well, no, I wouldn't."

"I never said that!" came Edwin's prompt and embarrassed reply.

"Yes, you did," Helen insisted.

"I honestly can't remember saying that," said Edwin untruthfully. "Anyway, if I did, I was probably joking, and anyway I don't know anything about her personal life."

There followed much discussion on a wide range of

personalities and matters appertaining to the parish life of St Peter's.

Eventually Alistair got up, admired a few ornaments on the mantelpiece, and inquired about a couple of pictures adorning the wall. Then he got his hat and took his leave.

What a nice couple, he thought as he walked back to the bus stop.

The rest of the evening was spent with Alistair trying to give his mind a break from what had now become the almost addictive mysteries of the case that he had been assigned. He reflected, I'm fed up with this case already and a fool to have got drawn into it; and yet, I'm intrigued and well, yes, fascinated by it.

"I know you've got something important on," said Donna, the receptionist of his hotel, as he wished her goodnight and went up the quaint old staircase.

As he cleaned his teeth, he found himself longing for the time when he and Zoe might have such a cosy little home as Edwin and Helen's. This led on to an almost painful feeling of missing her. He looked at his watch and calculating that it would be 5 p.m. in Chicago, rang what she had jokingly referred to as the emergency number.

There was no reply, which only exacerbated his loneliness and physical need for her company.

He was nearly asleep when she rang back, apologising for having been busy.

He explained in cryptic terms that he was having to stay in London. He referred to some business to do with his brother and felt an enormous guilt at deceiving her.

She in turn sounded apologetic, promising that her famous letter, as she called it, would be coming. Alistair, making a decision on the spur of the moment, said that she should stick to the plan of sending it to his address in Edinburgh and his spirits rose when she added, "Things are getting sorted." Somehow it sounded encouraging.

***

The next morning, even before he had finished his breakfast, Alistair was surprised to receive an early phone call from Edwin. He had something he thought he should have mentioned.

"It's easier face to face, isn't it, Edwin? I can pop round again this morning. I'll come straight after breakfast."

"Helen's away today, but that wouldn't matter. She's keen for me to have another quick word with you about something. Come on round. Sorry for the inconvenience."

Alistair soon returned to the scene of his previous evening's visit. Some houses look less cosy and homely in the morning, but Edwin and Helen's remained just as pleasant, he thought.

"It really isn't much," said a rather embarrassed-looking Edwin as he opened the front door and ushered Alistair once more into his cosy front room. "But to get straight to the point, to be honest there was just one occasion when Henrietta gave me the impression she had a past love life of some interest. It just cropped up naturally. I'd mentioned something about past girlfriends. I remember she said that people think we – meaning the clergy - never had such similar experiences to them. I remember being just a little bit taken aback when she said, 'As I say to Dennis, they'd be surprised.' It seemed a little out of character to me. Helen didn't agree with me about that at the time – said there was nothing in it."

"That was the only one time that she said anything like that, was it?" asked Alistair showing marked

220

interest and, sounding every inch like a professional detective.

"Do you know, as you're here I'll tell you. There was once when she was leading a short Bible study before our PCC meeting, and the passage which we had been studying was all about the person in scripture who asked after seven marriages whose wife would the widow be in heaven. Henrietta said, 'We're not going to meet all our exes in heaven.' That's all, but I remembered it. I wondered how the hell she knew, and realised she didn't!" he added with a laugh.

"You see," said Alistair like a tutor explaining a text, "the use of the word 'all' in that remark about not meeting all our exes in heaven suggests just possibly that there may have been a few in her life … I mean, as Helen's not here this morning I can say this, as you agreed yesterday, Henrietta was not bad looking was she, Edwin?"

"I suppose not," replied Edwin.

"Well, thanks for telling me all that, Edwin. That sort of snippet could prove very useful, you never know. I'm telling everybody that the police don't seem to have got anywhere with what you might call straightforward evidence, so my line is trying to find out people's hunches. *Intuition* perhaps is the word I'm looking for. You said your intuition told you your faith was correct – you see you can be so certain about your intuition being correct in some things…" The telephone interrupted him.

Edwin popped out into the hall to answer it, leaving the door open, and Alistair heard him saying, "Yes, I've got him with me right now. Yes, yes, yes, I haven't forgotten, I haven't got as far as that yet. I'll tell him before he goes."

"That was my wife," smiled Edwin returning to the front room. "Talking about intuition – she said

221

something made her feel you were here. How's that for intuition?"

"I couldn't help hearing you telling her that you would tell me something before I went. What was that?"

"She was reminding me to tell you about something that is probably totally irrelevant, but quite soon after Henrietta's arrival when Helen was still attending, there was a service and Henrietta was praying, doing what we call the intercessions, and she rather surprised us by saying, 'We bring before you those things known only to you that we need help with.' Then she seemed to clarify what she had just said by adding, 'The things we dare not say in public.'

"It was one of those moments we commented on as we walked home from church, but soon forgot about. I remember Helen said she thought it was rather a nice prayer, but we forgot about it. However after the crime, and after racking our brains so many times for just anything that might be in the slightest bit suspicious, or shall I say odd, or linked to such an extraordinary and horrible event … well, we did both recall her saying that. That's all. Helen was very keen that I should pass it on to you - tell you about it. She said at breakfast this morning that she guessed we would never know if Henrietta had had something specific in mind when she said that, or whether she was just making a general prayer – possibly just a theme she learnt about at theological college."

"And you were going to tell me, were you?" Alistair cocked an eyebrow.

"Yes, I must admit I had momentarily forgotten, but I think I would probably have remembered."

"Yeah, because as I say, absurd though it may sound, it's things like that, which the police never got to hear of, that may give a kind of breakthrough in

222

investigation. That was an unusual prayer, was it? I mean the previous chappie, sorry, previous vicar here, I never remember his name – Maurice, that's it - he never used that prayer, did he?"

"No. I couldn't imagine him saying something like that in a public prayer. It was a kind of Henrietta-style phraseology, if you know what I mean."

"You see, the former guy, Maurice, might not have had such an interesting private life," added Alistair with a laugh before continuing, "OK, Edwin, I'll say for absolutely the last time, please do let me know anything else like that. We're not going to get a breakthrough by just going over the same old police evidence that everybody's agreed about, like where, when and why they were at such-and-such a place and who their witnesses were etc., etc. I reckon the breakthrough may come when someone tells me something that they nearly told the police and then decided not to, probably because they thought it wasn't relevant or might be misleading or just wasn't helpful. That's what I'm going to have to try and spot and work on."

"No, I totally understand that, and quite agree," said Edwin as he helped Alistair retrieve his mackintosh from the many slung over the banister in the hall.

"I mean," said Alistair, "I respect and admire the police. I think they did a thorough job. Getting away from all this hunch business, if I do manage to make a breakthrough, it's going to be because someone tells me something or gives me something that the police never heard or saw. I'm not ever trying to be cleverer than them. I'm just after new stuff."

Like yesterday, they shook hands and bade each other farewell. Edwin, went back into his 'drawing room' and watched, amused, as Alistair struggled with the broken lock on the gate. Then he picked up the phone in the hall and phoned his wife.

"If anyone's going to get to the bottom of all this, Helen, it's going to be him," he said with some emphasis. "I told him what you said alright, and he said it was exactly the sort of nuance he was after. Anyway, where it'll all lead to is anyone's guess. Probably nowhere, but he's a wise old bird, and this famous intuition of mine is telling me that if anyone can find the solution, it's going to be him, OK. What a marvellous name, Alistair MacTavish!"

"Good, Edwin, we can't do more. Now remember our pact, we've got to look to the future and put this whole ghastly business behind us. Let's go down to the sea on Saturday."

"Looking forward to it already," he replied.

CHAPTER 18

(An interview with the owner of the house overlooking the crime scene)

I like Edwin, thought Alistair as he shaved the next morning. But, his thoughts continued as he washed his face, I'm not getting anywhere, and I must move more to the nitty-gritty of this case. It's time to meet the people whose houses overlook that allotment.'

Some time ago, in his mind Alistair had very clearly divided the people he had to concern himself with into groups. Obviously the first group was the congregation. The second were people from outside the church sphere, whom Henrietta had met during her life. This group might well include presumably some ex-boyfriends and lovers. The third, and possibly the key group, were the allotment holders; but the fourth and last and in a curious way most intriguing group were the house owners of the properties that overlooked the allotments. Something about their proximity to the crime scene made Alistair feel he would like to get his teeth into that as soon as possible.

Although the police had interviewed these good people, he had formed the impression that they were somewhat dismissive of the relevance of this group. As he finished his shave in front of the rather inadequate mirror of the hotel bedroom basin, it came into his almost mischievous mind that this therefore might be where a breakthrough lay and real progress could be made.

He decided to interview three of these people. The first would be Mrs Martin, whose house at Number 13 Lime Grove directly overlooked Helen's allotment, and who indeed had called the police on hearing Helen's scream. The second would be Philip, whose house at Number 11 overlooked Roger Brown's patch; and the third would be Aaron, whose abode beyond at Number 15 overlooked Sidney's little patch.

Yes, he confirmed in his thoughts, I'll start with the one that intrigues me the most, the house that directly overlooks Helen's allotment.

His luck was in when he telephoned Mrs Martin. "There's no time like the present," she said with gusto, and assured him that he was welcome as soon as possible that morning.

It was a fine morning as Alistair walked along the now familiar roads, and he was almost reluctant on arriving at the stately portals of Number 13 Lime Grove to have to commit himself to a morning indoors.

Mrs Martin opened the door with much enthusiasm, and courteously invited him in. The bright morning sunshine filled Mrs Martin's drawing room, and Alistair enjoyed the relaxed spaciousness of it while she bustled in the kitchen before appearing with a tray of coffee things.

She sat down opposite him and cocked her head as if she was expecting him to speak.

He broached the topic of the murder with what he feared turned out to be a rather longwinded mouthful.

"As you can imagine, I've read several times your account of the day itself. It's all very well documented, and I gather the police were particularly grateful to you for all the assistance you gave." This was a lie for he could clearly remember a rather dismissive note in the police file with the words, "Not much help" scribbled on the front against her name. "My role really, is to ask a bit of general background to what you know about life on the allotments over the years. The idea that Dennis is so keen on, and which I gather he's already contacted you about is, that you never know, it just might help throw light on various ongoing lines of inquiry both by the police and by myself, who Dennis has employed in this role of very private detective."

"Anything to help," she blurted out keenly as soon as he had finished speaking, "I'm really very keen to help if I possibly can. To be honest with you, there were times when I was a bit surprised that the police weren't more interested in what I had to say."

"Well, there you are," replied Alistair, relieved at her attitude and stretching out his arms in a friendly manner. He detected that she was a strange mixture of gentility and slight coarseness; perhaps she had had some kind of life change.

"I can assure you, I myself am very interested in anything you have to say," he continued.

She beamed at him and sat politely as if expecting him to start a cross-examination.

"Now, I thought I'd begin by asking you what's it like living next door to an area like this." He nodded towards the verdant view of the allotments from the window.

"Well, of course in one way we 'loved' the allotments. I say 'loved' because nowadays, to be honest with you, my daughter, Vanessa and I get the screaming abdabs – what's the word? - *collywobbles* every time I look over there – ever since the crime."

Alistair thought it was just possible that the police had found her overuse of the phrase "I'll be honest with you" as exasperating as he did.

"I mean, compared with a lot of what people look out onto from their windows we've got it made … lots of lovely greenery, as you can see … flowers and trees," she continued.

"It's looking beautiful today, isn't it?" interrupted Alistair, noticing a high vapour trail of an aircraft, which seemed to accentuate the blueness of the sky.

"Really lovely," he repeated.

"I personally never had any problems at all with any of the allotment holders," Mrs Martin continued. "They all seemed nice and friendly people to me. I know my neighbours had one or two altercations with them. I mean Philip, him in Number 11, on my right as you look at the allotments, he had words once. Not with Helen but with Roger, who has the allotment opposite his house."

Alistair thought he had better start as he intended to continue and remained quiet, feeling for his notebook in his inside pocket.

"It was quite a row one morning, over the back fence; went on for ages. About rats, it was."

"How bad was this argument over the rats?" asked Alistair, having retrieved the notebook and taken his first sip of coffee.

"Well, they were both blaming each other for the rat problem. Philip said it was due to all the rubbish left in the allotment by his end fence, and Roger said it wasn't and was probably due to Philip leaving food around during his summer evening parties on his own lawn. Philip said how clean he kept his house, and then Roger said they must be coming from Number 13 then. That put my back up, when I heard he had said that. Helen told me about that time that rats came in underneath her compost bin. She said compost doesn't attract rats, but in winter it's warmer in there for them and they like hiding there. Apparently rats on the allotments is an old problem, which has never really gone away."

Alistair threw one of his friendly smiles and commented, "It's funny how many little issues can arise when human beings live in close proximity, isn't it?" Then he added, "But they don't usually end in murder, do they, thank goodness!"

"One issue that very nearly did was my other

neighbour on the other side at Number 15 – dear Aaron," she said in a sarcastic tone, and continued, "He really did frighten the living daylights out of me when he had a row with the allotment holder opposite him. That guy Sidney," she said, getting up and pointing through the window at the allotment beyond Helen's, "complained to Aaron over the fence about his loud music – something I'd never dare do. I reckon the guy's a bit unbalanced. The balloon really went up. I thought Aaron was going to strangle him. The language was quite appalling."

Again Alistair acted dumb. He had learnt more about the rat saga by so doing and he would do likewise with this second situation.

"The poor chap, Sidney," she said, again pointing by now rather unnecessarily at the vacant allotment, "was whimpering, 'I only asked you to please turn it down a smidgeon,' and Aaron kept saying, 'you're only a f— allotment holder - get to hell away from my house.!" We didn't see that guy Sidney for ages after that. I don't blame him, either. He was well shaken by it."

"I'll have to look closely at that – anyone losing their temper badly in this little patch needs to be checked out in the circumstances. I mean, not to put too fine a point on it, it was one hell of a violent crime, wasn't it?"

"Good luck to you, mate," she replied theatrically and added, "but for goodness sake don't mention the church bells! It makes him go berserk – the church had to blinking compromise over how many rings they had, 'cause it woke him up when he had hangovers. Oh, he'll tell you all about it – give you an earful, he will. Please don't tell him I've said anything; I'll be honest, I'm afraid of him. I get bad vibes from him."

Alistair waited, expecting her to add her irritating

phrase "to be honest with you", but she did not.

"Ah, now that's the kind of thing I'm interested in. Vibes! You see the police have to stick to hard facts and evidence, but Dennis wants me to take this other approach and tune into hunches and vibes a bit more. I like your word 'vibes'. Do you get me?"

She nodded enthusiastically, as if pleased that it was nice to be taken seriously for a change.

Alistair stroked his chin thoughtfully before starting to speak.

"Now, that row about church bells, which you're talking about. It was actually with the vicar, was it?"

"With the vicar, and quite a few other members of the congregation."

"That sounds like quite an interesting little line of investigation for me to pursue, but you yourself never got embroiled in any such arguments?"

"To be honest with you, I'm afraid of arguments and disputes – hate them – bad for the nerves," she replied.

"Ah, I was going to ask you, how did you get on with all the allotment holders? You never had any rows yourself with them then, did you?" Alistair asked.

"Not once. Quite the contrary; Helen used to chat occasionally to me over the fence, and I remember Helen's husband, Edwin paid a compliment to my daughter, Vanessa. She was practising her flute in her bedroom upstairs one summer's day with the windows wide open, and he called out to her that he liked the music. Said it was a pleasant accompaniment to gardening, or something like that. Very kind of him, but it made her a bit self-conscious. I remember she came downstairs blushing and told me about it. I said it's nice to get compliments, but she wouldn't play it any more that day, and after that she'd always check that Edwin wasn't there before doing her practice. Anyway, no, we never had a cross word with any of the allotment holders."

Alistair stirred his coffee unnecessarily.

"OK. Is there anyone else? Any other allotment holders apart from these three near you – Roger, who is on the defensive about rats, Helen and Sidney, who doesn't like loud music almost as much as Aaron doesn't like church bells."

"Well yes, having said that, I must be honest with you there's one other guy - a guy there who walks around like he owned the place, and my word, he didn't half give me an unfriendly look one day."

These few words were sufficient to make Alistair realise immediately that she was talking about Charles.

"Do you know why he gave you an unfriendly look?" he asked.

"I can't think, though actually I reckon it must have been just because he found me looking at him, and I think he didn't want people knowing that he was nosing around. I remember thinking it was a bit odd, considering how friendly the others were. I mean, some of the others would even give me the occasional wave – even offered me beans and raspberries. Helen Archer gave me buckets of beans one year."

"Your phrase 'like he owned the place' makes me think it sounds like Charles," announced Alistair clearly. "He is actually in charge in some way. I gather he sees himself as a sort of liaison between the council and the whole allotments site. I've heard he's a bit full of himself."

"Yes, that's him. Charles. I heard someone call him Charles once," she replied speedily and continued, "well, I must admit, I had been watching him a bit, because of course I didn't know he was in charge at the time and I was just keeping an eye on him in case he was going to steal some vegetables or fruit, but he didn't."

Mrs Martin paused to take a gulp of her coffee.

"Once I realised he was a bona fide allotment holder I relaxed a bit, but I've seen him a bit over time wandering around, looking in the odd shed, through the window.

"Have you really? Now you see, that's interesting. You never saw him try a shed door?"

"Can't say I've seen him trying a door or anything like that."

"Never saw him at Helen's shed?"

"No, never saw him at that particular shed. Saw him take a good deck in Roger's shed, though, and Sid's for that matter, and even the old disused ruin of the old structure at the other end of Helen's allotment."

Alistair gave her a penetrating look. He felt a twinge of excitement, for here was a man who had been seen actually looking into other people's sheds, someone who he couldn't help feeling had a possible violent streak in him.

"You told the police all this, didn't you? And they seem to have checked him out and not got anything against him."

"I told 'em OK, but to be honest with you they didn't seem that much interested, which did rather surprise me. They never seemed to take any notes or anything."

"OK, well, tell me more about this chap Charles, who patrols around," Alistair insisted, still excited.

"What sort of things?" Mrs Martin remained uncharacteristically silent.

"Anything at all – anything you can think of?" pressed Alistair.

She continued to sit thinking for a moment in silence.

Alistair was tempted to prompt her once more. "You see, my job is to try and piece things together."

"Well, one thing I always remember," she said eventually, "I saw him helping Helen with the strimmer one day. That was the only time he seemed quite nice, and I must admit I felt sorry for him when he went and hurt himself with it. He didn't half swear, though - quite badly, let me tell you."

"Hurt himself? With a strimmer. *Ouch!* Tell me about it?" asked Alistair.

"Poor Helen, she couldn't get the thing to start. You know, it's like an outboard motor on a boat. You pull the cord, but she couldn't get the thing to start. Along comes Charles. 'Here, let me help you,' he says. Well, I shouldn't laugh, because he hurt himself well bad that day. Instead of cutting the grass, it seemed to start cutting his legs! Bled a lot. In fact so bad, I just had to call out through the bedroom window whether he needed any help. He looked like he was going to tell me to mind my own bloody business when Helen came running over to my back fence and shouted, 'Oh yes, please, he's bleeding a lot!' I come down with disinfectant, bandages, plaster - even scissors, the lot. Helen was magnificent. She bandaged him up."

"How did all this end?"

"Well, nothing much to add. Charles went off in a sulk, swearing at the strimmer. To be fair, he did say thank you to me, but rather grudgingly, I thought, and only because Helen told him to. Helen came round to my front door afterwards and returned the first aid kit. She didn't say much, but she said some of the grass was red instead of green, which made me feel a bit.....you know."

Mrs Martin held her throat and put on an ill expression before adding, "I think it was meant to be a joke."

Alistair wondered how someone so expert with such things could make such a bad mistake as to cut themselves with it. For a crazy moment the idea came to him that Charles might have been deliberately arranging an excuse for a bit of his blood being found at a future crime scene, but he dismissed it immediately.

"I suppose strimmers – well, they're tricky things, aren't they?" he said rather inanely.

"And loud – drives you mad after a bit – worse than bloody lawnmowers," Mrs Martin responded.

And so the conversation went on.

At length Alistair moved the little table away from him and stretched his legs.

"So, one way and another, you get to know what's going on a bit over there," he commented, nodding again towards the garden window.

Mrs Martin seemed strangely reflective and Alistair tried to soften his remark. "That's the impression I get; you're a kind of friendly neighbourhood policeman, sorry policewoman."

For a second Alistair was afraid he had said something wrong, as Mrs Martin seemed to continue her gaze at the horizon a little too persistently.

"I've been in a dilemma whether to tell you this or not. I did tell the police about my photos."

Alistair was only too aware that Mrs Martin had submitted some photographs to the police, who had studied them with the seriousness demanded by the tragedy, but had eventually dismissed them as not being helpful.

"Oh yes, I know about those; I've got a lot of information from Dennis and stuff the police have given him. Yes, I was going to get on to that...."

"But there's things I didn't tell them which perhaps I should have."

Alistair felt the beat of his heart quicken again. He had come to recognise this symptom of increased heartbeat as indicating possible interesting evidence coming. Yes, he seemed to have been born with an extraordinary yearning to solve mysteries.

He would try and get her to talk as much as possible and speak as little as possible. However, she remained unexpectedly and irritatingly silent.

"You tell me what you feel able to tell me," he suggested and tried to look even more relaxed, stretching back and extending his legs further.

Eventually Mrs Martin appeared to change gear, metaphorically speaking.

"Well, like I told the police, when I saw what I thought might be intruders out to pinch the harvest of all the hard work that I'd seen Helen putting into the allotment, it didn't half make my blood boil."

"Go on," prompted Alistair.

"That was one reason I started to keep my little camera by the bedroom window upstairs. I mean to be honest I was also afraid of our security here at Number 13. I mean it would be a good way for a burglar to come undetected and make a quick getaway – you know, across the allotments - so I'd been getting a bit security-conscious."

She pointed towards Philip Morgan's house, saying, "I mean, him next door is away a lot, and Vanessa and I are on our own here. A friend had said if a burglar was wanting to break in, he would almost certainly come from the allotments. Well, that made my daughter start having nightmares, so we had new locks put in all round plus an expensive burglar alarm. I mean, up till then I only had a dummy one – that one you can see from the street."

Mrs Martin paused as if expecting some words of encouragement from Alistair, but he was determined to keep his silence in the hope that she would speak more.

"You've probably seen the photos I showed to the

police."

Alistair remembered them well from the file the police had given Dennis, which he had shown him.

"When I heard you were coming I got the envelope out."

Alistair took the envelope carefully from her and refreshed his memory perusing them while Mrs Martin made various comments about which members of the Force were polite and which weren't, and who was handsome and who was not.

As he remembered, the photos were all rather indistinct, but one showed what his gut reaction told him was a lady with fair hair and what looked like a man in a mackintosh.

"That's the interesting one, isn't it, because it's not a million miles from the shed where Henrietta was found. I gather you couldn't recall much about them when the police asked you?"

"That's the funny thing. As I told the police, all I could recall was them talking nineteen to the dozen; looked like they might be solving the problems of the world, as the cliché goes."

There were various other images all pretty indistinct, though some were obviously children playing.

"Yes, you see, when I see children come in here I always think they must be after nicking all Helen's hard work – she gets such lovely raspberries."

Alistair waited patiently as she digressed, for running round in his mind were Mrs Martin's words that there were other things she hadn't told the police. He must not frighten her or get her to clam up, but he must endeavour to find out what this referred to.

He gave her a little prompt, asking her to please mention anything that may not have been taken as seriously as she thought it should. Sure enough, Mrs

Martin started up again. "Well, you know how awful the press were … "

"It was the usual sensationalism, wasn't it?"

"It was frightful – absolutely dreadful! Remember the picture they got their hands on, of Henrietta in her bikini?"

Alistair gulped. He remembered it rather too vividly and he remembered also Dennis's distress at it, and how staggered he was that they had found it. Henrietta had hardly ever been seen in anything other than her black priestly robes; indeed, to such an extent that jokes had been made that you wouldn't notice the difference if she rode a broomstick.

"Yes, I remember, it was very bad taste, and actually I know it caused a lot of distress," said Alistair sympathetically.

"Well, exactly, now I didn't want them putting pictures of my daughter like that in the papers, so I was very keen to keep her out of it all as much as possible. But you can imagine the media frenzy there was here and it seemed sometimes like they were asking me more questions about my daughter than about me."

Alistair was rather taken aback when Mrs Martin began to sob.

"I'm sorry, but you know this poor lady had been killed and they were even asking me what bra size my daughter was. It just made me cry."

Alistair muttered something about living in a fallen world, but then decided to wait till Mrs Martin composed herself.

"Only tell me if you want to," he said at length in kindly tone, "and if you think it helps, but you mentioned something about things you didn't tell the police, which perhaps you ought to have."

Mrs Martin continued her exasperating silence, and Alistair felt forced to prompt her again. "I mean, it's just possible that I could advise you if it was worth telling them or not," he offered eventually.

Mrs Martin now appeared quite flustered. She said, "You see, I wasn't really hiding it from them, but they were on an old camera, which my daughter had forgotten she had taken them with. I'd wanted to keep her out of it all – what with the press being so interested in her - and anyway, she only produced these ones recently. But yes, if you could advise if I should hand them over … here they are."

Alistair glanced at the photographs as he took possession. Again he recognised the familiar quickening of his heartbeat at the thought of interesting new material. He glanced at them with the immediate reaction that one of the figures shown could have been the person he had taken to be the man in the mackintosh.

"Thanks, I'll study these and if you and your daughter agree, I'll make sure the police get them for their ongoing review, file, records, whatever," he said, adding, "I really do assure you I won't do anything without your permission. I'll take good care of them, and I will give them back if and when you ask for them back."

When he felt he had stayed long enough not to appear departing too hurriedly, he took his leave politely.

"You've been so kind, Mrs Martin. I know poor Henrietta would have been so grateful that people were so cooperative in trying to get to the truth. You didn't know her, did you?

"Not at all."

"Not a church person then?"

"Absolutely not – don't believe in it at all."

"Ah well, there's no time like the present. I'll take pot luck and try your next door neighbour, this Philip

Morgan character, at number 11 – the rat catcher, as I think of him after what you said; and if he's out and I've got the energy afterwards, I'll gear myself up for the rather fearsome prospect of meeting the other fellow - the Aaron chappie at Number 15." He responded, making a gesture of farewell with his hat, and adding, "The chap who doesn't like church bells."

"Well, good luck with that one," said Mrs Martin ominously.

CHAPTER 19

(An interview with a volatile neighbour)

He found the rat man, as he now thought of Philip Morgan, out, so he went back past the front of Mrs Martin's house to the neighbour on the other side, and called with some trepidation and not very willingly at Number 15, Aaron's house.

The doorbell sounded ominously loud, in keeping with how he expected to find the occupant.

It had to be done, in the circumstances, but he would be glad when it was over and he was back in his little hotel having a wee dram. He would certainly deserve it after meeting this character with the daunting reputation.

The doorbell was answered fairly quickly and the grunt of "What do you want?" came in the same moment. Alistair explained who he was and muttered a few pleasantries, but received a rather stony silence. Wanting to get the main business over with, he rather abruptly broached the subject in hand.

"With the approval of the police, the late vicar's husband, Dennis, has assigned me the case as a private detective, and thought it would be a good idea if I just had a very quick word with you good residents here in Lime Grove," he announced.

Aaron maintained his stony silence, which Alistair found most intimidating.

"He thought it would be a good idea if I checked with the occupants of these houses near the crime scene as to whether there had been any troubles, rows etc.," he added, in what he was conscious sounded a rather cowardly manner.

Still there was this rather irritating, uncivil and unexpected stony silence, which Alistair broke by repeating, "So just got to check through re any rows with the allotment holders. Somewhere along the line someone reported some kind of a row involving you, about loud music - "

"The bloody cheek of it!" interrupted Aaron suddenly, revealing for the first time that he was capable of speech. "I mean, they don't even live here. Now if my neighbour had asked me to turn it down – well, that would be another thing, but a bloody allotment holder - makes yer mad. Frightened him off, I did, and I turned up the sound for the next few weeks to teach the sod a lesson. I mean, it's my house and he's only a bloody allotment holder. Bloke called Sid, it was - has the allotment opposite me. I mean, what about his bloody strimmer when I'm trying to sunbathe in the garden. Have you ever heard a strimmer going full blast?

"Anyway, that row blew over, did it? That was the end of that," said Alistair, stepping backwards slightly in case the memory of this incident induced Aaron to punch the air.

"That was the end of that," repeated Aaron emphatically. "But I mean the bloody cheek of it," he restarted, "Thinks he owns the place. I mean, what about the time when he refused to prune his ruddy tree so I could get some sunlight in my garden?"

"This is the sort of thing I'm here to ask about. Tell me about the tree pruning saga."

"Well, that tall tree at the end of his allotment was keeping the sun off my grass so it wasn't growing well. *And* ... " Aaron pronounced the word "and" as if he was about to wield a final blow... "I couldn't bloody sunbathe!"

"Was this allotment holder – this guy Sidney - not cooperative and helpful about this?" asked Alistair, sounding a little timid.

"*Cooperative?* Bloody hell! He kept saying, 'I'll attend to it,' but never did. Then he said it was the council's job. When I said, 'Don't give me that shit,' he said. 'OK, ask Charles.' I went to see this Charles guy, who reckons he's in charge, and I said, 'Listen, mate, if you're in charge then you bloody see to it that that tree gets lobbed, or else I'll come in here and pour petrol over all your ruddy little plants that you're all too damn lazy and too damn mean to go to the supermarket and buy like the rest of us.'"

Is this guy real? thought Alistair, stepping back a bit again, partly because of a rather strong smell of gin, and partly again because he felt some danger that he might be on the receiving end of some over-powerful gesture.

"OK, OK, old chap, but that was resolved too, I take it," said Alistair, determined to keep the upper hand.

"Listen you, learn some manners. Don't call me 'old chap'. OK, got that? I have a name. My name is Aaron."

"Sorry. Now, were there any more rows, Aaron?" Alistair's question hung in the air, while Aaron appeared to frown at the ceiling.

"Well, old chap, there was a time when this Sidney character, he had lit a bonfire, and unluckily for him the smoke was coming right at me, right in yer face. I said, "When you going to put that out? Like now, or in one minute's time?" He says to me, all poncy like - " and at this point Aaron started to do a little turn, as if dancing, before continuing – "'we're allowed it for an hour before sundown.' I said to him, 'I'll give you bloody sundown, mate, and I hosed his bleeding fire out right under his nose. He says 'I'm going to report you,' like he was a bloody schoolgirl! Well, we didn't have no more bloody bonfires after that, I'll tell yer."

Alistair could not refrain from a smile, which was

reciprocated by his interlocutor, who obviously enjoyed showing off in front of an audience more than anything.

"Sorry," repeated Alistair, "but there was one other row that had to be checked out, wasn't there? I believe you complained about the church bells."

"I'll say," came the instant reply.

Alistair felt it was his turn to make a joke. "I take it you're not a member of the congregation are you?"

"No, I'm bloody not! Those bloody church bells – drives yer mad on a Sunday morning. Honest, I told that vicar hundreds of times, 'Stop yer bloody church bells on a Sunday morning!'"

"And what did she say?"

"She said, 'I can see how you get road rage.' And I said to her, 'Road rage has got nothing to do with it,' and I basically told her to FO. I admit I was bloody annoyed, and it didn't help that I had a hangover. Cor, I was annoyed – and she had the bloody cheek to ask me if I was baptised. I bloody nearly baptised her! Could have stuffed her head in the water tank, that day, I'll tell yer."

As Alistair was unable to restrain his laugh, Aaron added, "She was standing right there by the water tank in the front garden when she said it."

"Church bells, though … I mean, it's not against the law, is it?" asked Alistair, rhetorically and still somewhat nervously.

"Bloody well should be – constitutes a breach of the peace, in my book. I told her - "

"Told who?" interrupted Alistair.

"The bloody vicar! I told her, 'The day you stop ringing those bloody bells, I might start coming to your something church,'" he blasphemed.

Alistair thought he heard the sound of somebody else in the house.

"Now here comes Sophie, my partner, so we're

243

going to have to terminate this deliriously happy little conversation," declared Aaron with an unpleasant beam.

Alistair looked round and saw what he thought was a pretty but rather goofy-looking little girl with a slightly vacant expression on her face. In his slight nervousness, he made some kind of rather bad joke to her about Aaron not liking the church bells. To his surprise, she answered quite promptly. "Not when he's got a hangover; anyone who makes a noise then better watch out. He goes berserk – I'm not kidding!"

"You be careful what you say," said Aaron, looking at the young woman. Then he announced, "Time to leave, mate," and began to close the door.

It seemed to Alistair more like an order than a suggestion, and recalling his father's advice that discretion is the better part of valour, first learnt when he turned back in cloud on Ben Macdhui, he turned and saying possibly the most disingenuous thank you of his life, waved goodbye and left the premises.

Alistair walked home, but in his ears were ringing those few words that he had heard the girl speak: 'He goes berserk.' Whoever had done this crime had gone berserk – it was the mot juste, he thought, and here was a man whose wife, or rather partner, had even said he was capable of going berserk; and not only that, but had also said he had an issue with the vicar.

In a book he would be near the top of a list of suspects, he thought, as Donna at the reception desk welcomed him back to the Concord Hotel.

"You look deep in thought again, sir," she said, not unrespectfully.

"I look forward to telling you and Cissie what it's all about someday, but for the moment it's got to stay under the old hat," he replied, smiling at her and removing the said hat.

CHAPTER 20

(An interview with a rat catcher)

Let's get back to the congregation, thought Alistair in the morning as the alarm clock brought him back from his dreams. I've had enough of the residents of Lime Grove for the moment.

During breakfast his thoughts continued. I need to let a little time pass to reflect on yesterday's interesting developments, so I'll leave those interesting people, the residents of Lime Grove, for a few days. He also decided to wait a bit before re-examining the new photographs taken by Vanessa, which her mother had handed him. He wanted to bring a fresh mind to those. With this resolution made, he determined to phone Fred Goodman, the ex-churchwarden, as soon as his toast, butter and marmalade were finished and he had cleaned his teeth.

Fred Goodman sounded like just the person who would help him consolidate his thoughts. More than a few people had taken the line that there wasn't much going on in the parish of St Peter's that Fred didn't know most, and a bit more, about. Yes, he would try and arrange a meeting today.

However, as it turned out, Fred proved quite difficult to arrange an appointment with. Alistair remembered that not a few people had told him that Fred liked to seem important, and always had to consult what he called his "little black book" before making even the most trivial of appointments. Fred was eventually pinned down to 2 p.m. on the morrow, so Alistair had to abandon his resolution and try and squeeze in a meeting with Philip Morgan of 11 Lime Grove, or as he had labelled him in his thoughts, the rat catcher.

Let's give him a try anyway, he thought, not for the first time recalling as a true Scot the line of Burns that "the best laid schemes o' mice an' men gang aft a-gley.' He pulled out his mobile and entered the number, which he had scribbled down in his notebook.

Ah, at least it's ringing, he thought as he leant back, indicating to Cissie, the waitress, that yes, it was OK to clear the dishes.

"Hallo, Philip Morgan here," came a decidedly Welsh voice.

Alistair explained his purpose in ringing at some length, wondering all the time what sort of response there would be.

"You're lucky to catch me, old chap. I'm hardly ever here, you know. In fact I'm only in today because I had to renew my passport, as I'm off abroad again in a few days' time."

"Oh, how fortunate. When would be convenient?"

"Well, no time, to be honest." Philip Morgan seemed very pleased with this irritating joke, laughing at length before continuing, "You see, I've so much to arrange before I go...."

"Well, you choose a time," suggested Alistair with a feeling of déjà vu, yet determined not to be put off a second time that day. One inconveniently pompous person was enough for one morning, he told himself, as Philip whistled irritatingly at the other end of the line.

"Oh, damn it, I suppose if we really need to meet up, you'd better come round this morning. It's the only time I've got. Come on, then, let's get it over, old chap. There's nothing I can tell you. I'm always away. The police told me I was the least helpful of all the people they interviewed."

Again there was quite a pause while Philip launched into another of his long laughs at what he seemed to regard as a joke.

This habit of laughing at his own jokes, which in other people Alistair could find endearing, was somehow in Philip's case immensely annoying.

At last Philip's laughter ended and he restarted. "The police were only joking, you know. I said to them, 'I wish I could have told you I saw a guy with a dagger between his teeth carrying a bloodstained axe, but I was in bloody Bangladesh at the time, wasn't I?'"

For a third time, the long and now increasingly irritating laugh ensued. When it stopped, Philip said quite abruptly, "Anyway come on round, old chap; the earlier the better would suit me, to be perfectly honest with you."

This last phrase, which rang in his ears, sounded particularly Welsh to Alistair as he got ready, put on his anorak, tied his shoelaces and got ready to depart.

Within an hour he was back in his haunts of yesterday at Lime Grove, knocking on the door of Number 11.

Philip opened the door politely enough, but it seemed as if he wanted to conduct the whole interview standing in the hall, as when the normal pleasantries of saying hallo were completed, Philip, instead of inviting Alistair into the living room as he expected, launched into an endless stream of talk.

"Fortunately I was away at the time of the tragedy," he burbled on, repeating his earlier telephonic comments, "and missed all the immediate hubbub - though of course it was still going on pretty much when I returned from abroad last September."

Alistair, who had originally been prepared to try and like the rat catcher was now beginning to find his style "really too much", as he was to say later.

Just when he was thinking that the lack of hospitality was a little marked, and was about to suggest moving into the living room himself, Philip apologised. "I would invite you in, but there's a lot to arrange at the moment, because I'm off out of the country again in a few days."

"Well, I don't mind standing here in the hall, if you don't; but my inquiry is a serious one, you know, and it's the victim's husband who has employed me ... "

"Oh, alright, I suppose I am being a little inhospitable. Come in and take a seat. You're making me feel guilty, but I mustn't make myself too comfortable There's one hell of a lot to attend to before I fly into the sunset."

"Literally the sunset, is it? Does that mean America?" Inquired Alistair.

"Yes, I do a lot of business – all over the world, actually - but in America mostly these days."

Alistair, who was missing Zoe more than usual that morning, said he only knew about Chicago. Somehow it helped to mention the city where she was. It was a link, however tenuous, with Zoe. Damn it, yes he was in love alright; even mentioning her city gave him a pleasant feeling.

He resolutely brought himself back to the matter in hand.

"I spoke to Mrs Martin next door at Number 13 yesterday and also her neighbour on the other side, Aaron MacQuarrie, at Number 15 beyond." He said the name Aaron with a slight twinkle in his eye, which Philip Morgan noticed.

"Oh, and you lived to tell the tale, did you? Yes, he's got a temper, that one. You know, I get teased if I get a bit hot under the collar and people say to me, 'Oh, it's the Welsh in you.' Now that annoys me, because, well, you should see old Aaron when he's annoyed about something - and he's an Englishman! Oh my, yes, I parked the car outside the front of his house one

248

Sunday and he came to his door and he said to me, 'Hey you, are you a bloody church-goer?' I said, 'What do you mean?' and he says, 'I don't want no bloody church-goers parking outside my house!' I said, 'Listen, mate, you may be new round here, and you may not have noticed it, but I'm your next door neighbour but one, and we don't behave like that round here."

Alistair laughed genuinely and began to think that maybe he had judged Philip too harshly. The picture of Aaron and Philip together having an altercation was a colourful one. He wouldn't have blamed Mrs Martin for spying on that one.

Pleased to find his new visitor so appreciative of his story-telling, Philip continued with slightly less of an eye on the clock.

"I said to Aaron, I did, 'Actually, if you really want to know, I'm a church-goer, but not here. I'm Church of Wales.'" He pronounced this in what seemed to Alistair as almost a caricature of a Welsh accent, before continuing at full throttle, "'That's where I go to for worship,' I said to Aaron. And as far as I know the nearest Church of Wales is in Chelsea, and that's where I go on the anniversary of my fiancée's death, if you must know, Mr Aaron McQuarrie."

Alistair put on his sympathetic look while Philip continued, "Yes, I was engaged to be married about twenty years ago to a girl from Swansea. She was the most beautiful girl in all of Wales. We met in a service station when my car broke down. I had to sit in the café where she worked for three hours, and by the time I left I had decided I wanted to marry her."

"I love a romantic story," said Alistair, knowing that it was a remark that would have been untrue before he had met Zoe. "Three hours to decide to marry somebody – that's quite quick, isn't it?" he joked, before correcting himself and resuming his sympathetic look. "But how sad that she died," he added.

"We were to be married in October. She was killed in a car crash the month before in September," replied Philip, staring down at the floor.

"It's nice that you go to church on the anniversary, as you say," Alistair responded, still in sympathetic tone.

"Well, I didn't at first, to be honest with you," rejoined Philip.

The use of this phrase about being 'honest with you' reminded him of how Mrs Martin had used it so often yesterday; perhaps one of them picked it up from the other.

"When it first happened," continued Philip, gazing out of the window with a sad expression, "I thought, How can there be a God? I was in despair. By chance I met the vicar here at St Peter's. In those days it was a man called Maurice. I didn't really want to talk to him, but I said to him, 'What would you do in my position?' He says to me, speaking like he was Our Lord himself, 'If I were you I would go to the Church of Wales in Chelsea, and I would pray that you will be reunited in heaven.'"

Alistair stared, genuinely enthralled, before saying, "That's interesting. I've heard good things about that chap Maurice before."

"Well, I suppose it was so unexpected. Anyway, you know, to cut a long story short, I suppose I was behaving a bit strangely at the time, and in fact I went and I did just that, and do you know? The funny thing was I found it helped so much. I don't know why, but it did."

Philip paused, staring once more through the window over the top of Roger's allotment opposite, and then turning his head to the left across Helen's, and lastly the more distant one of Sid Walsh's beyond that; but by now there were tears in his eyes.

"Helped so much," he repeated, nodding his head.

Alistair waited and then commented, "Well, you know I've never really been a believer, but to be honest with you" - this phrase is so infectious, he thought - "I've reached the age or the point in life when I'm reconsidering all this. I'm really interested in what you have told me. I suppose as well as trying to help solve this ghastly crime for Dennis's sake, I'm also, like a lot of other people no doubt, trying to help solve my own philosophical questions."

This remark seemed to bring about an uncharacteristic silence in Philip, during which Alistair brushed a speck of dirt off his trousers and added, "I really can't think of anything worse than a fiancée being killed."

He thought of Zoe, and rather pathetically, as it seemed to him, a tear came to his own eye. This is stupid, he told himself, I haven't known her long at all and I've such feelings for her.

Philip remained silent and the businesslike side of Alistair's character asserted itself.

"Well, I'd love to meet up and talk about these great matters one day if you're ever here long enough," he added with a chuckle. "But right now, if I could just get back for a short while to why I'm here, and ask you just a few questions about the crime."

"Anything you like," answered Philip, raising his arms as if to be helpful, "but I don't think I can tell you much more than I told the police."

"As I say, I saw Mrs Martin yesterday, and she told me you did have one little problem with an allotment holder," said Alistair, getting down to business.

Philip seemed to wake up from his trancelike state, and ignoring this reference to his dispute about rats with Roger Brown said, "Mrs Martin keeps an eye on things while I'm away. Makes sure there's no post sticking out the door and that sort of thing. I don't like to put it like this, but she's quite useful."

"That's very good of her, isn't it?" suggested Alistair.

"I don't think it's too much bother for her, mind you. I mean, there's no ruddy cat for her to look after when I'm away."

That is his trouble, thought Alistair, he hasn't got a cat and doesn't even like them,

"You should get yourself one, one day. Mark you, they're quite choosy who they'll accept as their owner. Or I should say, who they will own." Alistair tried to ease things a bit with this joke, which actually he knew had a lot of truth in it.

"Me, get a cat? No, I bloody won't!"

"Might help you with the rats," joked Alistair again, pleased with his subtle way of raising the subject again.

"Oh, she told you, did she? Yes, I don't blame her. It was a bit of a ding-dong, that was. That chap who owns the allotment opposite my house – I think he's called Roger Brown or something like that - am I right? Well, he couldn't get it into his head that his ruddy compost bin was attracting rats, and he started trying to make out it was me having parties on the lawn. I said, 'What parties?' and he couldn't answer."

Philip looked at his watch and interrupted himself. "Look, old chap, I don't want to be rude, but there's things I've just got to do this morning."

Alistair was somewhat disconcerted by this early and somewhat sudden attempt to end the discussion, so he asked rather abruptly, "I take it you never had any dealings with the victim – poor Henrietta?"

"Absolutely not."

"You never had anything to do with her church, St

Peter's?"

"Good God, no; as I say, I'm Church of Wales."

Once again, he made the word "Wales" sound like a caricature of a Welsh comedian, and seemed to turn rather suddenly less hospitable, adding, "Look, no offence, old chap, but I really can't throw any light on that terrible crime, and I don't want to be rude, but I haven't got time to make clever chit-chat with people who think they're cleverer than the police."

Now that really is rude, thought Alistair feeling quite annoyed and now determined to address Philip less respectfully.

"Sorry, mate, I won't take up your time, but felt it right not to leave you out in my … "

Alistair did not finish his sentence, and Philip's ushering him to the door made his annoyance reach unusual heights.

"Oh, whatever. Thanks anyway," he managed.

Philip did at least give him a hearty handshake, along with the slightly puzzling parting words, "No hard feelings, but I'm so terribly busy."

Alistair put his hat back on and strode firmly back down the pavement of Lime Grove, thinking to himself, I'm definitely on the side of the rats …

As he boarded the bus and slumped back into the seat next to an old lady, his irritation diminished and he found himself thinking, he may kill rats and not like cats, and at the end of the day I don't particularly like him any more than the rats or the cats do, but he's not a murderer, and is probably quite right that he can't throw any light on things. I suppose his problem is really that he just lacks grace – there's a lot of people like that.

As the bus jolted on and he witnessed one or two further examples of graceless behaviour, including shoving and pushing by the general public, his thoughts continued. But they're not ruddy murderers. They may be bloody rude, and they may throw their litter on the floor, but they don't go around murdering vicars!

CHAPTER 21

(An interview with a former and would-be churchwarden)

On his return home the last two evenings, Alistair had been too tired to start examining closely the photographs which Mrs Martin's daughter, Vanessa had taken. He had put them carefully in the drawer of his bedroom table to await such time as he could bring a fresher mind to them.

However, on the next morning, by the time he had finished his porridge, sheer curiosity began to get the better of him, and as his appointment with Fred Goodman was not until the afternoon, he returned to his bedroom, sat down at the table and with his magnifying glass in one hand and the photographs in the other, began to inspect them with the utmost scrutiny.

The intriguing thing about Vanessa's photographs was that they were slightly sharper and less grainy than her mother's, and there were always people in them; but alas, like those in her mother's photographs, these shadowy figures could be just about anybody.

He let the magnifying glass rest over one of the best pictures. One figure could have been a fat man; but he considered with some excitement that it could quite easily also have been a lady with a cloak blowing in the wind. He would have to contact Mrs Martin's daughter, Vanessa, and see if her recollection could throw any light on their grainy mystery. Surely the protective Mrs Martin would allow him a word with her, and not attribute to him the base motives that she had to the *Daily Express* photographer. One thing that struck him was that the mysterious, almost ghostly, figures in the two photographs of Vanessa's which particularly interested him, never appeared to be in any way working on the allotment. They seemed, for all the world, to be just a couple of people, going for a walk.

Having reached a point when he was satisfied that nothing more was to be gained that morning by continually staring inanely at the images, Alistair decided to give himself a good lunch before his afternoon appointment and descent on the citadel of Fred Goodman. It promised to be an interesting talk if nothing else, though he had decided not to cross-examine him about the little escapade with Gary, and the little matter of Fred having asked Gary to help him break down that fence; he would keep that up his sleeve.

By the time he caught sight of Fred's smart front door, he had quite got over yesterday's undercurrent of rudeness from Philip Morgan, which though less blatant than Aaron's had nonetheless been just as irksome.

He noticed how neat and tidy Fred's front garden was compared with his neighbours'. The porch was clean and tidy and the barometer within it looked smart, and somewhat superior to Edwin and Helen's old broken and inaccurate one, he noticed. Yes, Fred is a fastidious man, if ever there was one, he concluded. In addition to the particularly smart front door with its brightly polished brasswork, he was amused to see that the markedly clean and polished car parked in the little driveway had a registration number bearing its owner's initials, which seemed to give it an added grandeur that belied its years.

There's no doubt Fred likes to keep up appearances and create an impression of respectability. This interview is going to be interesting and possibly amusing, thought Alistair, recalling everything he had been told about Fred. He rang the extremely well-polished bell, and somehow knew by its strong and audible ring that it must have been heard. He waited for what seemed like a rather longer pause than etiquette required. He was recalling how Dennis had said, 'You simply have to interview the know-all,' and had then added how Henrietta's predecessor had said 'every parish needs its Fred.'

The door opened silently and easily. Fred was not a man to have a noisy hinge.

"Good afternoon, Fred, here I am at last," Alistair said, bowing slightly in his determination to show respect and get off to a good start.

"Well done," said Fred rather pompously. Alistair had to stop himself saying, "Well, I only got on a bus."

However, his slight irritation was soon banished, as Fred ushered him in with a courteous and reasonably welcoming demeanour.

"Come right in and take a seat in here. What do you feel like by way of refreshment at this time of day? Tea any good?"

"That would be perfect," answered Alistair, sitting himself down opposite the hearth. He had plenty of time, while Fred busied himself in the kitchen, to take in the ambience of the room. He liked the old prints of Cookington. Did it ever really look like that? he wondered, I suppose it must have. He was less keen on some of the Staffordshire pottery that various shelves and indeed the mantelpiece were bestrewn with. He noticed something on the latter that he would ask Fred about when he returned from the kitchen.

"I like your clock, Fred – lovely old one," he ventured.

Fred put the tray down rather carefully on the little table and replied, "Yes, our children and grandchildren gave it to us for our ruby wedding anniversary. To be honest, I hinted rather strongly that that was the one I'd like – had to be Roman numerals and largish. I'm rather particular about clocks. There's another one upstairs, which I was presented with after my fourteen years as churchwarden."

"I've always liked Roman numerals myself," replied Alistair and then continued, "I was going to ask you; what's that on the mantelpiece, Fred?" His eye once again rested on an object that seemed slightly out of place in such a neat display.

"Oh, that – that's a piece of old clay pipe. I don't exactly collect them but I pick 'em up when I see 'em."

"Oh, so you're another of these collectors of pieces of old clay pipes, are you?"

"Well, as I say, I don't exactly collect them, but well, as I say, I pick 'em up when I see 'em."

Fred went over to his mantelpiece and lifted the object up, admiring it for a while. "It was from the allotments, and it was the best preserved and largest bit I ever found. You see, it's got the bowl and most of the stem, which is quite rare. Often wonder what the guy was like who took this out of his mouth and threw it away. Course, all that area was market gardening for as long as anyone can remember, so I suppose it's not that surprising that there's so many around. Don't know much about the subject," he continued, "though, like everything, I gather some people take it all very seriously."

"Yeah, I know someone else with your little hobby," put in Alistair.

"Who else does, then?" asked Fred, cocking an eyebrow.

"Edwin, the churchwarden," answered Alistair promptly, having decided not to mention Fred's partner in crime, Gary.

"Really? That surprises me, though I suppose if his wife's got an allotment that makes sense. I've heard there are a lot on that particular patch up where she is. Can't imagine him doing any gardening, so I suppose picking up bits of old pipes would appeal to him."

Having made this dig at Edwin, Fred then compounded it by saying, "While his wife does all the work."

Cor, thought Alistair, don't these Christians love each other!

Alistair could not resist stirring it up. "Why? Don't you rate Edwin much as a worthy guy to be churchwarden?"

"Well, he takes a very back seat. Told me once he believed in carrying out his duties with a light touch. Understatement of the year – 'Light touch' – I'll say! In my opinion, they should be more careful who they give these appointments to," came the reply.

"Florence is great at the job, though, isn't she?" responded Alistair, as if to smooth things over.

"Well, she did very well during the interregnum before Henrietta arrived, and she's doing well during this new situation, I'll give her that. There's a lot to do, you know, ensuring the services are all arranged and people contacted to take them and preach etc. She was the star churchwarden, so she would have been the official contact for all the correspondence, documents and the like during the interregnum, and of course now in the current situation I know the bishop's put a lot on her shoulders. Ha, when that first interregnum ended, I think she was a bit put out; lost her pivotal role – no longer the key person she used to be! Yes, she's good at biting her lip, but I could see she was seething with annoyance underneath. Didn't approve of quite a lot of Henrietta's innovations, I can tell you. Of course, one day she'll be replaced and I admit at first that is difficult. You get used to being churchwarden and it doesn't seem quite right when you stop."

"Of course, you were in that role for ages, I gather, Fred."

"Yes, I was star churchwarden. I was ... fourteen years doing that little job, to be exact. Everyone thinks I wish I still was churchwarden but I really don't. Much prefer just poking my nose into anything I think is interesting. I grant you I missed it a bit at first. Who wouldn't, after fourteen years? But, as I say, now I just poke me nose into anything I find interesting."

Again, Alistair could not resist a rather rash retort. "I expect you found the crime 'interesting', to use your word," he said, not unkindly and with a twinkle in his eye.

Fred remained oddly silent, and Alistair used his reference to the crime to tackle the subject more explicitly.

"Now, Fred, I reckon you're the guy who, if anyone, can throw light on what may be behind all this – this ghastly crime."

For once Fred didn't beam or purr but quickly retorted, "Can't make it out at all. We're all completely foxed. You can imagine a lot of us have discussed this business till we're blue in the face. My own view is it's got to be some old grudge probably from way back when. I mean as far as the congregation are concerned they really are the last people who would seem capable of such terrifying breaking of commandments."

"Well, I know some of them have broken other commandments," responded Alistair.

"What – you mean petty pilfering?" Fred cocked an eye.

"And coveting, and the odd bit of adultery, no doubt," added Alistair.

"Oh, I wouldn't know about that; or perhaps I do. Really...who?" Fred said enigmatically.

Alistair would not be deflected, "You know, Fred,

for Dennis's sake I'm so desperately keen to get this matter finished with, over, tied up. Is there absolutely nothing that you can think of that might help me to do just that? I can't help feeling you're one of my best hopes for making a breakthrough."

There was a pause while Fred looked with rather a confused stare at his hat, which, as it seemed to Alistair, lay rather carefully placed on the table beside him.

"Anything?" repeated Alistair, leaning forward earnestly.

"Of course, I know everyone in this parish pretty well, you know," started Fred rather pompously, "Some I like – most, I'm glad to say. Some I don't, but there's no one I could imagine committing a crime like this. Funnily enough, the one person I don't know is the victim's husband, Dennis. I've never got to know him, and he's not easy to get to know, because he tends to keep to himself. He doesn't attend parish events, shoots away after morning service to get his Sunday paper. Do you know, he didn't even attend the annual meeting? I call it the AGM. It's properly called the APCM – annual parish church meeting."

Fred stretched the words out in a lengthy and deliberate manner, which seemed to emphasise their importance, and then continued while looking at the back of his hands. "I mean, there's a problem there. He should have, shouldn't he?"

Fred paused to flick some dust off a cushion with a cloth that seemed to have conveniently and miraculously appeared.

"Alistair, you've asked me to be absolutely totally honest with you, and that's difficult because I know Dennis is your friend … "

The doorbell rang. Fred excused himself and went to answer it. Alistair heard him mumbling something to the effect that yes, he went to church.

"Blinking Jehovah's Witnesses," he chuckled as he came back. "Everyone in our congregation has a go at them, but they're good people really, searching after truth. I usually engage them in some interesting conversation."

"The interruption came at a bad time, Fred, because you were just about to tell me something," resumed Alistair.

Fred looked as if he had lost his place.

"You were saying you knew Dennis was a friend of mine," prompted Alistair.

"Ah yes, I was going to say … But to be, using your words, totally honest with you … "

"Sorry, I've picked the annoying phrase up from Philip Morgan, who probably picked it up from Mrs Martin," apologised Alistair.

"I've wondered sometimes," continued Fred, "if Dennis just flipped; you know, found it all too much." His face assumed what could only be described as a markedly serious, if not grim, expression.

Slightly taken aback, Alistair managed to retain a demeanour of calmness and, leaning forward, asked, "Can you think of anything that supports such a theory?"

Fred seemed to relax and indeed smile again before continuing.

"Well, as I say, it's somewhat embarrassing, with you being his friend, but I'll try saying it. It's mostly just the distance he keeps from the life of the church, the impression he gives that there's something not quite right – even, I'd go so far as to say, gives the impression that everything is such a nuisance … "

Alistair was determined not to interrupt Fred but the pause became too long.

"Go on, Fred. Elaborate, please."

"Well, Karen," he continued, nodding towards the staircase visible through the open door, "and I used to think maybe he's just shy. Odd though, because he goes off to his business every day, and his kids aren't shy, and his wife wasn't."

"Keep talking, Fred, this is interesting," responded Alistair, trying to appear a little more nonchalant than he was at hearing such aspersions cast on his old friend.

Fred remained silent, looking at the floor.

"Apart from all that, is there anything you've seen that might lend support to such a theory – your theory that he flipped?" pressed Alistair.

"It's so difficult with you being his friend … " mumbled Fred into his hand.

Alistair interrupted him swiftly. "He's well aware that by asking me to do this investigation, some people will say all manner of things about him, of which not a few will be not to his liking. He accepts that, but still wanted me to take the job on. Fred, please, for Henrietta's sake, tell me anything that you feel would help to get to the truth, or help eliminate false trails. Is there anything specific that makes you have that feeling?"

Fred straightened the creases of his trousers with his fingers and thumbs for what seemed like an inordinately long time before saying, "I've never told anyone this, except for her upstairs, but I saw him by the allotments once. I was on the way home after a little meeting at the vicarage. Henrietta had said he was out at his evening class learning Italian. Well, the college is in a different direction. He was walking past the allotments – that's all – nothing suspicious, but just not where I'd been told he would be … and by the allotments," he added rather slowly and deliberately. "I can anticipate your next question, so let me say it was some couple of months before the tragedy."

Alistair deliberately waited to see if Fred would add any further fascinating little snippets of information, and sure enough he continued, "When I heard about the murder, I remember thinking, it can't be him; I mean if he was going to do that, well, he could have pushed her off the top of the church tower."

"Why do you say that?" asked Alistair, again rather taken aback.

Fred laughed. "Well, do you really want to know?"

Alistair nodded silently as Fred, appearing to rather enjoy the suspense, stared straight ahead at the picture over the mantelpiece as if it was the first time in his life he had seen it, and continued speaking.

"I was up there once with his wife – yes, the vicar - and she said something which really annoyed me, and I thought how easy it would be ... "

"You're teasing me now, Fred! Come on, that's bad taste, isn't it? What did she say that annoyed you, for goodness sake?"

"Well, if you really must know," Fred repeated himself, "I made some comment about someone being pretty - a new girl in the congregation - and Henrietta ticked me off. I felt offended. I felt like a schoolboy who has been reprimanded. I said even the old have their feelings, and she turned round sharply and literally spat the words, 'And so do priests, but we don't go round expressing them!' It was a rather unfortunate, even nasty, little conversation, which wouldn't have happened with Maurice, whose departure I regret; anyway, I thought it was a bit odd, and as I say told my wife, but honestly I never thought to connect it with what happened."

Alistair tried pausing again to elicit any further intriguing titbits. Fred remained quiet, so Alistair asked, "What did your wife say?"

"Her upstairs agreed with me. She said that

conversation wouldn't happen with a normal priest ... sorry, I mean a *male* priest."

"OK, Fred, I have to ask you one or two things; I don't know if you and Henrietta were close?"

He paused and as there was no response from Fred, he added, "Or if she ever confided anything to you about her personal life – say, about boyfriends, lovers …"

"Good Heavens, no … certainly not!" Fred seemed genuinely shocked.

"Well, that answers that, Fred. I don't like putting suggestions and questions like that to people, but as Dennis said, if I'm to do this properly – well I just have to, don't I? Wasn't it Shakespeare who said that nothing will come of nothing."

"King Lear," said Fred, to Alistair's astonishment.

After a little more discussion of personalities and matters in the life of St Peter's, Cookington, Fred got up as if to indicate that time was passing, and that he had other things to do.

"Well, I think I've told you everything. As I say, it was almost certainly of no consequence, but I did see Dennis there by the allotments that time I mentioned. Thought I saw Henrietta over that way once too. Asked her at church whether she was thinking of putting her name on the waiting list for one and she said, 'Fred, many a joke comes true. There aren't many places in the modern world where you can get peace from the bustle, but over there,' she said, 'well, it's kind of cut off – cut off from the world, like being up the tower – it's quiet and private – almost secret, like a hiding place.' It's funny, I remember those words almost verbatim and it's so ironic, because she said she might get one when she retired."

It was not long before Alistair found himself catching the bus back to his little hotel, and as the usual jolts helped it on its way, he reflected on the day's interview. There was this new big question. Why had Dennis been so adamant that he had never been to the allotments? What was he doing there? Fred would not have made that up. Also, on a totally different tack and even more intriguingly, what he wondered had Henrietta meant by "and so do priests"?

The words rang in his ears even after the bus reached his destination and he had showered and was happily enjoying the simple little dinner provided by the Concord Hotel.

"You're thinking again," said Cissie in her teasing voice.

"I sure am, Cissie, and I've got to do a lot more of that."

Over and over again as he fell into slumber, he heard those words, "and so do priests".

Was there something of interest and of relevance to her awful end, hinted at, however tentatively, by such a remark?

He was too sleepy to answer that question in his thoughts, and soon slept the sleep of the just.

CHAPTER 22

(The interruption of an unexpected tale)

When Alistair awoke in the morning, he was immediately of the opinion that the time had come to turn his attentions away from the parish and investigate Henrietta's past life, and particularly her love life. In his ordered mind it would be best to do this chronologically. He would travel to his own dear city of Edinburgh and eliminate from his inquiries this first boyfriend of Henrietta's, who by all accounts had been more smitten by her than she by him.

As always, when a prospect of returning to Edinburgh was on the cards, he felt an uplifting sense of joy.

The more he travelled the world, the more he loved Edinburgh. He smiled to himself as he recalled Zoe asking him why he loved it so much, and how he had replied that he just could not explain. It was like people asking a great explorer why they went; people who asked the question could not understand the answer. To get to Scotland, for years now he had always used the plane, so what was once a novelty had almost become the norm. In early years he had driven sometimes up the east coast and sometimes up the west. How familiar he was with those routes! However, as the years passed he had found the distance increasingly tiring. On the east coast route, Yorkshire had seemed to go on for ever, and on the west coast Carlisle had always seemed further than expected. He had tried breaking the journey with stops at places like Ripon and Boroughbridge on the eastern route and Carlisle on the western. Although such halts were interesting and enjoyable, and he had even grown fond of Ripon,

Boroughbridge and Carlisle, they were, he used to say, a bit of a palaver. For ages he had used the train, but it had so often proved crowded and plagued by delays and track repairs. Before long he found himself saying, "Flying is the only way."

Nonetheless on this particular occasion he had deliberately elected to travel by train. He had wanted time to think, and it was one of his curious personal gimmicks, for want of a better word, that he always thought most clearly, analytically and usefully when jogging along on the train. Why? He would have to ask a psychologist one day. He would use this journey to mull over all the information he had acquired and to put the facts in perspective.

He had hoped to spend that day pleasantly, packing and relaxing with a book and to all intents and purposes having a day off, in preparation for the morrow's journey.

However, life always took one by surprise, and he was somewhat astonished to receive a rather breathless phone call from Fred Goodman asking him if he could make a second visit to his house, as there was something which he'd omitted to tell him yesterday, but which on further consideration he was determined to tell him, for what it was worth.

Fred had terminated the phone call with the words, "I'd feel better if I got it off my chest."

Somewhat ruefully, but not without curiosity, Alistair accepted the need to cancel his proposed day of sybaritic self-indulgence and before long found himself once more at the smart front door of one Fred Goodwin, BA.

Fred launched straight into a little speech in the hallway.

"It's so good of you to come back. I really thought and thought after you'd gone yesterday, and the more I did, the more I felt I shouldn't have held back on this. Sometimes it's very difficult to know what's wise, or I should say correct, and what isn't. Anyway, I've changed my mind and I'm going to tell you."

"I'm all ears, and I thank you for feeling that you can share it with me, whatever it is," added Alistair, with what he hoped was a friendly smile.

They entered the smart little living room and Alistair took the same seat as on the previous day.

Fred at last sat down himself, after pottering about in the back of the room and opening a drinks cupboard.

"It's an embarrassing sort of thing, and I thought we'd indulge in something a bit stronger than yesterday," he said with a twinkle in his eye, muttering, "I've heard you're not averse to a wee dram of your national drink."

Fred cocked his eyebrow as if awaiting approval of his knowledge of Scottish terms before continuing with a kindly beam, "Anyway, makes a change from tea and coffee."

"At this time of morning? I don't usually. However, that looks a good one, Fred."

"Look, I'll spit it out straight away. As I say, it's embarrassing, and my only reason for telling you is that, as you said, to get to the whole truth, we've all got to tell the whole truth and well, it's probably totally irrelevant but just possibly might not be; because the way I see it, if people can go off the rails one way, they might just possibly go off another way, if you can follow me."

"You've got me on tenterhooks and I'm staying quiet until I hear what you've got to say, Fred," replied Alistair, genuinely agog and somewhat impatient by now.

"Well, what I'm going to tell you happened well before the crime – indeed, well before Henrietta even came here. It was during the interregnum."

Alistair, in his impatience, had to practically bite his tongue to stop himself breaking his own vow of silence by urging Fred on.

"While the vicarage was empty, we had a lot of work done in it, redecorating and that sort of thing. Plumbing, cleaning, repairs all over the place, the lot," started Fred, adding in rather a disapproving tone, "all paid for by the Church, of course, I might add."

Alistair made no comment in his eagerness not to hold the story up.

"The electrics needed attention, too and that's a field I've a certain experience in," said Fred rather pompously, indulging in his favourite mannerism of looking at his fingernails.

"And I went round to the vicarage one evening," he continued, "to try and deal with the flickering light problem. There was trouble with the lighting going dim and that sort of thing. I wasn't officially meant to be there, but I knew about the electrics there, and I didn't want them landed with a big bill from some cowboy electrician, who I'd heard Florence and Edwin were all in favour of calling in."

Fred paused and looked through his whisky glass at the window.

"Anyway, I was in there working away where I admit I shouldn't have been; well, imagine my surprise when Florence came round. I was going to appear out of the darkness and confess my trespass and say something like 'old habits die hard', when I heard her on the phone, which was about the only thing left in the empty house. I heard her speaking to Edwin, the other churchwarden. I always remember those first words I heard her saying. She was sort of saying, 'You did say you would take me up on the suggestion to come round and have a look at what's going on at the vicarage, didn't you?'

"Of course, I could only hear one end of the conversation. She said things like, 'No, it's still convenient for me; Roy's away off to his parents in Aberdeen. I've nothing on this evening – a good evening to show you round. There's a lot going on.'"

Fred leant forward, and putting his head in his hands, chuckled with what Alistair began to think was mock embarrassment,

"Well, anyway, I'm not proud of it but the devil got into me, and instead of coming forward and saying hallo, I thought, this will be a laugh, and I hid myself in the fuse cupboard there."

Alistair sat spellbound by the vivid picture that Fred was painting.

"I didn't have to wait long. Sure enough, Edwin arrived and did his bit of appearing interested. So disingenuous, that guy – he can really annoy me. Well, Florence showed him round everywhere on the ground floor, mercifully not coming into my cupboard. I heard her say, 'That's the fuse cupboard. I'm not touching anything in there. We'll get that firm in for the electrics.' She was damned rude and said, 'We won't let Fred get his hands on it.' That really annoyed me, so I thought if they're going to slag me off like that, I'll blinking well eavesdrop on them! Then of course they went upstairs and she showed him the bedrooms. They were talking about how the lights had been dim and flickering, and so Florence was using torchlight only, but I heard her say she would put this one small lamp on in the bedroom. Of course, when they got on to that subject, I was scared stiff they'd come down and find me in the large fuse cupboard where I was hiding.

"I don't know why I did it. I'm sorry. It was just sheer mischief; as I say, I suppose the devil got into me, and just when Edwin and Florence were getting rather

271

shall we say pally, talking about their difficulties....."
Fred interrupted himself and went and got the whisky.

A part of Alistair wanted to cut in and rebuke Fred
for eavesdropping, but he determined to keep his self-
imposed vow of silence till this amusing and vivid story
was all told.

Back from the drinks cupboard and sitting
comfortably in his chair, Fred took what looked like
more of a large gulp than a wee dram before
continuing, "I suppose I didn't want the excitement to
end and, fool and terrible fellow that I am … Well, the
devil got into me. I switched off all the electricity at the
main switch."

Alistair could not refrain from gasping, "Fred!" in a
tone that could only be described as one of horror;
however he immediately recalled Gary's account of
how Fred had mischievously called in aid his services
to break down the allotment fence.

"I know, I really regret it, and I feel terrible about it
and on a serious level I've asked to be forgiven."

Alistair, who for a moment was slightly perplexed
by this last comment, had to remember that it was a
church congregation he was dealing with.

There was a pause that seemed so long that Alistair
felt compelled to ask, "Why are you telling me all this,
Fred?"

"Well, I was waiting for them to start coming
downstairs, and then I was going to make a bolt for it. I
listened carefully for the first sign of them coming
down the stairs. I was mighty perplexed because I
couldn't hear anything. Then I realised they weren't
coming downstairs. They were staying up there and
talking quietly in the dark. I strained to hear their
voices. At first I laughed to myself, thinking they
sounded like a couple of lovebirds. Then, I couldn't
believe it, but I'm sure of it, they started making love.

I'm sure of it!" Fred now beamed at Alistair with a look that also contained a sense of relief that he had got a big secret off his chest.

For a moment, the stunned Alistair seemed not to react.

"As I say, I couldn't believe it," Fred continued, "I mean, there was no furniture in there. All the upstairs rooms were completely empty."

"You mean they were on the floor?" asked Alistair incredulously.

Fred shrugged his shoulders. He took a further gulp of his whisky and said, "Well, there wasn't any furniture up there. I knew that because I'd had a quick deck round when I arrived before going into the fuse cupboard before Florence came."

"You surely can't be sure they, shall we say, went all the way, can you?" asked Alistair, recovering somewhat from his astonishment at this most unexpected and colourful information, and trying to help Fred by smiling in an amused way at him.

"Well, if they didn't, they deserve an Oscar, I'll tell you. Anyhow I scarpered as quietly and as quickly as I could. Oh yes, they were both in church the next Sunday, looking like butter wouldn't melt in their mouths."

"Well, I'm staggered! But I'm still not totally sure I understand why you're telling me all this," Alistair said plainly.

"Well, I never told the police when they were investigating the crime, because, as you will probably say yourself, it was totally irrelevant, and I suppose I was embarrassed at having hidden in there and eavesdropped; but when you said you were approaching things from an entirely different angle and all that kind of line, well, I thought I'll just tell everything, you know, and something may come to light. I mean, personally, I can't help feeling that if people can go off the rails one way, then perhaps they can go off the rails in another way too. But look, I don't for a moment think Edwin and Florence had anything to do with this crime – not for a moment. However, it was a crime of passion, and oh, I'm just trying to say things are never what they seem, are they?"

"Fred, can I be absolutely terrible," asked Alistair, "and ask you for a refill? It's damn good whisky."

"No worries, Alistair, there's plenty more where that came from. I was presented with a whole crate when I'd completed my time on the Deanery Synod. I hope I haven't made a fool of myself telling you about all this – it's just that when you were saying about looking at things from different angles and all that, I found myself thinking that I just couldn't exclude the remote possibility that it might be relevant."

"Well, thanks for taking me seriously, Fred. I expect it's probably totally irrelevant like 99 per cent of what I'm coming across; but that's the nature of the game of private detective work, I suppose." Alistair lowered his voice and asked, "I suppose you told Karen, your wife."

"You tell your wife everything, but I never told anyone else – not a soul. Sorely tempted to, once or twice, I can tell you, but I never did."

"And Karen would have kept it to herself, wouldn't she?"

"Oh yes, in forty years I've never known her break a confidence. She said she was mighty surprised, but I remember she said, 'Well, you know, sex appeal can be very strong,' which made me laugh. I mean, no offence to Florence, but she's hardly in the same league as Edwin's own wife, Helen. In a way I regret telling Karen; but you know, Alistair, I've heard you're a bit of a bachelor type, however, if you ever do eventually get married, you'll find you don't keep any secrets from your wife."

Fred, seemingly somewhat emboldened by the whisky, shot him an interested glance. "Do you think you might ever get married, Alistair?" he asked.

"Well, you've told me a secret and a half, so I'll tell you one. I've got a reputation for being a bit of a bachelor boy; I've allowed that image to develop, because I got a bit hurt in my early days, I suppose. Anyway, don't tell a soul, Fred, but I've got to admit to being a bit smitten by a girl I met on the plane flying over to Chicago recently. We met up a bit over there. She's still out there sorting her life out, as she put it, but I've got a funny feeling it might come to something."

"Good on you," replied a beaming Fred in friendly tone. He continued, "Apart from my wife Karen, nobody will ever hear a word of your secret from my lips, I promise you."

"Oh golly! I'm an old blabbermouth, aren't I? It's funny how when you feel like that, you want to tell people, isn't it?" said Alistair.

They changed the subject by mutual consent, and going out into the hall, stood for a while admiring another barometer. Soon they were shaking hands and saying their goodbyes.

CHAPTER 23

(Alistair goes to Edinburgh)

To say that Alistair returned to his hotel at lunchtime in a bit of a daze would be an understatement.

At first, he could think of nothing else but the extremely colourful and vivid tale that Fred had told him. It was a reminder to him that people are not always what they seem. He weighed Fred's emphasis on how if one commandment could be broken, perhaps another might be more readily broken; however, serious though adultery was, surely murder was in a field of its own ... Trust old Fred to give me something to think about. Maybe he just imagined it; could have just been all in his mind, he mused. The likelihood was that whether it was true or just a bad case of getting hold of the wrong end of the stick, it was probably utterly irrelevant to the case he was assigned to. For the moment he would put the story in abeyance and carry on undistracted by it.

Indeed, as the hours passed his thoughts returned more and more to the prospect of seeing his own city again on the morrow, and Fred's extraordinary tale seemed more and more like a bad dream. As sleep overcame him that night, he felt back to his calm self and was looking forward immensely to the return to his native city on the morrow.

Indeed, the next morning the alarm found him dreaming happily about the Pentland Hills, which he had climbed as a boy and knew like the back of his hand, but he was soon up, shaved and breakfasted. Then something happened which was more than he dared hope for. Every morning he had rung to check with his landlady, Mrs Davidson, in Edinburgh, if there was possibly a letter from America, and every day he had felt disappointed that there was nothing. Perhaps Zoe has lost my card with my address, he thought or perhaps she's deliberately not replying. Whatever's happened, I must look to the future, he mused; but then he heard the phone ringing, and within seconds Donna, having got up from the reception desk, collared him in the foyer, telling him that there was a phone call for him from Edinburgh.

"It's a lady, but I could have sworn she said her name was David,' said Donna, passing him the phone with her pleasant smile.

Excitedly, Alistair went to the desk and took the phone. He recognised immediately the unmistakeable tones of his excellent landlady in Edinburgh, the incomparable Mrs Davidson.

"Alistair, that letter you've been asking about, I think it's arrived. Looks like a lady's hand, I think. It's from Chicago. Do you want me to forward it to you today?"

"Oh no, Mrs Davidson," he replied, trying to sound calmer than he felt. "I was truly just going to give you a wee bell to tell you I'm actually coming up to Edinburgh today," he said, putting on a more matter-of-fact tone.

Despite the increased beat of his love-struck heart, he calmly gave Mrs Davidson his expected time of arrival, made some pleasant chatty observations and bade her farewell with a friendly "see you soon."

A few further quick preparations, and within half an hour he was waving goodbye to Donna and off with a spring in his step on what he told her was "a wee break", but to him was a busman's holiday; for the tracking down of this enigmatic figure with the weird name Buzz, from Henrietta's past, was his main objective.

The Piccadilly Line was its usual crowded self.

Gradually the people with luggage seemed to change from air travellers to train travellers. King's Cross lived up to its reputation as a melting pot of all the world, but curiously he loved it, seeing it as the gateway to his home. How familiar he was with the whole procedure, the wait for the platform number to be shown on the departure board, the confusion over reserved seats, the whistle, the mumbled incoherent and garbled announcements over the train's loudspeaker, usually to the effect that the buffet was now closed …

He could not resist the tradition started in boyhood of looking out for the cathedrals, first of Peterborough, then York and Durham, but during the bulk of the journey he had plenty of time to churn the recent interviews which he'd had with people over and over in his mind. Gradually he began to think clearly and even to jot down a few notes. Yesterday's interview with Fred was, of course, the most recent and lay vividly in his mind, but each interview had raised questions. The mystery and difficulty of his assignment seemed to increase rather than to diminish. The more he thought about it, even his old friend Dennis had not seemed at all himself. Both churchwardens had also seemingly added to the mystery by not really being able to help at all. The three allotment holders likewise had raised more questions than answers, and one could say much the same for the residents of Lime Grove in their three overlooking houses. What he had learnt from the stranger on the hill about this enigmatic character called Buzz just completed the whole extraordinary question, and of course came more and more into his mind as the great city of his boyhood and indeed life came, mile by mile, nearer and nearer.

This is one hell of a mystery, his thoughts continued, as he gazed across at the Bass Rock and then at Dunbar Church, as the train sped past. His thoughts broke off for a moment at the sight of that familiar landmark, and he contemplated how this teaching of Christianity had certainly conquered everywhere, and sure took some explaining. To all intents and purposes and in 99 per cent of ways, it stood for the same creed as St Peter's, Cookington. He strained his face against the train window as it disappeared from view. It struck him fleetingly what a great tribute to Christianity that sturdy old wind-battered tower was.

Yes, when this case was over, he must grapple with that even bigger mystery – the mystery of life. At the age of forty-six it was time to engage the brain about that. He still called himself an agnostic, but some of the remarks made to him by the parishioners whom he had investigated had made their mark, and he was aware that he was reflecting more and more deeply about these great matters. He was aware of a change in himself since his last time in Edinburgh. The mystery of the universe was occupying his thoughts more than before. Perhaps, not least because it would please his late father, he would pay a visit to St Cuthbert's in Princes Street, where as a boy he had suffered boredom beyond imagination during long Sunday sermons, while his father, dressed in tails, had performed the duties of an elder with a solemnity that contrasted so much with his roars of laughter across the table at home.

However, he had a crime to solve, and with an effort of will he made his thoughts return to the relatively more mundane mystery of St Peter's, Cookington, as his eyes rested on the hill of North Berwick Law moving into the distance.

It was his first return for some time and as he stood on the platform a friendly railway official chatted to him.

"Nice to be back in my home city. Who's doing best these days, Hibs or Hearts?" he asked amiably and jokingly.

This went down badly at first as it transpired this railway employee supported Livingston; however he soon clapped Alistair on the back and said, "Livingston's a great little place. Supported it ever since I met my wife there."

Yes, he thought, I'd support the Chicago Bears if Zoe did.

"No," said Alistair, declining the offer of a taxi. He would walk. He had been slightly shocked to discover how close his rooms, which he rented from Mrs Davidson and which he amusingly referred to when talking to his brother as "his other favourite wee hotel" in the New Town, were to this mysterious character Buzz, whom he must try and track down. It really would be a sensation if the murderer turned out to be a near neighbour of mine up here, he mused.

He walked across Princes Street, enjoying the sunshine that had come out to greet him. Edinburgh was looking at its best. The inevitable piper, welcoming the tourists much the same as when Alistair had left on his journey south a few weeks earlier, was playing 'Loch Lomond', and from this distance the music was perfect. It made Alistair imagine Zoe standing on the shore of that beautiful loch, and a tear came to his eye. Yes, he was in love with this girl Zoe, whom he had only just got to know. This was the first time he had been back to his native city since meeting her, came the next inevitable thought. Zoe was the only girl for him, but it did not stop him welcoming the smile which an Edinburgh lass gave him when she inadvertently bumped into him.

It did not take him long to cross St Andrew Square, where an American tourist asked him whose statue it was on the top of the column. He felt a certain satisfaction and pride in knowing the answer, due to his fascination with local history. He knew that even many an Edinburgh man was not too sure, but he was on his own patch and this was not the first time that a lifetime of interest in local history had come in useful to an enquiring tourist. Now he was going down Dublin Street admiring the view of Fife across the Firth of Forth. This is what they don't have down there in Cookington, he contemplated: no hills, no views of hills across the Firth. That's their problem.

It did not take him long to reach his rooms.

"Nice to be back in the wee hotel," he greeted Mrs Davidson as she came out of the ground floor flat to welcome him.

"Before I do anything else, I'll give you your letter, Alistair," she said, handing it to him and adding coquettishly, "you know, putting two and two together, I'm just hoping it's what I want it to be."

"Enough of your romantic aspirations for me," he said out of habit as he placed the letter carefully in his inside pocket, almost beside himself with anticipation.

He picked up his holdall and said, "I'll meet up for a good chat with you and give you all the goss before I return south, Marjorie; right now I'll just settle back in, and maybe go out for one of my wee evening strolls in an hour or so."

He was conscious of falling back into the old Edinburgh jargon, more infectious even than American.

It did not take him long to settle in, and shortly he was indeed indulging in just such a pleasant evening's stroll, having decided to stick to his original plan of visiting this former boyfriend of Henrietta's, nicknamed Buzz, tomorrow.

In his pocket was the letter; somehow he had summoned the self-control to wait until his conversations with Mrs Davidson were over and he had washed and unpacked, and had decided that he would open it for reasons only he understood while sitting on a particular favourite bench in Princess Street Gardens. He sat down, sharing the bench with a lone lady and her dog. He pulled the letter out from his inside pocket and took one last look at the smart unopened envelope with its flashy American stamp. Opening it neatly, his first reaction was how short it was. He read avidly.

How nice to meet you on the plane and get to know you in Chicago. Enjoyed myself immensely in Washington and am now back in the windy city. Hard at work trying to sort out a complicated situation. Will be returning to UK in not more than a month's time and will give you a tinkle at the number on your card on arrival. Till then, Zoe.

This short message was followed by an *X*.

It would be hard to describe how elated Alistair felt. Having reread it several times and stared repeatedly at the *X*, he returned the letter to his inside pocket - near his heart, as he thought to himself. He had dreaded that she might write to terminate their short, barely begun relationship.

It was hard for Alistair to be polite to the dear old lady sitting on the bench, who obviously wanted to chat. Funny how whenever you want time to think someone talks, thought Alistair. He could have moved, but somehow he just wanted to wait here and savour the moment. The stranger was not to be silenced. She asked him many questions, to which he courteously replied, and as he warmed to this typical Edinburgh lady of the good old days, he found himself enjoying her endless chat. He decided to enter into the spirit of her convivial conversation and questions. Which city did he like best after Edinburgh? That had to be Chicago. What was his favourite girl's name? That had

282

to be Zoe.

As the conversation continued, Alistair, no doubt appearing rather distracted to his chance companion, realised more than ever that he'd been encouraged by the letter, and really was in love with Zoe. Eventually the good old lady left, wishing him good luck with a friendly wave. How true that saying about passing like ships in the night is, he thought, as he watched her shuffle away, throwing some breadcrumbs to a grateful pigeon. Had she ever felt like him in distant days? he wondered. Alistair was left alone with his thoughts, now increasingly taken up with recollections of his flight to Chicago, the few precious days spent sightseeing with Zoe in that noble city, and the heartrending farewell he had made at the airport.

How amazed Zoe was going to be when he told her how he not only knew her brother's former lover, the tragic Henrietta; but as if that was not enough of a bombshell, how in the absence of any police progress, he had been assigned this investigation by her poor widowed husband …

Despite the excitement of everything in his life, he slept well that night and, pleased to be on the job, set off early the next morning for the address of the intriguing Buzz.

When he did arrive at the house, which was only a few streets away, he noticed, as in his childhood, the old lamplighter marks on the outside walls by the big front door. He knew that these were made in olden days by people striking the lights for the gas flames, but on entering it was the big hallway with its high ceiling that struck him most, so contrasting as it was with Cookington. He was familiar with such places, having lived in Edinburgh all his life, but never ceased to admire them. He noticed the three little piles of mail for each of the three flats laid out on the bench of the entrance hall. He had become unused to these Edinburgh stairs but found himself counting them and remembering the old trick of walking diagonally to help make them seem less arduous. Did it work? He was never quite sure, though his father had assured him it was so. He was just passing the middle flat when a man's voice, which he assumed to be that of Buzz, shouted down from the top flat above.

"Welcome!" came that loud booming voice, in what Alistair felt was indeed a warm and welcoming manner.

"I'd forgotten about the stairs," puffed Alistair, waving his hat.

"Now what would you like at this time of morning?" offered Buzz, even before Alistair had reached the final step.

Buzz was not as Alistair had envisaged him. He was so much more serious, though he was undeniably friendly and pleasant.

"You know I never have it at this time of morning, but just one wee dram of that," said Alistair, having shaken hands and pointing through the hall door at the whisky bottle on the tray, where coffee and tea appeared also to be options. It crossed his mind that if he had imbibed a dram of whisky given by Fred Goodman, who was the epitome of an Englishman, then surely he could accept one here in the heart of the New Town.

They were soon ensconced in the comfortable and large living room, looking out at the tops of the tall trees of this fine New Town Square. He could see the London plane flying in to the airport at Turnhouse, and for a moment it made him think of the Concord Hotel, imagining Cissie engaged in her perpetual clear up between the dining room and the kitchen, and the slightly smarter Donna, sitting pertly at the reception desk. For a moment he was struck by the paradox of being homesick in his home city, but then began to repeat his by now rather well-rehearsed explanation of why he was there.

Opposite him, his new acquaintance, the mysterious gentleman who went by the curious name of Buzz, followed his every word and nodded with an understanding and helpful demeanour.

"I have to admit to being a bit surprised when you rang, but of course I know the crime is still unsolved," said Buzz with a final nod, when Alistair finished.

"Anyway, I thought I'd start by trying to dig out some really ancient photos I've kept all these years," he said brightly, as he got up from the chair and moved backwards towards the door.

"I haven't had them out since the year dot, but I've got some OK – they certainly seem distant days. I've always kept them buried deep in a cupboard out there," he added, disappearing out of the room.

"I find digging up the past rather painful," he continued from the depths of the outside cupboard.

Left alone for a moment, Alistair sensed for the first time a slight melancholy enter into the atmosphere. It did not last long, but it was enough to make Alistair's imagination run riot. He had time to dream a bit while he continued to hear Buzz rummaging around outside in the cupboard.

In his mind's eye, he could see his host catching a train in a fleeting moment of unbalanced passion and committing the crime and, as it were, getting the next train back.

He was roused from such farfetched daydreams by Buzz shouting out again through the doorway, "I've found it!" followed by "Oh my Gawd – look how awful my hairstyle was in those days – enough to put any sensible girl off me for a lifetime!"

He came in with a bundle of old photographs and sat

alongside Alistair on the sofa. "This is back in nineteen something something," he said confidently. "There aren't many, but though I say it myself, they're quite good. Look at this one."

He passed the already faded photographs to Alistair one at a time, saying a few words as his guest scrutinised each one.

Alistair held one up and said cheerfully, "That's you and Henrietta, is it? She looked quite dishy in those days; I shouldn't say that, but you know what I mean; you say you've got over it all many years ago."

Alistair felt guilty and expressed the hope again that he had not offended by his choice of words.

"Oh no, of course not, but I can't help feeling wistful about it all. I know it's stupid, but you can't help these feelings, can you?" He looked up and seemed to be waiting for an affirmative response from Alistair.

"Everyone has to accept the way things turn out, you know," Alistair offered helpfully, wondering how on earth he himself would cope, should Zoe reject him.

"It was all so complicated and tangled, what happened between us," Buzz began, with what seemed like an effort of will; and then, as if finding something impossible to explain, he turned to Alistair and said rather sharply, "Anyway, I didn't go down to London and murder her, if that's a theory."

Alistair tried rather unsuccessfully to laugh and answered, "I'm not suggesting that for a moment, but I did wonder if you knew anything, however small," he stressed, "which might help me get to the bottom of the mystery. Frankly, it is one hell of a puzzle at the moment."

"I would really, really love to help, but I really don't think I do know anything helpful. I'm sure I don't. I was staggered when I heard the news of her murder –

286

absolutely staggered. In some ways I found it curiously cathartic. You know, death is so final. It really was the kind of finale."

There was a silence, during which Alistair again gazed out of the window at the tops of the trees in the square's garden, conscious more than ever of how Buzz had been so deeply affected by this distant relationship, of which it would seem only these few rather faded photographs remained.

He heard Buzz's earnest voice restart the conversation. "Of course, I'd made a decision not to make contact or be involved in any way, but her death kind of removed even the remotest possibility, and curiously I found that quite helpful."

"But before her murder, you didn't think about it all as life went by, did you?"

"Yes, every day," said Buzz, "or it seemed like every day. I mean, I've been a bachelor all my life, and I suppose you wonder how life might have been very different."

Alistair switched his gaze from the treetops to the inside of his whisky glass. Just for a moment he wondered again whether this ancient affair had just become too much for Buzz, and again it entered his mind that perhaps he had just tracked Henrietta down, literally got a train and murdered her, and as his mind repeated, as it were got the next train back. He checked his thinking. No, that's the second time I've had that crazy thought; but surely if that were the case, Buzz wouldn't go on about it, but just say it was all in the past?

To Alistair's astonishment he found himself within a very short space of time accepting a second glass of whisky from Buzz. Maybe it was the whisky which made him put it to Buzz straight, "You know, I don't for a moment think you've got the remotest thing to do

287

with Henrietta's death; but would you agree with me that a theory could be made that it all got too much for you - this wistfulness, as you call it - and you just kind of flipped? I mean, in theory that could happen to someone, couldn't it?"

Buzz didn't say anything but just sat looking intently at the empty fireplace.

"I mean," went on Alistair, "you were terribly affected by what you call a fleeting romance, weren't you?"

Alistair, who was now studying the design of the carpet suddenly became aware to his astonishment that there were tears in Buzz's eyes, and in a moment the man was sobbing.

"I'm sorry, I'm so sorry, really I am," said Alistair quickly and sincerely. "You know, Buzz, I really don't think this for a moment. I'm literally just trying to eliminate that wild theory that someone might ignorantly suggest."

Buzz recovered himself quite quickly and Alistair deliberately changed the subject, and before long they had moved on to football and old matches from way back, which they might have quite possibly both watched, unaware that life would lead them to bump into each other in later years. Ships in the night can pass twice, mused Alistair.

Buzz, who seemed rather taken by such a possibility, left the room to search for an old football programme, saying, "This should be easier to find. I look at my old programmes a bit more often than photographs! I find that following the football makes me happy."

Alistair sat back and dreamily cast his eyes across the now empty room and over the nearby bookcase. The book which caught his eye almost at once was an old Latin primer, which he recognised from his own schooldays. How could he not? Had he not struggled many a lesson and many a homework session over that very same school book, whose cover he had been more familiar with than his own hand. Enthusiastically he got up and reached for it, pulling it out with a look of excited recognition. Immediately, an old open-ended return train ticket to London fell out and plopped on the floor. Alistair picked it up and was about to return it to the book when he noticed that it was dated just before the date of the murder.

In one of his rare split-second decisions, he slipped it into the top pocket of his jacket and replaced the book. He returned to his chair and pretended to be avidly studying Buzz's latest magazine, when, after what seemed like a long time, Buzz came back in carrying the old programme.

"Here it is," he said avidly.

Alistair had made a very quick decision not to mention either the old school primer or more importantly the old train ticket. He managed to hide the slight feeling of fluster which this discovery had caused, and kept up a normal conversation until it was time to go. He would allow himself time to think this extraordinary find through and consider what to do.

He therefore quite hastily arranged with Buzz to meet up for a second and final time on the morrow and took his leave.

As he descended the long flight of stairs of the typical Edinburgh tenement building, he was already glad to have some privacy to mull over this extraordinary find of the railway ticket.

He made a deliberate decision to give his mind a rest and spent a pleasant afternoon in the Botanic Gardens, admiring the beauty of nature. More than ever the sheer beauty of these plants began to make his thoughts contemplate the possibility of a creator. Yes, life was the even bigger mystery that he must turn his mind to as soon as he was finished with this case. His life called out for an explanation just as much as this death of the poor vicar of St Peter's, Cookington.

He managed to continue to keep his thoughts uncrowded during his early evening meal, but during his postprandial stroll he began to go over and over everything that they had said to each other in the morning's conversation.

There was no doubt about it: Buzz was a suspect alright. He had obviously been very much in love with Henrietta, if not infatuated, and by his own admission thought of her every day. On top of this, he had made a trip to London at the time of the crime, which he had chosen to keep quiet about, and which Alistair would have been completely ignorant of, if the ticket had not fallen out of that old Latin primer. Why did Buzz keep the ticket anyway? he wondered, 'and why did he put it in that Latin primer, which would have been a perfect hiding place, unless some nostalgic old codger like himself, who happened to be so familiar with it, had not pulled it out to give it a look over for old times' sake?

Alistair's evening stroll was twice as long as usual as he pondered these bald questions. Round and round he perambulated in the New Town square that he had access to.

Theories raced through his mind, but he had disciplined himself to be patient and sleep on such questions, and he sensibly decided to wait to see what tomorrow's chat brought to light. It would be interesting, to say the least, for Buzz would have to offer some explanation both for the journey and the withholding of the information.

The morrow dawned and found Alistair gazing affectionately down from his own top floor window at the well-known street below. Yes, he thought, this is my city. I'm looking forward to getting back to live here when this little attempt to solve this friend's tragic mystery is completed. Then again, he thought, looking wildly into the future, if Zoe wanted to live in Cookington – that would be OK with me.

Once again Mrs Davidson's fine Scottish breakfast was completed, and Alistair was on his way back to Buzz's imposing residence.

I'm getting back to being used to the stairs already, he thought as he made his way up, finding them easier than yesterday. Buzz was once again standing at the top landing, waiting for him, and once again, with a friendly gesture towards the living room door, he was ushered in.

He sat down on the same chair as yesterday without waiting. Buzz gave an impression of impending conviviality, which did not quite agree with Alistair's now more businesslike approach.

"Look, Buzz, I'm sorry about this, but I am here investigating a crime and I've got to get on and get it over with, so come on, I'm going to ask you straight. Why did you tell me you hadn't been to London for ages when you had?

It was almost as if Buzz had been expecting such an enquiry. In a quite unrattled way, he said, "I just thought it would save an awful lot of hassle. It was just for a sporting event – a football match. OK, I made a mistake, I should have told you. God knows how you found out about it. I should have known you people have ways of finding things out. I should have told you; I'm not saying my judgement's perfect, but you see I'm fed up with all this. I just wanted to be shot of the whole matter."

"I mean, Buzz, I've got to say this to you, and I'll preface myself by stressing I'm personally as sure as a man can be that you are innocent of this crime, but it is kind of incriminating to say you've never been somewhere and then have to admit it when a train ticket is found – especially when that train ticket is to the city where the crime occurred. You'd agree that, wouldn't you?" asked Alistair in conclusion, thinking, to be fair, he doesn't appear in any way flustered or disconcerted by my springing this on him.

"Alistair, it was a one-off, and I just wanted to save all the palaver. I'm really fed up with the whole damn case. I'm sorry, I can see what you're saying is right and I've learnt a lesson." He paused and ran his hand through his hair in a gesture of frustration.

"You see, now it's going to have to be investigated more thoroughly than ever, simply because you kept quiet about it. Oh, Buzz, I hate being in what must appear such an unfriendly role, but you know the system must take its course."

"Out of interest, how did you know I went?" Buzz enquired with genuine curiosity, adding, "are you going to tell me?"

"I don't know what the police would say or what a professional private detective would say, but I'm going about this my way and I'm telling you - you left the ticket in that Latin primer," replied Alistair, nodding towards the said book, "and it just happens to be a primer I wrestled with too in my schooldays up here in Edinburgh, so I just grabbed it out of sheer nostalgia when you went out of the room to look for that football programme yesterday – and the blinking ticket fell out."

"I wasn't hiding it," pleaded Buzz earnestly. "I looked something up the other day for the crossword – a Latin phrase - and honestly used the ticket as a bookmark. Look, I'll show you my diary, and you can read for yourself what that trip to London was all about."

Buzz produced as if from nowhere a diary and started opening it for Alistair to read.

Without looking at it, Alistair said, "You see, Buzz, the police would say, 'How do we know you didn't write that carefully to deceive?'"

"Surely I wouldn't have put all this in my diary if I had anything to hide!" said Alistair defensively.

"Not necessarily," came Alistair's riposte. "You might have had that ready in case some proof that you had been was discovered."

"Well anyway, I went to see a match."

"Can you prove that? Is it something you do a lot? Do you have a match ticket, or is there anyone who can support your story?"

"I keep match tickets and I can produce it if you must," said Buzz wearily.

"You're short on alibis, Buzz. Look, as I say, the police would probably go about all this in an entirely different way. They probably wouldn't tell you what they found and try and trip you up and all that business. Well, I'm different. I'm not even a private detective. The whole point about Dennis assigning me to a private investigation, before hiring an established private detective agency, is to approach it all very differently to them. Now, I'm trying to be honest with you, because I'm investigating for a friend, who has asked me privately to help for his own sake of coming to terms with what's happened. I don't want to have suspicions of people; I want to eliminate them from suspicion. Buzz, for goodness sake tell me something that can show how you're beyond any reasonable doubt innocent of having gone south, flipped and committed a crime and got the train home. I mean, it was at the time of the crime. Where did you stay, for heaven's sake?"

"You see, that's the problem. I didn't tell you

because I didn't want all this palaver. I can't prove the truth of what I'm saying. I didn't stay with anyone. I went down for the match. I had a good walkabout, and to use your words, as you say, got the train home."

"You didn't stay anywhere?" asked Alistair in a dumbfounded tone.

"No, I slept on the train and saved myself quite a few bucks, old chap," replied Buzz with a flourish, before continuing. "You're a bachelor, you should understand. Sometimes it's just easier to do that, there's no one to inconvenience. Now come on, I know you like a wee dram."

Alistair was in a dilemma, on the one hand wanting to keep up the momentum of his new-found businesslike approach, but on the other wanting to glean more about Buzz's movements by having a more light-hearted chat.

Buzz proceeded to give details of the football match, which he had travelled down to London to watch, and indeed volunteered details of his exact movements. He assured Alistair that he had not visited the suburb of Cookington.

Alistair noted that a receipt for a snack which he produced was however located only a few miles from Cookington.

A whole host of questions came into Alistair's mind, why did he keep the receipt? Again, was it to use as a kind of alibi?

"Yes, I've got the programme tucked away in my little glory hole. I'll get it for you," said Buzz convivially as he left the room.

Alistair sat back, aware that there were a whole myriad of questions needing an answer, and he knew he was not going to be able to answer all these questions immediately.

He decided to take the softly-softly approach, and

discussed the match for all the world like a sports correspondent.

He did however throw in the question, "Were there any other sudden unexpected trips to London for any reason, sporting or otherwise?"

"No, not in recent time," replied Buzz in a matter-of-fact tone.

"Presumably you don't always deny yourself the basic comfort of a roof over your head when you visit the capital?" Alistair said, aware that it sounded a little sarcastic.

"Well, I've stayed with friends in my time; but no, my previous visit would have been at least a year before that particular match," answered Buzz, maintaining his matter-of-fact tone.

"I'll probably think of a whole raft of questions when I get south, so I expect I'll be in touch. Please be honest with me, Buzz. I want to help you, and I can if you're honest with me."

They parted amicably at the top of the stairs, with Alistair admiring a tall plant on the landing before descending the long stone staircase. He touched his hat to a gentleman entering the middle flat, who was carrying his post in his hand, and continued down to the large hall by the ground floor entrance. As he did yesterday, he glanced at the post remaining for the other floors set out neatly on a chest. He was startled to see that in one of the piles, sitting on a little heap of circulars and leaflets, there a letter addressed to Buzz with the clear postmark of Cookington staring him in the face as clear as daylight. On an impulse he grabbed it and slid it under his coat. He calmed his conscience by thinking that he was after all here on an investigation, not a holiday, and he would get this letter back to Buzz by some devious means or other, so it would only be delayed by a day or so.

When he got back to his digs he was glad to find that Mrs Davidson was not on the lookout for him and hurriedly climbed the stairs to the sanctuary of his top floor.

He sat down on his favourite armchair, and without further delay apart from a quick scrutiny of the Cookington postmark, excitedly but skilfully opened the letter.

It was somehow shorter than he was expecting in that he was surprised to find it was only one sheet of paper.

Avidly he read the scrawled words :

Hi Buzz,
How's things?
Sorry to give you a blast from the past, but have been meaning to drop you a line for some time now – just to tell you, met a total stranger recently and fell talking to him in the pub – the dear old Antelope at the top of the hill. Remember? People still discussing the crime and we fell talking – didn't say anything terrible or anything I shouldn't, but I found out the other day from the usual tittle-tattle people that he's a bloody private detective.

Thought I'd better let you know that the fellow's on the job – seems pretty amateurish, to say the least. Don't think I said anything I shouldn't have; but it makes you realise why you should keep your mouth shut, doesn't it? Sorry.

I assure you I never, never mentioned your staying with me when you came down to that match. I agree with you it would be unnecessarily complicated trying to prove what an innocent coincidence it was – better just not to mention it, like we agreed we wouldn't with the police. It'll save the poor fellow a lot of time anyway, won't it?

I'll get up to Edinburgh one day and hope you can come down again some time – and this time there won't be a crime that makes you have to keep it secret!!!

Cheers for now,
Yr v old mate,
Eric

Alistair sealed the envelope as skilfully as he could and popped out to the letter box at the corner of the street, where he dropped it in.

On return he allowed himself a dram of the finest whisky in his collection. What an extraordinary coincidence, he thought to himself. But didn't I always think that Eric chappie on the hill seemed remarkably well informed about this and that?

After five minutes staring at his fireplace, Alistair said almost out loud to himself, Of course it could be a bluff – maybe he even knew I was coming to Edinburgh.

He walked over to his window.

"Very interesting anyway," he said to himself, "but I won't delay my return to Cookington; not least because this development needs a lot of thinking through."

When Alistair said goodbye to his landlady, Mrs Davidson, the next morning he was at pains to emphasise to her the importance of both giving his London number to any caller by the name of Zoe, and also to be so kind as to let him know if there had been such a call.

"I will, Mr MacTavish," said that stalwart lady earnestly, "but I just wish that one day such a request might concern your personal affairs and not business."

Alistair chuckled to himself. If she only knew, he thought, and with a parting wave of his hat said, "just wait and see – time will tell!"

Now that's unlike him; what did he mean by that?

wondered Mrs Davidson all morning, as she busied herself cleaning the hall in an effort to miss his company less. Perhaps, she thought, he just possibly might get married one day – it's not impossible. She gave the brasses an extra rub, lost in thought. I would definitely get an invitation, I'm sure of it, she mused, flicking her duster for the last time at an unlucky spider that had so nearly escaped her weekly clean.

CHAPTER 24

(An interview with the chairman of the Finance and Fabric Committee)

In some ways Alistair was glad to be back in Cookington, as he had found the Edinburgh visit with its unexpected twist to have been more demanding than he had expected. The whole journey south had found him preoccupied with the thought that Buzz had certainly been in love with the victim, and also with the incriminating matter of Buzz's suspicious trip to London, which he had earlier failed to mention. Somehow, he managed to put all these matters in abeyance and get back into Cookington mode.

Cissie told him that Fred Goodman had phoned that morning with some message about clay pipes, but interesting though that sounded, it too could wait while he kept his prearranged appointment with the chairman of the Finance and Fabric Committee.

He had been told that David Davies was a busy businessman by more than one person, and as he strolled along in the morning sunshine he thought, good for him to find time to help the church in this way.

David answered the smart door of the grand-looking house and ushered him in to an opulent drawing room at the back. The carpet was so clean he hardly dared put his foot on it.

This is the most spacious house of the parish I've been in so far, apart from the vicarage, he thought, laughing to himself as he took his seat on the ample sofa.

Kate, David's wife, came in with the coffee chatting amicably, and placing the tray carefully down on what seemed to Alistair to be a rather interesting and valuable old table.

"David regards it as a hobby, all this church accounts business – Finance and Fabric Committee, or whatever it is," initiated Kate with a slight giggle. David looked a bit nonplussed by his wife's friendly teasing, "But you do, don't you, David?" she said, giggling again.

David took a deep breath and started. "I have been known to go to church, if that's what you're getting at … "

She interrupted him. "He goes to special services, like Christmas Eve - "

It was his turn to interrupt her, "And others, Kate, be fair, but I admit I'm not the most regular of attendees. However, I do this to try and help. I suppose a psychiatrist might say I do it to compensate for not going to church, but to be honest it makes Kate happy, and she in turn lets me off most Sundays. I love accounts, though, and the parish accounts are so totally different to work. It's fun."

"A busman's holiday?" suggested Alistair, interrupting with one of his friendly smiles.

"Well, hardly. As I say, it's so different to the sort of accounting I do at work," said David firmly.

Alistair asked about his work but this seemed to make David clam up a bit, he thought; so he changed gear to get his inquiry going.

"Tell me, how do people feel about giving money to the church, I mean generally?" he asked, stretching his legs and making himself more comfortable. The room seemed to demand that one made oneself comfortable.

"Oh, you get to hear a few grouses about the church always asking for money, and all that line of talk. Sometimes I feel quite sympathetic towards remarks like that, and I know you do too, Kate; but at the end of the day we always say you can't run a church on good cheer."

"Who's we?" asked Alistair.

"Oh, the Finance and Fabric Committee. I'm the chairman. Our remit covers among other things the planned giving scheme and all that. Donations generally."

"It's voluntary, of course, I assume," offered Alistair.

"Yes, but I must admit we have these fairly regular campaigns, and I know some people feel it's a bit coercive. I've definitely picked that up from some sources."

Again he looked to his wife for support. "You have too, haven't you, Kate?"

Kate looked serious and commented, "What worries me is the way some people feel they have to give for the wrong reasons, you know, not from the goodness of their heart, but because it's a black mark if they don't – that sort of wrong thinking."

"But no one's going to murder the vicar over that, are they?" laughed Alistair, before turning to her husband and continuing, "but nonetheless, David, I'll ask this to get it out of the way. When you heard this news, did you ever link it with anything you had come across in the church, for example the finances, or as I say, anything else to do with running the church?"

"No, I really didn't. I mean, I had a good laugh because I'd received this note from churchwarden Edwin, saying if there was one more reference to the church being hard up he would personally strangle the vicar! We had a really good laugh about that. He and Helen are really good friends of ours; I actually phoned him after the crime and quoted his note and said you're number one suspect."

"I didn't approve of you doing that," put in Kate reprovingly.

"And he had a good laugh too, I presume," suggested Alistair, ignoring Kate's disapproval .

David stared down at the floor and responded, "No, to be honest, I hadn't realised, but I think he was still in shock. I remember he said, 'Doesn't that just show you how careful you have to be before you say anything?'"

There was a pause while Alistair for some reason seemed to be writing rather a lot in his notebook.

David continued, "No, actually, to get back to your question, people are extremely generous. Very much so; I mean, here are the figures."

He groped for a document below the coffee table, which he eventually found and handed over.

"That's a list of parishioners' names with their committed amounts," he said. sounding every bit like the chairman of the Finance and Fabric Committee that he was.

Alistair took the document and, raising an eyebrow as he made a cursory glance at it, asked, "Did you immediately think this terrible crime must be completely unrelated to the parish and its parishioners? I mean, when it first happened, did you think it's got to be related to something outside the parish?"

There was a pause while David seemed to be thinking.

Alistair clarified, "I'm interested in people's immediate reactions to the tragedy. Dennis wants me to take a very different approach to the police and kind of delve into peoples thoughts, even their innermost thoughts, about it all."

Again there was a pause, but as Alistair felt he had made himself clear enough, he would wait and let David speak first.

As it happened, David and Kate both started to speak, saying the same thing at once, though David prevailed.

"At first I thought it must be a maniac on the loose; though Kate and I have struggled with the question of why the hell it should be a broken-down, dilapidated old shed on the allotments, and one that belonged to our dear old friends Edwin and Helen. They of course were even more surprised than us."

"Surprised would be an understatement," put in Kate, "they were utterly dumbfounded, bamboozled. I spoke to Helen the day after she found the victim. I deliberately didn't contact her on the actual day when it was all breaking on television etc., but even the day after she was just completely shocked – absolutely utterly shocked. She later told me that she and Edwin both had to take sleeping pills for a long time after that. I mean, I noticed it myself; they really weren't able to converse normally for a long time," she stressed, adding, "Edwin is normally so chatty and bubbly, but it was like he was struck dumb."

"A crime like that, if it's not done by a maniac, is usually the result of some terrible family situation or dark secret," suggested David, going off on a different tack and adding, " but I mean, Dennis is such a normal sort of regular guy … "

"I like your phrase 'dark secret'," cut in Alistair. He continued, "It's going to have to be a dark one for the police to have missed it, after their amazingly thorough investigations. They drew a blank in this direction and, as I keep saying, Dennis has asked me to take a different tack, which is what I would think of doing anyway, and asked me to try and unearth any 'dark secret', to use your words. Yes, he didn't actually use those words; I think he said something like 'any motive completely unknown to anyone else apart from the murderer and certainly unknown to the police at the moment'. He was kind enough to imply that if anyone could unearth that it would be me, but I'm not sure I'm going to be able to, and I'm not even sure that we aren't just dealing with a complete maniac alone on the prowl."

Alistair paused as David sat with his head in his hands, and was surprised to find that he actually seemed to be sobbing.

"Yes, I'm sorry," said Alistair, hastily and sympathetically, "I've got used to thinking of it all as an abstract problem to be solved, an academic exercise, and I realise to you, who saw Henrietta so frequently, it must be just so devastatingly upsetting still."

"I often get upset like that too," said Kate, patting her husband, who was still sobbing, on the shoulder, "but somehow I do find my faith helps a lot. Actually, the crime put David off going to church more than ever just now – I mean, since this has happened - and I can understand that."

"I think what upsets me so much," said David in slightly more composed voice, "is that she tried a few times to get me to go more often, and to be honest I kind of palmed her off with a few false promises."

"She'd understand, darling," comforted Kate, almost stroking his arm. "She *did* understand, she told me. She said we're all different; I remember she said, 'Look at Helen,' who had rather abruptly stopped coming when Henrietta arrived, having suddenly found her Presbyterian roots again."

Alistair found himself entranced by Kate's kindness and gentleness. He tried to imagine his hoped for future, and was sure that Zoe would be an equally helpful wife in such circumstances.

"I suppose all murders are unpleasant, but this was a particularly unpleasant one, wasn't it?" he suggested after a while, when he felt that David was beginning to recover himself, but still appeared a little embarrassed. It seemed to him that his remark must have sounded a bit inane, but Kate nodded her head in agreement.

"As I say, I just wish I'd responded a little more in the way she had hoped for," reiterated David, now seemingly fully recovered and getting up out of his seat and going over to collect a file from a shelf.

"I wish I'd gone more when she suggested it, but there doesn't seem much point in trying to please her now that she's not there. Yes, I know, I know, I know, you don't go to church to please the vicar; but I wish I'd tried to please her more by going. I got to know her so well at all those finance and fabric team meetings which we had."

Alistair noticed the file, which he retrieved, had written in big red letters on it. 'LETTERS RECEIVED RELATING TO PLANNED GIVING STEWARDSHIP CAMPAIGN'.

David apologised for his somewhat unexpected moment of grief and said in a sprightly tone, "When it first happened, rather stupidly Kate and I had a second look at one or two of the more heated responses received from parishioners during our stewardship campaign. I'm afraid we did it as rather a sick joke, but you know – it was a classic whodunit! It seems stupid now, but this one," he paused checking it through, "which asked, 'Can't we get rid of her?' seemed a bit over the top, or shall we say unchristian," he added, even managing a smile and handing over a letter.

Alistair started to read it and his countenance began to show some astonishment.

"Wait till you get to the last sentence," said David watching him intently.

Alistair read on :

Dear David,
I shall not be responding to this latest appeal from the vicar for increased giving to the church. I think it

utterly ridiculous that a pensioner in my position should be begged to in this way in order to pay for the upkeep of a vicarage, which is much bigger than any house I could possibly hope to live in. She has no mortgage like the younger generation and no utilities to pay. It makes my blood boil.

And another thing, I don't accept this theme that the so-called "leafy suburbs" should support the inner city churches, where I know from my own experience there are churchgoers with bigger incomes than myself.

I found particularly offensive the remark in the vicar's sermon, when she launched the campaign, that we should support Our Lord with the wallet as well as the heart. That was the final straw, after so many irritating innovations, changes and gimmicks. The sooner this lady is got rid of the better.

Yours, a disgruntled member of what used to be a pleasant church.

"Phew!" was all Alistair could summon on concluding his read.

"Phew indeed, eh? That final phrase - 'got rid of' - intrigues me," remarked David, before continuing, "I mean, even if he or she had put 'the sooner that lady goes' it would be a bit softer, wouldn't it? Kate and I have anguished over this for ages. Why would you put something like that? Imagine someone sitting down and writing that. We haven't a clue who wrote it."

"Really? Not a clue?" queried Alistair, adding, "I would have thought you must have your hunches."

"No, honestly, we don't," they replied almost in unison.

"If you had to guess somebody," pressed Alistair.

"Well, I think it must have been a visitor to the church that day – someone who got rattled by that remark about the wallet. There were some unfamiliar visitors that day, I've always remembered."

"You can't remember what they looked like, can you?" Alistair asked, looking up sharply.

"They're just a vague blur, but I do remember there were some," said Kate quietly. "Henrietta asked Edwin to invite one to coffee in the hall after the service. I remember Edwin told me he thought the lady was rather rude, as she had said to him that she had come to church to worship God, but not to drink coffee, and then made some sarcastic comment that she was surprised we could afford it! Mark you, I think in a way Edwin sympathised with where she was coming from. Edwin must be the only churchwarden in the country who doesn't do planned giving. We're not meant to know that, but David gets to know things like that."

Alistair seemed to be in rather deep thought for at least a minute after that. Then pointing his pen at Kate he said, "I'd like to ask more about visitors later – you know, another time when I've had a moment to think and do a bit of research."

"There is the famous visitors' book," commented David helpfully. "Edwin had the bright idea that we ought to have one."

"He got the idea from a church in Scotland, which he goes to when he's up there visiting Helen's mother. They send a Christmas card to their visitors. I think that's rather nice, isn't it," said Kate sweetly, adding, "I think St Peter's should do that. I mean, it's good if churches pick up good ideas from each other."

"Were the police very interested in the visitors' book?" asked Alistair rather unexpectedly, as if his thoughts were still on the previous part of the conversation.

"Oh, they certainly took a deck at it, but I suppose it didn't lead to anything."

"Funny, that; I should think it could just possibly be

the sort of thing that could contain a lead," answered Alistair, adding, to the amusement of his hosts, "is that the word detectives use?"

After inveigling David and Kate into a little more parish gossip, which confirmed him in his opinion that David was a man with a very detached view of it all, Alistair took his leave, raising his trilby hat and waving from the front garden gate.

Yes, he thought as he strolled down to the station, I'll need to study that visitor's book with the utmost care.

When the bus arrived, he got on and was so deep in thought that he almost said out loud, "*with the utmost care.*"

CHAPTER 25

(A meeting with an old soldier in the park)

In some ways Alistair was irritated by his lack of progress, but it had been an enjoyable day and he thought not entirely unproductive regarding the case. After saying his thank yous and goodbyes to David and Kate, he had gone off to a pleasant pub to refresh himself and collect his thoughts. After lunch, he had decided not to interview anybody further or specifically, but he would use the spare key which Dennis had given him and would let himself into the church and take a photograph of certain pages of the visitors' book. Then he'd spend the time ambling around the parish having the odd word with a variety of total strangers, ranging from shopkeepers to park attendants.

It did not take more than five minutes to get the pictures of the relevant pages, and soon he was on his way, strolling around as inconspicuously as any private detective ever did. As he said to himself, he had more than ever really got the feel of the place. He had read local notices, enjoyed the ambience of the local library, and even assisted a council worker engaged in clearing up litter. "There's no standards these days," the latter had said to him, adding, "just met my old mate, Len, going to the park – soldier in the war, he was – said to me he wonders what they were fighting for; said the country is going to the dogs."

It was now late afternoon and Alistair allowed himself a little stroll along by the river. Then he'd indulge himself with a tasty bite to eat at a new local restaurant which was beginning to intrigue him, followed by a drink at the Royal Oak, which he was now genuinely fond of as a suitable place for the quiet contemplation of his day's work.

He was aware that as well as contemplating this ongoing mysterious case, he was also beginning in an unprecedented way to contemplate where his own thoughts stood on faith and indeed on life itself. As he continually reminded himself, that also was a mystery to be solved – albeit a different sort of mystery. It would be good to solve both, he laughed to himself.

As he was strolling casually along by the river toward his gastronomic destination, the beauty of the park and the pleasant evening light bobbing on the river gave him a sudden and uncharacteristic whim to take a seat on a bench by the path.

The old man sitting next to him at the other end left him in silence for a bit as Alistair drank in the scene more fully, then showed a willingness to chat by commenting on the ducks swimming in the river.

"It's as good as watching telly sitting here in the park," beamed his neighbour.

Alistair assented.

"Nice to come out, get a bit of fresh air, have a break from me house," offered the old man, obviously keen to have a chat.

Again Alistair agreed. "Very pleasant," he said. He would have preferred to be left alone with his musings, but he sensed a certain kindness in the old man's voice. He would have a chat if the man spoke again.

"Nice to see the little ones enjoying the river," came the inevitable further comment.

"You been coming here a long time, then?" Alistair asked, again feeling sorry for a kind of tangible loneliness which he felt clung to this old-timer.

"I should say so. Been living here in Cookington since the war. Was in the Italian campaign; got back home and found some of the family had died, and my sister had married a chap with a little money; she only went and bought the house for me – well, I mean, I don't own it; it belongs to her husband. She died some years ago now, but the husband, well he let me stay on in it; course, he'll get it when I move on, which can't be so very long now. Nice of him though."

"So you're a real local, then?"

"I'll say! Course, I used to live in Southall before the war. I was a plumber. Worked with me dad all over the West End. My dad played for Queen's Park Rangers."

"How interesting, I'll have to look him up. I'm interested in football. He must have been very good."

"I don't think you'll find any records of him. I'm talking about the days before they started keeping records. I mean, in them days they would play the match and then as like as not go and do a plumbing job after, like. I mean if Her Ladyship wanted it, I mean if she had a problem with her toilet or something like that – well, you just had to go."

"You used to help him, did you?" asked Alistair, warming to this fellow human being.

"I'll say. Worked with him till of course he got too old. He became ill and died, but I carried on the business because of course he had built up rather a lot of clients and all that sort of thing. Hey, look at that swan! Sorry what was I talking about?"

"You were telling me about the family plumbing business and how you took over."

"Well, of course, then the war came. I had to leave it all. We had to do our training – it was over in Wales or somewhere over in the West Country. I can't remember the name of the place. I get muddled now, you know; well, I'm ninety-two, aren't I?"

"That must have been a bit of an upheaval for you, going off suddenly to train like that."

"I'll say."

"Where did you go afterwards? Saw a bit of action, did you?"

"I'll say!"

"Tell me about it."

"I was in the Italian campaign, wasn't I?"

"Really? How interesting."

"You know about it, do you?"

Alistair was tempted to use the old man's catchphrase of "I'll say", but said, "I know of it. It's history. I'm interested in history."

"I was with the lot that came over from North Africa. We landed in Sicily." The old man started to draw a rough outline map with his walking stick in the earth on the path. "Three of my mates on my landing craft got killed." He pointed the stick at the blob which represented Sicily. "We was under heavy fire. It wasn't just the Germans shooting at us; we had the bloody Italians loosing off too, didn't we? Bloody frightening, it was. Water was much deeper than we was expecting. One chappie got drowned." The old man stopped; his eyes filled with tears. "It still makes me choke, you know. He was my mate, you know. He had red hair and he always used to wink at me and he always used to say that we would meet up in Piccadilly Circus when the war was over; course, we never did. 'Cause of that I've never been to Piccadilly Circus since the war ended. Course I've seen pictures of it. Him, Trevor, he was one of the lads on the landing craft with me that got killed. I've got an old photo of him at home."

Alistair felt emotional too; the old man had painted such a vivid picture of his fallen comrade with such few words. He genuinely felt the need to remain silent. He knew the old man would continue shortly and he did.

"The fighting went on for weeks. Then I landed in Italy: Salerno. We had the weather to contend with too.

Bloody zero visibility, they used to call it. Yes, I captured Rome."

Alistair saw the tongue literally in the cheek as the old soldier turned and smiled at him.

"Did you really?" managed Alistair, at a loss for words.

"Yes, I was at Monte Cassino too."

"Blimey!" Alistair allowed himself despite his dislike of swearing, but fond of this new expletive he had picked up in London, "I'd like to hear about that sometime, that's a story in itself, I know."

"I'll say. It was a monastery, you know."

"It's funny. I think of it as a battlefield. I forget it was a monastery." Alistair found himself thinking of how Christianity had gone just everywhere. Yes, it was time he worked out what he believed and what he did not.

The old man brought him back with a start.

"Course, I ended up in Austria at the end of the war."

"What happened after the war? Were you able to carry on with the plumbing business?"

"No, had to get a job. Mark you, plumbing came in useful. Got a job, kind of handyman sort of job, at a young offenders' place not many miles over there," came the reply. The walking stick was now up in the air and away from the map of the Mediterranean, and pointing in a westerly direction as he continued. "It was convenient, because as I say my sister had got me this house here in Cookington. My old house just wasn't there anymore."

Alistair was lost in thought.

"Course, I had to retire from the young offenders' place when I was sixty-five – that was twenty-seven years ago - but I've lived there since the war: sixty three years."

313

"Phew! Happily, I hope?" Asked Alistair with an eyebrow raised.

"Yeah, it's not a bad life," philosophised the old man, before turning the conversation to his main interest and hobby and saying with extreme abruptness, "I'm interested in transport."

"*Transport!*" said Alistair with some astonishment.

"Well, my main enthusiasm is trams, but I like trains and buses. People offer me a lift, but I say no, I prefer to get the bus. I've got lots of models and pictures back home. Can show you if you're interested."

"One day," said Alistair, looking at his watch and now ready for his evening refreshment. "Well, I must be thinking about going."

He sensed a certain disappointment in his new-found companion's glance, and thought he would go the extra mile and ask one more question.

"So you know this area pretty well, then?"

"I'll say."

Although, as he kept reminding himself, Alistair had mentally called it a day as regards the investigation, and was now looking forward to his evening meal and drink with even more joyous anticipation than usual, he thought, why not, and asked the old man if he'd heard about the crime.

"I'll say," came the unexpected answer, but framed in predictable phraseology. "I should have! I only bin to that church every Sunday of my life for forty years."

Very taken aback by this unexpected news, Alistair knew that duty demanded he probe more than a bit. That much anticipated drink would have to wait a bit longer. He would have an extra one to make up for the delay. He sat there expectantly, waiting for the old man to speak.

"See, we was brought up Nonconformist. Yes, I

liked the chappie who was there before her; I could take him, though even he went in for a bit of this and that."

"What, you mean he was a bit High Church too?" asked Alistair excitedly, knowing that this type of conversation could well prove useful, giving quite an insight for his purposes.

"I'll say. I mean, compared with what I'd bin used to as a young man. I mean, as I say – we was Nonconformist; but the chappie before her – Maurice, that was his name - he didn't go in for her gimmicks. But you can't change at my age, and you see I thought I've got to go along with her, because after all she'd be taking the service."

"Which service?"

"My funeral service."

"Oh, you shouldn't think of that."

"Well, the way I saw it, I gave twelve pound a month to the church, and when the time came for the service, well, she'd do it all properly and that; but trouble was she went and got murdered. Who would have thought that she'd go before me? Funny old world! I just hope, if I don't kick the bucket before, whoever comes next after this 'ere interregnum, if I'm still here, will do it proper, like."

"Do what properly?" asked Alistair, just checking for clarification.

"The service, my funeral service."

"That's a long time off," assured Alistair with one of his most benign beams. He felt a basic human inclination to tap the old gentleman reassuringly on the shoulder.

"Well, I outlived her, didn't I? Who would have thought it would be that way round? I mean me, I'm ninety-two, she must have been about forty. She wasn't even born at the time of the Italian campaign."

Alistair decided that he must probe further and make inquiries, however ready he was to call it a day; but somewhat to his surprise the old soldier got to his feet. "I'd better be going. Wanted to stay and chat very much, but it's come on me again. I'm OK, but it comes over me sometimes. Don't feel too good sometimes, passes, and then I'm alright."

"Are you sure you're OK?" Alistair was taken aback, not to say alarmed by how old and frail and indeed thin the old gentleman seemed suddenly to appear, now that he was standing up.

"Do you mind walking with me?" asked the old man with a beam that Alistair could not resist.

"I think I'd better," he replied, and remembered that phrase about how being good mattered more than church-going.

"It's not very far. Kingfisher Row is where I live. Do you know it?"

"Yes, I think I do. I'm getting to know this area a bit. We'll see how you are when we get there, and I could call a doctor if necessary."

"Don't think I need a doctor. Probably be fine when I get there. Happened the other day, and when I got home, was as right as rain. Just age, you know. You'll be able to see those models of trams and pictures after all," managed the ailing old gentleman.

They did not talk much as they walked to the house in Kingfisher Row. Alistair thought his companion seemed a bit breathless, and he advised him not to try and speak. His thoughts were now entirely taken up with the problems of old age.

What a wretched thing it is. Yes, it needed some kind of explanation. Maybe this Christianity with its message of eternal life, which defied science, is the answer, he mused, as he shuffled along the streets with the old man clinging tightly to him.

When they got there, Alistair was invited in. He smiled to himself on finding the hall strewn ankle-deep with leaflets, advertisements ranging from Indian restaurants through every conceivable type of charity to double glazing and the services of tree surgeons.

"Do you want me to pick these up?" he asked helpfully.

"You can if you like," replied the gentleman somewhat enigmatically, "I do every now and again, but you see they just keep coming, so what's the point? I just leave them there."

"It's like walking through snow," joked Alistair, and then thought to himself, What a stupid thing to say!

The old man beckoned him down the hall to the back room. Alistair was aware that he passed a rather tidy, smarter-looking front room.

Glancing through the door of that room he espied a cat sitting in front of an empty fireplace.

"Goodness, you've got a cat!" he exclaimed, "I wasn't expecting that. What's he called?"

"No, it's an artificial one. I mean at my age, it wouldn't be fair, would it?"

"I was going to ask you its name," said Alistair, laughing.

"It's got a name. Just because it's not real, doesn't mean it can't have a name, does it?" joked the old man.

"I suppose so; but why don't you have a real one?" asked Alistair.

"Well, I mean - you know - after I've gone, who would …?"

"Oh, don't say that," Alistair coughed, but now thinking to himself that it could be any time soon and adding, "I must say it's so realistic, and that's just where a cat would sit, isn't it? Right in front of a fireplace."

"Everyone gets a shock when they find it's not real.

Even the vicar, when she came round here about the service, she didn't half scream when she poked her head in there! I told her, 'Look, I only got it from one of your bloody jumble sales, didn't I?'"

"I bet she was amused."

"Ticked me off for swearing, she did. I said I was in the army. She said 'Yes, but you're a Christian now, Len."

Alistair suddenly realised that this was the first time he had learnt the name of his new-found companion. Fancy asking the name of the artificial cat before asking the owner! He laughed to himself.

"Yes, she said to me, 'You're in a different kind of an army now, Len.' Always remember her saying that. Made me think – oh yes, she had her good points. We had a good chat about my old army chaplain. He risked his life to try and save one of my mates, he did. That's really why I started to go to church proper after the war."

These words were not lost on Alistair, but by now they had reached the back room - Len's citadel, as he saw it. It reminded Alistair of the film *Crocodile Dundee*, with the socks drying on the string across the fireplace.

Len seemed to get a new lease of life, now that he was in his own house. He offered Alistair some tea, which he readily assented to, but when it came he found the cup was just too dirty to drink from, so he excused himself and went into the very small kitchen next door and washed it.

"Sorry about that, me kitchen hygiene ain't too good. It's the eyesight, you know. Mark you, we'd drink out of anything on the Italian campaign. Stupid, but I've known soldiers drink dirty water at times on the campaign."

Genuinely interested though he was, Alistair steered

the conversation away from the war, and Len started to talk about a wide range of matters, including his early family life and pre-war days. Alistair who was a good listener and, sensing that the old man must be a lonely person, sat back opposite him and braced himself for a a lengthy stint of conversation, from which he was hopeful that he might just possibly glean some information relevant to the crime.

At one point Len broke off and said, "Here, let me get you a G & T."

Alistair was surprised. The last thing he expected was for Len to pour him a glass of one of his favourite tipples. It turned out to be from a Marks and Spencer can, which Alistair had never seen before.

"Haven't you ever seen one of these before? There's plenty more where that came from in the kitchen."

This could be a good evening, thought Alistair, as he decided to change his plans. Len's house was warm and strangely comfy, and as good as any pub. He was already used to the absence of lightshades, and he would try and learn as much as he could from his host.

As expected, he knew it meant, before long, a thorough tour of all Len's pictures and models of trams.

That indeed was what happened next, owing to Len's insistence, and it involved a slow and tricky climb up the stairs and inspections of pictures, books, models and much else.

Back again in the comfy back room, Alistair was determined to make the most of this unexpected opportunity to learn more relevant information about the parish, and he gradually brought the conversation round to the subject of parish personalities.

Len seemed to equate information about the parish with information about the late vicar, and Alistair decided that he should just let him ramble on with the hope of picking up something of value.

"I'm really interested in anything you have to say about the vicar. This is what Dennis wants me to do – try and learn as much as possible," he urged.

"I'll tell you anything you like," said Len. "I'll answer anything you throw at me, if I can."

For a moment, he seemed better, and Alistair thought he would take the opportunity to ask, "Did she ever say she was having trouble with anybody - real trouble, I mean? You see, apart from maniacs, I guess murders are often the result of real trouble." Alistair was annoyed with himself that he sounded so crass and had not expressed himself more clearly.

"Well, it's funny she did tell me once that there was a lady she had had a bit of difficulty with. I never got to the bottom of it. She wouldn't tell me, but I remember she said she never felt at ease with her – 'Bad vibes.' she used to say. Think she might have had a bit of a fright with her once. I think this lady must have said something or done something that upset her. Told me she had never told her husband even, what with it being so difficult her being a priest and that. I said, 'Why don't you tell me what all this is about?' She said she was only telling me because I told her of a fear I had – kind of nightmare I used to get when the war ended. I mean, in them days we never got no counselling. If I was looking a bit down one day, the sergeant used to come round and he'd say, 'Sharpen up Stephenson, sharpen up!'"

Alistair was slightly taken aback to find the old man had such a fine surname. Somehow he had expected it to be something short and comic.

"Well, in a way I like that attitude," continued Len Stephenson. "Don't go along with all this more help for the criminal than the victim malarkey … country's going to the dogs. Only said that to a mate of mine the other day."

"Oh, that'll be the guy I met clearing up the litter not so very far from here this morning."

"That's him – Geoff."

"Small world," replied Alistair automatically.

"But anyway, those bloody nightmares," continued Len, as if keen to revert to the previous remarks, "after my mates got hit on that landing craft! I suppose I kind of never got over it. She said, 'Don't worry, Len, in heaven all will be healed; meanwhile take comfort that you are not alone.' She said something about how hard it was to forgive and how I should just try; I don't know, it was all very muddled, but I said something like she had never seen a good friend shot down right in front of her – never been in a landing craft; and she said something about the bastard who had fired at us was probably just a soldier doing his duty. I remember she said, 'The bastard had been a kid once, with a mum and dad who loved him. Made me think. Up till then I'd hated that bastard. She told me not to use that word. She said, 'Call him an enemy soldier.' But after what she said – well, it made me think. Well, I suppose he had been a kid once. Anyway, she said she had got something to forgive, which was very different, but no less difficult, she said."

Alistair leaned forward, listening earnestly.

"I said, 'How can it be more difficult than losing three of yer mates?' She said, 'Come on, Len, you know matters of the heart – the most painful of all, aren't they?' I told her how she didn't realise how close you were to your mates on a landing craft. Anyway, I said, 'Matters of the heart? But you're happily married with a nice family, aren't you?' She said something about someone had got it in for her, because they thought she'd done them down."

Alistair, aware that his heart was beating faster at hearing such relevant utterances concerning his assignment, wondered if he should pull out his notebook and jot down the answers to a few clarifying questions.

"Len, would you mind if I asked you a few questions? You see, this will be a surprise to you, but I didn't tell you this, because obviously I never in my wildest dreams thought we would be having a conversation like this, but you see the vicar's husband, Dennis, got so frustrated with the police inquiries getting nowhere that in kind of desperation he asked me, as an old friend, who fancied himself as a kind of sleuth and had a hankering after a life as a private detective, to carry out an investigation."

There was a pause while Len sat gaping at him with open mouth, from which eventually the word "Blimey" emitted.

To his own surprise, Alistair felt slightly embarrassed, and tried to clarify his situation. "I mean when I sat down on that bench next to you, I had no idea that you were someone who might be able to throw a bit of light on things. I hadn't a clue who you were, or that you even went to St Peter's. I promise I didn't know you went to St Peter's when I sat down next to you on that bench – it was pure chance."

He paused again, but wanting to get on with things, added, "It strikes me you might just possibly be able to throw some light on things. I mean, did the police ever ask you about any of this?"

Len seemed to recover his equilibrium. "The Old Bill! I offered to speak to them when I heard they were interviewing people, but everyone always said, 'No, Len, just keep out of it and let them get on with it.' I heard once they grouped me with a few other of us old-timers in the parish, saying we didn't know what day of the week it was. They couldn't be doing with ninety-two-year-olds. That bloody annoyed me! No, nobody ever talked to me about it. Kept saying, 'No, Len, don't trouble yourself with it, mate.' Course, after a bit I said to myself, OK, fuck off ... Sorry to swear, but what with the vicar being gone I've got back into the habit of it. I'm quite broad-minded, you know. I mean I was in the bloody army, for goodness sake. No, I'm only too happy to tell you what they didn't seem too interested in."

Alistair smiled. "Do you know, this is exactly the sort of thing Dennis wanted me to do – to learn about things the police didn't cover," he said hopefully.

To his surprise, the benign old gentleman momentarily became quite cross looking, as if he was really annoyed or at any rate suffering high blood pressure, if not an apoplectic fit. Then to Alistair's horror he sank back in his chair, looked up as if to heaven, and seemingly collapsed.

"Len, are you alright? Len, are you OK? Len, Len, Len!" came Alistair's urgent voice.

Len's reply was a kind of delirious burble of incoherent words.

"Len, I think I should call an ambulance! Len, Len, Len!" continued the anxious Alistair.

Although Len waved his hands as if to decline the suggestion, he slumped further back.

Alistair reached for the telephone and dialled 999, then turned back to Len. "It's just to check you over. They think it's wise," he offered helpfully.

Leaving Len as comfortably as he could in his chair, he went to the front door, wading again through the mass of leaflets and advertisements that littered the hall floor. He stood on the porch waiting for a distant siren. All was strangely silent. A cat scurried across the road, escaping some crisis of its own. He thought he heard an owl, but it could have been his imagination. Then unmistakeably, loudly and clearly and surprisingly closer than expected, came the sound of the approaching ambulance's siren.

In a moment he was ushering the ambulance crew into the house.

"What's your name, sir?" the ambulance man asked Len, having walked past Alistair and ignored his efforts to be helpful.

Alistair was surprised and relieved when Len answered.

"And how old are you, Len?" continued the ambulance man.

"Ninety-two," said Len with some pride.

"Ninety-two! Right – well, I'm catching you up fast, Len; now we're just going to get you into the ambulance and we'll get you checked over. That's all we're doing, Len. You know what a check over is, don't you, Len? Expect you had 'em in the army, didn't you."

"I was in the Italian campaign," were appropriately the last coherent words Alistair heard the old man say.

While the ambulance man was helping Len to the ambulance, the ambulance woman stayed behind talking to Alistair as they moved to the hall.

"This where he lives then?" she asked rather ungraciously.

She asked him a few further questions as the flashing blue light continued to invade Len's snug little home.

"Yes, I'm a friend of his," said Alistair with some feeling, omitting to mention that he had only just met Len a couple of hours or so ago.

"He got family to inform, then?"

"No, he doesn't have any family, but I've instructions to tell the churchwardens of the local church here, so I'll do that straightaway. Thought I'd better wait till he was safely in your hands first – you know, before doing that."

"Before doing what?" She asked.

"Before telling all his church people, who look after him and care for him, what's happened. They are his family, as it were."

Alistair was momentarily a trifle disconcerted when the ambulance woman asked, "Not that one where the vicar got murdered, is it?"

"Actually, it is," he replied. "Len's a very loyal and stalwart member of the congregation there."

"Doesn't seem to have helped the poor old chap much, does it? I mean religion, what the hell's the use of it? We had a vicar knocked down in the High Street last month over in Redbridge." She pointed rather inanely in the direction of the town beyond Cookington. "You still get knocked down in the street, don't you?"

"Well, that may be just when religion becomes important," mumbled Alistair confusedly, surprised to find himself in the role of defender of the faith.

In fact this was the first time he had ever said anything like that, and he felt an indescribable feeling as if something was changing in him.

She seemed stupid and certainly ungracious, but markedly attractive, he thought, standing there with her blonde hair shining under the bare light bulb of Len's hall. How strong physical attraction is, he thought, and almost felt like kissing her, but checked such an inappropriate thought. Besides, it was Zoe, still somewhere an astronomical distance away in America, who he wanted to kiss. Zoe was better-looking too, and so much nicer. This girl has looks but isn't nice; you couldn't marry her, he thought.

Soon she was back with her colleague and he was watching the ambulance leave, its light still flashing, but no siren. He turned back to the house. He went back and walked down the hall into Len's inner sanctum and, as he said afterwards, closed the room down. He turned the fire off, switched some lights off, and pressed a button on the television that made the energy-saving light go off. He checked that the back door from the kitchen was locked. Curiosity and a sense of occasion made him go quickly upstairs again to check that they had turned everything off when they had come down.

Again he noticed how surprisingly neat Len's bedroom was, although the bed was unmade, just as Len must have left it when he got up that morning. He remembered his mother saying, "We never know when we get up each morning what's going to happen during the day." He had another look at the picture of the tram that had seemed to mean so much to Len. He took a closer look at the frame with the medals in, which he had only been able to catch a cursory glimpse of during the few minutes earlier when Len had been with him.

The bathroom was cleaner than the kitchen, he was relieved to find. The other two bedrooms were very bare. In the larger of them he noticed a visitors' book on a table. Another visitor's book, he mused to himself, recalling the morning's conversation with David and Kate. Sheer curiosity made him pick it up and look at the last entry. It was dated seven years ago. His sister had visited him. In the comments column she had written, *Very comfortable and pleasant, well done, brother!* Somehow, it highlighted Len's loneliness.

Alistair found a large bunch of keys on the floor and picked them up, putting them in his pocket.

Once downstairs again, he made a quick inspection of the front room with its unlived-in atmosphere. He glanced quickly at Len's artificial cat, gazing into the unlit gasfire. He saw the old-fashioned bureau, which Len had referred to as being the depository of all his important documents.

He returned to the back room with its more cheering and lived-in ambience despite its untidiness. Conscious that time was passing, he hurriedly dialled the churchwardens. He rang Florence first.

"There being no vicar, I guess you are the one to inform first," he said with a touch of irony.

At first she was surprised and a little suspicious. However within a moment she was saying, "Oh, Alistair, it's you! Goodness me – it was only the other day we had our little interview, wasn't it? How have you been getting on?"

He cut in with his news of Len's departure in the ambulance and the briefest of explanations for his having been there.

She sounded genuinely upset and concerned, but thanked him for what she called "doing the right thing".

He rang Edwin and left a message on that good gentleman's answering machine.

He carefully closed and locked the door. He had half expected an enquiry by a naturally inquisitive neighbour, but there was nobody around. They were all going about their usual business, whatever that was, he thought. He could see a television set on in one of the houses opposite, with the people watching some fictional story and unaware of the real life drama outside. He momentarily toyed with the idea of informing the neighbours, but Len's unexpected crisis seemed to have made him tired now.

Having satisfied himself that the house was properly closed down and secure, he went to the little corner shop at the end of Kingfisher Row and bought a bottle of red Spanish wine, which somehow seemed to match his feelings. Then he waited for the bus, which eventually came looming out of the darkness at the end of the distant main road, and thus he journeyed back to his little hotel, content to have time to collect his thoughts on the lumbering bus.

The combination of the hot muggy atmosphere in the bus and its droning engine and rhythmic jolts soon made him soporific, despite the excitement of the day's extraordinary and unexpected events. He would have a nice evening in, and enjoy the combination of the Spanish wine and his thoughts. On arriving at the small reception desk, where Donna sat doing a crossword, he decided that first he would ring the hospital; that was only right, and besides he wanted to, as he had formed quite an attachment to such a benign old gentleman.

The switchboard at the hospital was very much more efficient than he was expecting, and within minutes he was being told, "Len Stephenson is still waiting to be assessed by one of the doctors."

He decided he would ring again in the morning, and gradually the evening passed, at the end of which Alistair was a little surprised to find he had drunk the whole bottle.

Even in his mild alcoholic haze it struck him how odd it was that this old soldier - the one man who really had killed people in real life, albeit in war - was the one man that nobody could possibly suspect.

***

When he woke the next morning, he immediately realised how stupid he had been. He had a headache, but even before breakfast he rang the hospital.

"He is in Heron Ward. Visiting hours are twelve to eight," came the helpful voice, as if it was the most common occurrence in the world to collapse and be admitted to hospital.

Birds seem to follow Len around, thought Alistair.

Destiny has led him to Kingfisher Row, and now on to Heron Ward …

After his breakfast, during which he was irritated by Cissie's rather cheeky comments about him having a hangover, he decided to have a quiet morning before setting off to visit Len promptly at noon.

The place reminded him of an air terminal more than a hospital, but as he progressed in the direction of Heron Ward the atmosphere became more as expected.

On arrival at the ward, a nurse at the desk eventually asked him who he was after, and pointed him in the right direction. He went looking amongst the several elderly patients there for Len.

Suddenly he found him. He was propped up on a pillow and looking at him with recognition, and pleased to see him, but seemingly unable to speak.

Alistair kept repeating over and over again that there was nothing to worry about.

"I found your keys, Len. Here they are." He produced them like a conjuror from his inside pocket, adding, "I will give them to the churchwardens, Florence and Edwin. Your keys are safe. Everything is under control."

On hearing this, Len seemed considerably relieved and began to relax; he leaned back, much as he had done in the backroom chair the previous evening.

"I'd better go now, because I mustn't tire you," mumbled Alistair, who never felt at ease in hospitals. He waved goodbye, and Len raised his arm in response.

He thought he had better have a word at the desk in the ward on the way out. Eventually one of the nurses finished her telephone conversation. She produced a file with Len's name on and invited Alistair to put down his details, as they had what she called a bit of a blank. Alistair wrote his name, the address of the Concord Hotel, and a telephone number in a space marked 'Contacts'. Then he added in neat handwriting on the side of the page, *I'm the guy who called the ambulance.*

"Have you got any information on his condition? People are asking, you know," he asked, not entirely honestly, but sincerely.

"The assessment is ongoing. He has a chest infection, so we've got him on antibiotics. Things should be clearer next week."

"Next week!" responded Alistair with some astonishment. He then left the ward and the hospital, not quite sure where he would go next, or indeed what he would do that day.

On arrival at the bus stop, he decided to go on to the middle of London and enjoy a museum. He needed a day off after the traumas of yesterday, with its ambulances and artificial cats that made you jump.

A very good day off it was too. Alistair even forgot about the case completely, and poor Len as well, as he engrossed himself in exhibitions and displays of a historical nature that he was particularly interested in.

However, reality returned to him as he left the museum after his absorbing day. He was sad to think of poor Len in hospital, for he had warmed to him immensely, and quite surprisingly so, considering he had been a perfect stranger. These old heroes of the war are dying off, he reflected, as their heroic exploits sank into the silent pages of the history books.

As he walked from the Tube station back to the hotel, he wondered if he would be met by some further development. He had a hunch that he would; he'd learnt that things happen so quickly and unexpectedly. He climbed the few steps of the hotel entrance, and almost in answer to his thoughts, Donna called to him from her reception desk that there was a message for him from someone called Florence.

"Called herself a churchwarden, or something weird like that," said Donna, handing it to him.

He took the little bit of green paper headed 'Telephone Message' and read it, taken aback by its terseness: *Len has died.*

CHAPTER 26

(An interview with a vicar's former lover)

When he woke the next morning, Alistair was immediately of the firm opinion that he needed a break. The intensity of the last two days' experience demanded one, for he needed time to think through the vividness of it all without the artificial words that would be needed when in the company of a member of the congregation. However, after a very few days he felt the urge to keep the momentum of the investigation going. He would still keep clear of the congregation, but ease himself back into the case by interviewing someone from outside the borders of St Peter's, Cookington; someone indeed who came more and more into his focus. Hadn't Len said something about Henrietta suggesting that someone had got it in for her, because they thought she'd done them down? Yes, it was time for him to meet this Rhys chappie. Rhys Williams, her previous lover, must be spoken to without delay.

Although Alistair had quite a lot of difficulty in tracking him down, which after many calls to the New World Hotel he eventually did, at its neighbour, the Runway Hotel near Heathrow Airport. He found Rhys to be cooperative, and quickly arranged a meeting for that afternoon in the Bar In The Sky of that exotic-sounding establishment.

This will indeed be another world, surely, in a Heathrow hotel, he thought as he studied the map to locate his rendez-vous. He could put his contemplation and meditation about Len's last hours with him into temporary abeyance and make headway with the investigation in this other world of big business, where wrongly he imagined that church probably meant only christenings, weddings and funerals.

Rhys was already there when Alistair arrived and seemed to be enjoying both his drink and his chat with the barmaid, who was thanking him for a drink, when Alistair put out his hand and said, "Hi, you must be Rhys."

"That's me, sir, nice to meet you. Can I buy you a drink?"

Rhys seemed cocky. Alistair did not particularly like him from the word go.

When the welcoming pleasantries were over, they moved over at Alistair's suggestion to a comfortable sofa, carrying their drinks.

Alistair noticed Rhys's appreciative look at a young lady guest at a neighbouring table as he launched straight into his interview with him.

"It's a wretched business, this crime, but as I said on the phone, Dennis asked me to see if I could make a breakthrough, as the police seemed to have come up against a brick wall."

Rhys gave a slightly too loud laugh and said, "He doesn't suspect me does he? Only joking, but he never liked me. I don't know why, because I never did him any wrong."

Alistair thought to himself, well, you may not know why, but I think I do, as Rhys winked at one of the waiters and, nodding at the barmaid, made some kind of a crude gesture.

He is cordial enough, thought Alistair, but has an underlying arrogance that revealed itself from the start.

"Look, Rhys, I'll come straight to the point, because both of us want to get away. Henrietta was your girlfriend before she married Dennis. It was pretty serious, I mean, you lived together, didn't you? Then she married Dennis and now she's murdered. I'll be honest with you," said Alistair, using the old infectious phrase which he had picked up, even though he did not like it, "a lot of people in the congregation of her church have told me they feel sure it must have been something outside parish life, something to do with her personal life."

"She had other boyfriends, though, didn't she?" was Rhys's defensive response.

"Who?" asked Alistair abruptly.

"You know about this guy called Buzz," he offered. "He asked her to marry him – you know that, don't you?"

Alistair's countenance revealed nothing, but he was puzzled. He had thought that Buzz would have been regarded as just being a young lad smitten by a passing crush. He paused, and deliberately taking his time, made a bit of a palaver of finding his notebook and pens. He wanted to slow this guy Rhys down a bit.

"Do you know anything about Buzz? he asked.

Rhys seemed to be silenced by this question.

"He seems rather a shady mysterious figure, from what I've heard," bluffed Alistair eventually.

"Do you know, I don't; but whenever we had a row she used to say, 'I could have married Buzz.' And well, she seemed quite impressed." There was a pause and then he added, "No, wrong word; I would say not impressed so much as flattered by this young guy having proposed to her. I don't think he did impress her too much."

Rhys lit another cigarette while Alistair waited for him to continue, noticing for a fleeting second that a rather sad expression came over Rhys's countenance. The head barman asked him to put the cigarette out and he obliged with a curse.

"I asked her one day to tell me more about him, but she only said he was a young guy who would find the right girl one day. She said he was young for his age – a bit under the thumb of his parents - but to be fair she used to say he was a really nice guy. That's all she said."

"You never felt jealous, or even threatened by this?"

"Good heavens, no! She hadn't seen him for years - never mentioned him unless I asked. There was no communication at all, no letters, phone calls, visits – not even a Christmas card. I think he had accepted it when she gave him the dump because apparently he had dropped her a line by return of post, saying he understood. She never heard from him again."

The rest is silence, as Shakespeare would have said, thought Alistair, unless … no, I'm as certain as I can be that guy Buzz is as innocent as they come.

He reined back his thoughts and asked, "Is there anything you can say to help me with this investigation, to give it a pompous name? You know, Dennis only asked me to take it all up as the police had got nowhere."

Rhys studied the back of his hands in a way that reminded Alistair of Fred Goodman and proffered what sounded like a final comment on the matter. "Well, she kept that last note from Buzz for a while, but when we were having a clear-out one day, she just tore it up and chucked it in the waste-paper basket."

"You mean the last note Buzz wrote when he accepted that she was going with you and looking to marriage."

"Yes."

"You seem to have a vivid memory of that."

"What do you mean?"

"I mean you actually remember the waste-paper basket."

"Do you know," began Rhys, looking just a trifle flustered for the first time, "that's because she seemed to be saying a prayer as she did it – you've got to remember she became a vicar. She was always bloody religious. Got on my nerves; it became a dividing issue between us. I remember I kind of challenged her on that occasion and said to her, 'You looked like you were saying a prayer over the waste-paper basket then,' and she said, 'Maybe I was.'

"Somehow that answer annoyed me, and I said, 'What the bloody hell for?' Then she said, 'Well, maybe for Buzz to find the right girl one day.' I don't know why but it really annoyed me. I remember I asked her what the hell we were doing suddenly talking about that adolescent kid who had a crush on her. She ignored me and started jabbering on that there was something about our differences in the Bible, and I got even more annoyed; I guess it's no surprise we eventually split up. Maybe I really would have murdered her if we had got married!" He seemed to think this was a good joke and laughed rather longer than Alistair thought seemly in the circumstances.

"What were your feelings when she left you for Dennis? I mean, she gave you the Buzz treatment too, didn't she."

"Ah no, by that time I'd realised it just wasn't going to work out. I'd nothing against Dennis; I'd met him a few times, and actually we got on very well. He always seemed a bit embarrassed, and I admit it was an odd feeling for me sensing that he was in love with her; but then again, oddly enough I realised that it wasn't bothering me. You get used to anything after a bit, don't you? No, I certainly never contemplated removing Dennis."

Again he laughed, and again a shade too long, Alistair thought. The use of the word "removing" gave Alistair a shiver of discomfort, which oddly he had not had hitherto during the investigation. Someone removed Henrietta, alright, he thought, and felt the need to take another swig of his drink.

"I mean, in a way he made it easier for me to make the split with Henrietta," continued Rhys after a pause. "Some people even sympathised with me. You know, they took the line, 'Poor chap, he's had his wife stolen from him.' I answered all these questions with the police. They acknowledged I'd never shown any signs of jealousy."

"People probably thought it wasn't very nice for you, and of course, poor chap, you were no stranger to break-ups, because the Lucy relationship didn't turn out well and she'd walked out on you; but you're happily married now ... "

"Exactly. Things, as they say, turn out for the best. Third time lucky I was - with my darling Sheila."

"And we're left with this extraordinary mystery of who murdered Henrietta."

"Well, I always say it must have been some mad lunatic – I mean, the way they found her and everything."

"It's an isolated murder, though," said Alistair into his glass. "I think lunatics often have another go, don't they?" He paused and allowed another of his very serious expressions to come over his face.

Aware, after a moment, that Rhys was not going to respond, Alistair continued, "Unfortunately for you, by a diabolical coincidence you were in England at the time of the crime, weren't you?"

"I really can account for my movements almost to the hour during that visit. When I wasn't on business with several colleagues to vouch for my movements, I was practically always with the missus - Sheila. We were either out visiting friends, shopping together or just being together – chilling out in the old country, as you might say. We did a bit of sightseeing – a surprising amount, considering I was here on business."

He held back his head and laughed out loudly as he continued. "The police really did check it all out, Alistair old chap, and they pronounced me innocent."

The laugh became unpleasant again; it really did not seem appropriate in a discussion about a murder victim with whom he had lived.

"So I'm going to drink to that, and you've really got to accept it," Rhys said finally, getting up and moving towards the bar, as if he had trumped a trick at bridge, and adding to Alistair's feeling of distaste.

" OK, they were satisfied with your movements," said Alistair haltingly, when he came back with his full glass, "but you realise I have to ask you this. What about your wife Sheila's? Are you able to account for her movements all the time?"

"The police checked all that out too, and they really practically always could. She was nearly always with someone else, if she wasn't with me, when she left our hotel, and it was always either shopping or sightseeing, when she wasn't with me or my colleagues. They were pretty thorough, as you might expect. I remember she had to find receipts, old visa slips, old admission tickets – you name it. To give the police their due, they were thorough OK – they studied the times and dates on endless bits and pieces. It was distressing for both of us at the time. Sheila said the only thing that kept her going was the thought of having a good, really exotic holiday when it was all over."

Alistair sighed. He was not enjoying this. Somehow the parishioners, with all their foibles, were more pleasant to interview. He had thought he would welcome a break from them, but now the boot was on the other foot, and he felt the need of a break from the likes of this chap Rhys, who was too loud for him. He did not really mind swearing too much, but Rhys could do with a mouthwash.

"So Sheila, I understand," continued Alistair, mustering all his reserves of patience and tolerance, "claimed she never went over in the Cookington direction. In other words, curiosity about her husband's former lover and the church she was now vicar of never struck her as a place to go have a deck at."

"Good God, no!" exclaimed Rhys. "The only time she mentioned it was when I asked her if it would be a fun thing to do, and she looked quite shocked – went quite white, she did - said she'd never thought of doing that and wouldn't want to."

"You suggested it, did you?" asked Alistair, seeking confirmation.

Rhys nodded.

"And you didn't have any feeling that you'd put an idea into her head that she might take you up on one day?"

"No, and I'm sure she never went over there. Goodness me, she'd have told me all about it if she had. She always tells me everything. We don't have any secrets."

Alistair checked his mobile while Rhys continued, coming out with the old "I'll be honest with you" phrases followed by "She used to say she liked mooching around – that's the word she used 'mooching' – on her own in London exploring its byways and alleys. Yes, 'byways and alleyways' is another of her phrases. She loved visiting the old City churches – redolent with history, she used to say. If there was something she disapproved of like a new extension or suchlike added, she'd put her disapproval in the comments column in the church's visitors' book. Told me once she felt a bit guilty, because she had put 'Disapprove of the shocking reredos' or 'Hate the horrible screen' – comments like that. Said it got it off her chest! I could never be doing with that, so yes, there were a very few times when she went off without me for one of these mooches around, but she never mentioned going to Cookington, and whenever she got back she always told me where she'd been. She used to show me brochures and tickets … mark you, her favourite thing was visiting places a bit off the beaten track for tourists – that sort of thing."

Alistair had deliberately maintained a silence throughout all this, and now the two of them sat without talking, while Alistair flipped the pages in his notebook.

Rhys eventually broke in again. "She had a little book entitled *Hidden Corners of a Great City*, and another called *Secret Byways and Alleyways of Forgotten London*. She loved those little 'exploration trips', as she called them; told me once it was her new-found hobby."

Alistair was now scribbling in his notebook.

"I gather on the day the crime occurred she went to the Museum of London," he said abruptly.

"That's right; the police checked it out and were satisfied with her account of the day," came the prompt reply.

"You've never wondered whether she went anywhere else that day?"

"I think she threw in a City church, but apart from that absolutely not. The London Museum would tire out even a girl as strong as her. I can't remember the name of the church that she went on to visit, St Something or other … St Botolph's, that was it."

Alistair made a mental note to visit that church on one of his City strolls, and for the fun of it take a look in the visitors' book – a stupid idea, but he pinned his chances on stupid ideas.

Rhys's voice cut into his thoughts. "Look, I've

never known her tell me a lie ever. As I say, the police checked out everything, and to be honest, Alistair, you're wasting your time talking to Sheila and me, because we just can't offer more than what we've told the police."

It was time for Rhys to light another cigarette, while Alistair metaphorically speaking, bit his tongue. For the second time, a disapproving signal from the chief barman made him put it away immediately, and he pulled out a bit of chewing gum, seemingly as an alternative.

"Sorry," put in Alistair, "I realise it's going over well-trodden ground for you – I realise that. Dennis has asked me to carry out this last different kind of investigation in a desperate hope of finding closure. You appreciate that it's Dennis's wish that we're sitting here having this deliriously happy conversation."

"I took the trouble of checking with him that you were bona fide this morning. I'd like to help, but truly, I really can't help you any more than what I've told you," declared Rhys with his usual disregard for grammar and rather too gleeful a tone for Alistair's liking.

He moved as if to get up, and Alistair was cross with himself for being too polite to this brash fellow, but determined he would continue in the same vein for just a little longer.

"Can I just trouble you one moment more? These letters here," he said, producing the bit of paper, "do they mean anything to you?"

"'T A T T,'" repeated Rhys very deliberately. He seemed to think for a moment, then said quite convincingly, "No, doesn't mean anything at all to me. 'TATT' – doesn't mean a damn thing to me."

Alistair remained studying Rhys's countenance carefully and satisfied himself that he genuinely

341

seemed somewhat intrigued with the question.

"That's interesting," he said looking at Alistair straight in the face, "are you on to something? The police never asked me that one."

"Oh, it's probably nothing; we're – that is Dennis and I - are just trying to pick up anything the police may have missed. I'll explain and fill you in more later."

The conversation continued for a little while and became a little bit more cordial. Alistair sensed that Rhys was still wondering about the letters.

However, soon enough Rhys rose from the table, and excusing himself that there was a meeting to be prepared, took his leave and went up to his hotel room.

Within minutes, he pulled out his mobile and phoned Sheila, who had been waiting for him in another lounge, to ask her if 'TATT' meant anything.

"Doesn't mean a damn thing to me," answered Sheila, "but how did it go? Did he report any progress?"

"Doesn't appear to have any leads at all. Mark you, I don't know what this 'TATT' means. I'm wondering what the hell all that's about. No, I reckon this is just a complete nonsense – Dennis getting one of his mates to carry out an investigation. Says it's to be different to the police's – says it's to have a different kind of approach – kept using the word 'hunch'. He kept asking me, 'Do you have any hunches?' Well, no, I bloody well don't have any hunches, unless a homicidal maniac is a hunch!"

He quickly changed the conversation to other more immediate arrangements, and suggested they give Alistair time to 'push off' and then have a late meal.

Down below at the Bar in the Sky, Alistair stayed behind, jotting down notes for quite a few minutes, and then with an expression of some distraction, got up, smiled at the barmaid (receiving more of a response than Rhys had, he was pleased to note), and took his leave.

He was somewhat surprised in the foyer to bump into Rhys with a strong, well-built but decidedly attractive lady on his arm, whom he presumed was Sheila, and was indeed confirmed to be her by a rather more flustered-looking Rhys.

"Ah, Sheila, this is the great Alistair MacTavish," he began rather cheekily to his wife, to whom he gave a gesture as if to suggest they shook hands, before continuing in sarcastic tone, "the world-famous private detective, who is going to solve the unpleasant goings-on at Cookington."

Funny he didn't mention she was so nearby, thought Alistair, as he courteously greeted her and, ignoring Rhys, made some cliché about it all having been such a horrid business.

Aware that he was being rather sidelined, Rhys butted in, "I'm sure he would appreciate a few words with you too."

"I think that would be a good idea," replied Alistair, now turning to Rhys and adding, "as I told you, Dennis wants me to speak to as many people as possible, and I'll probably take you up on that suggestion, if that's OK with you, Sheila."

Sheila gave him what he could only describe to himself as a somewhat sickly smile, but he had to admit she was an attractive lady, though with something of a tart about her.

"I thought Sheila had gone off for the day on one of her rambles," remarked Rhys, "but I found her here. There's a health club here that she likes. She likes keeping fit, don't you, Sheila? Look at these muscles – not bad for a lady. Disapproves of the bar here … only bar she likes is the parallel bars – oh yes, she likes her gymnastics."

He waved his old-fashioned hat and took his leave.

A suitable wife for Rhys, Alistair said to himself as he travelled back, and then an uncharacteristically sordid thought came into his mind. But for most men, more of a one-night stand than someone to marry.

He returned to his own considerably more modest hotel and it was not long before he'd showered and was back down in his favourite saloon bar. This was his kind of hotel; so different to Rhys's, he reflected.

Although content, he had a lot to think about. This old friendly bar seemed a good place for a think. He studied his photographs of the pages in the church visitors' book. He was intrigued by the fact that there was seemingly the same signature on both the date that David and Kate had referred to and also the date of the crime. Frustratingly, it was written in an almost illegible scrawl, which if he had to guess at looked more like 'A.Wilson' than anything else.

Unfortunately he allowed himself a glass too many. It was all such a horrid business. Sheila was probably completely innocent, but seemingly had had a window of opportunity for such a crime, however unlikely such a scenario was. She could easily have put in an appearance at a museum and then scuttled off somewhere else. Yes, the police might assume she was still gazing at the Elgin Marbles, but she could be on her way to … "Cookington, for example," he said out loud in his half-inebriated state.

That made him realise it was time to retire to bed, and soon he was up the stairs and dropping off to sleep in his little room – feeling, as he recorded later in his diary, slightly pickled for the first time in ages. As sleep overtook him he found himself wondering what had happened to Rhys's first girlfriend, Lucy. It seemed the good lady, whoever she was, had seen the error of her ways fairly early, for Rhys had hitched up with Henrietta fairly soon after. All Alistair had ever gleaned about Lucy was that she had short urchin-style blonde hair, and he imagined her to be rather cute. He slept well.

CHAPTER 27

(The return of the girl of his dreams)

The next morning he was woken rather early and unusually by a knock on the door. He jumped out of bed, rather bleary-eyed, fearing there might be a fire or some such emergency, calling, "Yes, here I am, what is it?"

Surprisingly, it was Cissie's voice that came through the door. "Mr MacTavish, Donna asked me to knock on your door as there is an urgent message for you."

"Oh yes," he managed, composing himself.

"It was a phone call from a lady in Scotland. Donna has got it written down."

Alistair dressed faster than on any other morning of his life and appeared with a remarkably composed demeanour at the reception desk.

"Here it is," said Donna, passing him a scribbled note on the familiar green telephone message form. He read it avidly. *Caller: Mrs Davidson. Of: Edinburgh. Message: Lady called Zoe called from Chicago, Arriving on flight 936 at 12.15 Terminal One at Heathrow tomorrow Thursday 5 October.*

"Thank you," he said calmly to Donna, as if he had just taken receipt of a dental appointment card. Then he added, "I'll just give Mrs Davidson a call to thank her and acknowledge this."

He proceeded to make the call immediately and thanked Mrs Davidson just a little too warmly, so that that good lady's curiosity was aroused even more. Later that day she said to her great friend and confidant (in the flat below), "Love is so strong, it can conquer anyone – even that Alistair."

To hell with the whole blinking case, thought Alistair deciding that his first job after breakfast was to journey to Heathrow, where he intended to check on flight arrival times and familiarise himself generally with the layout, and particularly with where international arrivals would first appear. It was time to put a little self-interest to the fore.

Seldom had he been so full of the joys of life as on that trip to the airport. Absurdly, he found himself singing, 'I'm getting married in the morning.'

On arrival at the air terminal, he bought a paper and strolled around looking at people arriving, and had to pinch himself to think that tomorrow it would be Zoe there, struggling with a suitcase.

Confident that he knew where everything was and feeling as prepared as he could be, he caught the Tube back and spent what little remained of the morning writing out notes about his inquiries so far, and deciding in his mind how he was going to broach the subject of the investigation to Zoe, who would know nothing of it. How could he be sure that she realised his wanting to see her had had nothing to do with the investigation, which he did not even know about when he had handed her his card? His main concern would be to assure her that he had had no ulterior motive. Would she believe him? he mused. Well, she would one day, his ardent heart replied.

In the afternoon he went for a stroll in the streets around his hotel. What strange comings and goings, what secrets and emotions were in these good peoples lives? he wondered; for in the same way that they must surely be so ignorant of all his thoughts and emotions, so likewise must he be of their affairs. An old lady smiled at him in a way that reminded him of his mother. What was her story? he wondered. How was her luck when she was my age? Next he saw an elderly gentleman, moving slowly along the pavement with two sturdy walking sticks. He thought of Len. Was this old guy a landing craft man too? he wondered.

Late that evening in the little hotel lounge, he looked up the flight arrival times on Teletext. There was the list of flights, some landed, some expected at different times, some with no information yet. The list continued until 11.00 a.m. on the next day. He must wait a few hours until her flight would be shown. Meanwhile the seconds changed relentlessly on the screen. Yes, I'm excited alright, his thoughts continued. I haven't felt like this for years!

He did not sleep well that night, being as excited as when he was a child before the first day of the holidays, but sleep he must have had, because when his little alarm clock brought him to his senses, he realised that he had been dreaming a strange dream in which he and Zoe were being married in St Peter's, Cookington, with Dennis saying that in the absence of his wife, who was no doubt looking on with joy, he pronounced them man and wife …

Weird dream, he said to himself as he shaved and cleaned his teeth, but good, it meant I must at least have been asleep, and be better rested than I feel.

"You're off your food a little bit," said Cissie, with what he sensed was a slightly teasing tone in her voice.

Donna seemed to be joining in the teasing, and started quietly singing some refrain, which seemed to go something like, "Can't sleep, can't eat, I'm glad I'm not young anymore." He felt a little embarrassed. Was there some kind of look on his face that betrayed his emotions? He excused himself politely from the table and withdrew upstairs.

Curiously, he remembered his mother telling him that he looked smart with a handkerchief in the top pocket of his jacket, and after a last glance in the mirror to make sure he was as smart as he could make himself, he left for the nearby Tube station.

The air was fresh and invigorating on the Piccadilly Line platform, and a strange quietness mixed with his anticipation of the train's arrival.

When it came, it was more crowded than he expected, and brought him back with a jolt from his daydreams. He reminded himself that life was not a fairy story, as he had to stand, keeping his balance between suitcases labelled for faraway Eastern European countries. An airline steward smiled at him across the carriage. Maybe he was gay, he thought; but it could just have been the friendly gesture of a fellow human coping with his lot.

On arrival at the terminal station he joined the irritatingly large herd of people shuffling towards the escalator, and then upwards and onwards to the concourse, dodging and occasionally bumping into luggage trolleys.

When he eventually reached the arrivals department of the terminal, he was momentarily mesmerised by the milling throng of people coming and going, but within seconds was studying the monitors earnestly. There it was with the correct flight number, staring him in the face unmistakeably, and there too was an expected time of arrival, which showed only a couple of minutes' delay. He would take a seat until the plane landed, indeed until it was shown as 'baggage in hall', for he could just make out from that distance what the monitor was saying.

For a while he amused himself studying the currency exchange rate figures at a nearby currency exchange office. People came and went, couriers delivered packages. To think this goes on every day, he reflected, as he raised his feet for a cleaner to sweep the floor underneath.

With a start, he looked again at the monitor. The expected time of arrival was delayed by a further five minutes. After one or two further delays, he suddenly saw the word 'Landed' alongside the flight number.

His heart beat a little faster. How ridiculous to be so excited! he checked himself. He had a strange, rather novel feeling, like he was watching a play; and then he saw that the monitor had changed again and was signalling 'Baggage in hall'.

He got up from the seat and stood staring down at where the arrival passengers were groggily perambulating with differing amounts of luggage. He would wait a few minutes here and then edge nearer.

He wondered what she would be looking like. What would he say? In an isolated and extremely brief moment of panic he wondered if he would even recognise her. The question returned again. What should he say?

Should he kiss her? Yes – he would. But he banished such thoughts, for life must go spontaneously.

Suddenly she was there, unexpectedly early. How smart she looked! How sensible and efficient her bags were.

He kissed her spontaneously on the cheek and she responded more than he dared hope.

"At least you recognise me," he joked.

"Of course I do," she answered warmly.

She explained that she had been able to come right through ahead of the other passengers, because her baggage had come off first, and thanks to a friend, who worked for the airline, had been able to travel first class and get to passport control first.

He explained that the monitor had only just changed to 'Baggage in hall' and he had been just about to edge nearer.

He suggested a taxi and led the way by a quick route, which he had noted yesterday. The old adage of 'Be Prepared', which he had drummed into him in his scouting days, had a certain undeniable wisdom in it, he thought.

With one eye on the chaos of the myriad of taxis arriving and the inevitable queue-barging, he heard her telling him of her hope and intention to stay, during this relatively short return to her native land, with her friend Elsa in Chelsea.

In spite of her not looking so, she insisted that she was tired, and he was at pains to tell her that he completely understood. They agreed that he would escort her in the taxi to Chelsea, just say hallo to Elsa, and then on the morrow, when she was more rested, they would meet up for dinner. He would book a table at his favourite little Chinese restaurant in Cookington.

"I think I know the one," she said. "I've always wondered what it's like inside."

Within a short time they were at the front of the queue.

"Chelsea, please," said Alistair, hoping he was giving an impression of helpfulness, politeness and a businesslike quality as he lifted the small amount of bags into the boot.

"It'll cost you," said the taxi driver ominously.

"Don't worry – it's a one-off," he said, noticing Zoe's concerned reaction.

It suited him that despite a few efforts of friendly conversation, the taxi driver was uncharacteristically of a taciturn nature.

He asked Zoe several questions about her visit to America and how the wedding had gone.

With a combination of jolts, hoots, curses from the driver, traffic jams and unexpected bursts of speed, the taxi progressed through the concrete jungle of West London.

A bit unnecessarily, they went over the arrangement that he would arrive at six o'clock the next day and they would travel over to Cookington for the dinner.

He was conscious that he was a bit distracted by the prospect of telling her of the assignment, and knew that it must wait; however, he stupidly worried that the secret was affecting his style, and again stupidly felt that he must say something in case it was.

"There's something I've got to tell you," he blurted out, rather too abruptly for his liking. "It's not about us – it's totally unrelated, but you'll understand when I tell you."

He sensed her surprise, and was concerned that she seemed slightly less relaxed after that, but within minutes the taxi had slowed down and the taxi driver turned his head to the glass behind him and said what was probably, "Somewhere near here, is it?" and then began peering out of his window for Number 16.

Zoe, who was leaning forward, was muttering, "I know it's on the right near here. It's somewhere near here."

"Gotcha," shouted the taxi driver, "Number 16, clear as blinking daylight."

A smart-looking woman with red hair came to the door and started waving frantically.

"You've got to be Elsa," shouted Alistair waving as he turned to pay the taxi driver. In his joie de vivre, he gave the man a good tip and saw him wave as he disappeared into the melting pot of London.

Zoe introduced him to Elsa on the doorstep, but unwillingly he felt he must not overstay his welcome, for she had indicated she was tired and wanted a good sleep; so with an aching heart, he declined Elsa's heartfelt invitation to come in at least for coffee.

Trying not to appear too ardent, he gave Zoe a peck on the cheek, and then, like the taxi driver, he too disappeared into the said melting pot of that great city.

Alistair returned home by Tube. It was not until the train neared his station that he came out of the romantic daze that had engulfed him, though to some extent it remained with him all day.

Despite being full of joy at his new situation, he found himself preoccupied with questions like how, when, where to tell Zoe of his assignment concerning the murder mystery. Such is the power of love, though, that he was able to put the dilemma out of his mind and slept the sleep of the just that night.

***

The next morning saw him up early and whistling, as he got ready for a quick visit to one of his favourite museums. He was careful not to overtire himself, and returned in time for a refreshing shower. Then, after a final check in the mirror that he looked as cool as it was possible for Alistair MacTavish FRGS to be, he set off to the Tube station.

He got to Zoe's station, as he called it, too early; but solved the problem with a pleasant stroll, again being careful not to allow it to take the edge off his freshness.

He looked at his watch; the magic hour had arrived. With difficulty he managed to wait a further couple of minutes so as not to appear too prompt.

There was the smart door of Number 16, which he remembered so vividly from yesterday, but today he immediately noticed new things about it, including the pleasant plant standing neatly in the corner of the porch. How odd that he had not noticed that in the excitement of yesterday.

Zoe swung the door open and appeared like a conjuror's assistant out of a magic box.

"I'm ready if you are," she said.

"Let's hit the trail," he replied, mimicking her

swashbuckling vein.

In a moment they were on the Tube and talking sweet nothings. A couple came in at the next station and sat opposite them. The man played with the girl's hair. Alistair longed to do likewise with Zoe, but knew he must wait.

The train started to empty as it approached the suburbs, and soon the couple opposite were gone too. Ships in the night again, thought Alistair, I wonder what their story is?

How fresh the air felt at the terminus in comparison with central London. Now all they had to do was get a bus. They waited for it, chatting. He saw one in the distance and said, "There she blows!" which made her laugh.

"It's not a whale," she said teasingly, and stuck her finger playfully in his ribs.

"Sorry, I tend to say foolish things all the time," he replied.

They went to Alistair's favourite Chinese restaurant in Cookington and he was pleased that the staff there were so friendly, treating him like a local, and polite to Zoe.

There was still much for him to ask about her time away and her brother Greg's wedding.

Gradually the conversation drifted towards his life in Scotland, and she asked quite suddenly why he was not in Edinburgh.

"Ah, now, that's what I was referring to in the cab yesterday when I told you I had something to tell you. The trouble, is I don't want to spoil the evening; I mean parts of what I have to tell you are quite dark."

Momentarily, he thought she looked defensive and even uncomfortable. He kept repeating that it had nothing to do with him wanting to see her – that was totally unconnected.

"What are you trying to tell me?" she asked, almost impatiently, "are you going to tell me you are married, or you've got children, or something like that?"

"No, no, nothing like that. Good heavens, no!" Alistair laughed and then added, stutteringly, "I want to tell you, but first, please believe me."

"Of course I believe you."

"Zoe, I had no idea when I was on the plane and slipped you my card, that I was going to be asked by Dennis to investigate Henrietta's murder. I passed you the card because I wanted to see you again."

The emotion of getting it off his chest came to him, and fighting back the surprising tears that came to his eyes, he blurted out again, rather rashly, "Because I wanted to see you again and I had feelings for you. It had nothing to do with this ghastly investigation, which I didn't even know about when we were on the plane."

Despite her total shock at what he had just told her, she saw how worried he appeared by such a thought.

"Of course, of course, of course I believe you," she repeated, sounding rather relieved, as it seemed to Alistair.

They sat in silence for a bit.

"I wondered if you were going to say you were married or something like that," she said, recovering a bit from the surprise, and hoping that humour would help him to relax.

"Good heavens, no," he repeated. "But it's complicated everything, it's got in the way. It's such a blinking nuisance that I have to be worrying myself and you with it all, when I'd just like to be able to be normal, like everyone else. I'd like to just be with you in a carefree way, same as every other couple, but this whole matter has blown up and I'm in it up to here."

He raised his hand to his neck to stress his involvement in the case, which he felt sure she would underestimate.

"Other couples have annoying things, Alistair. We don't live in a perfect world. We live in a world where, for all its beauty, these horrible things like murder are about; but that doesn't mean it's going to be a problem for us," she said sympathetically, squeezing his hand for the first time in England.

The hand squeeze made his heart race, but he sat silently for a moment pondering her words.

"Let's shelve it till tomorrow. Let's have what we'll jokingly call a formal chat about it tomorrow," she suggested, with a twinkle in her eye.

"Oh, I like that – that's a great idea." He nodded, and was about to try and thank her for being so understanding and her superb suggestion, when the waiter came up and asked if everything was alright.

He was conscious that they had been there slightly longer than his usual sojourns, so he asked for the bill and paid, declining Zoe's offer to contribute.

They walked to the station, again talking sweet nothings, and were lucky with catching a train straightaway. Soon they were in Chelsea.

"Here's my favourite front door," he said smiling, as they approached Number 16.

"To save you coming all the way here, I'll get the train out to Cookington tomorrow for a change. Meet you at the station at twelve, and we can have a bite, take a walk in the park and talk it all through. Lets take advantage of these few days while I'm here before visiting my relatives."

She would not allow him to resist her suggestion by travelling in unnecessarily to Chelsea again.

"I know when I'm beat," he joked, "so see you at twelve at Cookington Station."

On the porch, he gave her a kiss on the cheek, which he could feel all the way home.

Alistair slept well that night.

***

The next day he turned up at the station at twelve. He made sure he was there first, knowing that waiting on her own at the station might not be to her liking.

When she arrived, he thought she looked more beautiful than ever.

Within minutes they had popped into a nearby pub for a quick bite of lunch, but kept off the subject throughout their pleasant snack, talking mostly about the things they agreed were better in England than across the water.

They set off afterwards towards the park.

"This is simply a lovely place," she said appreciatively as they entered the grand gates.

"Ah, one day I must show you real country," he rejoined, "up in the Highlands."

Then he took the initiative and plunged straight into the subject with no holds barred. He told her everything: his astonishment when he found his old friend Dennis was serious in asking him to carry out the investigation; how, like the rest of the country he had followed the case in the papers and in the media; and with particular interest, having been a good friend of the victim and her widower, Dennis.

Inevitably he explained far more than was necessary why he had not mentioned his friendship with Henrietta and Dennis, when she had referred to the case on the plane.

"Didn't want to get bogged down in the whole sorry affair," he reiterated for the umpteenth time. "I wanted to chat to you and get to know you. You can understand that, can't you?"

He felt great relief that she seemed to understand

357

what he was saying, and very shortly she was telling him all about her brother, Greg, and how he had told her, as a confiding sister, about his ill-fated romance with Henrietta, and how he had been "cut up by it all" - although it was more him choosing to break up with Henrietta than she breaking it off.

"He confides in me," she said rather proudly, as it appeared to Alistair, who nodded seriously.

"He fancied her, I think, but they had differences in attitudes about things. I told him once she wasn't his type, and I think eventually that comforted him. He said to me that I was the only person he would listen to saying that. Of course, Henrietta had actually left him for Rhys, who I gather she was rather infatuated with, but who, from what I heard, was rather a loud, coarse businessman."

They discussed how strange it was that Dennis had not referred to Greg, when listing Henrietta's previous lovers.

They agreed that the question arose whether Dennis had even known about Greg.

"Buzz didn't appear to know about it either," commented Alistair, stopping to point out a rather grand stag that stood stationary, staring at them. Like the cat near Len's house in Kingfisher Row, it too seemed to sense a problem of its own, turned and trotted off.

"Well, Buzz never mentioned it to me, poor chap; but then it was all long after his halcyon days with her," resumed Alistair, stooping, picking up a twig and throwing it into the blue yonder.

"Unless they are both not letting on about it," responded Zoe, continuing, "seems strange that both should be keeping quiet about it. Maybe this is the great secret in her life. However, one thing I can assure you, Alistair, and that is my brother, Greg, is a totally impossible person to have been a criminal."

"I absolutely accept that," said Alistair, concerned that it sounded somewhat formal.

By the time their walk had ended and they were back at the Tube station, Alistair had a rather satisfying feeling that nothing had been left out in the résumé of the situation.

 He kissed her goodbye and returned contentedly, but somehow paradoxically feeling a little lonely, to his hotel.

On arrival he found to his surprise that he was really tired. All that fresh air and exercise is probably the reason, he thought, and it must be the relief at covering so much ground and getting all that over with. He lay back for what turned out to be a long sleep.

However, Alistair had an unpleasant dream that night, in which Greg was congratulating him on his engagement to his sister Zoe, but was hiding an axe behind him as he did so. He woke with a start in a sweat. It was five o'clock in the morning. He didn't care how tired he would be the next day; he would get up and sit and think this whole matter through.

Curiously, he was in some ways glad that Zoe had felt she had to visit relatives some distance away. It would give him a little time by himself to get back to what had been becoming his normal lifestyle as a very private detective.

It was ridiculous, but a tear came to his eye. How sad that their romance had this evil crime louring over it. He tried to imagine how things would have been if they had just met up in more ordinary circumstances. He reminded himself of her words that life was not a fairy story. Hadn't she said that nothing was perfect in this life? On the positive side it was true, that already what she had said about Greg had made him feel strangely closer, and almost admitted into family secrets.

As Zoe said, one must take life as it comes, his thoughts continued. Joy and sorrow were so often around together. Had he not sat through a sermon on that very theme, a lifetime ago, when his father was an elder, sitting alongside him in his morning coat at St Cuthbert's, Princes Street, in Edinburgh?

He heard the birdsong, so loud outside his hotel window – even here in the busy conurbation of West London. Another day starting, he mused, such a precious gift from the Creator - what would He do with it?

He needed a break, and yet he must keep the momentum of his investigation going. He must do something to further his thoughts on the matter, but now how about someone completely different? Everyone had praised Emma Duncan as being the best example of a true Christian that St Peter's, Cookington, had produced. Yes, why not? He would track down this Emma Duncan, who seemed to have such a good reputation in the parish. Why! Had not even the critical Fred referred to her as a "good 'un"?

CHAPTER 28

(An interview with a flower arranger)

Of course, he was early for breakfast that morning. Cissie began irritatingly to sing her erroneous version of the refrain again, "Can't sleep, can't eat, I'm glad I'm not young anymore."

Realising that he was tired after his nightmare and early rise, Alistair felt more than ever that it would be a suitable day for a relaxing tea and chat with Emma Duncan, the stalwart old lady of the parish. Accordingly, he phoned her and arranged to make a call that afternoon for tea. She sounds welcoming, he thought, and after all, she was the one who had said at a chance meeting in the street, "If it all gets too much for you, give us a call and come and have a cuppa with the old flower arranger – I may be able to help you more than you think."

What did she mean by that? Alistair's ever questioning brain wondered now. Originally he had thought she meant that she knew a lot of tittle-tattle and gossip about the parish. Perhaps she was referring to her intention to convert him to the Faith, which at the time he had sensed and rather backed away from. But did she mean she knew something specific about the case that might lead to a breakthrough? No, he concluded, She just meant a little tittle-tattle. He needed a quiet day, and this would be a quiet day, OK. Afternoon tea with this dear old lady – what a charming quintessentially English prospect, he mused, stirring his breakfast teacup.

I've certainly got a less hectic schedule than the prime minister, he chuckled to himself that afternoon on his way to her house, as he passed a billboard announcing the latest political crisis.

He was surprised to find that Emma's house stood a little apart from the other homes belonging to parishioners that he had visited so far. It was on a main road, which was even busier than Edwin and Helen's, and not very prepossessing from the outside. However, having rung the doorbell and been ushered in, he soon noticed how neat and tidy it was. Surprisingly spacious and definitely cleaner, he thought, that any other house of the parish that he had been in. The armchairs and sofa seemed extra large and comfortable. He sank back in sheer luxury and looking up, expressed his admiration for such a nice room. Even before noticing the well-arranged and lovely flowers, his eye fell on the fine photograph of a gentleman in naval uniform.

He assumed it was her husband, whom he knew had been killed in the war, and she confirmed this.

She talked interestingly about the work of the church, and it seemed to him that what he had heard about her was indeed true and she was very holy, for want of a better word, albeit in a slightly unexpected sort of way.

Gradually the conversation imperceptibly moved on to the subject of the crime.

"Did you ever suspect anybody about this?" he asked, pleased to be getting down to business at last as he stirred the tea.

"I really can't imagine any of our lot doing a crime like that. Myself, I feel sure it's got to be someone with a quarrel with her from outside."

"You mean outside the parish?" Alistair sought clarification, liking her use of the phrase 'our lot'.

"Yes, someone involved in her life but unconnected with our parish."

"That's interesting and helpful," Alistair added after a pause, giving her a penetrating look.

"You know, when you worship with people over a long period of time you really do get to know them in an odd sort of a way. I mean," she interrupted herself, "are you a church person, Mr MacTavish?"

"No, I'm not."

There was a silence as he again stirred his tea unnecessarily; then he added, "Sorry."

He expected her to laugh, but she did not. Then, as the pause continued, he remarked, "However, I'm going to have a big think about all that when this is all over. Funny, I haven't told anyone else that."

He smiled at her as she in turn looked penetratingly at him.

"I'm glad you said that," she whispered.

"Said what?" He barked.

"About the big think," she replied and added, "I'll keep you in my prayers."

Alistair was not sure whether one was meant to say thank you, so remained silent.

Emma Duncan placed her cup and saucer down on the table and continued, "No, I've administered the chalice to them for years, and I kind of feel it in my bones … they just couldn't have - "

Alistair interrupted her. "But I mean they have feelings, passions; you can't be sure, can you? You can't really know what people are like – what secrets there are in their lives. I mean, people put on public facades, don't they?"

She looked a bit shocked.

He sought to clarify his point. "It's not a criticism of them – it's human nature. They don't go round with a placard round their neck saying, 'I'm capable of a crime of passion', do they?"

"I'm pretty sure I couldn't commit a crime of passion." A twinkle came into her eyes. "I'd use poison, I think."

Alistair laughed, "You would?" And then, warming to her more at finding that she did have a sense of humour after all, he added, "But what about some of the others?"

She threw her head back and laughed. "Oh dear! No, honestly, I truly can't imagine any of them doing a crime like this! I feel it's got to be something completely unrelated to the church."

"But she was a vicar, and for a vicar, isn't the church the biggest thing in their life?"

"Apart from her family, and I mean vicars are ordinary people, even though some of them try and think they're not. No, I'm certain it's either something to do with her personal life, maybe from way back, or..." She broke off.

"Or some passing maniac?" suggested Alistair helpfully.

"Exactly," beamed Emma.

"Can I ask you why you said that about vicars being ordinary people, and all that?"

"Oh, no particular reason; but it's true, isn't it?"

"Come on, Emma, I've got to try and pick up on any little nuance that people let drop. That's what makes my little investigation different to the police's. Picking up on little nuances," he repeated rather deliberately, "and I thought I detected just possibly a little meaning in the way you said that about her, without me saying anything. Did she ever say or do something which made you make that little comment about vicars being ordinary people?"

"I spoke to her once about my husband's death. It was weak of me; I was just after reassurance, I suppose, though my faith is strong and I suppose I didn't really need reassurance from a priest; but I asked her if she was sure I would be reunited with George in heaven."

She nodded towards the naval photograph, and

pursed her lips before continuing.

"We were so in love. George's ship went down about a year after we were married. Torpedoed, or 'tin fished' as he and the lads used to phrase it in those distant days. Anyway, he was lost at sea. There's no grave. It's been such a long wait – this waiting through youth, middle age and now old age. I've pinned everything in the doctrine of survival of death – I mean the Resurrection - but I didn't want to bombard you with religious terms."

He gazed at her intently, impressed by her sincerity.

"Not yet, at anyrate," she added, raising her eyebrow and giving him that wry look.

"And did she give you reassurance?" asked Alistair abruptly.

"To my astonishment, she asked me what would happen if you had two husbands, or for a man, two wives. Rather oddly, she said that she wasn't sure she wanted to meet all her exes in the next life. That's all. It's just that it wasn't what I was expecting. It was a bit disappointing, if you know what I mean. I made a slight fool of myself." She paused and coughed in an embarrassed sort of a way.

"Go on," prompted Alistair. "What did you say?"

"Well, I don't know why I'm telling you this … I haven't told anyone else."

Again she paused and gazed at the fireplace before continuing.

"It was totally stupid of me, but I suppose I hadn't received the reassurance I was seeking from her, and I felt the need to ask to see the bishop and get my reassurance from him. You see, in the Anglican Church, we believe the bishop has care for each one of his flock, as we say in our quaint old biblical language. Anyway I wouldn't have troubled him about anything else – just that. It's the most important thing in my life

365

obviously – this looking forward to being reunited with George in heaven. That's what keeps me going. That's what it's all about – all this church business. That's why I put the flowers on the altar every Saturday evening."

"And how did the bishop react?" inquired Alistair, somewhat moved.

"Well, if you must know, he quoted the famous line from scripture: 'He that believeth in me shall never die,' and then he just gave me a personal blessing. I just felt completely at peace after that. Funnily enough, within a second, he asked me how Henrietta was settling in, and of course I said 'Oh, fine.'"

Alistair bowed as if acknowledging the privilege of being told something very personal and important.

"Very interesting," he managed. "I'd like to talk more about all that sometime, and I'm not just saying that; I really mean it. But to get back to Henrietta. I just want to get this clear. Are you saying that there was something in the vicar's life that made it difficult for her to believe that love survives the grave?"

Emma Duncan thought carefully before replying. "Well, it was as if the answer to my question caused a problem to her; yes, as if it might be a bit complicated for her. How can I put it? I detected that her private life hadn't been what you might call straightforward."

A quite lengthy pause followed this observation, during which Emma's expression changed from a beam to take on a more reflective appearance, and it was only broken eventually when Alistair, realising that he must revert to the investigation, raised his hands in a gesture of resignation.

"Well, you know the police have pursued all the conventional lines of inquiry, and having discussed it with Dennis, I know he takes the view that my new tack should be to investigate people's hunches – that sort of line of inquiry – a bit different to our beloved constabulary, who have drawn a complete blank."

Emma Duncan looked as if she was about to speak, but then she waited for Alistair to continue, which he did.

"Of course, I've been doing quite a bit of what you might call conventional investigation – checking train times, times and dates and all that sort of thing - but I'm aware that in most cases the police have been there before me. Where they haven't been is on these interesting little roads down people's hunches. That's really where, as Dennis put it, I come in."

They chatted on a little bit, mostly about other things, particularly about plants and trees and birds, before saying their goodbyes.

As Alistair walked home he was deep in thought. More than ever he felt that enough people shared his own hunch that there was something in Henrietta's past that was sufficiently in her thoughts for it to manifest itself when certain germane questions were raised. Sure, it was only a hunch, but the old mantra returned to his brain: weren't hunches what his old friend Dennis wanted him to chew over?

By the time he had got to the pub at the crossroads his thoughts were switching, and he was earnestly going over and over in his mind the meetings he had had with both Buzz and Rhys, but particularly the latter. He decided on a whim to allow himself 'a quick one' in a pub of which the doors were alluringly open.

The old-fashioned interior appealed to him, and choosing a corner table away from the fruit machine, he sat down by himself with the firm intention of thinking undisturbed for a good few minutes.

On and on his mind repeated that he had to go particularly, not only on other people's but on his own hunches, vibrations and gut instincts too.

Why did his own thoughts keep leading him to wonder about Rhys's wife, Sheila? She might well be someone who, no doubt with a woman's intuition, could help him a lot. He resolved on the morrow to try and make contact with her; but the evening was yet young, and he ordered a second drink with a good feeling of enjoying free time after working hard, because in some way his chat with Emma had helped him clarify his thoughts.

He would get some crisps too. He sat back in the pub chair and watched the football match distantly on the overhead plasma screen. That old phrase, 'This is as good as it gets', came to him, and he passed a pleasant evening. Yes, I rather admire Mrs Emma Duncan, he thought, as he ordered a third glass.

CHAPTER 29

(A day off, an unexpected phone call and an adventurous evening)

Alistair had to admit to himself that he had a weakness for days off, and the next morning he woke with the rather pleasant feeling and resolve that he was entitled to one. He would attempt to make an appointment with this rather enigmatic and somewhat sinister lady, Sheila, and after that it would be good to give the old brain a break and return on the morrow with a fresh approach.

Breakfast was spent with rather more than usual conversations about sweet nothings with dear Cissie, the waitress. When she left much earlier than usual on some urgent matter of her own, he mused on how he might spend his day off. He loved museums and art galleries, and perhaps most of all just strolling around the city and admiring both buildings and vistas, watching the bustling scene around him from some pleasant café, or not least having his head buried in some journalistic comment on the topic of the day.

He stood up to return to his room, stretched his arms in the warm sunshine which was streaming through the dining room window, and then his mobile rang, vibrating in his pocket.

Blast! he thought. Can't I even have one day off?

It was Fred Goodman. He sounded quite excited, even breathless.

"That you, Alistair?" asked the unmistakeable voice, with its peculiar mixture of pomposity and mischievousness.

"None other, Fred. What's up?" responded Alistair curtly.

"Are you free today?" came the equally curt question, which Alistair did not want to hear.

He took the immediate decision to be absolutely frank. "To tell you the truth, Fred, I was going to give myself a day off … "

"A day off? From what?" Fred could be comically cutting if he wanted to.

"It's harder work than you give me credit for, Fred. All this going to see people and going through everything they say. You have to listen hard and concentrate, you know, and then think it through quietly afterwards. Anyway, what's up?"

"Well, it's a bit of a long shot, but you know all these break-ins we've been having at St Peter's over the last year or so. Well, five out of seven have been on a Tuesday, and I've had the bright idea that we should lie in wait, as it were, and catch them red-handed. I mean, if they're kids I reckon they probably come before the early hours and I'd say that if there were say four of us we could handle them. I mean, if the fuzz aren't going to try and catch them, why don't we?"

"Who are the other members of your gang?" asked Alistair with pleasant sarcasm.

"Well, I've got Edwin and Bill, the insurance officer, lined up, who I gather you haven't met yet, and David Davies says he's game, if you are, as he's got a day's leave tomorrow; and I reckon, as he is meant to be the chairman of the Finance and Fabric and has been going on about this, it's kind of appropriate," answered Fred, unable to resist his usual swipe at poor David for his lack of attendance.

"Oh, so I've got David to blame for this, have I?"

"No, it's just we wondered what you would think, and felt we ought to keep you posted about it all."

"Well … " Alistair hesitated, looking wistfully at the beckoning sunshine and blue sky through the little dining room window.

"You can still have your day off," joked Fred, "only you won't be able to round it off at the Hell Fire Club in Soho or anywhere, because we were thinking of assembling, for want of a better word, at about 10 p.m., when the hall users have left and locked up. I think it's the badminton club tonight, and apparently they shut up shop pretty promptly – unlike the blinking cycling club, which I used to have to turf out at about eleven."

"This sounds like what I call an adventure," chuckled Alistair, warming to the idea the more he thought about it.

"Great! Welcome to the gang then, Alistair. It may be and indeed probably is a complete non-event, but boy, would I like to round those scoundrels up. Bloody vandals, sorry – *wretched* vandals! Funny how when the vicar's not there anymore, you do start swearing a bit more."

Far from spoiling Alistair's day off, he felt the plan enhanced it. For added to the pleasant sensation of ambling around in the City and enjoying everything from views to coffee, was now the agreeable prospect of a fun evening meeting up with two likeable enough chaps and one other, who if nothing else might inadvertently throw further snippets of useful information his way.

As it turned out, he did indeed have a good day, at least in his book. It was spent wandering around intriguing alleyways in the City and sampling a couple of pubs and a café.

He also took the opportunity to visit the church of St Botolph's, which Rhys's wife, Sheila, had claimed to visit on the day of the crime. He made a point of looking carefully in the visitors' book at the pages around that date and found no signature. He did however notice that there was a signature, which struck him as not unlike that of the 'A. Wilson' that he had noticed for those two days in the St Peter's visitors' book. Though infuriatingly inconclusive, the signature struck him as sufficiently similar to make him get out his camera and take a photograph of it, to the astonishment of an off-duty guide. "My old friend visited here earlier," he said rather lamely, as he turned the pages back to the present day and beat a fairly hasty retreat.

He sat for a moment on a bench and contemplated how it would be perfectly possible to visit both St Botolph's and St Peter's on the same day, and indeed be met by Henrietta, and then stroll deep in conversation in the allotments, as witnessed by Gary and Fred and possibly Vanessa's camera. Was his train of thought getting too far-fetched to the point of being ludicrous? he wondered. You could easily read far too much into everything, he knew, and yet, and yet and yet … what other theory was there? None bar a passing homicidal maniac.

With an effort of will, he checked his wild thoughts and strode off to continue his day in London.

He would head west, for the next best thing to going to the theatre for him was to walk outside one and study it from every angle, which custom he did indeed indulge in, having drifted past fascinating office buildings, plaques and statues.

In the late afternoon he returned eastwards and allowed himself the luxury of climbing the Monument, from where he gazed out in all directions at the hubbub of London stretching out to the horizon beneath him.

Somewhere over there, just out of sight beyond the horizon, lay Cookington, with St Peter's and its yet unsolved mystery. The thought of Cookington from here, in the very centre of the bustle, made it seem quite a homely place, not least because his temporary home, the Concord Hotel, lay just beyond and for the first time he felt a strong, almost emotional affection for the suburb, which was paradoxically so sleepy and so bustling. He turned to face north. 400 miles in that direction lay his real home, the only home, the New Town and dear Mrs Davidson, his landlady, as he called her; and of course also the enigmatic Buzz.

The thought of Buzz brought him speedily back to the increasingly onerous task in hand, and more immediately to the need to get back for what he termed Fred's adventurous vigilantism.

Alistair decided not to return 'home', as he was beginning to call his brother's hotel, but to have a nice meal in a reasonably priced restaurant and then go directly to St Peter's to link up with the rest of the gang.

When he eventually arrived there, he reflected, in philosophical mode, on how now it was the Monument and the City of London that was in turn just out of sight, over the horizon, as it were. By now he was walking down the short, familiar street, so delightfully christened Apostles Way, and in a moment found Fred Goodman, Edwin, David and a third rather rough-looking fellow, whom he presumed to be Bill Thompson, the insurance officer, all sitting in a car in the car park.

Fred Goodman jumped out on seeing him, and immediately gave an impression of being in charge - for all the world, thought Alistair, like an older more slow-moving Captain Mainwaring from the celebrated *Dad's Army* series.

"We've only just arrived in David's limousine," said this alternative version of Captain Mainwaring through the front nearside window. "Come and join us; we're just going to have a little council of war. You haven't met Bill Thompson, our insurance officer, yet, have

373

you?"

Alistair climbed into the rather spacious and opulent vehicle, shook hands with his new acquaintance, Bill Thompson, saying, "We haven't met before, nice to meet you," and sat back for an evening of fun.

"Nobody's met me!" joked the gruff, seemingly inebriated insurance officer, "and the reason is I never go to church. Got landed with the role by old Maurice, the previous chappie here. Told me the idea was to inveigle me into the congregation, but I said, 'Maurice, old man, you're going to have to pray a little harder, because I prefer to lie in bed on a Sunday morning.' Well, at least I'm honest – more than some of this lot, I'll tell you."

Alistair could not help rather liking this new-found member of the cast, as he saw it.

"Don't do yourself down," put in David, "I saw you there on Easter Day."

"That was only because of break-in number three – bloody kids! If we catch 'em tonight, I'll make sure they never come to church again."

They all laughed and sat chatting for a while in the growing dusk.

Eventually Fred announced, "When the last of this badminton gang pushes off, we'll move into the hall and take up positions to watch. I reckon we can push off at midnight if nothing happens, because I honestly reckon you're right, they are kids who have been causing all this trouble."

Two tardy members of the badminton club stayed irritatingly long.

"Those two are obviously having an affair," said Bill Thompson, adding, "can't say I blame the fellow, she's pretty dishy."

"Just cool it, Bill, and try and behave for once," responded Fred.

Eventually the amorous couple strolled off down the road past Florence's house and disappeared into the depths of Cookington.

"We do a pretty good show at weddings here at St Peter's," joked Fred as he watched them go, adding, "right, chaps, it's down to business."

With almost military precision the four sentries moved to their positions as outlined on Fred's hand-drawn map of the premises, and commenced the long watch.

Fred had allocated to Edwin and David a position behind some bushes, from which there was a very good view of the great West Door, the main entrance of the church, which all members of the congregation normally used on a Sunday.

Alistair had been assigned a position in the hall, giving him an excellent view through the window of the south side of the church and its chapel at the west end, and at its east the choir vestry, which had been the method of entry to the church in some of the break-ins.

Fred himself took up position at the east end of the church outside the little used door which was called the ambulatory door, on account of the fact that on going through it one found oneself in an actual passageway behind the altar.

Just as the church clock struck eleven o'clock, Alistair saw a flash. It was an unmistakeable flash, coming from the chapel window, and it could only mean one thing, he immediately thought. *There is someone inside taking a photograph.* However almost at once he corrected himself, for he saw what could hardly be mistaken for anything other than torchlight.

Alistair immediately walked hastily towards Fred Goodman's position. He found Fred transfixed on the rusty old chair he had perched on during the watch. Alistair noticed that Fred was shaking markedly.

At Alistair's arrival, Fred managed to get up, and seemingly taking a grip of himself, said, "Someone came running out of that ambulatory door, and goodness knows how, seemed to disappear over the wall beyond it! Let's all meet up and work out what to do."

"Well, Fred, I came over to tell you that I saw torchlight in the chapel. There's someone in there now, unless it's the fast mover you saw coming out and legging it over the wall."

"Right, into the chapel we shall go," responded Fred impressively. "Let's get together with the others at the west end and go in."

Aware that something had happened, the others met them as they approached, and they all stood for a moment in a group just outside the big West Door.

Edwin, who knew full well that Fred almost certainly had his own key, nonetheless produced his key with its large key ring saying 'Churchwarden'. "Do you know, the bishop said to me at Henrietta's induction that it was always the sign of a good churchwarden to have the key."

"Shh, no silly talk!" came Fred's reprimand as he reasserted his authority.

In seconds they were in the porch, or narthex as it was called. Fred found the light switch without even looking. After fourteen years as churchwarden he could find most switches in the dark.

They all stared round looking for any signs of damage or loss and then Fred ran bravely to the chapel, where Alistair had seen the torchlight, but reported it empty.

It was Alistair who noticed it first. "Look, looks like they stopped to sign the visitors' book!" he said with a laugh in his voice. Then he changed his tone and added in some astonishment, "Hey, is that coincidence or what? It's open at the page of the week of the crime."

"You're joking!" put in David.

Alistair was by now studying, not for the first time, the dates and names on that page carefully.

As he opened the inside door leading from the narthex to the church, Fred, more like Captain Mainwaring than ever, summoned them and whispered, "We had better check the whole church thoroughly. I guess it would be so easy not to notice something missing."

"The candlesticks are all here," contributed David, trying to be helpful.

"Well, at least the choir vestry is still locked," joined in Bill, adding in very much of an insurance officer's tone, "so they can't have got the violins."

"Unless the sacristy's been gone through, and they've entered from the ambulatory."

They went over to the big door to the left of the altar that went from the inside of the church to the sacristy.

Edwin turned the ancient handle, exclaiming, "Oh no, it's unlocked!" He turned to the others. "As you know, Fred, that's always the last check we do after counting the collection and locking up of a Sunday morning. We always check that's locked. I can guarantee Alan will swear blind that he locked it after the last service." He turned to Alistair and said, "Alan's the guy who counts the collection after the services and locks that door up afterwards. He said to me once, 'If ever I forget to lock that door, you can book me into the care home.' We'll give him one of your buzzes when we get back, Alistair."

Unnerved by this unexpected easy access from the church to the sacristy, they all looked hurriedly round within, but found nothing missing.

"I would say there's nothing out of place," said Fred eventually, putting his hand through what remained of his hair and leading the little gang on through another door into the ambulatory, which linked the sacristy to the choir vestry on the other side.

"As I knew, the ambulatory door is certainly open. That's where our friend fled through before legging it over the wall. I was sitting outside, but it was so quick and unexpected that I can't help identify who the hell it was," said Fred in a troubled tone.

In the darkness Alistair gave an amiable beam towards Fred, rather liking the way such an old gentleman used such youthful language, as the old man continued, "The good news is that the door from here to the choir vestry is still locked, so yes, Bill, as you said, those violins should be safe."

For a few moments, they remained standing in a huddle and looking anxiously around, until Fred broke the silence. "It seems like whoever was in here got wind that we were around and scarpered mighty quickly from the chapel, into the narthex, through the church, through the sacristy, round the passage we call the ambulatory and then out through its door and heigh-ho – unbelievably - over the wall."

"I reckon you're right, Fred," agreed David, "that would all tie up. Didn't you get even a fleeting glimpse of the damned rascal?"

"I couldn't see the person at all; it was like a shadow – that's all," replied Fred, shrugging his shoulders.

"Couldn't see any clothes at all?" pressed Alistair, knowing that first reports were often the most useful.

"Nothing," was Fred's frustrated reply.

"How tall?" continued Alistair, very much taking on the role of a policeman.

"Honestly, I can't even say that. It was just a shape – literally a shape - presumably from this ambulatory door, flitting across that little bit of car park and up

378

over the wall."

"And of course, once over the wall – well, that's it - they've disappeared," put in Bill, trying to show that he had sobered up a bit.

Fred appeared to be thinking rather hard, before saying, "Yes, I suppose that's something I can say – they were agile OK."

"Well, there you are, we're looking for someone who is agile," said Alistair encouragingly.

"That eliminates half the congregation," joked Edwin, adding, "as you say Fred, it's blinking kids. It's their parents who deserve a stiff punishment, as much as them."

Alistair had walked down the aisle and back into the narthex, where he appeared immersed in studying the visitors' book.

Eventually the others called him back.

"Look, guys, we need somewhere warm and private to discuss this; Helen's away tonight, come back to my place," suggested Edwin.

Having satisfied themselves that the church was empty and that nothing seemed to be missing, they left the church, carefully locking all the doors, particularly the one from the church to the sanctuary, which they had been so surprised to find open.

Alistair suggested he would have the quickest of looks at the ground between the ambulatory door and the wall, but do it more thoroughly on the morrow.

He rejoined the others carrying a cheap child's bracelet

"The trouble is, anyone could have dropped that anytime," observed David, thinking it was time he made a contribution.

"A coincidence, though, because it's directly opposite the ambulatory door, is it not?" pronounced Fred in rather lordly tone, and then added, "I reckon I'd have seen that if it had been there on Sunday when I swept that bit of the car park."

Soon they were all back aboard David's grand limousine, and in minutes had travelled the short distance and drawn up outside Edwin's house.

Edwin's grown-up children did not seem too keen on the prospect of an impromptu parish meeting elbowing them out of the front room, where the television blazed away, so Edwin ushered them all into the dining room, with a muttered comment to the effect that kids and cats ruled in his house. In a moment they were all sitting round the table.

"It's good sitting round a table, it'll make us concentrate, and the whisky will be just as good, Alistair," laughed Edwin.

Alistair smiled. "We'll never be able to disassociate the wee dram from our nation."

There followed what could best be described as a council of war, in which they all agreed to keep watch at the church for the next few nights. They would finalise arrangements in the morning when they were fresher. Finally, they agreed not to tell the police about the evening's goings-on. "Or not yet, at any rate," confirmed Alistair, getting up and looking for his hat before adding, "don't want my pitch being queered just yet, if you know what I mean."

He had said goodbye to the others and was on his way to the station when curiosity got the better of him and he determined to turn and just make a last evaluation of the height of the wall, where this fugitive had last been seen.

He had to pinch himself to contemplate how the day's unexpected adventure had added such a twist to his investigation; because, although he had kept such a secret thought to himself, he could not exclude the possibility that there was a connection between this break-in and the crime he was investigating. I mean, he thought, nothing has been taken; but I saw torchlight. Was somebody looking at something, or looking for something? I'm probably barking up the wrong tree.

It seemed even darker now than before, but once back in the car park of St Peter's, and as his eyes grew more accustomed to the dark, Alistair could find his way to the wall easily enough.

He would just have one more look at the area by that wall, he thought, and as he peered through the intense darkness at the black outline of the masonry, his first thought was that there was no way that he himself would have been able to scale it.

It must surely have been a young person, and a fit young person at that too, he mused, as he turned to leave with his eyes now firmly on the ground, looking for any obvious clue that might fortuitously have fallen.

Then it came. Crashing down from the tower, not a stone but a large slab of concrete thumped into the ground beside him.

With reflex action, he quickly swung round and looked up to the top of the tower. He saw it beyond doubt. It was only for a second, but it was a light, and he just knew that it was the same torchlight that he had seen earlier. But now it was there, between the ancient parapets of this sturdy landmark.

The realisation rushed to his mind: they hadn't checked the tower. They had assumed that no intruder would have gone there; but quickly the ghastly truth came to him that this was no ordinary intruder. This was someone who had seemingly just tried to murder him. This must surely be one and the same as the horrific killer of the late Rev. Henrietta Carr.

For a moment his whole being told him to rush away to safety, but something, whether sheer curiosity or a sense of duty, made him instantly calculate that

381

this was his chance to find out who it was at this church who was not averse to a little murder now and again. If he did not seize the opportunity, the mystery might remain unresolved for ever.

Annoyingly, he did not have the spare key to the church which Dennis had given him, and unless his would-be murderer inside had keys, he or she would presumably be locked in now. Of course, it might well be that they did have keys. Either way, he must summon help and keep an eagle eye out for any escape bid from the building. He felt a strange unfamiliar sense of real fear come over him and now again, as he backed into the darkest shadow he could find, part of him wanted desperately to summon the police.

He felt sure Edwin and David would want to call the police in this new situation; but as well as fear, the common fault of human nature - namely pride - made him for a moment yearn for this to be *his* moment of glory, not the police's.

He crouched in his new-found total darkness, considering his position. The idea came to him in a flash. Fred was his man. He had a set of keys that no one had had the heart to ask him to return when he retired. Not only did he have a set of keys, but he had the necessary mischievousness, which had led him to ask Gary to help break down that fence and indeed to hide, eavesdropping in that fuse cupboard in the vicarage. Yes, Fred had the sheer spirit to be game for such an adventure; or to use the modern jargon, as he humorously mused, "up for it"; but was it right to summon an old man of that state of health to such a precarious situation?

However, such doubts were answered with the thought that no one else, outside their little gang of vigilantes, would be able to take on board his incredible position, for they would not know about the evening's

382

earlier events; and of course it was Fred Goodman, who had told him about the tower.

The phone conversation which ensued between Alistair on his mobile and Fred, who had only recently returned home and was engaged in cleaning his teeth in the bathroom, must surely have ranked amongst those claiming to be the most bizarre in the history of human telecommunication.

"*Fred*," gasped Alistair and added, without managing to disguise his anxiety, a rather ridiculous, "is that you?"

Fred, not entirely able to conceal his surprise, confirmed it was indeed him, and he was trying to be as quiet as possible to avoid disturbing his dog.

"Well, I'm trying to be as quiet as possible to avoid disturbing a murderer," replied Alistair, experiencing one of those surreal moments when he could hardly credit what he was saying.

"What was that?" came the quick response, tinged with anxiety.

"Fred, curiosity got the better of me, and as I was going home after our little post-mortem at Edwin's, I turned and went back to the church just to have another quick look at that wall. Sorry… sheer bloody curiosity. I wanted to remind myself just how high it was. Anyway, just as I was examining it and standing there thinking … whoosh, down falls this dirty great slab of concrete, missing me by inches! I just knew it came from the tower and instinctively looked up and, sure as eggs are eggs, I could see someone up there in the turrets or rather, I'm sure I saw a light – a torchlight – just for a second; but it was just like the one I saw in the chapel earlier this evening when you placed me on guard, looking through the hall window.

"Where are you now?" asked the incredulous Fred, who was by now walking down the stairs and no longer concerned with attempts to keep quiet.

"I'm crouching by the back entrance to the car park. The guy must be still in there. I need someone urgently to help apprehend this maniac. I can't call the police in the circumstances – I mean, at this stage I'm not sure I could explain everything to them. David, Edwin and Bill would want to call them I'm sure – in fact I know they would. I've just got to spot who this person is, but I need reinforcements, if you know what I mean. This whole evening's entertainment was your idea in the first place, Bill told me; so do you think you could come round?"

There was probably not another man in all England of that age, who in such circumstances would have answered with such alacrity, "I'm on my way. Stay there and don't move! I'll park outside in Apostles Way to avoid causing a stir, and walk in to where you are. I should be able to get there in about ten minutes."

For Alistair it was the longest ten minutes of his life. He kept his eyes firmly fixed on the looming outline of the tower, though occasionally glancing at the West Door as if he was half expecting some fiend to emerge. But soon, visions of Fred either crashing his car or being stopped by the police for speeding seemed to flood his brain so vividly that he wondered if he had really been watching carefully.

Twice he thought the distant sound of a car must be Fred's, only to find it was a cruel false alarm.

Now there was the sound of a car arriving in the street and coming down Apostles Way. Intuitively, he knew it was Fred. The sound of parking, a door closing, footsteps and finally the gait of a shadowy figure approaching, confirmed it was Fred alright. He had a bag round his shoulder and fastened across his front. Although it was obviously switched off, Alistair, whose eyes were now well accustomed to the dark, could see that he carried his ubiquitous torch.

Not the first council of war of that evening now took place. Fred, who somehow gave an impression of a man enjoying himself and only too glad to be engaged on such a scary mission, explained he had brought various bits and pieces with him, adding with a chuckle, "Just for self-defence, of course." Alistair could sense the beam of his smile in the darkness.

"I suggest we go in. We'll say the police are surrounding the church and we want to do a deal with them," said Fred with the authority of a platoon commander, adding wryly, "it won't be the first lie told in that church."

He rebuked himself for making silly chatter and said, "We'll know that whoever we confront is, if not a murderer or indeed *the* murderer, at any rate a would-be murderer."

Together they walked resolutely, almost as if marching, to the West Door. Fred inserted the key firmly into the lock, turned it with the experience that fourteen years as churchwarden had ensured. They entered the narthex and turned left towards the tower door. Fred shone his torch and yelled out in a loud voice, "Police are surrounding this building. Come down and your safety will be assured." Again he added rather humorously to Alistair that he was sure it wasn't the first lie told in this holy place.

A deathly, almost tangible silence prevailed. Alistair, with his love of Shakespeare was reminded of the line, 'not a mouse stirring'.

They reached the door to the tower. With sickening concern they realised it was not only unlocked but open.

Fred looked at Alistair with an eyebrow raised and a

385

nod towards the stairs. "We never thought of checking the tower, did we? he commented, still in his new kind of James Bond style.

Alistair was amazed at his own courage as he followed Fred up the steep spiral stone steps of the tower.

Somehow it helped to banish fear to keep shouting. Fred and Alistair in turn continued to shout out the agreed rather abrupt false message to trick the intruder into a quiet surrender. "The police are surrounding this building. Please allow us to negotiate with you for your safety!"

The silence prevailed, somehow more marked in contrast to their shouts.

"This tower is dangerous!" added Fred in a further shout, with, had Alistair been able to see it, a twinkle in his eye; adding, "quite apart from the prospect of a bit of fisticuffs halfway up, I'm glad I've got a bit of backup!"

Alistair, aware that he was extremely nervous, also sent pretend messages into his lapel to give the impression that he was in communication with a large number of reinforcements. For impromptu improvisation, it was remarkably convincing, and worthy of Rory Bremner himself.

They reached the little anteroom, which was situated about a quarter of the way up the tower. It was a curious, rather soulless, empty space with one or two very old pictures of bell ringers from yesteryear.

Fred went quickly to the door, which led on further up the remaining and much larger number of stairs.

He whispered to Alistair. "Are you prepared to continue?"

A little while ago, thought Alistair, I might have been. But I've so much to lose now with Zoe …

Fred's thoughts were of a different nature. The wife

is dying, I dread being without her. I think I'll go …

"You stay here," ordered Fred, "and I'll go on up. The spiral staircase changes to a ladder after a bit, and I know which rungs of the ladder are safe and which aren't. I know where there's a railing and where there isn't, and this is not an occasion to teach you."

Within a second Fred was gone, and after a few further moments the sound of his footsteps became less loud as he made his way up and up and up.

Alistair sat straining his ear to hear of any movements of Fred above him.

Suddenly there was a tremendous clang below him. He knew it could only be one thing. The door to the tower, which they had used to come in at the bottom, had been banged shut. He also heard the unmistakeable sound of the large key turning. They were locked in the tower, with him alone in the anteroom and Fred, by now, high above him.

Fred too had heard the huge door at the bottom being banged shut, but decided that as he was so near the top, he would go the few extra steps up to the summit. He hoped with all his heart that the sound had simply been Alistair going down and having a look in the church. The cold night air hit him like a knife, but as always, the old mountaineer in him felt a certain satisfaction at having reached such a lofty summit. He went quickly to the parapet and scanned the area round the church below, but as he expected, from that height in the dark could see nothing, though his torch showed that there was a little line of concrete slabs left by a builder, with one obviously missing. He would have loved to look around for what he had a hunch was a hiding place of Henrietta's, but the combination of the cold, the darkness and the growing realisation of their being possibly trapped, combined to make him turn hurriedly and descend the steps quickly.

Alistair, waiting tensely in the little anteroom, far below, heard Fred's approaching descent.

When Fred's footsteps indicated that he was only one twist of the spiral away, he called out asking Fred if he had heard the tower door shutting. Fred, who had by now begun to wonder whether it was his imagination or whether it had been Alistair going down to have a look in the church, now realised with dread that they were almost certainly incarcerated. They decided to check, and agreed that if it was the case, they would return up to this anteroom where they were, which was at any rate less claustrophobic, and where they would be less likely to be victims of eavesdropping, should this sinister intruder be still there with an ear to the door with which he had incarcerated them.

Together, with Fred leading the way and his torch beaming brightly, the two descended from the anteroom.

Fred tried the door and with sickening fear, they realised beyond doubt that their dread was confirmed and they were locked in the tower.

As agreed, they returned up to the anteroom.

"Let's wait and think the situation through before phoning. Thank goodness we've both got mobiles," came Fred's slightly more agitated, but still authoritative, voice.

Alistair was impressed by Fred's calmness in this extraordinary situation and commented on it in flattering tone.

"Army training," responded Fred unable to conceal a tone of pride in his voice, adding with a chuckle, "a lot of people don't realise that I was in the army – only wear my medals on Remembrance Sunday. Long time ago now, all that training, but coming in useful, eh?"

There was a slight pause while Fred adjusted his

torch.

"I reckon we're safe enough here for the moment," he continued. "Whoever's playing silly games knows we're locked in; they probably aren't going to hang about too long, because they probably think there are people who know where we are, or they may think quite correctly that we've got mobiles and will summon help immediately; so I reckon they will have probably scarpered by now. So, let's just hold our horses a minute or two and work out a plan of action."

"You're making me feel better, Fred. I had visions of some monster suddenly appearing," remarked Alistair, very aware of just how frightened he was.

"Unless there's some kind of children's secret hiding place or passage that I don't know about," responded Fred, pleased with the compliment, "I'm confident that there's nobody in this tower except us. I mean, there's just the spiral staircase, which becomes a ladder at the very top. There's this anteroom, and of course there's the actual top, which I can assure you is empty. Bloody cold up there, I can tell you! We'll summon help on the old mobile in a minute, but let's get our thoughts straight first; because I take your point, you don't want the police in on this, not yet at any rate."

"Of course it may be completely unconnected," said Alistair, "but if we are on the trail, I'd so love to solve it all myself – 'the guy with the hunches', Dennis called me when he roped me in on this. I'm rather proud of being called that. Always fancied myself as a sleuth, you know, Fred, ever since I was a kid practically."

By mentioning Dennis, Alistair had reminded himself of what Dennis had said about Henrietta's remark that the tower was a good place to hide something. Fred seemed very taken aback when Alistair mentioned it, and said he'd like to ask more about that later.

"But, no, I agree," continued Fred reverting to the question of the police, "let's keep 'em out of it for the moment."

He paused, collecting his thoughts, and then rather slowly and deliberately continued, "So, it's quite simple, isn't it? He, she or they either left the tower before we went in, then once we had gone in and were well up, they quickly moved out of the shadows and bolted us in."

Alistair could see that Fred was thinking, so held his silence.

"Yes, in which case," continued Fred, very deep in thought and mumbling, "they must have been hanging around in the dark somewhere and just waiting for us to walk into the trap. I knew there was a danger of that, but I didn't want to risk having to tackle an assailant on my own on those first steep steps."

"And I don't think I'd have fancied being left waiting without reinforcements down in the narthex," acknowledged Alistair.

Another seemingly long pause ensued and then Fred started up again.

"You said, didn't you, that you've been watching the church door since seconds after the flying missile nearly poleaxed you?"

"Yes, I'm as sure as I can be that nobody left by the main West Door after that, because I looked up immediately at the top of the tower, saw a momentary torchlight, and within seconds took up position hiding in the shadows within sight of the West Door. Without taking my eyes off it, I contacted you on the mobile from my hiding place in the shadows and waited there till you arrived," affirmed Alistair.

"Well, unless we find that the only other door - the ambulatory door - has been used again since we shut it earlier this evening, they can only have left by some other way. I mean, I suppose for a kind of cat burglar type there are other means, aren't there?"

"I thought we didn't know of any, if we rule out a world rock climbing champion's descent," responded Alistair, trying to ease his own tension.

"It may surprise you to hear, Alistair, that even I abseiled down the tower at a fund-raising event for charity we had a couple of years ago!"

"You're joking, Fred!"

"Go on say it – even at my age!"

"Goodness me, no, I didn't mean that Fred; you're very fit, otherwise I wouldn't have summoned your help. I mean, I didn't realise you had that skill – of abseiling."

"It's not a skill," retorted Fred modestly. "The experts come here and fix up the ropes, and to all intents and purposes they bundle you down like a package ... well no, I suppose to be fair to myself, I bundled myself down like a package. Emma Duncan, our flower arranger, was the eldest. She did it no bother. Sang all the way down, she did! Gave me the creeps, it did, when she was coming down, because she was singing 'I'm on my way to heaven'. Told me afterwards that if anything went wrong it would only mean she'd be reunited with her husband sooner rather than later. That's faith for you."

"She's a gutsy lady, that one. I was impressed by her. So you reckon someone could have been abseiling down the tower after chucking the missile at me, and then pop round to the West Door and lock us in the tower."

"All I'm saying is, it's not impossible to do that. Blimey, even our local MP joined in."

"Old Stewart, did he? Typical bloody politician – even risk their bloody neck for a few votes! Sorry, I'm swearing, and in church too; it's just that I'm nervous – bloody nervous," emphasised Alistair.

"It isn't the first time bad language has been used within these hallowed walls, I can assure you," quipped Fred, adding, "I can remember when old Maurice caught his finger in the church cupboard door. Used to think he was a saintly man, till I heard that."

These humorous recollections did help to ease the tension, but only very temporarily, as their nerves were frayed by their extraordinary plight.

Alistair found himself subconsciously allowing Fred to take on the role of commander in this 'little night operation', as he called it afterwards. He had forgotten till now about Fred's military past.

"I reckon," said that old soldier, with great deliberation, "we wait half an hour and then I'll start phoning. I'll phone Edwin first. He's on the list as being first keyholder in emergency. He's down as officially having all keys. Whether he can find them is another matter. Anyway, do him good to get him out of bed. Can't really phone Florence in such a perilous situation. Sounds sexist, but I'm a product of my times and it just don't seem right to me to put women and children in even a remotely dangerous situation." He paused for a moment. "Henrietta wouldn't have liked to hear me say that," he added jokingly, revealing a sense of humour even in these dire circumstances.

Having originally been so impatient to get out of the tower and away as quickly as possible, Alistair now found himself with a paradoxical feeling of security at being locked in. Who knew what perils might lie in store, should they venture out from the sanctuary of the tower? A hit on the head in the dark from a homicidal maniac, perhaps? Thus ran his wild thoughts.

The fact that they both had mobiles and that Fred had taken the precaution of leaving a note both at home and in his car saying where he was, relieved his sense of being trapped.

"OK," announced Fred after a final of many looks at his watch, "I reckon our half hour is up, Alistair. Let's give our dear friend, old Edwin, a wake-up call."

Moments later he stared in frustration at his mobile, muttering, "Bloody call minder!" and adding rather unconvincingly in an effort to keep calm, "I suppose it's funny."

Alistair looked at Fred, waiting for his next bright idea.

"Of course, I think Edwin said something about unplugging the phone at night," Fred said softly, "because Helen's mum up in Glasgow who has Alzheimer's kept ringing them during the night. But wait a minute, that was ringing a good seven times or so before call minder cut in, so maybe he was just slow getting up. I think I'll keep trying."

At that moment Fred's mobile rang loud and clear with an incoming call.

"What's up, Fred? You just rang my number, just now in the middle of the night. It's bad enough with Helen's mum waking us up at all hours! What the bloody hell is going on?" came Edwin's voice, so clearly that Alistair could hear it himself.

Alistair thought that Fred explained the situation to Edwin just about as clearly and as succinctly as could be done, not least explaining why he thought it best to leave the police out of it at this stage. To Alistair's immense relief, arrangements were made for Edwin to come urgently round, armed with more than just the church keys and to release the captives.

Compared with the recent wait in the anteroom for Fred to come down from the top of the tower, the wait for Edwin to arrive seemed to Alistair to take an eternity. Again his imagination started to produce images of ambushes and other unpleasant possibilities.

Fred's assurances that it took longer than you think to get up, walk or get in the car and drive over from Edwin's place, did nothing to ease his anxiety.

"You know, Fred, I don't mind admitting it: a private detective is meant to solve mysteries, not get caught up in them himself like this."

"Reminds me, when I was a kid – about ten years old, if you can imagine such a transformation…" began Fred, in an attempt to calm his agitated companion.

Alistair's imagination, which had been working overtime, could not actually stretch as far back as Fred Goodman's youth.

"…it used to seem so long to wait till the end of term," continued Fred.

"And your point is…?" said Alistair rudely, owing to his constantly agitated nerves.

"The point is, it did come, eventually."

"Sorry, Fred, I was losing my nerve there a bit," apologised Alistair.

"Don't blame you. I was just talking sweet nothings to try and keep you calm."

At that point they both heard a fairly loud noise, and both thought it must be the big West Door of the church.

"Well, someone's here," came Fred's ever calm and reassuring voice.

Within seconds they heard shouting. It was certainly more than one voice. It sounded like several people were trying to be as loud as possible. It also sounded like the word "Police" was being used a lot.

As fervently hoped for, there then came the unmistakeable sound of the lock on the tower door below being turned.

Some innate sense of self-preservation had made them stay in the anteroom, but now they heard Edwin's voice loudly and clearly calling them, so they descended the spiral staircase as quickly as possible. Fred went first, carrying his torch, which shone brightly, illuminating the old round wall of the spiral staircase.

"Fred, Alistair, are you there?" came the welcome, familiar and unmistakeable voice of Edwin Archer who, for all his sins, was churchwarden of St Peter's, Cookington.

They shouted back, and within seconds had descended to the bottom, where they found the door swung open. There in the torchlight was a rather dishevelled-looking Edwin, looking both pale and fraught.

They both noticed with surprise that behind his shoulder stood the permanently dishevelled insurance officer, Bill Thompson.

"Are you alright? asked Edwin urgently, adding rather unconvincingly as he constantly looked around. "There's nobody here, as far as we can tell."

"Nice to see you, and you too Bill," said the ever polite Fred.

"Thought I'd bring reinforcements with me," chirped Edwin, looking over his shoulder at Bill and adding, "I'm rather a coward when it comes to midnight murderers in spooky towers."

"Don't blame you, Edwin," interjected Alistair, patting him on the back and saying, "there's no way I could come on my own. I'm shaking like a leaf as it is."

"We've been shouting out that we're the police to give us courage, just in case they're skulking in some dark corner," explained Edwin.

"We had the same idea," responded Fred, as Edwin continued self-deprecatingly, "Yeah, I thought I'd bring old Bill with me. I may be churchwarden, but I couldn't for the life of me remember which switch was which just now … ”

"Well, I don't know! What are you like? Churchwardens ain't what they used to be," came Fred's expected and not entirely jocular retort.

"Edwin says he woke me up because he knew I was on my own and it wouldn't disturb any wife or whatever. I told him, 'You can't bank on that another night!'" laughed the rather cheerful insurance officer, who seemed to relish the chance of a little excitement. "If it's those bloody kids that have been causing all that damage and doing all those break-ins, I'll bloody strangle them if I get my hands on them," he added with some vehemence.

Alistair thought in other circumstances such a remark would have put him straight on the suspect list.

The ever practical Fred was already planning a next move. "I vote we check the building out, and then leave it securely locked and go somewhere to discuss and thrash out this mystery – who and why was this person or people up there, and what we do next."

"I've got something to tell you straightaway Alistair," said Edwin earnestly. "As we drove past on the main road, we both saw a light on in the vicarage. Maybe Dennis was disturbed in some way by something connected."

"If he wasn't disturbing us," said Alistair wanting to remind everybody that he was the hired sleuth here.

"I tell you one thing for sure," commented Fred. "That person legging it over the wall, who we saw earlier this evening, could not be Dennis. He's been limping like crazy lately; and if the person who Alistair saw at the top before he called me, escaped by abseiling, which I'm beginning to think they must have, well, Dennis positively refused to join in that, despite Henrietta's vow that she would persuade him to do it."

"But you see, that could all be part of a cover-up.

I'm not saying I think that. I'm just saying you always have to bear it in mind," commented Alistair.

"I suppose you're right," replied Fred, "but if he was acting with that limp, well he deserves an Oscar."

Not for the first time that night, all four of them searched the church thoroughly, and everything appeared in order, as it had when they had gone round locking everything up.

Alistair again seemed drawn and intrigued by the visitors' book being open at the date of the week of the crime. There certainly had been visitors that week. Had someone been looking at that for some sinister reason, possibly even to check there was no evidence against them, and been unexpectedly interrupted and had to rush away? Am I going mad to have such a thought? he wondered. But there had to be an explanation for it being open at that page, and word had certainly gone around that there was a private investigation going on.

His thoughts were also preoccupied with his recollection of Dennis telling him that Henrietta had said she found peace up there in the tower, and had talked about how you could hide up there from the world. The conversation came back so vividly; even his words about how she used to say that Our Lord had gone up mountains and got strength to come down and continue His work. How she used to quote a former bishop of London, Robert Stopford, who used to say, *"Churches are great places to go out from."*

Alistair was also deep in thought at the possibility of two people working together. The person who had fled over the wall earlier in the evening could surely not be the same person who had hurled the concrete slab down from the tower, and presumably later locked him and Fred within. It made him wonder, in his extraordinarily imaginative mind, if there were perhaps two people up to no good here. He even wondered if they were deliberately creating false clues.

I must always try and have a different line of thought to what the police would. That is the role that Dennis asked me to take on, he concluded.

The others had left him for a while as these thoughts had wafted through his mind, and it came as something of a jolt when Fred roused him by saying, "This time there is evidence of a search. I've just discovered the drawers of the little table in the chapel, where we keep the book of remembrance and turn the page each day, have been gone through. I may have missed them earlier this evening when David was with us and we were checking.

"Also, look that drawer at the back of the church hasn't been opened in years," chuckled Fred. "Hang on, I remember curiosity got the better of me one day and I tried to open it, and it was locked. I remember I asked Henrietta about it, and she laughed and said, 'No one knows where the key is.'"

"Well - what's in it, then?" asked Alistair with genuine interest.

"It's bloody empty! Sorry, I do sometimes forget I'm in church. It's empty," replied Fred sheepishly.

"Is empty, but not necessarily *was* empty, eh?" said Alistair, rather slowly and deliberately, and again appearing deep in thought. Eventually he mumbled, "It definitely looks as if somebody was looking for something and something rather specific, because nothing has been pinched. This is a rich burglar, if you know what I mean. It ain't kids; they would have swiped that tape recorder, for example, and that video recorder."

The combination of a deep weariness and their satisfaction that the premises were now empty made them return to Fred's car, and soon each member of this intrepid gang of heroes was back in his own bed in differing degrees of somnolence.

CHAPTER 30

(Another unexpected phone call, and another adventurous evening)

To say that Alistair woke feeling tired would be an understatement. The adventures of the preceding night had left him more exhausted than he felt well with, and it immediately struck him what a blessing in disguise it was that Zoe was away visiting her relatives. He determined to take a day off, and this time he would not let any unexpected phone call interfere with his intention.

By ten in the evening he had managed to maintain his plan and was not only feeling rested but revelling in the glow of a day spent relaxing and reading and doing just what he wanted to do and not what anyone else wanted him to do.

He would take an uncharacteristically early night and return fresh on the morrow to hunting the dragon, as he had now come to think of the whole investigation.

The early retiring to bed was a novel and pleasant sensation for him and he felt slumber approaching, happy in the thought that an hour before midnight was worth two afterwards, as his mother had taught him.

However, Alistair of all people, a true Scot who loved his poetry, should have remembered the famous line of the national bard, that the best laid schemes o' mice an' men gang aft a-gley.

Yes, it was his mobile.

"Damn it," he muttered. He had meant to switch it off and swore, cross with himself for not having done so.

For a moment he thought he would leave it ringing, but it was persistent.

Knowing that the wondering of who it was would wreck his early sleep every bit as much as actually answering it, he struggled for the light switch and then grabbed the mobile.

"Yes," he grunted, not very welcomingly.

"Sir, I'm sorry to trouble you at this time of evening," came the rather cautious but unmistakeable voice of Mrs Martin of 13 Lime Grove.

"It must be important for you to ring me at this time of night, Mrs Martin," he replied not impolitely, but stressing the word "night".

"I was in a terrible dilemma whether to do so or not – really I was," came her timid response.

"What's up?" he asked, adjusting his pillow to a more comfortable position and beginning to feel less irritated, telling himself as much as her, "After all, I'm not staying down here in big brother's hotel for the fun of it; I'm meant to be solving a mysterious crime."

"I thought I heard foxes creating a racket out on the allotments and I went to the window in the dark to see if I could see them, and I saw a torchlight down there at the far end of Helen's allotment. My lights were off so I thought I could watch a bit without being seen. The torchlight kept going on and then intermittently going off. It was kind of going round in circles, and it was almost like something was being looked for."

"Could you see who the person was?" a now alert Alistair cut in.

"No, I could only see the torchlight going round and about," she reiterated.

"Is the person still there?" asked Alistair.

"I haven't seen any sign of anyone for some five minutes now. I didn't know whether to ring you or not, then I thought I'd be awake all night with the dilemma if I didn't ring you, so I thought I'd call you straightaway and get it over with. You did say to do that if I saw anything of interest; though I know you didn't think it would be an immediate sort of thing like this, did you? I haven't told Vanessa yet. I think she'd have the screaming habdabs if I did."

"I was going to ask you to give me five minutes to think what's best to do and then ring you back, but I don't want your daughter being woken up. Stay on the line and keep watching while I think what's best to do."

Alistair was by now sitting on the edge of the bed, holding his mobile in one hand and his brow in the other. His immediate reaction was to leave the whole matter till the morrow, but his restful day meant he felt curiously energetic, and soon enough his conscience came into play. Then emboldened by his survival yesterday, he realised he must go and investigate. The question was, who could he summon to go with him? Fred, despite having sworn that he never wanted such another adventure as last night, would no doubt rise to the occasion; but it would take up valuable time and certainly would not be welcomed by that mischievous Captain Mainwaring doppelgänger after the previous night's experiences.

He did not want to call the police. Again, vanity made him want to make progress with this mystery without their help. They had tried and failed he thought to himself; so he'd be justified in leaving them out of it for now.

"Still can't see any more torchlight," broke in Mrs Martin's voice, sounding stronger and braver, now that she had recruited reinforcements - albeit telephonically - in the form of Alistair.

"Sorry to keep you, Mrs Martin. I'm just deciding something. You see, I'm going to come round; but I'm wondering whether, instead of just pouncing from nowhere and confronting whoever it is on the street or even there on the allotment, it wouldn't be cleverer to come to your house and go over the fence from there, and take the line that we're charged with looking after the security of the allotments. I think your dear daughter, Vanessa, is going to either sleep right through this or you're going to have to explain."

"By all means," said Mrs Martin warmly, already imagining a fine picture of herself in the *Daily Express*, perhaps even alongside this handsome private detective, Alistair MacTavish. As long as Vanessa wasn't in it; but no doubt that was who they would be interested in. No, this time she wouldn't allow them to make her daughter dress up in a bikini. It was her turn, and it would be she herself smiling out at their readers.

"I'll come round straightaway to your house on my own, then. I'll be on my way in minutes," Alistair said, trying to imitate Fred's impressive style from last night.

Woken from her reveries, Mrs Martin reiterated, "Still no more torchlight, Mr MacTavish."

Alistair took only a few minutes to dress, and having ensured that he had both his torches with him, he set off at a good pace for Mrs Martin's house.

It was not an occasion for admiring the stars, but such was their grandeur that he could not help but do so, and for a moment that other great mystery, which also was preoccupying him, came into his mind. It would have to wait. On the immediate front was a crime that needed to be solved.

When he arrived at Mrs Martin's house, he found the front door ajar, with her standing there in the dark.

"I saw you coming through the dining room window," she whispered, adding, "Vanessa is still asleep. I still haven't seen any more torchlight."

"Shall I come up and see where you saw it from?" asked Alistair rhetorically, in the quietest audible voice that he could manage, striding towards the staircase without waiting for reply.

"From here," she said, now slightly breathless with the combination of the excitement and the unusually fast ascent of the staircase in his tracks.

"Show me exactly where the light was, please," came Alistair's immediate and businesslike next question.

"Over there, at the end of Helen's allotment. You can just make out an old disused shed at the end, about halfway to those distant trees by the path," she replied.

"I'll stay watching for a short while, and then probably just go and confront whoever it is. I can't admit to liking these adventures, and I could do with a whisky, to tell you the truth," came Alistair's unexpected comment.

"Your wish is my command," came Mrs Martin's ready response.

"I was only joking!" he said with embarrassment, "But gee, I sure could do with a dram, if you've really got some. No, I don't like this sort of situation. You don't know what to expect, do you? I'll let you into something top secret. I had an adventure like this last night."

Whether it was the whisky or a sudden rush of conscience and sense of duty, he never knew; but, having imbibed a 'wee' dram of his national drink, he summoned himself and said rather dramatically, "Right, I must go. I'll climb over your fence at the point you showed me and look around and find out who's disturbing our night's sleep. I have a whistle. If I blow it you can summon the police, because the fun of trying to deal with all this single-handedly is rapidly diminishing. Yes, one blow on this whistle will mean I'm in distress and need help urgently."

Mrs Martin noticed how at this point Alistair clenched his fists, and admired his resolute walk downstairs, through the kitchen to the back door and out into the garden.

She left the back door ajar as arranged, in case of a sudden retreat being required by Alistair, and went upstairs to watch proceedings through her window. She marvelled that Vanessa was still asleep, but that was good. It could harm someone so young, in her opinion, to have their picture in the paper for all to ogle at.

This is better than television, she thought as, after a not ungenerous slurp of whisky herself, she took up position by the slightly pulled back curtain at the bedroom window.

The most accurate way to describe Alistair's mood down below as he crossed her garden lawn would be to say that he was alarmed by his own courage.

Within moments he had crossed Mrs Martin's fence by the dilapidated old stile and walked resolutely down Helen Archer's allotment, to where Mrs Martin had reported the torchlight to have been.

He stopped for a moment and stood still. Somehow, his survival of yesterday's adventure had given him a certain confidence.

A distant recollection of a sermon, heard in school days, about occasions in life, when you have to say to yourself, "take courage!" came into his mind. Hadn't the preacher said, "There is no alternative but to trust the Lord, be brave and battle on"?

Alistair was brave, but like many brave men, courage could desert him inconveniently on occasions, and it did then.

He shouted out loudly to the blackness of the night, "Can I help you?" Only he knew that it was in fear rather than in courage.

The silence was deafening, and made him shout half bravely and half timidly, "This is security and we want to help you! We think you may have got lost."

Again, only a little wind rustling the leaves in the

nearby plum tree could be heard, by way of reply.

"Please let us help you find your way out!" he shouted again, in what he feared must by now have sounded a fairly timid voice.

He became aware his legs were shaking with fear. He was used to that symptom now. It had happened the previous night, when he had heard the tower door bang shut below him at St Peter's, while Fred had been 'summiting' - as only Fred could call it.

"Please let us help you leave the allotments; this is a security operation!" he continued to shout, trying to appease whatever homicidal maniac might be lurking there in the shadows; but yet again, still only the wind replied.

Somehow his nerve held and he managed to keep that famous imagination of his at bay. Having walked all the way down to the central path and then right to the main allotment gate, which he found securely locked, he returned by the same route to Mrs Martin's house.

Considerably relieved to be still in one piece, but somewhat frustrated, he joined her, not a little breathless, at their lookout position at the same first floor bedroom window, and together they waited, watching for more torchlight.

"I swear I didn't imagine it," said Mrs Martin lamely.

"Of course you didn't! It may interest you to know that I've used that very same phrase myself last night after seeing torchlight that my companions didn't see."

Some hours later, as dawn broke and he finished the umpteenth cup of tea that the animated Mrs Martin had brought him, he announced that it was getting light enough for him to return to the allotment and have a more thorough look around.

However, the cold light of day revealed no further

clue than had his torchlight of the night.

He looked carefully around that very spot, frustrated by his total lack of any kind of clue.

Just at the moment that he had decided to give up and return, he tripped over an old root and fell awkwardly, crashing into the old ruin of the disused halfway shed, mouthing expletives that even Aaron would have been proud of. The somewhat bizarre statue of the garden gnome on the ledge inside which had glared irritatingly at him on previous inspections, fell to the ground, shattering into pieces. From it, a ring rolled out in ever decreasing circles and eventually coming to rest lying on the disused shed floor.

Alistair picked it up immediately.

He immediately noticed that on the inside of the ring were two letters, 'SA', intertwined.

Being Alistair, he immediately wondered whether it had been put there recently as a plant to put him on a false trail; but soon he found himself pretty sure that it must have been what the bearer of last night's torch was searching for.

Someone's been looking for that, I wouldn't mind betting, he thought, as he placed it carefully in his wallet.

On what was now his second return from the allotments to Mrs Martin's house, he was met by a concerned Mrs Martin informing him that Vanessa was now awake, and she had told her that he would be able to explain everything to her. She added with some relief that Vanessa was planning on spending the next night away, which would make it easier for her – Mrs Martin - to keep watch through the bedroom window, should that be necessary.

"Please do that, Mrs Martin," Alistair replied, simultaneously making the decision to keep quiet about his discovery of the ring. If ever a new development needed a bit of thinking through, this was it.

Soon he was busy giving the undeniably attractive Vanessa a summary of his night's work on the assignment.

"And I slept through all that, did I?" she gasped in astonishment.

"Yes, you did," he replied, quite understanding why the *Daily Express* might like to have her picture on the front page.

CHAPTER 31

(A sister contacts a brother)

The remainder of that day passed in a bit of a daze for Alistair. He was conscious of being every bit as tired again as after the previous night. These last two nights had indeed been what he called a double whamee of adventures, and he was aware of not being able to think clearly. He was also distracted by the planned return of Zoe to London on the morrow. Thank goodness that these two nights of adventure had occurred most fortuitously when she was away staying with her relatives.

However, by evening he began to feel more settled and to think more clearly. For a start, he was very keen to talk through his recent experiences with Zoe, and, as he said to himself, get her take on it all; but he also decided that this diabolically sensitive matter of her brother, Greg, being the unknown lover of the poor late Rev. Henrietta Carr was blatantly one that had to be investigated. Excruciatingly embarrassing though it would be, he could not shelve such an overwhelmingly intriguing lead, and would have to contact Zoe quickly and start checking it out. What had made him move so slowly about this was the feeling that returned to trouble him beyond words: that old nagging question of whether she would think that this was the real reason why he wanted to see her and befriend her. That would be too awful to contemplate.

He must, to use one of his favourite phrases, take the bull by the horns. He must contact her, and there was nothing for it; but it would, he realised, mean having to lay his heart bare and express his feelings about her openly and much sooner than he would have in other circumstances.

Though he frequently used his mobile, he sometimes liked what he called the old-fashioned method, and went to Donna and asked to use the phone.

"Don't forget, you've promised to tell me what's going on," she laughed coyly, "and what all this is about some time when it's all over."

"When it's all over," repeated Alistair clearly, adding, "you and Cissie will be the first people I'm going to explain everything to. You're both being very good and discreet and patient. For the moment, let's just say I'm on an assignment, shall we?"

Donna giggled. "I like that – an *assignment* – sounds very grand!"

He got straight through to Zoe, who sounded cheery, and after the most hasty of questions about her visit to old friends and his equally hasty references to some of the extraordinary escapades that he was longing to tell her about in more detail, they speedily arranged to meet for coffee. As soon as he put the receiver down he worried how he had sounded. How annoying that he was now always having to worry in case he was giving a wrong impression, and if the wrong end of the stick was being got. Crime investigation and romance don't mix, he thought.

The next morning, he made a point of getting to the café first, and chose a secluded corner table. "I'll just wait for my companion," he said politely to the waitress.

When Zoe arrived, she looked more beautiful than ever, he thought. Everything was perfect, even her expressed wish to have some good old-fashioned English tea.

What a pity, he thought, that he had to rush things along, but the investigation demanded it; and though in reality it was unnecessary, in his mind he would have to try and convince her that the investigation had nothing to do with his wanting to be with her. He felt he just had to make that clear before pursuing inquiries about Greg. It would mean, he thought, telling Zoe of the strength of his feelings for her.

He would have to choose his moment. His heart was racing a bit as he reflected that things would never be the same after this.

Within a moment she was there, sitting opposite him, smiling radiantly.

They chatted a bit about her visit to the north of England, and she recounted various amusing incidents and escapades, most of which seemed to imply that her relatives were colourful characters, and he referred, with a skilful lightness of touch, to his own recent adventures, which had occurred in her absence.

For a moment he caught her looking rather sadly out of the window, or so he thought.

It had the effect of making him start to tell her rather earnestly what he was determined to do.

He started to speak, a trifle jerkily, "I've got to tell you this, Zoe. I hope with all my heart that you realise this already."

Now she was staring at him earnestly, as he continued, "But what I'm trying to say is I would have wanted to meet up with you and stay in touch with you, even if it wasn't for this incredible coincidence of our common acquaintance and link with St Peter's. In the circumstances I've just got to stress that to you." He paused and then astonished himself by adding with tears in his eyes, "Please believe me."

She looked at him without saying anything but breathing rather heavily, as he always thought afterwards when recalling the scene.

"We've been through all this already, Alistair," she began, not unsympathetically.

In a moment he repeated rather emotionally, "Please

believe me," and added, "it's important to me that you see the truth of that."

She did not say anything but took his hand across the table and squeezed it. He looked up and found her staring into his eyes as if she was looking right through him. "I thought we got that all cleared up in the pub and in the park, didn't we? I do believe you, and yes, I do understand."

This moment of intense personal drama for Alistair was interrupted by a rather unexpected and mundane enquiry by the waitress as to whether they would like another choice of cakes.

They both laughed and he relaxed considerably.

"I guess," she began, still in american parlance, "you're going to ask me something about Greg, or possibly even to get Greg to help."

"I probably would have already, in other circumstances," he replied, adding, "I've been holding back for obvious reasons."

"I'll help all I can," she promised, and added words to the effect that it was everyone's duty to help the police and get justice following such a despicable crime. He could only nod his head, as his thoughts were still on other things.

"One thing's for sure," she continued, "my poor darling brother, Greg, would rather die than hurt a fly, so you can eliminate him alright. But I'm sure he'll be able to give you some interesting titbits about his rather short relationship with Henrietta. I know him so well, naturally. Of course I'll ring him up and get him to speak to you. No problem. What's more, I'll record our call so you can hear for yourself just how he is."

"Wouldn't he be furious if he knew you were recording him...?" began Alistair.

"Well, I'll tell him afterwards that I've done it, and I just know that he won't mind me recording my chat with him, when he finds out that it's in pursuit of truth, as it were. He'll be really pleased he was able to help. He was actually really cut up about the police not making progress with their investigation. He did actually say he would do anything in the wide world to get to the truth of what happened to Henrietta. I promise you, Alistair, at the end of the day, when he realises what's going on, he honestly won't mind me recording the conversation."

Everything in Alistair's instinct made him want to insist that she advise him that he was being recorded, but he knew it would probably be more interesting, and that Greg would probably speak more naturally, if she did not let on till afterwards.

"He's been back from his honeymoon a little time now," she continued, "I must admit, not even I could possibly have contacted him about a former lover on his honeymoon!"

"Of course not," agreed Alistair rather sheepishly.

"OK. Well, I'll give him a ring tonight," she reiterated resolutely, "and I'll record it and we'll see what happens. I'm sure to get his new wife, Samantha. I suppose he won't be able to speak freely in front of her. Anyway, I'll play it by ear and let you know how I get on, and if he's in and it all goes to plan I'll get the recording to you tomorrow. Then, as soon as you've listened to it, I'll own up and tell him and I'll stress it was my idea and that you disapproved etcetera."

What a situation! thought Alistair to himself, after they had arranged to meet on the morrow and kissed goodbye.

CHAPTER 32

(A tape recording is handed over)

Despite Zoe's assurances, Alistair had worried over the arrangement of her ringing her brother and recording the conversation, and rang her first thing after breakfast to express these qualms.

"I can't explain why, but I just would be happier if you were with me when I listen to the recording for the first time. I think I'd somehow feel less of an eavesdropper. I wouldn't feel so bad if it was anyone else; I mean, it's the kind of thing investigators do all the time I suppose, but it being your brother - "

"OK, OK, OK," she cut in.

"Do you mind, Zoe?" he asked once more.

"Of course not. To be honest, when I woke up this morning, I did rather wish that I'd told him I was recording it, but I stuck to our arrangement. I played it back to myself last night. There's not much in it of interest but there is something – well, you see – see what you think. I've got it at the ready – all ready to start from where I finished chatting about our various comings and goings since we had last seen each other and broached the subject."

They arranged to meet hastily at the rather inappropriately named café, the Racing Page, knowing that for all its faults it had the great advantage of privacy.

Again he got there early, and again Zoe seemed more beautiful than ever when she arrived. They sat in the little enclave of the café with the tape recorder on the table in front of them.

"Shall we go?" she asked with her finger poised above the 'Play' button.

"Go for it," he joked, trying to ease his own slight

tension, which he had felt all morning.

Alistair listened avidly with his ear cocked a few inches above the tape recorder.

He took in every word, every nuance of this sister-to-brother conversation, which went as follows:

"Greg, I've got to ask you something really crazy now."

"What's new, sis?" came a male voice jokingly in reply, inevitably sounding rather different to what Alistair had imagined.

He heard Zoe's unmistakeable voice emanating from the little machine.

"There was this remarkable coincidence on the plane over to your wedding. I was chatting with this guy about why I was travelling to Chicago and your forthcoming wedding and sorry, I don't think it was the champagne, but I let slip how you'd had a romance a long time ago with that vicar who hit the headlines when she got murdered on those allotments."

"Oh Zoe, for goodness sake, why did you get on to that? What was the point? I told you not to ever mention all that to anyone ever again. I bet it was the bloody champagne that got your tongue wagging. Not very nice, really, when you're on the way to my wedding with Samantha."

"I'm sorry, I'm sorry, I'm sorry. Anyway, all he said at the time was that … something like - oh yes, he remembered the case. Well, anyway, this guy chatted me up all the way to Chicago, and he only slipped me his visiting card when we said goodbye, didn't he?"

"Oh, bloody hell, Zoe! And you've gone and fallen for him, I'll bet … Come on, why are you telling me all this? What's all this about?"

"Greg, I'll put it in a nutshell. We've kept in touch."

"Who? What? I'm not understanding."

"This guy and I; I looked him up when I got back

415

here and we've been seeing each other – seeing each other a lot."

"Zoe, where the hell do I come into all this?"

"Don't jump down my throat, Greg, but this guy has turned out to be a private detective, who has been assigned the allotment murder case by the victim's husband."

"Look, Zoe, I can't be doing with all this bullshit."

Alistair winced. He was a man of the world, but for some inexplicable reason bad language offended him, and it seemed to jar that the brother of such a sweet girl could use such language. He momentarily got pleasure from realising that Zoe would have noticed that he himself did not swear – perhaps he had earned a few brownie points for not doing so.

"No, no, no, listen to me, Greg, listen to the end and then loose off at me. I'll explain, I'll explain, I'll explain everything."

Alistair could hear Greg's voice complaining inaudibly but harshly at the other end of the line before Zoe's melodious voice cut in.

"As you know, the police drew a complete blank and as I say the victim's husband asked this guy Alistair, who is an old friend of his, to take on the case and carry out a different kind of investigation – approaching it all from a different angle, and forming impressions and that kind of thing … OK, have a go at me now"

"Well, where the hell do I come in to all this, Zoe?"

"Well, of course on the plane I let out that the victim used to be your girlfriend."

"Bloody hell!"

"You see, I was talking about going to your wedding and weddings and lovers and girlfriends. You can't blame me, Greg, and of course I didn't have a clue that Alistair knew the victim, and I didn't have a clue that I'd ever be seeing him again."

"Will you please stop calling her the victim! Call her Henrietta, for goodness sake."

"I thought it might upset you if I did."

"Why the hell should it? I got over Henrietta years ago. She went with that guy Rhys, didn't she? I didn't even know she married this Dennis chappie until the murder hit the headlines. I must admit I was surprised; from what she told me, she and Rhys were made for each other, but of course I'm always proved wrong about that sort of thing. Anyway she gave me the push alright."

"Would you be prepared to come over and have a chat with this Alistair guy sometime soon? I mean, he just wants to meet as many people linked to the whole tragic business as possible. I don't feel he can go to you and start asking about it all in front of your new wife."

"A word of warning, Zoe, I know you're a big girl now, but sounds to me like this Alistair guy is probably chatting you up because he thinks it'll help get him to interview me, and I don't like that sort of behaviour. It's using people and playing on their emotions."

"You are so wrong there, Greg, so very wrong."

What pleasure Alistair felt at hearing this response!

"Oh yeah? I was right about Leonard, wasn't I?" continued Greg.

Alistair's heart sank as he heard tell of this former man in the life of the girl he was smitten by. She had never mentioned Leonard. Was this Leonard part of what she had referred to as "this business that she had had to get sorted out and think through" while in America? He put such distracting thoughts quickly to the back of his mind, and lowering his ear even more, concentrated on the recording, which reeled relentlessly on.

"You'll really like Alistair, I promise you, Greg.

417

You'll really warm to him. Please do me this favour. You remember how you said in your wedding speech that as I'd introduced you to Samantha, you had rashly promised that you'd have to agree to anything I asked. Well, I'm asking this."

"Zoe, I wasn't thinking of something like this. I meant something personal, something to do with the heart … "

"This is personal, Greg, it is to do with the heart."

Again, Alistair's heart quickened.

"Please, Greg," continued Zoe's voice from the tape recorder. "Please won't you just agree to meet up with us? It'll only take a half-hour or so."

"Well, you're right, I said I'd do anything for you, Zoe, but I hardly had this in mind. What's going on here? You don't sound your usual self. I think I'd better come and check up on you. Look, Samantha's going to her friend for the day tomorrow, Monday; I'll come over to Cookington and have a chat with you."

"And meet Alistair, please, Greg. I'll explain more when I see you," pleaded Zoe's voice crackling from the machine.

"OK, I'll meet this Alistair guy; but Zoe, I won't be able to help him any more than I could help the police."

"Greg, you're a super brother! Look, we'll finalise arrangements later, but come and have lunch then on Monday at one o'clock at that restaurant you like – the Three Horseshoes – that's the one you like, isn't it?"

"See yah, sis."

"Bye."

Zoe clicked the off button and as the recording stopped, she said, "Well, that's it, Alistair. I don't think it looks like it's going to bear much fruit, but I'm glad you're meeting my brother. I think you'll like him, and I'm pretty sure you'll rule him out as a suspect," she added, laughing.

Alistair gazed into his empty cup. What on earth would I do if I did suspect him? he asked himself, but it was a silly thought and he dismissed it.

The waitress arrived with the bill and they were soon up and leaving the café.

They said goodbye and agreed to meet up at Greg's favourite restaurant on the morrow, Monday.

Alistair strolled back towards the station, but as he waited at the bus stop, the thought came back to him, what would I do if I suspected her brother?

The bus took a long time coming, and by the time it did, he had answered himself, it wouldn't make any difference to me and Zoe.

CHAPTER 33

(Meeting a lover's brother)

The Three Horseshoes was a suitable restaurant for business, thought Alistair, though he much preferred the local Chinese one from the point of view of both relaxing and food. He wished he was going there instead, and with only Zoe, but as he strolled nonchalantly along the pavement towards their chosen rendezvous, or more precisely the street corner nearby, he reminded himself that this was, beyond doubt, an important matter that had to be clarified.

Noticing that he was a little early, and despite the drizzle of rain, he stopped to look in a shop window and even sat down for a moment on a convenient bench under a shelter. As he reflected on the forthcoming meeting with Greg he found himself on the one hand happy to be meeting up with Zoe again, but on the other slightly apprehensive about his talk with Greg. He could not help referring in his mind to Greg as the lover whom Henrietta had never mentioned. Why not? he wondered. She had spoken enough about Buzz and Rhys – what was it about Greg that had made her so reticent? Why also had Dennis made no reference to him?

He met Zoe at the corner of the High Street as arranged, and they walked the short distance to the restaurant, appearing to the passing strangers like any ordinary couple without even a tenth of the mystery that engulfed them.

They sat down at the table and took a deliberately long time studying the menu and explaining to the waiter that a third party was expected. Alistair normally only indulged in wine in the evening, but the ambience of a restaurant that he was not entirely unfond of, led him to plump for a nice bottle of Beaujolais. This had just been ordered when a man arrived at the door, that Alistair took to be Greg, but who turned out to be another customer, who had placed himself conveniently distant from their table. This mistake of Alistair's gave much merriment to Zoe, who kept saying, "I can't believe you thought that guy was my brother."

The merriment increased when Greg actually did arrive, as Alistair had presumed that it could not possibly be him, for the image he had built up in his mind was so very different.

Recovering from her laughter, Zoe kissed her brother and helped him off with his mackintosh as he complained about the weather and struggled with his umbrella. She made a rather formal introduction, and Greg having shaken hands equally formally, plonked himself down alongside his sister with his back to the road, facing Alistair.

"It's great to meet you," uttered Alistair warmly, passing him the menu.

After much chatter on various topics ranging from the weather to the menu, Alistair said in a firm voice. "Now, there's one thing I want more than anything to make clear to you from the start, Greg. When I first met Zoe I had absolutely no idea she was connected with all this business, and although it came up quite naturally on the plane very quickly, I can promise you I had already decided I wanted to be a friend of hers. Besides, I truly had no idea that I was going to be asked to take on this investigative assignment at that time. As you're her brother, it's just so important to me personally that you realise the truth of that. I feel very shy having to spell it out like this, but I feel I must. So please believe me."

Zoe looked at Alistair in a way that her brother knew meant she agreed.

421

"I'll believe you," he said, "and that really is the case, is it? You really hadn't been asked to take the assignment on at that point when you met my sister? Dennis really hadn't asked you?"

Alistair was nodding vigorously and giving short sharp assurances. He was worried that he was overusing the word "absolutely".

"I know why I'm here right now today," said Greg, civilly enough. "Zoe told me on the phone that you would want to speak to me about the crime."

Alistair interjected, "Greg, because it's so important to me that you believe me about my wanting to be a friend of Zoe, even if this case never existed. I'll be absolutely straight with you about something else. I just hope you realise that I wouldn't say what I'm about to say if I wasn't. Greg, I want you to know that Zoe recorded that phone conversation which she had with you the day before yesterday. I didn't ask her to. She suggested it and insisted on doing so, even though I was against her doing it. She said she wanted to prove to me what I obviously believe already - that you are entirely innocent."

Greg seemed rather taken aback and looked somewhat reproachfully at his sister.

"I promise you that's true, Greg," Zoe said. "I wanted Alistair to hear you speaking about Henrietta naturally with his own ears."

"OK, OK, OK – I'll accept that; but sis, don't you ever do that again! I could have said the most outrageous things – I didn't, did I?"

He looked at Alistair and said in a noticeably friendlier tone, "I never swear when my sister's about, you know; she doesn't like it."

"Alistair never swears," put in Zoe swiftly and almost with pride.

"Well, I wouldn't say never – you should have

heard what I said when my shoelace broke this morning - but no, I try not to. I don't like it in other people," stressed Alistair, glad to note that Zoe's nods showed his remarks met with her approval.

"Do you mind if I get down to business?" he continued, adding, "it's not really my style, but I have to discipline myself to cut the cackle and adopt a direct approach."

"No, I prefer that," said Greg, with a noticeably more pleasant air. "Besides, I haven't got all the time in the world this morning."

Alistair launched straight into it. "It seems Henrietta never mentioned you to anyone. Why was that, do you think? Why do you think nobody seems to know about you? I mean, I've come across a few people who seem to know about other people in her earlier days, like this chap Buzz, and Rhys."

"I think it was probably because with Buzz and Rhys she left them. With me ... I left her."

Quick as an arrow Alistair asked, "Did you ever regret that?"

"No, not at all – let alone go round murdering her lovers or stabbing her in an allotment shed! Sorry, I know I shouldn't speak the way I do, but a lot of time has passed since the tragedy, and I had all the right feelings of horror and revulsion about it all at the time, and for a long time after. But now I find I can cope with it best by talking in the way I do."

He swigged some Beaujolais - rather a lot, thought Alistair, as he himself turned to the waiter and ordered another bottle.

Alistair, now deciding not to rush things too much, deliberately let the conversation wander over other subjects, before bringing it around again to the question of Henrietta's former boyfriends.

"I wonder if she regretted your leaving her. Did she

ever mention previous boyfriends when she was with you?"

"I'm surprised you know about that character called Buzz, because actually she never talked much about him. I think she mentioned him once; said he was some kind of kid who had had a crush on her," commented Greg, and continued, "come to think about it, she didn't talk much about Rhys, either – you know, the guy she nearly married - or the girl Sheila, who he did marry, for that matter. I don't think she liked Sheila much, but you know, I didn't know much about Sheila, till I got an unexpected visit from her."

"Hey, you never told me that, Greg!" said Zoe with a slight tone of rebuke.

"Well, I'll promise not to be secretive in future, Zoe, and you've promised not to play tricks on me with tape recorders, so we're quits sis."

"Please tell Alistair everything, Greg, please, for my sake; it's so important to me," pleaded Zoe urgently, sensing from Alistair's demeanour that he found this latest information most important.

"Yes, well, this lady Sheila - she turned up unexpectedly on my doorstep one day and asked if I knew whether Rhys was still seeing Henrietta, and I said I hadn't a clue, which was the absolute truth. It was all a bit strange, because she said she knew I wasn't still seeing Henrietta – how the hell she knew that, I don't know – but she seemed very suspicious that Henrietta had met up with Rhys again since she'd married him."

"This really is absolutely fascinating and could be crucial – please continue, Greg," managed Alistair, rather conscious that his pulse rate had quickened, and realising that this was exactly the sort of thing his investigation must get to the bottom of.

"Well, I mean I just kept saying, 'I don't know, I

honestly don't know.' I must say she didn't seem to accept my assurances, and well you know, seemed in a bit of a stew. She found it difficult to accept that I didn't know; accused me of keeping something back from her, which annoyed me."

"When was this, Greg?"

"I can tell you that exactly, because it was exactly a month before the crime."

"Did you tell the police?"

"No, I didn't. Not long after the crime, I was just thinking that I should, when the police, who had cross-examined me at some length, contacted me again and told me that the people concerned had been eliminated from their enquiries. If the police say something like that, you kind of accept it, don't you?"

While Alistair looked a trifle stunned at this answer, Greg glanced at his watch and said, rather arrogantly as Alistair thought, "Time's up!"

"That's a bit quick, Greg," came Zoe's sisterly rebuke.

Alistair wanted to press him more, but not wanting to lose the goodwill of his lover's brother, stood up politely as Greg retrieved his coat from the furthest depths of the restaurant.

He regretted that he had spent so much time during the meal on small talk, though it had seemed tactful and appropriate at the time. In seconds, Greg had shaken hands with Alistair, kissed his sister goodbye with a half-serious, half-teasing rebuke of "Don't you do that again, sis," collected his mackintosh, umbrella and hat, and disappeared into the rain.

Alistair and Zoe sat down again at the table in near silence for some time.

At length Alistair somewhat triumphantly said, "Well, we know something now that nobody else does."

"Sheila's visit to him," said Zoe emphatically.

"There are so many questions whirling around in my head," continued Alistair, literally putting his hands to his head.

"He never told me about that visit of Sheila's. I would have told you, Alistair. You know that, don't you?" said Zoe emphatically.

"Of course," he replied, "but oh dear me, so many questions now, and still that odd one, you know, how come Dennis never learnt about Greg, or if he did know of him, why did he never mention him to me?"

Zoe looked genuinely speechless for a moment, and then Alistair continued, "Why did Sheila never mention her visit to Greg to anybody? I mean, I asked Rhys if he knew of any other relationships that she might have had." He paused. "You know, how can I express myself?" he asked, brushing some crumbs away and adding, "up to now everyone's been completely baffled, including me of course."

She sat in silence for a moment, looking at him lovingly.

"And I'm still baffled," he added with a self-deprecating laugh, "but now suddenly we know something that nobody else knows."

"Are you thinking ... could this be the missing link?" added Zoe, having refound her voice, which now had a more urgent tone.

"The breakthrough, I've been calling it to myself," said Alistair with a frisson of excitement, before deliberately calming things down by saying, "I just don't know. Probably not, but it's interesting how we now know something new. That's what I've been wanting – something new."

He leant back and stretched his arms in the air and added with a warm twinkle in his eye, "And it's all thanks to me meeting you on that plane and learning about how your brother knew Henrietta and … "

"You're going to have to confront Sheila about why she visited Greg, aren't you?" suggested Zoe, interrupting him in an attempt to be helpful. Then she added, "Oh dear, I so didn't want all this to cause Greg any aggro, especially when he's just settling down to married life. Oh dear!"

"I, or rather we, need to think it through, don't we?" Alistair responded, with a premonition of an appalling dilemma. "We mustn't plunge in without considering the effect it will have, and all that."

He took another sip of the pleasant red wine and seemed deep in thought before adding, "It might be wiser to keep this to ourselves for a while, eh?"

"I notice you said we, and not I, need to think it through," said Zoe with a smile, relaxing a bit.

"Did I? Sorry, Zoe. Oh golly, I just wish we had met in other circumstances, without this whole horrendous saga going on!"

"Oh, not that old chestnut of yours. Can't you see, in a funny way, it's making us quite close? Why is it such a bugbear to you? Look at it as a positive thing."

"But, Zoe, it's so unromantic! I want to be talking about other things with you - not death and murder and rage and....."

"Alistair, we've got to take life as we find it or as it finds us. God willing, there'll be plenty of time for everything else … " Her words tailed away and she looked out of the window rather distantly.

That distant look, though so attractive, worried him. What, and more particularly who, is she thinking about? he wondered.

"Plenty of time for just normal things that couples do and talk about, is that what you mean?"

"Oh yes, I did mean that."

He never understood afterwards how or why he said

it, but the words just came out. "Plenty of time for love," he added rather distinctly.

She stretched her arm across the table and squeezed his hand, nodding and looking at him intently.

After a longish silence, he spoke with a new cheerfulness in his voice, "Thanks, Zoe, you've no idea how much you have helped me; just knowing that you understand how I just want to get this whole investigation over with quickly so that we can get on with the rest of our life – that means so much to me."

She squeezed his hand one more time and then withdrew it.

"Look, I've got a good idea," she remarked pertly.

"Another one?" He laughed, feeling cheered.

"I know you said you don't believe in deadlines and so on, but why don't you take the line that you'll give it your best shot until, say, the end of the year. Then, if we're still drawing a blank, we'll say 'Well, we tried, and you know – no can do, Dennis old chap. Sorry and all that, but we say ditto to what the police said; it's like it's got to remain a mystery until another day.'"

"I like that idea," responded Alistair warmly. "It's kind of light at the end of the tunnel, even if there isn't any light, if you know what I mean. I'll call it Zoe's deadline."

"No, it's *our* deadline, not Zoe's deadline." She thumped her fist down on the table, adding, "After that, our time begins."

"Oh, that's a wonderful thing to say," he responded cheerfully. "After that our time begins: no more investigations, then we can be just a normal couple without having a dirty great horrid crime hanging around our necks, which has to be constantly examined and chewed over."

She cocked her pleasant eyebrow, saying, "I take it you agree, then, do you? It's our deadline."

He agreed, and to the curiosity of the waitress, who he was unaware of standing behind him, shook hands yet again; but in his mind it was and always would be Zoe's deadline.

"There's one thing more I want to say, Zoe. Do you mind if, before *our* deadline expires," he said, stressing the plural pronoun, "I engage your help with all this? I mean, ask you to help me big time."

"I don't think I'll be much help," she commented.

"More than you realise; but seriously, though, I need someone to bounce ideas off and generally chew over lines of inquiry," he stressed.

"Well, I'll certainly do my best, and we'll keep that pact about not letting it drag on past the end of the year," she agreed helpfully.

"That's absolutely agreed," he said in conclusion, putting both hands on the table and looking as if he was ready to go.

"You never know, we may get that lucky breakthrough, and it might all end very much sooner," came her final comment, as she started gathering her things to leave.

He was sure it was not just due to the fine red wine, which had now come to an end, but to this new pact, that for the first time for a while he felt not only strangely serene, but also animated and cheerful.

"We had better go, else they'll think we want dinner here too," he laughed, getting up from the table.

CHAPTER 34

(Two lovers discuss their suspicions)

Alistair's feeling of joy lasted all afternoon, but by early evening he began to find himself being both more and more hopeful of a sudden breakthrough and more and more intrigued by this unexpected development of Sheila's visit to Greg. Over and over again, he contemplated how strange that this would have remained unknown had he not met Zoe on the plane.

He was increasingly of the opinion that he should take Rhys up on his offer to arrange a meeting between himself and Sheila. To keep things calm, he would make out that he was coming to a conclusion that there was nothing more he could usefully do in the way of progress.

He phoned Rhys and leant back in the little armchair in his hotel room, trying to relax, for he felt a certain frisson of excitement.

He was just beginning to wonder if there would be no reply when Rhys's voice burst suddenly into the ringing tone with a sharp "Yes?"

"Rhys, it's Alistair MacTavish here – you remember, the very private investigator."

"Oh, that's a surprise. You're the amateur chappie who came to see me the other day in the Runway Hotel. Of course, I remember. You're not arresting me, are you?"

Alistair, irritated by the stress on the word amateur, ignored the joke.

"Look, Rhys, you were kind enough to say that whenever I needed a word with Sheila you would arrange it. To be honest, I'm just about to throw in the towel on this mystery, but to wrap things up I was hoping to just have a word with her, tying up a few loose ends before submitting a final report; and I notice she's the one person I haven't had a word with. I know Dennis would expect me to – in fact I think he may have asked me to do that," he lied.

He did not like pretending to be a bumbling idiot, but it would help if the nascent wild ideas in his mind were to prove true.

Rhys's response was surprisingly helpful.

"Let me see, Alistair old chap. Let me get the diary out. I write down all her comings and goings in there. She's arriving back from the States any day now."

Alistair, who was by now more than hopeful of marrying Zoe, wondered how anyone could fail to know exactly when their wife was arriving. He waited patiently while Rhys uttered a few more "let me sees" and there was a distinct noise of pages turning in a diary.

He watched the clock ticking on his mantelpiece. How strange a thing time is, he mused as he waited there, watching the second hand of Sparky move inexorably on its circuits, and listening to Rhys's incoherent mumblings.

Eventually Rhys said in clear, sharp tone, "Ah, of course, that's it, she's arriving 6 p.m. on Wednesday."

"Oh well, she won't want to see me that evening – that's for sure. Or the one after, I imagine. Perhaps I'll try and give her a ring on the next day and arrange an appointment."

"Sounds very thorough, your investigation," commented Rhys.

"Well yes, just thought she might be able to confirm one or two things."

"She's not a suspect, is she?" Rhys joked, adding, "if I've been eliminated, I should think she has."

This was followed by much laughter, which to be fair Alistair thought sounded genuine and not that of a guilty man.

"Good heavens, no!" he replied disingenuously, knowing that probably every nuance would be relayed back to Sheila.

"Look, Alistair old chap, I'll let her know you want to have a word with her. Now supposing she can manage Friday – that gives her a whole day to get over any jet lag on the Thursday – what sort of time on Friday, and whereabouts would you like to meet her?"

"Well, let's make it afternoon – sort of post-lunch. Is two o'clock too early?"

"Two o'clock if she can make it, and do you want to come over here to the hotel, what we jokingly call 'airside', or...?"

"Dennis has given me the use of the vicarage while he's away, and he's not going to be back until late that night. For one reason and another, it would be very convenient if she could make it over to St Peter's vicarage in Cookington."

"Oh, I'm sure she can. She knows her way there alright, I'm sure. That will appeal to her – be able to have a good look round – loves old churches and hidden byways and all that jazz. Think I told you about all that."

"Yes, you did," replied Alistair and in his thoughts only added sarcastically, thanks for reminding me.

"St Peter's vicarage it is, then, at two o'clock on Friday. I'll contact Sheila and check with her and get back to you to confirm that, obviously."

The confirmation came sooner than he had expected. For Rhys, transatlantic phone calls were commonplace. From across the vast expanse of the Atlantic, Sheila had confirmed the appointment.

Now, he thought, all I have to do is wait. Friday seemed a long time off, but it was already Monday afternoon and he must think positively. The good part

432

of it was that it would give him time to think it through carefully with Zoe.

That was exactly what he did do, phoning her early the next morning, Tuesday.

"I've got a meeting with Sheila arranged!" he said with excitement, "I set it up through Rhys. He says she's returning to the UK tomorrow, Wednesday and has agreed to see me on Friday. It's in the vicarage at 2.00 p.m. I have a feeling I'm going to learn a thing or two."

He was already worried that he was taking up too much of Zoe's time with the case, but his latest development particularly required a bouncing board for ideas, if anything did. And anyway, she was on a six-month sabbatical leave from her university teaching. It would be a good change from her academic research.

"That's great, Alistair, but play it carefully as regards what Greg told you – please, for Greg's sake. Please keep him free from any aggro, if you possibly can."

"Well, that's why I'm ringing. I would welcome a run-through of everything and everybody with you first."

"I realise, we've just got to thrash this one out. Let's not muck about in restaurants; you come over to my place and we'll go through every aspect of this darned mystery, peruse all the evidence, consider all suspicious points and … "

Alistair completed the sentence for her. "Then decide what action we're taking."

"I can't do tomorrow, Wednesday, as I'm away all day; it's going to have to be today if you can make it. I'll cancel my silly coming and goings today. Can you make it today?"

"I sure can. That's wonderful, but are you sure you can really manage that at such short notice?"

"For you …" she began jokingly.

He did not remember much of that journey, because he rehearsed all the matters he wanted to raise and get her take on.

When he arrived at her street, he marvelled that he had not bumped into a lamp post, considering how deep in thought he had been. Making an effort to change his thoughts, he looked around. Somehow her house appeared slightly different today. Despite being there before many a time and oft, now he found himself noticing several charming details about the steps and front door: tubs and plants and window boxes; and even the door knocker looked more interesting than before.

She welcomed him in her usual loving way, ushering him into her front room, where the morning sunlight streamed in.

For two people who were lovers, he realised it was absurdly businesslike; but they really did cover all the personalities, all the circumstances, all the sightings, all the possible motives.

Alistair had a nice feeling that now he had hidden nothing from her as he recounted first the adventurous night at the church and then the equally alarming one at the allotments. Zoe had been totally alarmed for his safety as both these extraordinary tales unfolded. He actually had great difficulty in defending his decision not to involve the police as yet.

"I can only say, I strongly disagree with you about that," she said firmly, and he found himself reassuring her and being persuaded to promise her that the events would very shortly be reported to the police.

"Pride comes before a fall," she said. "You just want to be the one to solve it all on your little lonesome, don't you?" She spoke jokingly and playfully, and not for the first time she threw a cushion at him.

They agreed there were odd, indeed suspicious, matters relating to practically everybody he had spoken to; though in most cases murder seemed an unlikely and disproportionate result.

Zoe seemed very wary of Dennis. "Why had he denied going for strolls to the allotment?" she asked, more than once, and he agreed that he had no answer as yet to that.

Even Dennis's assigning the investigation to Alistair seemed to raise her doubts about him.

"It's not a natural thing to do," she reiterated, to the point where Alistair had given up trying to defend such a course of action.

Equal in suspicion with Dennis she placed Charles, not least because of his rather sinister prowling around on the allotments, supposedly in a supervisory role, combined with his temper and drink-related bursts of outrage and tantrums. "It's like road rage. People like that are highly unpredictable; it just takes a small thing to tip them over the edge," she commented in a matter-of-fact tone.

When it came to bursts of outrage, he however, personally thought that Aaron would win hands down; but she had oddly regarded him differently, saying that from Alistair's account of the matter he was just hot air. She said Aaron was born like that. Charles had become like that due to the buffets of life.

"There's a difference, Alistair," she said, as if she was a psychiatrist.

Whilst they both agreed that Ben and Faye had reasons for not liking the poor unfortunate Henrietta, blaming her for matters of the heart, Alistair was surprised that unlike him she was more suspicious of Faye than of Ben.

"That's why it's good for you to have a woman helping you," commented Zoe, adding, "Faye really had it in for St Peter's, hadn't she? Didn't you say she had said that St Peter's had ruined her life? I mean, that's a pretty strong thing to say before a vicar gets murdered, isn't it? *Ruined her life!* I'd never say something like that."

Sid and Roger she did not seem to consider to have any motive at all. Roger's memory failings sounded genuine enough. Curiously, she had often said that if it had not been for Alistair's strong hunch that Edwin and Helen were above reproach, she would have been suspicious of them. He remembered her saying that before, because it was the only time he had ever heard her swearing, and he recalled her exact words. "I mean, why the bloody hell did the crime happen on their allotment? Why did Helen run home? Why did she ring her husband so promptly?"

"She rang the police first," put in Alistair in Helen's defence.

On and on their discussion had gone; not in a gossipy way, but in a sincere attempt to grapple with a seemingly insoluble mystery. Sometimes they agreed, as for example regarding Fred, who neither of them with their knowledge of human nature could see in the role of a murderer.

She did a lot of listening as, one by one, Alistair gave as succinctly as he could a summary of all the different characters and facts of the situation. He left no one out, and so colourfully did he depict them that although Zoe had never met many of these people she felt almost that she knew them well.

Sometimes when he had finished discussing one character, she would say in conclusion something like, "I don't think I like the curate," or, "I think I rather like Buzz."

She made Alistair laugh when she eliminated Barnaby with the words, "Ex-policeman becomes lay

436

reader and murders vicar? No, I don't think so."

It was the photographs that had particularly preoccupied them. Together they had pored over them. They agreed Mrs Martin's pictures were really hardly any help, as the figures depicted in their background were far too grainy and indistinct, but her daughter Vanessa's ones were relatively clearer and more intriguing, not least because of their date being shortly before the crime.

Not for the first time, he went through with Zoe how Mrs Martin had told him how she had set herself up as a kind of vigilante, guarding Helen's allotment in particular but others too. That had been her motive in taking the photographs. He explained how Mrs Martin had meant to show these pictures to Helen, but hadn't done so because she had begun to think the shadowy figures were her friends or family, for Helen's allotment did have visitors. For example, Helen's husband, her son and her daughter went there, and even her mother had been seen picking sweet peas on one of her visits from Glasgow.

Zoe well understood that Mrs Martin would want to keep her daughter out of the whole horrid business, especially after the press had suggested photographing her in a bikini. "But you know, Alistair, these pictures should be taken very, very seriously," she added.

She held the first of Vanessa's photographs under her reading lamp and peered again at it with her magnifying glass, which itself had an inbuilt light.

Alistair watched her, beside himself with her attractiveness as the lamplight sparkled on her hair.

Eventually she said, "In a court of law, the position of the shed and that tree would surely identify Helen's allotment."

"If only the two grainy figures could be equally clearly identified," said Alistair, in a tone of frustration.

437

Zoe continued silently to study them.

"My gut reaction is that they are both men. They are definitely walking, aren't they, and seemingly deep in conversation. It's as much their gait and posture – I think they've just got to be two men, haven't they?"

"Is my imagination running away with me?" said Alistair. "But I've found myself wondering so much whether one could be Henrietta, with her cloak blowing in the wind..."

"I don't think so. Honestly, it's your imagination Alistair. Anyway, what about the other figure?"

"Well, her assailant," answered Alistair jokingly.

"You really cannot deduce that from these two pictures, Alistair!" she said, laughing.

Alistair remained silent. Zoe knew that silence always meant he was deep in thought.

Eventually she prompted him. "And this phantom assailant, who … "

It was Alistair's turn to cut in abruptly, as if he was just putting words to his recent thoughts.

"It's not just the pictures, you see, but anyway as regards them, I agree the second figure has a more masculine posture, but you can't rule out the possibility that it might be a slightly tomboyish girl."

"Don't agree … but who could you possibly have in mind?"

"For example, Sheila," he suggested earnestly.

Zoe laughed that one out of court, saying, "You're attaching far too much to this information from my brother, Greg, that he had a visit from Sheila. I trust him that it was just a complete nothing. I know my brother even better than I know you, and if he says there was nothing sinister about it then believe me there isn't. Anyway, the police told him the people concerned had been eliminated from their inquiries. Greg's a bit upset about all this, and I really don't want his connection coming into investigations at all."

She laughed, playfully threw a cushion again at her new-found lover, and seemed to take it as a cue to get up and go and make tea in the kitchen.

As he sat back listening to the clatter of the crockery and the sound of the kettle, he had time to quickly summarise his thoughts.

It had been an extremely useful day, covering a lot of ground, and what was more they had agreed about practically everything, with this one latest and rather awkward exception that Alistair had entertained definite doubts about Rhys's wife, Sheila. Zoe had not only disagreed, but had seemed surprisingly concerned that her brother Greg should not get enmeshed in trouble after revealing this admittedly mysterious secret visit of Sheila.

Zoe came back in to her cosy living room, carrying tea on a tray.

"I do worry for Greg's sake," she reiterated, as if she too had been thinking about it again while making the tea. She placed the tray carefully on the table.

He did not reply, seemingly lost in thought; but he looked up suddenly with a somewhat shocked expression as she said, "I was going to get round to telling you, Alistair, but I hadn't quite worked out how to put it. It's just that Greg rang about half an hour before you arrived this morning. He said he wanted you to keep silent about that visit from Sheila, which he told you about. It's so difficult for me, because I'd do anything in the wide world for my brother; but he told me not to tell you he had rung, and here I am telling you."

With that, she burst into tears. Alistair suddenly realised that he had not seen her crying before, and was struck by how it had the effect of making him love her more than ever. It also had the effect, for the moment at any rate, of making him agree to shelve that whole matter until another time.

After tea they continued in their deliberations on the case, avoiding mention of either Greg or Sheila. However, both were aware that they were very much going over old ground, and gradually their conversation moved on to other matters - not least of which was what they might do when this assignment was over.

He agreed to leave her in peace until Friday evening, when hopefully the interview with Sheila would be over, and any mysteries attaching to her explained. Then they would go for a relaxing dinner at their favourite Chinese restaurant.

He stood on the porch, and after a further appreciation of the plant that he had admired on arrival, said goodbye with a cheerful show of optimism and even bravado.

"I'm going to get this whole thing tied up very soon, Zoe, and then we can get on with the rest of our lives."

"Well, I stand by my idea of that deadline, remember; that's why I suggested it, because as you say then we can get on with the rest of our lives," she responded supportively, having cheered up considerably.

He nodded and kissed her tear-stained cheek.

'Time was so inexorable,' he mused as his Tube train thundered westwards through the tunnel in the direction of Cookington. He tried rather unsuccessfully to put the case out of his mind, picking up a free newspaper from the seat opposite, and helping some lost tourist to track down her way to the mysteries of Oxford Circus for the first time in her life.

Yes, it was now already Tuesday evening; who could tell what will have happened by Friday? He glanced at his watch and wondered what would be the state of play that time on Friday.

On returning to the Concord Hotel, he greeted Donna politely, but curtly. He was conscious that he needed to unwind, to rest his overworked thought process.

He did not feel like going to the bar that evening, but sat in his room reading. It helped a bit as it always did.

Maybe when I'm actually lying down with the lights off I will finally unwind and get the rest I need, he mused.

That proved an optimistic view, as over-imaginative theories constantly whirled round in his head.

He analysed what was troubling him.

It was quite simple, really. He was more suspicious of Sheila than Zoe was.

To make matters really difficult, she was quite noticeably critical of any suggestion to cross-examine Sheila in a confrontational way, which he was moving towards. It was true that she had taken her usual pleasant line of it being up to him; but on the other hand she had actually said, "I really don't want you to reveal that Greg told you about Sheila coming round and paying him that surprise visit."

She had said that it could create a whole lot of trouble for Greg. "He's mighty unhappy that I got him involved in all this again. Actually said he had hoped he wouldn't have such irritations in the first weeks of his marriage."

Round and round his troubled thoughts whirled; for, as he reminded himself again, left to himself he was inclining to tackle her head-on about the reason for her visit to Greg. A visit unknown to the police, his thoughts kept repeating – a visit she had wanted kept confidential.

One by one now, these thoughts came to him like arrows, but always ending in the knowledge that Zoe did not want Greg's disclosure referred to, and was adamant that he should not trouble Greg again.

He literally sat at the little table in his room, absurdly holding his head in his hands.

Then it came to him in a flash. He could ask someone else to contact Greg. In a literal sense, he would be keeping his word to Zoe. Yes, he would ask someone to do this for him. He was overwhelmed by this excellent idea. He mustn't let go of it. A good idea is nothing worth if not acted upon. Hadn't Zoe herself actually said that to him?

He stood up and paced the few feet of his room at least three times. Who should he ask? That was the question that he was now grappling with. Edwin came immediately to mind, because he was so skilled in diplomacy, tact etc. Was there anyone else? he asked, almost out loud. One after the other, for varying reasons he dismissed the wide range of different personalities that drifted into his mind. Florence seemed too brash, Barnaby too ponderous, and like Fred and Dennis, not totally cleared of all suspicion in his mind. Yes, Edwin seemed to win hands down. He was about to thump his fist down on the little wobbly table to settle the matter, when an inexplicable mental vision of Emma Duncan came to him. He glanced at the friendly face of Sparky, his alarm clock. It was exactly nine o'clock. Hadn't Emma said to him the other day at their chance meeting in the florist that she always said a prayer for him each evening at that time? Yes, she too would have been a possible choice, he started to think. For one thing, she was of such high moral stature; she could be invaluable in defending him if Zoe was outraged by his plan. Edwin and Emma were both suitable people to call in aid in this quandary. Within a second, who of the two to choose became itself another dilemma.

He lay down on the bed, almost in tears, which made him realise he must be more tired than he had thought. However he could not get to sleep and heard midnight striking in the distance. 'It's already a few minutes into Wednesday, Sheila's arrival day, followed by a day of rest – how ironic – *I'm the one who needs the rest …'*

Then he solved his dilemma of which of the two people to ask by the decision to contact them both, and therefore in the end slept quite well in the circumstances.

CHAPTER 35

(A flower arranger to the rescue)

In the cold light of day, the plan seemed more problematical. Wild thoughts raced through Alistair's mind. What would be the reaction of Edwin and Emma? It would surely appear bizarre to them.

During breakfast he managed to give these thoughts a rest, helped by the fact that at the next table there were some overnight guests who were on their first visit to Britain, and who asked him intelligent questions about London. Their cordial chit-chat ended in an invitation to call in next time he was passing Los Angeles.

As he climbed the stairs back to his room, an old phrase learnt at school about grasping the nettle came back to him.

'Right, it's nine o'clock now,' he registered after glancing at Sparky, and taking out his mobile, rang the number.

He stood there in his empty room listening on the mobile to Edwin's house phone ringing away. Then something happened that stupidly he had not anticipated. The dulcet tones of the call minder invited him to leave a message. He had hoped to catch Edwin before work, and if not him, his wife, Helen, whom he could go on trying to contact all day. He felt however that he really could not leave a message on call minder.

Oh Emma, he thought as he dialled her number, if prayer can help, I pray that at least I find you in.

There was a click at the other end of the line.

"Is that you, Emma?" he blurted out rather ridiculously.

"Hallo," came the response, "I won't ask you how you're getting on."

"I need your help," he blurted out, again rather gauchely, as he thought.

"I would have thought that the only help I can give you is of a spiritual nature," she said in a slightly lame tone.

Not as expertly as he would have liked, he explained his reason for calling.

"I'm very flattered that you should think of me. I really can't for the life of me imagine why on earth you should think that someone would be prepared to chat to an old lady like myself."

"To be honest," replied Alistair, conscious that he had picked up this unappealing phrase from so many people, "I think you're the person who could most stress to Zoe my absolute reservations and concern at going against what she wants."

Somehow, by saying this, he seemed to have embarrassed himself, and went hastily on to explain that he had not yet been able to contact Edwin.

"Well, yes, I think I would like someone to be with me," chirped Emma, adding, "you're right; God has given Edwin a really great gift of expressing himself well. I commented on it once, and his wife Helen said it was because he'd been in so many awkward situations."

"Do you know, I'm so relieved you think it's a good idea. I've been worrying something stupid that Edwin will think I've gone stark raving bonkers." He explained the situation clearly, remembering every nuance of what he wanted to convey.

"Look, Alistair," came Emma's voice, still kindly, but with a change to a more businesslike tone, "Edwin won't think you've gone bonkers. Let me explain all this to Edwin. I know him so well."

Alistair was conscious of the stunned silence of his response to this unexpected suggestion. However, a

445

kind of relief came over him as Emma eventually ended the conversation with, "You leave it to me, Alistair, I'll get this arranged. I'll let you know if I've managed to contact him – or if you don't hear from me, just possibly after we've been to see Greg. We'll speak on the phone this time tomorrow."

As Alistair turned off his mobile, it was almost a shock for him to find that he did not have to do anything more than just wait to hear from Emma. He'd had a similar sudden realisation before in life. It's when you quite unexpectedly find that there's nothing more you can do, it's all out of your hands and you haven't even moved from the chair in your room.

Alistair passed the day in a restful manner, and his state of calmness continued to the extent that he slept well that night.

**

The next morning, Thursday, broke and the weather had changed, with rain lashing against the window. Even the breakfast was very different to the convivial one of yesterday, and the dining room was empty, which made the rain all the more audible. An empty dining room usually meant that Cissie would find time for a good gossip, but she was fortuitously in a hurry too as she had a dental appointment.

Yes, normal life must go on for other people, I suppose, Alistair thought.

He kept looking at his watch.

He would wait till nine o'clock before ringing Emma. How on earth had she got on? He clung to the old adage that no news was good news.

It was 8:55. He got up and, wishing Cissie good luck at the dentist, made his way swiftly past the reception desk, waving to Donna as he went up the staircase to the sanctuary of his room.

He was shocked to find how nervous he was. His pulse was racing and he was thirsty.

He laid the mobile out on the table in front of him and found the anticipation, of he knew not what, made him almost feel like praying.

Then it rang, vibrating like mad and jumping all over the table.

"*Hallo!*" his voice boomed out in contrast to the silence of his empty room as he grabbed it.

"Yes, I have some news for you," came the soothing voice of Emma.

"Tell all," he managed.

"I'll tell you in a nutshell," said Emma, very much in her businesslike tone, but adding, "it's going to have to be a fairly big nutshell, but I'll tell it all as quickly and succinctly as I can."

Alistair found that his nervousness actually prevented him from speaking.

"Right. Well, I couldn't get an answer yesterday, either, when I rang Edwin and Helen's house," continued Emma, "but I went round there in the afternoon and found Helen in. Sorry, Alistair, but I had to let her in on what's going on. Honesty is nearly always the best policy, in my experience. Anyway, she was very good and said she'd ceased to be surprised by anything since that day she had found poor Henrietta's body. She contacted Edwin straightaway at his office and he drove straight to my house yesterday evening after work, arriving about 6.30 p.m., and the two of us set off for Greg's house in Edwin's car."

"Just like that?" Alistair commented, now able to speak, having been considerably calmed by Emma's soothing tone and seeming efficiency.

"Just like that!" She laughed, adding, "are you a Tommy Cooper fan too, Alistair?" She did not wait for

447

an answer, but continued, "when we got to Greg's house, there was no reply, but just as we were leaving, along comes this chappie and joins us and asks, 'Are you looking for Greg?' Anyway, this chap told us that Greg was in the pub down the road, so off we went, Edwin and I, and turned up at the pub. First pub I'd been in for a long time; but great fun it was."

Alistair had one of those rare moments in life when the old phrase about having to pinch yourself to believe what you're hearing came to mind.

"Greg was there, OK. He was with this guy who he introduced us to as Eric," continued Emma. "Edwin's so tactful, so diplomatic – he really should have been foreign secretary or something. Anyway, he went up to Greg and said he had very important news for him – said it was confidential. I have to say Greg was a little the worse for wear. Said something about Eric being an old friend of his from schooldays. 'If it's about the case,' says Greg, 'you can say it all in front of my mate, Eric.'"

Emma cleared her throat and continued, "Rum sort of a chap, that Eric. Half pickled himself. Kept mumbling, 'It wasn't buzz' - whatever that means. I said to him, 'Tell me, Eric, what do you mean by saying it wasn't buzz?' Then he started saying, 'Here, there's been a chappie round here investigating all that – had lunch with him up the hill at the Antelope.' It's difficult to report this, Alistair," continued Emma, "because the chap was talking nonsense. It's frightening what a demon drink is…"

Reluctantly, Alistair felt he just had to butt in. "You don't know if this Eric chap was called Eric Watson, do you?"

"Yes, that was his surname, I asked him. How do you know that?"

"You forget that I've been carrying out a bit of

investigation myself," answered Alistair, glowing with satisfaction, "but I don't want to stop you – please carry on."

"Of course, it was quite noisy. There was a lot of convivial background noise – you know the sort of thing, conversation, glasses clinking, the odd shriek, the odd guffaw of laughter.

"You're painting a very vivid picture, Emma. I can really see this in my mind's eye," cut in Alistair, encouragingly.

"Well, the conversation continued," Emma began again. "Edwin was asking 'Can't we go somewhere quieter?' 'Oh, God no!' says Greg. 'This is my night at the pub. Whatever it is you've got to say, spit it out!' At that moment he departed for what, being slightly old-fashioned, I call the conveniences.

"'Do you know, honestly,' I said to Edwin, while Greg was away, 'I think the more tiddly he is, the more we're going to get out of him.' Edwin just had time to make the brilliant suggestion to me that we should stick to Coke and plough Greg with beer to make him talk. I just had time to say, 'Excellent idea Edwin, but I can take a couple of my favourite tipple, G and T for starters.' And he just had time to say he'd start with a couple of beers; but we did agree we had got to get Greg to open up and, you know, get him talking loosely.

"Right, Alistair, to cut a long story short, this is what you need to know. This is what Greg came out with. It was difficult to catch, what with Greg being so inebriated and incoherent. He said Rhys had given Henrietta a couple of rings: a couple of valuable gold ones with some sentimental message etched in both of them – 'EUS' - apparently the last letters of 'Love You Always', something soppy and sentimental like that, to quote his actual words. The other ring had some intertwined letters engraved inside. He said the letters were the last letters of their two names – 'S' for Rhys and 'A' for Henrietta - intertwined. Greg's not very discreet when it comes to deciding who to tell things to and who not to; anyway, he only went and told his new lover and now his wife, Sheila, that he'd done that! Of course, when Sheila heard this, she wanted Henrietta to give the rings back to either Rhys or herself. Rhys said it wasn't because of the money value of it, but the 'emotional aspect of it' - to quote his actual words again. Poor old Greg was so sozzled when he used the word 'emotional' that it sounded more like evolutional!"

"Well, to get back to Greg's story. Henrietta didn't feel she had to give the rings back. Felt quite strongly apparently that it was nothing to do with Sheila. Apparently they had met up once or twice to try and thrash the matter out amicably. I tried to find out where that might have been for you, but Rhys could only say somewhere round and about, and not a million miles from their hotel.

He was pretty slurred by now, but he made it clear that Henrietta had annoyed Sheila by saying she had hidden the two rings in different places somewhere, and Sheila would never find them.

"Poor old Greg, he was in such a bad way. Excessive alcohol is such an evil. Anyway he kept saying, 'I don't mind telling you all this; but there's nothing to it.' He told us quite simply that Sheila had called on him and asked him straight if he knew where those hiding places were, and he had told her, 'No, I bloody well don't!' Sheila had said to Greg that she felt really stumped. She'd told Greg that she thought Henrietta would have told him since he was, to quote, 'the whore's next one' before she married Dennis."

Emma interrupted the flow of her narrative. "Are

450

you still there, Alistair?"

"I'm listening in wonder ... carry on, please," replied the dumbfounded Alistair, keeping his secret that thanks to Mrs Martin's vigilance he had found one of the hiding places.

"Well, Edwin was doing most of the questioning. It sounds incredible, but old Greg was so away with it by this time that I was actually able to scribble the odd note under the table without him even noticing that I was writing. My main worry was that Greg was going to become too sick and we would have to abandon the whole thing, and I did have to advise Edwin to put the brakes on as regards plying him with drinks. Anyway, meanwhile it was a case of in vino veritas. Let me read you out some of the quotes from our inebriated friend that I managed to scribble down under the table, so to speak. I've got them here in front of me - "

"This is fantastic work, Emma ..." Alistair interrupted.

If Alistair had seen the blush his compliment produced he would have been surprised.

"Let's see, here we are," continued Emma, seemingly ignoring his compliment, "he said Sheila seemed really obsessed with getting those ruddy rings back. Sheila had seemed to accept that Greg had never given Henrietta a ring, but seemed to think Henrietta had confided to him where she hid things. Seems extraordinary, but then life is always stranger than fiction, isn't it? Ah, here's another of his direct quotes, if I can read my writing. It's not easy writing under a table as opposed to on it, you know? Yeah, here are some more of Greg's actual words. He said, 'I kept telling Sheila, "Look, just forget about it!" But like I say, Sheila seemed obsessed – offered me money even – but I genuinely couldn't help her, because I honestly didn't know where any bloody ring was!'

"Ah, here's another line that Greg kept repeating. 'I kept saying, really I don't know.'

"Now get this Alistair," Emma went on, slightly raising her voice.

Astonished though he was by all this, Alistair could take a second to marvel at Emma's use of modern jargon.

"Sheila asked him, 'Do you know about her secret hiding place in the tower?'

"Here's another direct quote from Greg that I scribbled down. 'I said I don't know what you're bloody talking about!'

"This is quite incredible," interjected Alistair in genuine awe.

"Now, Alistair, neither Edwin nor I could believe what Greg came out with next. I really can't believe it, and Greg himself said he couldn't believe it, but Sheila had told him that she had found out about Henrietta having a secret hiding place at the top of the tower, by seducing Dennis. You see, before asking Greg about these rings, she'd asked Dennis about the ring. Where it was, and everything … Apparently, Dennis had let the cat out of the bag in return for what I believe are the usual favours. Then she blackmailed him by saying to him that if he opened his mouth about telling her, she would expose his immoral behaviour, or even accuse him of rape. Under all this pressure, poor old Dennis told her as much as he knew about her hiding places; but of course it wasn't 100 per cent accurate, because Henrietta had really been pretty vague, saying 'in the church' and 'on the allotments'. Shall I just keep going with all this, Alistair?"

"Yes, please," managed the very private and dumbfounded detective, scarcely able to speak.

"Greg said she swore him to secrecy too about the conversation. He was really drunk by the time he was telling us all this, but he kept saying, 'I didn't even tell Zoe – "Didn't even tell my sister," he kept repeating. "Only told her and that Alistair chappie, who she's getting hitched up with, the half of it, when they were asking me at the Three Horseshoes. Only told them I'd had a visit from Sheila, that's all. Never told them what she had been wanting, or … I mean, I didn't want her going telling my sister about my slip-ups … I mean, she's a bloody blackmailer!'"

"I can't believe I'm hearing this!" managed Alistair, almost giving up his attempts at note taking.

"Well, I'm afraid it comes to an end there," replied Emma and added, "because poor old Greg now became quite ill with his overindulgence. It was really horrible, and of course highly embarrassing. Oh, there's one last thing I fortunately managed to get in, moments before he collapsed …"

Emma did one of her characteristic coughs, usually signifying a slight forthcoming embarrassment.

"I took the liberty of asking him, 'Did you tell the police all this?'"

He replied rather enigmatically that he had told the police everything they needed to know, and they had told him they had checked Sheila out thoroughly, and there was absolutely no evidence against her."

Emma's story came to an abrupt end here. Greg had apparently passed out under the influence of what she called "that demon drink", so intrinsically good, but so evil when taken in excess, "like the modern generation do".

Alistair thanked Emma warmly for her sterling detective work, and soon the telephone conversation was completed and silence reigned again in his homely little hotel room.

His reaction to the quite extraordinary tale he had heard was a series of wild thoughts. Hadn't he always felt that the person who jumped over the fence might be the same person who went back into the church and locked him and Fred in the tower? Hadn't he sensed that someone was looking for something in the church, and looking in such a way that they hoped not to be detected?

He put his head in his hands and told himself, thanks to Mrs Martin's vigilance, combined with a lucky trip on the allotment, I've found one of those rings, the one with 'SA'. Now I'll have to find that other one with 'EUS' etched in it ... My guess is that it's somewhere in the church, and my hunch is the tower.

CHAPTER 36

(Barnaby's bombshell)

Alistair was by now totally preoccupied with the thought that he must challenge his old friend, Dennis, about the truth of Greg's drunken and almost unbelievable tale. He smiled to himself at the pun that it had the 'ring' of truth, for thanks to Mrs Martin's vigilance, combined with a good bit of luck, he had one of the rings, neatly hidden in his bedroom at the Concord Hotel.

With Dennis away, there seemed nothing for it but to phone him. They were old friends, but perhaps less close than one might have expected. The preamble would be the difficult bit, but Alistair would manage to lead up to the situation rather skilfully, he liked to think, and stress that he was trying to help him.

However, he was well aware that Dennis might quite reasonably and understandably refuse to talk, and might even just put the phone down. Yet he must try, for how much more sure he would be about his growing theory if he could ascertain the truth of this incredible report of Dennis being blackmailed by Sheila.

He looked at the little mobile on his desk. Had he really got the nerve to ring up Dennis and confront him with this extraordinary revelation? Their friendship would be for ever changed; but Alistair had already realised that possibility was on the cards the moment he took on the assignment.

If I'm to be brave enough to confront Sheila, I've got to be brave enough to cross-examine Dennis, he thought, as he sat there a moment longer in a kind of trance.

Soon he found his thoughts digressing along the

lines of how odd life was, and then on again to the other great mystery that he wanted to turn his mind to when the crime was solved.

He was brought back to earth from these philosophical contemplations by the mobile ringing and doing its usual dance across the table.

"Alistair, it's Barnaby here. Got the answer at long last from the bishop this morning. He had wanted time to consider whether it was my duty to tell you this or not, and I'm glad to say this morning I got the following letter from His Grace. Shall I read it to you?"

"Fire ahead," replied Alistair, aware that another day of miracles seemed to be unfolding.

"OK, it goes like this. *'My dear Barnaby'*," began Barnaby, and continued to read out the letter uninterrupted.

"'After much prayer and thought on the difficult matter you brought to me, it is my conclusion that for the sake of truth and for the sake of triumph of good over evil, you should feel free to tell all you know to a proper and legitimate investigator. When you swore on the Bible never to repeat the matter in question, there had been no murder of any one of those closely concerned. In view of the subsequent murder and the blank that the police drew in their investigation, you should in my opinion reveal your secret to this properly assigned investigator, Mr Alistair MacTavish, whom you refer to, and if I may recommend it, to the police also.

"'May I take this opportunity of thanking you for the many years of excellent service that you have provided as a lay reader at St Peter's, Cookington, and assure you that I am very much aware that it is people such as yourself who are the strength of our beloved Church of England.

"'Yours in Our Lord's Name, Patrick Kensington.'"

There was a pause while Barnaby put the letter back in its envelope.

"Shouldn't really have included that compliment to me at the end when I read it out to you," he mumbled, feeling rather pleased that he had.

"Well, that's good, Barnaby," said Alistair. "How do you want to deal with this? You've obviously got something interesting to tell. Do you want to speak face to face, or is it something easier to say over the phone?" It was now beginning to seem to him that the problems of the whole world could be sorted out through the medium of his dear little mobile.

For a moment Barnaby seemed to dither about which engagements of the day were important and which could be easily deferred.

Alistair interrupted him. "To be honest with you. Oh dear, there I go again with that wretched phrase! I'm at a rather critical point in my inquiries, and speed is of the essence, but I am pretty free today."

"I think it might be easier face to face," replied Barnaby sincerely. "Are you able to come over again to my abode on the edge of the parish?

Much though he liked the Concord Hotel, Alistair was glad enough to have a break from its confines, and enjoyed a nice sunny journey over to Cookington, followed by a pleasant walk to Barnaby's outpost.

As on his previous visit, he received a friendly welcome from that benign if slightly pompous gentleman. This time the house was otherwise empty, however, and Alistair detected a more efficient and businesslike approach on the part of his host.

Having been ushered to the seat he had taken on his previous visit, Alistair sat back and tried to relax, with a distinct sense of déjà vu.

"It was a time when Henrietta was away, and I was

457

actually quite busy anyway, I remember," began Barnaby, getting straight to the point. "Well, I got this call from Dennis. He wanted to speak to me urgently. I kept saying, 'Spit it out, man' – that sort of thing. But he said 'It's a pity we can't discuss this face to face. As you will realise, I'd find it so much easier to tell you sitting in the same room.'" So anyway, round he came, and sat in that very seat that you're sitting in."

"Basically," continued Barnaby, letting his favourite word hang in the air a while, "he said that he'd had a slip-up in his marriage. It had made it so much more painful when she died, but Henrietta had forgiven him, when he had confessed to her. However, for some reason, he wanted to confess to me too – said he would feel better if he did."

Alistair put on a good act of being surprised at such information about his old friend.

"Of course I was sitting there, trying to be understanding and nodding my head," continued Barnaby, attempting to keep everything straightforward, which was the style he faced every matter with.

"Thank you for sharing this with me," Alistair put in, adding, "it's as well that I should know about it, in the circumstances."

"Yes, poor Dennis," resumed Barnaby, "he went on a bit, saying how Henrietta had said, 'I know men are like that.' It was a tad embarrassing, because he was sobbing a bit, especially when he was saying that oddly it somehow made them closer, because apparently she had said she was no saint herself. He kept saying those were her words, and he said he thought she was a saint to forgive him."

Alistair's acting abilities still managed to show a degree of astonishment at what he was hearing, as Barnaby continued, inevitably repeating himself slightly, "It was a rather unpleasant experience, sitting there and seeing him and listening to him sobbing."

Barnaby put his hands together almost as if he was praying and continued, "Poor Dennis! He said he was so weak, so susceptible to temptation. He had allowed himself to be seduced by someone. Didn't say who the fallen lady was. Said he'd like to blame it on the alcohol which he had drunk, but he thought to be honest he would have done the same sober. She was a very attractive woman. He had always thought so."

Alistair stared at the floor.

"It was unlike Dennis to have confided to me as much as he did, and I suppose it's only human nature that he never revealed the name of the person who seduced him," said Barnaby, staring out of the window as if he had brought the matter to a conclusion.

"Was there any talk of blackmail?" asked Alistair, trying not to sound too eager to hear the answer.

"How do you mean?"

"Did this lady, whoever she was … was she after something in return for her favours?"

"He never mentioned anything like that."

Alistair sat gazing at the empty fireplace and keeping his silence.

"Might as well tell you everything, though. What is particularly painful to me, as a St Peter's man through and through, is that this breaking of the commandments occurred in our dear vicarage here - before he and Henrietta had moved in, I hasten to say. Dennis told me that he had gone to scout out the place where he and Henrietta might be moving to. Henrietta had been before a couple of times and formed the impression that she quite liked it, and was showing signs of agreeing to the move. She had liked the tower and been up it a couple of times and explored the vicinity of the church, walking along Lime Grove and all round the allotments. She'd more or less plumped for our parish in her mind, I think, and was pretending a bit that she was waiting for the green light from Dennis. So naturally dear old Dennis had wanted to see whether he liked it or not. Actually, I think he might have already agreed. Anyway, to get back to the matter, according to him (and I've no reason to doubt him because, to give the devil his due, he seemed to be being very honest), this lady who seduced him had met him a few times, and happened to be around. They met up and chatted, and she had gone with him to have a look and help him form an opinion."

Barnaby couldn't help a slight smile at what he was about to say next.

"Apparently there were no lights working there at that time in the interregnum, and they entered in the dark by a back door with a key that Henrietta had been given for her look round. Dennis told me that they had a bit of a close shave avoiding an embarrassing meeting with our two churchwardens, Edwin and Florence, who had just been checking on maintenance."

Alistair was flabbergasted to realise that this was where Fred's tale came into the equation. It was them, and not the churchwardens, who he had heard on the floor of the upstairs bedroom as he had hid in his fuse cupboard. Trust old Fred to get his wires crossed! However, who could blame him in the dark, and considering two people had just left the empty vicarage and two had just arrived.

Well, well, well, thought Alistair, leaning back and stretching his arms up towards the corners of the ceiling, while Barnaby disappeared into the innermost reaches of his kitchen..

Yes, what Greg had revealed in his drunkenness to Emma and Edwin seemed to be borne out by this. It looked like Sheila had indeed blackmailed Dennis to tell her where the hiding place was.

Alistair felt the return of wild thoughts, even crazy ones, racing through his head. For all he knew, Sheila might have seduced and blackmailed other people too, even the police.

Barnaby returned with a welcome beverage. He began to wax on about the temptations of the flesh being very hard for the young these days, as if the world had ever been any different.

"Well, dear old Dennis is hardly young," said Alistair, aware that it must have sounded a bit inane. He decided to put his thoughts in abeyance while he eased what he felt was a slight tension by speaking in a friendly way with Barnaby about a wide range of subjects.

He was glad to say goodbye at long last, and be able to think long and hard as he strolled home, without interruption or the necessity to make polite conversation.

Like a lurid movie, the possible sequence of events of his growing theory began to unfold in his mind. After this seduction of his poor old friend Dennis, presumably Sheila had gone looking for the ring, armed with the information that she had extracted from her victim. He had sensed that Dennis knew the tower was a special place to Henrietta, and Dennis had probably come out with that, though probably not with any exact details of the actual spot. Somehow she must also have got wind that there was another hiding place on the allotment too, which of course would fit in with what Dennis had said about her finding peace from the bustle of life there; hence the torchlight that Mrs Martin had seen and summoned him to witness. Yes, somewhere in the tower and somewhere on the allotments …

Was his imagination beginning to run away with him? But that could well have been her, up there at the top of the tower, hurtling a concrete slab down and narrowly missing a second act of murder, where he himself would have been the victim.

His nascent theory was beginning to hold water. It was at least a theory that nobody else had come up with.

If it proved right, and even if it did not, surely now Zoe would not blame him for involving her brother, Greg, contrary to her wishes. But what if the result of his actions was that Sheila started coming out with all sorts of lurid scandal about Greg? Would Zoe ever forgive him?

There was just so much to think through, and the task ahead of establishing what had happened seemed taxing in the extreme.

He tried extending his walk back to the station, but it offered no respite to his tormented thoughts.

The idea came to him rather suddenly that he would have one last thorough look himself at the top of the tower before catching the bus back to the Concord Hotel. He had been lucky finding one of the hiding places almost by accident when, having been summoned by Mrs Martin to investigate the torchlight, he had tripped over that root at the allotments. Maybe he would be lucky in finding the other hiding place in the tower. If it was him choosing a hiding place, he would opt for the very top of the tower, so why not give it a whirl? He had talked a lot about hunches. Now it was time to put a hunch to a test.

It was a long walk from Barnaby's home on the edge of the parish to the stately edifice of St Peter's Church, with its striking tower.

He stopped for lunch in a welcoming pub and allowed himself to spend the afternoon relaxing in the park.

Setting off in the early evening, Alistair was struck, not for the first time, as he approached the church down Apostles Way, by what a fine tribute to Christianity this robust structure was. He found himself recalling how once on a train journey to Edinburgh he had found himself gazing through the window and counting towers and spires and had ended up contemplating how the whole country was dotted with these fine landmarks, which had all started when an outcast was crucified on a cross on the very edge of the Roman Empire.

Such thoughts were soon banished when he arrived at the foot of the church tower next to the vicarage, which with Dennis away looked more forlorn and desolate than ever. For some reason, today it also seemed a somewhat daunting venue to have chosen for confronting the woman whom he was increasingly suspicious of being a murderess.

To avoid being inveigled into conversation if anyone was around, he went through the deserted car park and entered the church through the ambulatory door. There was enough light to make his way down the side aisle to the west end of the church, and into the narthex to the foot of the tower. He unlocked the door and went in, up the spiral staircase to the anteroom, and then on up the next lot of steps. Then he climbed up the hair-raising ladder, and negotiated the difficult bit just before pulling himself up onto the very top, which he had jokingly christened the Hillary Step.

He pushed the trapdoor open and emerged out onto the small area of flooring. He was immediately taken aback by the strength of the wind. As usual, the parapet seemed dangerously low. How the hell did Emma Duncan manage to abseil down from here? he wondered. Yes, it was clever of the local MP to have joined in too, for anyone abseiling down from this giddy height would get his vote alright.

Although he had a torch, he determined to carry out his final search for any hiding place before it got dark. He had been here before without success, and called himself a stubborn fool for thinking that this time it would be any different. Hadn't he always been accused of a certain obstinacy, of banging his head against a brick wall and not knowing when to stop.? He checked the same stones for any sign of looseness, but as before they seemed as firm and well set as ever.

A sense of the ridiculousness of his situation came to him, and he thought that before he descended he would take a final look at the view from up here, because he had no desire to ever return. Henrietta might find peace and solace up here, but he wasn't sure that he did – not this evening anyway.

As expected, a very slight feeling of vertigo came over him. He held on to the parapet in the corner with a hand on each side. The strengthening wind momentarily disorientated him and gave him an increased sense of insecurity. To reassure himself that the building was strong and secure, and that the tower could withstand the onslaught of even a hurricane, he gently kicked the bottom stone in the corner.

With surprise, he sensed the stone moving loosely. With an unpleasant feeling of insecurity bordering on fear, he immediately knelt down and examined the area. Yes, the stone was loose. He pulled it out, finding a cavity behind, into which he put his hand. He was not looking for a hiding place now, but trying to reassure himself of the sturdiness of the structure. Opposite his hand and to the sides, he was pleased to find the stones were as strong as ever, but when he put his hand downwards, he realised there was a space almost like a hotel safe. He pulled out what felt like a matchbox. It was indeed a matchbox. In an instant, he had opened it, and there shining remarkably brightly was a gold ring. He picked it up and examined it closely. The now familiar letters 'EUS' showed clearly in the light of his torch, which he had by now brought into use.

An extraordinary sense of wonder came to him, along with the realisation that this must surely be Henrietta's secret hiding place; and sure enough, inside there had been only one object, namely the second of the two rings that Sheila, for whatever mad obsessive reason, must have been searching for.

Several minutes of astonishment passed before Alistair resumed more rational thinking and behaviour. He removed the ring and placed it securely in his wallet – the second of such rings to have been thus lodged for safety. For some inexplicable reason, he replaced the now empty matchbox inside the hiding place, and indeed put the loose stone back, jamming it tightly so that, for all the world, it looked as secure as all the other stones. Henrietta would be proud of me, he thought.

Then, after a last look round, as used to be his custom before descending his beloved Munros of Scotland, he descended the staircase and carefully locked the tower door behind him.

With a wind like that, my little joke about the Hillary Step is not so inaptly named, he thought.

Once down from the tower, he found it was by now dark in the church, but with the aid of his torch he was able to make his way back from the west end to the east end, through the sacristy. He was about to open the ambulatory door out to the car park, when out of the darkness appeared Fred Goodman. To say that Alistair had a fright would be the understatement of the year.

"Good God, you gave me a fright, Fred! What the hell are you doing here?"

"I'd like to ask you the same question," came Fred's

465

voice in his controlled but cocky tone.

"I was having a last fruitless search for any secret hiding place of Henrietta's," replied Alistair, composing himself a bit.

In the torchlight, Alistair could see that Fred's countenance looked somewhat disbelieving.

"And what about yourself, Fred?"

"I won't try and deceive you, Alistair. It would be easy for me to give you a hundred different reasons why I might be here, as Florence is away and Edwin could probably not even find the key to the church if I rang him up. No, I'll tell you straight. I too was having a good look round to see if I could find anything to help throw light on the mystery. I told you, didn't I, that Henrietta always said a church would be a good place to hide something."

To smooth things over, Alistair unwillingly invited Fred to the nearby pub for "a quick one", before eventually catching the bus and journeying back towards the Concord Hotel. For the moment he had decided to keep his find a secret. There would be time enough to explain his secrecy to Fred another day.

Back at the Concord Hotel, it suited him to find that both Donna and Cissie were off duty, so that a courteous "Good evening" to the stand-in receptionist was all that was required, and he could retire quickly to his room.

CHAPTER 37

(A bad night)

He had a premonition that his overactive brain would deny him the gift of sleep. Indeed, the combination of Emma's remarkable account of her and Edwin's meeting with Greg, plus his own conversation with Barnaby in the morning, followed by the visit in the evening to the tower, which had yielded its secret, to say nothing of his planned confrontation with Sheila tomorrow, all combined to make the prospect of sleep well nigh impossible.

If only Zoe had agreed with me ... If only I hadn't drawn her into the investigation so much ... How can I go ahead and do exactly what she doesn't want me to? On and on his thoughts buffeted him, like a choppy sea.

He turned in his bed for the umpteenth time, annoyed that he had got himself into such a difficult situation. He heard a distant church clock striking midnight. Somewhere a dog barked. He lay there unable to stop his racing thoughts. He swore out loud in the darkness of the room and got up and sat at the little table on the chair. He put his head in his hands and said very deliberately to himself, in his thoughts, that he must make a decision. It came to him that he must either wallow around in continuing mystery, or act on this growing hunch and confront Sheila. He thumped his fist on the table. Damn it! His thoughts raced. He would confront Sheila and challenge her with his suspicions. It would clear the air; it might make her talk more. Hadn't Dennis said I should work on hunches? Hadn't Zoe, despite her strong reservations about any further approach to her newly married brother, nonetheless used that rather good little phrase that "hunch was the name of the game"?

467

That entry in the diary with those mysterious letters "TATT" in Henrietta's diary kept flashing in his mind, almost taunting him as to what their impenetrable meaning might be. Was it just one of those bizarre coincidences that those letters were the last of, say, "Meet Sheila at allotment"? If that was what they stood for, it would indeed have been an occasion for Henrietta to have used her private, indeed secret, code by writing only the last letter of a word. However, it worried him that he was making everything fit what might be only a crazy theory emanating from his obsessive mind.

For a moment, he checked himself. Staring through the crack in the curtains at the night sky, he asked himself, was Zoe right? Was he being too far-fetched for words? And for a moment an image of her calm, sympathetic, cheerful face came into his mind and soothed him.

Then his wild thoughts began to reassert themselves and seemed to answer that very question. But, damn it, those mysterious letters - they must mean something, and Henrietta did have the habit of making cryptic diary entries using the last letters of words when extra privacy was most required. Was this guess of his the sort of hunch that Dennis had asked him to seek? Was this the sort of hunch that the police were trained to dismiss for lack of evidence? Had the police not told Greg that the people concerned had been eliminated from their inquiries?

He thought of the photographs which Vanessa had taken, and which in a way her mother had rather understandably kept hidden from the police, to protect her daughter from the eager cameras of the press. It was new material, unseen by the police, he reminded himself. He did not want to look at them again. He had studied them for hours in his room, moving the

468

magnifying glass forwards and backwards like a machine, to the point where they were so vividly etched in his mind that there was no need to actually look at them again, for he could as it were see them with his eyes shut. For what he vowed would be the last time, he listed the points about them in his mind. One could at least say that one of the photographs definitely showed *two* figures at the allotment. The position of the shed and a tree almost certainly identified Helen's allotment. One of the figures appeared fat, but as he had suggested to Zoe, and as it had crossed his imaginative mind a hundred times, it could well be the vicar's clerical dress blowing out behind her in the way that more than one person had commented on, making her look fatter and bigger than she was. Had he not seen other photographs of her in Dennis's house, and indeed in the papers, showing her in a not totally dissimilar style? Zoe had not agreed with that particular jump of imagination, but hadn't a great many people commented on how Henrietta was never out of clerical dress? Hadn't some wag rather unkindly joked that if she was holding a broomstick, you wouldn't notice the difference?

To and fro his mind went, and on and on his eager thoughts chased themselves, as he struggled to clarify the case he was making. Admittedly, the other figure looked like a man, but only by posture. It could just possibly be the tomboyish stance of Sheila. Hadn't he always thought she had a certain tomboyish style about her, ever since his fleeting meeting with her at the hotel? Perhaps that was what his friend Dennis had found so irresistibly attractive, for she was certainly well built, and though strong, not losing her femininity. "Tomboy" was a fair description, and didn't Rhys say that she preferred parallel bars to drinking bars? So if anyone was agile enough to vault over car park walls it was her. She certainly had some very tomboyish, interests, for didn't she enjoy watching rugby and even boxing? These points he stressed to himself, nearly speaking out loud as if he was a prosecuting lawyer in court. He would not irritate himself by looking again at Vanessa's photograph, but thinking of it he felt strongly that, apart from Sheila, no one he knew put their hand on their hip in quite that manner.

Sometimes, as the days had gone by, he had looked at that photograph and thought, No it's preposterously far-fetched. Other times he had looked at it and thought it could be; and once, only two days ago, after a drink too many, he had thought it must be, and to his shame he had broken his rule and sworn out loud, there and then in his small bedroom, "*You bloody murderer!*" At that time he had corrected himself and indeed rebuked himself, telling himself he must be tired, and he'd gone down to the bar for a drink to calm himself. Later he had shown the photographs to Zoe, who had thought it was too far-fetched, telling him that he was trying to make things fit together to support a preconceived theory, and saying that no jury would accept it as evidence. This had quietened him down, but in his heart of hearts he had never completely agreed with her about that.

If only they had agreed about that, it would make it so much easier for him; but maybe this was an occasion when he must trust his own judgement. It was the first time that he used a phrase to himself that he would come to use often, namely, that they couldn't be expected to agree about absolutely everything, and after all she had never claimed to be interested in detective work. He however had been enamoured of it over the years, though he was rapidly going off it now, tormented as he was by these constant interminable dilemmas.

He thumped his fist on the little table again. Yes, he

would not delay; he would change tack. Instead of the long days of contemplating everything in a slow and leisurely manner, which had so appealed to him at first, he would now expedite matters. From now on speed is of the essence, he said to himself. He wanted to get on with the rest of his life, and that was not one where murder was so inextricably linked with the family of the lady he hoped to marry. He drew up a rough plan of action and laughed at his old joke about a plan of inaction, for now he would go to the opposite extreme.

Sheer curiosity made him yearn to confront Sheila and note her reaction. In his excitement, he could hardly wait for two o'clock in the afternoon, and the prospect of this confrontation. It would clear the air. It would make him feel better. At any rate she would have to admit she had visited Greg. That would shake her, he mouthed again almost out loud to himself, in his new ruthless and brazen mood.

He was indeed determined now, as he strutted around the room in a mixture of impatience and nervousness. It was time a few people got challenged baldly, face to face. Yes, he would do it; he would act fearlessly on his hunch and pursue this at all costs. It seemed like his only break. If he was wrong and there was a big hoo-ha about it, he could consider resigning honourably from the voluntary role that he had taken on more or less on a whim, as much to help an old friend as to indulge himself in a passion for detective work. Indeed, he was rapidly beginning to think it might be a case of having bitten off more than he could chew. He might like a good mystery, but one that had totally foxed such experts was a little unfair for a novice.

He found himself staring at one of his most precious and oldest possessions, namely Sparky, his old alarm clock. It showed the time to be exactly one o'clock, and the idea came to him that he would try and give himself one hour's reflection only, as calmly as possible, literally going through the theory that had gradually developed in his mind to the point where he was thinking of it as 'my theory'. He would jot down notes as he thought it through; but after the hour was up, he would make an effort of will to stop thinking about it.

He began to scribble note after note in a barely legible scrawl:

Someone had been looking for something in the chapel of the church. The person had got wind of being discovered and so ran away, leaving the church through the ambulatory door and crossing the wall in agile style. Then gone back a little while later when the coast was clear (sometime during the post mortem at Edwin's house). When I went unexpectedly back to the church, whoever it was had by then returned to the church and gone up the tower, seen me with his torch from the tower and tried to put an end to my investigation. I suppose it's a kind of compliment! He laughed to himself.

What was the person after? It must be something specific, because a thief would have taken any number of valuable things from the church, which had been left. It could be anyone, but that included Sheila. At any rate it would seem the person knew the intricacies of the church pretty well.

Of course it could be Dennis, who knew at least vaguely of Henrietta's hiding place and certainly knew the intricacies of the church, because to all intents and purposes he lived there – well, as close as damn it.

Fred Goodman would have also known the premises like the back of his hand, because he had been churchwarden for fourteen years.

Florence, a most conscientious churchwarden, probably knew the place well by now, though she had used the phrase that she 'was getting to know it'.

472

Edwin Archer, like Florence, must be getting to know it well enough, albeit to a lesser extent, given his rather detached approach to the role.

Bill Thompson, in his capacity of insurance officer, had of course learnt a lot about the ins and outs of the building over the years.

It was Sheila, though, who would appear to have been the one most likely to be engaged on a search. Whatever motive the crazed workings of her mind had created, she had by Greg's account sounded desperate to find those rings.

Although Vanessa's photographs did not identify the two figures clearly enough, Gary's reported sightings added considerable force to the nascent theory that the two figures could have been Henrietta and Sheila. Gary had thought they were possibly two women. He had reported that one of them seemed to cross herself.

Alistair turned his mind to the diaries. There was no "MSAA" staring him in the face from their silent pages, which could have meant something like "Meet Sheila At Allotment", but there was "TATT". Could that be explained by her having used the last letters of that phrase? Had not Dennis said that she had the simple technique of using the last letters of words when it was a very private matter. Far-fetched – far-fetched in the extreme - but there was no getting away from the fact that she had this custom - what Dennis had called "this endearing idiosyncrasy". For a moment he was sidetracked, wondering if Zoe had any endearing idiosyncrasies. Then he reminded himself, wasn't his only chance of succeeding where the police had failed to pursue far-fetched ideas?

He had to admit that if it was not for his long-held friendship with Dennis, he would have been a little suspicious of certain things. Right from the beginning he had wondered about many odd little facts, even why

473

it was tricky for Dennis to put him up, and why Dennis had gone on about there being quite a lot going on. What had that meant? Was he too trying to find the exact spot of Henrietta's hiding place?

He remembered how for one wild moment at the beginning of his investigation he had wondered if Dennis was in league with Helen. Why had he told her first about thinking of employing himself as an investigator? He knew Dennis was fond of Helen. Anyone could see that by the look in his eyes. However, he had asked Dennis once why he had not asked him first about taking on the assignment, rather than checking the idea out with Helen. Dennis had replied, "Well, she found poor Henrietta, and anyway you were out of the bloody country when I had the idea."

Roger, the allotment holder, had reported walking with Dennis back from evening class, which at first Dennis had not remembered, and indeed there was this extraordinary disagreement about which pub they had gone to. All very odd! Was it just a genuine memory problem that presumably Roger had, because his wife supported Dennis's recollection that it was the Griffin and not the Turk's Head.

He laughed to think he had ever found it suspicious that Roger's phone had failed when he had asked him about that, and how he had wondered whether Roger wanted time to think so kept cutting the conversation off.

This had made him recall how Zoe had wisely often stressed to him that in an investigation such as this, there would be many coincidences and many red herrings. Well, there certainly were plenty about his old friend, Dennis. Puzzling questions too, he mused, for example, did he really not know of Henrietta's affair with Greg?

Did he really not know that the parish directory, which he had seemingly randomly selected without looking from a bottom drawer to give him, had contained so many notes and names and addresses, in particular that of the poor forlorn Buzz?

For a moment Alistair rebuked himself for having such dark thoughts about a friend, saying to himself that if Dennis had been going to do his wife in, he wouldn't choose the allotment. Immediately his fevered mind asked, Or would he? Maybe it was not premeditated, and was just a chance site …

As for Buzz himself, he mused, that's a name I will never forget! Zoe is right about how many coincidences there are in life. I mean, this case has a Buzz and an Edwin … why am I thinking of the moon?'

Buzz himself, who could have had such an obvious motive, had seemed such a suspicious character when his ticket to London had fallen out of that old latin primer that Alistair had picked out of the bookshelf in a moment of nostalgia for his old school days, particularly when he had lied about travelling straight back to Edinburgh; but the letter Alistair had cheekily intercepted from Eric Watson had to his mind satisfactorily shown his innocence.

He reflected on Henrietta. He recalled how one of Len Stephenson's last words had been to mention that Henrietta had had a bit of difficulty with a lady. Had told him that she had bad vibes from this person.

Poor old Len, he thought wistfully, I remember him so clearly telling me how the police had told him to "keep out of it, old man." Well, any progress he was going to make would be with something the police did not know about, because on the material they had, they had done a good job.

He looked at his old friend the alarm clock, which he had christened 'Sparky' for some extraordinary reason.

He returned to bed, but though he felt calmer, sleep still eluded him. He lay there wondering if the cold light of day would make him check his resolve as he eventually drifted momentarily into and out of a light, fitful slumber.

***

The next morning broke wet and murky, with raindrops hitting the windowpanes as noisily as if kids were throwing things. Was it this that gave him such a strange sense of foreboding? Why were his feelings so changed from the serenity of early yesterday and the resolve of the early part of the night?

An eerie new fear came over him that if she was the murderer, she might attack him. He tried to pull himself together and calm such racing thoughts. He metaphorically kicked himself for pondering whether this was his last Friday morning before being strangled by an irate and wild Sheila, but his imagination about her reaction had run wild with possibilities; had he not dreamt once before of her attacking him and woken with a scream so audible that he had felt self-conscious the next morning, when entering the dining room for breakfast?

To that same dining room he now went, and was glad to find Cissie in more sympathetic mode as she brought him his breakfast, and he ate it without any irritation.

"How was the dentist?" he asked, without much sincerity, and did not register the reply. It annoyed him that he was so tired, but he would just have to put up with that. Not for the first time, a photograph of the prime minister glared up at him from his morning newspaper on the table beside his side plate. He is

476

probably tired too, I shouldn't wonder, he thought, trying to cheer himself up.

"I'm going to be extra busy for a couple of days, Cissie. There's a lot going on, believe you me. After that I'll let you and Donna know what I've been up to all this time, because both of you have been so good, not bothering me with questions any longer. I've got a lot on my mind and I'm afraid it makes me rather rude. Please forgive me."

"Ooh … can't wait!" responded Cissie, adding, "One of our customer's asked me if you were a spy. I said, 'I really don't know what he is.' Thought you'd be proud of me being so discreet. I am discreet, aren't I?"

He knew Cissie was proud of this new word, "discreet", which he had taught her.

"Yes, you're a paragon of discretion, and I'm proud of you, Cissie," he replied affectionately, putting an arm round her shoulder and pecking her on the cheek. "You've been great through all this. Arthur's a lucky man."

She blushed, and he walked upstairs aware that he was behaving slightly oddly and saying unusual things, and that he must be even more on edge than he thought.

He was puzzled that he should be so nervous. The whole meeting with Sheila would probably end in nothing more remarkable than a good laugh and a cup of tea; and yet what explained that chilling feeling that it might end in something very different?

Should I pray? he asked himself, and reflected, Emma Duncan would; even Fred had admitted to prayer when they were trapped in the tower. Surely that had been a more desperate situation, and it had ended without any misfortune. So, why shouldn't this be a doddle too?

His mobile began to vibrate and rang out clearly

from his jacket pocket.

He turned round, leant on the little windowsill, and felt an inexplicable joy and contrasting tranquillity as he recognised Zoe's ever lovely voice.

"I know we agreed not to have another chat till we meet this evening at the restaurant, but just thought you might need this one."

"How sweet of you and I think you're right," he responded.

"You see, I'm getting to know you so well … "

"I don't like going against your will … "

"That's why I'm ringing; I knew you'd be in a dilemma after our chat on Tuesday, and I just wanted you to know I support whatever you decide."

He felt an overwhelming feeling of relief and an extraordinary renewal of energy flowing through him, and he said with feeling, "That means so much to me, Zoe. I'm not sure I could do anything you disapproved of."

"I support your decision, whatever it is," she pronounced, as if it was her final word on the matter.

"OK then, we'll go for it," he replied in similar parting vein, adding, "wish me luck, and looking forward to that Chinese meal tonight. Goodbye."

"Good luck, Alistair, take care," came her last words, followed by the click of her putting her phone down, which rang in his ears.

He stood for a moment staring at his phone, knowing now beyond doubt that he would confront Sheila that afternoon. To turn back now would seem to Zoe like cowardice. He reflected that it was the worst moment of nervousness that he had felt since he had become momentarily stranded as a boy on a mountain rock high in Glen Coe. He remembered Emma Duncan's phrase, "There are times in life when you feel you are on your own, but we believe that actually you're not."

Then it came to him. Well, now I'm not on my own. Zoe is still supporting me and has given me carte blanche.

As he had often noticed before, it was funny how a chat like that with Zoe could calm him down, and he was surprised to find himself, within about an hour, drifting into a semi-wakefulness followed by the gift of sleep, which had eluded him for so much of the night. Such was the calming effect of a wonderful lady.

At Zoe's end, a minute ticked by while she sat in thought. At first she found that she was unexpectedly pleased with the arrangement to "grasp the nettle", as Alistair had put it, but within a short space of time her unease returned.

Why does this uncanny sense of impending danger refuse to go away? her thoughts went. Suppose he got into difficulties? I can hardly hover around on the off chance that he might call help at some unarranged time.

Then the idea came to her in a flash. She would ring Emma. He was always going on about what a wise old bird she was. For goodness sake, she had even got him to read some passage in the Bible and he had threatened to ask her about its meaning before giving his views to Emma.

Before she could change her mind, she grabbed the phone and dialled Emma's number, surprised at her relief in finding her in.

In a sheepish and embarrassed tone she expressed her concern about Alistair's planned confrontation with Sheila that afternoon, and made her request. She explained how he had made an appointment for Sheila to come to the vicarage at two o'clock that afternoon. She explained how Dennis had given him the keys while he was away and encouraged him to use the vicarage as a venue for interviews.

Emma coughed to hide her surprise at this unexpected request. "I would have thought he would go bananas if I unexpectedly turn up out of the blue – he'll never forgive me."

"You're the only person he really trusts in this whole sorry business, you know, Emma."

"Apart from you," said Emma with a calmness that belied her continued surprise, but which almost seemed to make Zoe's call sound expected.

"Well, that's sweet of you to say so, anyway," responded Zoe aware of a glowing feeling within her.

"No, call it women's intuition, to quote you; I think you'd make a great couple."

Zoe was glad that her blush could not be seen.

"Do you mind, Emma?"

"Well, anyway, OK, my dear. This sounds like something one can't say no to. I'll go round that way about two o'clock and see what's cooking, as he always says."

"Yes, he always uses that phrase; clever of you to have picked up on it." Zoe found herself feeling proprietorial about Alistair's language.

"You're a lucky woman, Miss Zoe," said Emma with a firmness tinged with embarrassment; then added, "if I was a very good few years younger, you'd have to watch out, and I certainly wouldn't be doing you any favours."

For a moment they both laughed, but to Emma, as she put the phone down, such an urgent cry for help demanded the true Christian response.

'No great sacrifice,' she said to herself. 'It's clearing up a bit now into really quite a nice sunny day, and I feel like getting out and about this afternoon. I'll go round to the vicarage at two o'clock and check that all is peace and quiet.'

CHAPTER 38

(Confrontation in the vicarage)

He arrived at the vicarage and let himself in with the key that Dennis had given him. He felt better now, reminding himself how pleased Dennis would be that he was getting on with the job.

He sat down and was conscious of a welcome calmness coming over him. The worst that could happen would be that she would feel extremely insulted and hurl abuse at him. He could cope with that.

He was waiting for her at Henrietta's old desk when he saw her through the window arriving at the porch. He walked promptly to the front door and invited her in, taking her coat with many jokes about feeling like a vicar about to interview a confirmation candidate etc.

Sheila looked a little nervous, he thought, but nonetheless responded in the same jocular theme and took a seat opposite the desk as he sat down again.

He started proceedings by explaining in what was now routine fashion how Dennis had given him this assignment and wanted him to speak to as many people as possible, and with that in mind had actually given him the key to the vicarage, while he was away, so that he could use it to invite people round for a chat.

She seemed more relaxed now and smiled back at him by way of response. There was something in the smile though that unnerved Alistair a little, and he rather timidly pursued his questioning.

"Please tell me anything you know about Cookington – anything that you think might be helpful. I've decided if I can't make any progress after a little time to call it a day and get on with other things. Dennis feels he owes it to Henrietta to have this one last shove for truth – the old extra mile business. So please just tell me anything you can – anything that you think might help me get to the bottom of this whole horrid business."

"Yes, I was with Rhys on his business trip. I wasn't particularly keen to come with him but he was determined that I should. Unfortunately, it would have to have coincided with the time of the crime, which has proved a bloody nuisance and meant an awful lot of police questioning; but Rhys and I were able to account for every movement we made as we were practically always together. The police checked it all out thoroughly, what with Rhys having been Henrietta's boyfriend. Occasionally, when his business demanded it, I did go off on my own, and would do a bit of sightseeing and visiting friends."

"Well, that's reasonable enough," said Alistair, as much to reassure himself, as to put Sheila at ease.

"Yes, as I say, the police were satisfied with my movements," she continued, "and as they rather pompously phrased it were no longer wanting to pursue their enquiries relating to either Rhys or myself."

An unexpected feeling of impatience came over Alistair and somewhat impetuously he decided he would broach the challenge straight away. If nothing else, an interesting discussion should follow.

"Yes, I know that. There's no suggestion whatsoever that you're involved in the crime, but I have to report to those who have employed me," lied Alistair, "how you came to be there with Henrietta at that time."

There followed one of those silences that is louder than sound.

He had not expected silence; a loud and long denial and complaint maybe, or a desperate attempt to strangle him but not this.

Finding it difficult to interpret her reaction, he felt

482

the need to speak again. "Look, Sheila, I know you liked, shall we say, mooching around. Well, it's quite natural that you'd want a mooch around Cookington."

His heart was beating and he felt momentarily afraid at the recollection of his dream.

He felt the need to keep talking. "No one's accusing you of anything," he began again tentatively, "but we just have to get a truthful clarification of everything we know about people's movements. I'm sure you can understand the importance of that, can't you?"

It fleetingly crossed his mind that if the time ever came to tell Zoe of this unpleasant situation he would hide from her how afraid he was feeling; there was no need for her to ever know.

A further silence ensued, during which he curiously heard the clock ticking. Ticking away to Zoe's deadline, he thought.

"What do you mean?" asked Sheila eventually, in a defensive but menacing tone, which shattered the silence like a mirror being broken into a hundred pieces.

"You know, we have to ask people," Alistair continued, taking courage from using the plural pronoun, "why they went places and all that. I reckon of all people you had the best reason for going to check out Cookington; just sheer natural, understandable curiosity, I imagine. I'm sure that's all it was."

"Well, you're right, that's exactly what it was!" she shouted back. Calming down a little, she added, "Just sheer curiosity – amusement, you might say. I was intrigued to see the sort of set-up that my poor husband, Rhys, so nearly got, shall we say, caught up in."

Alistair relaxed. Though still unsure of his interlocutor, he now felt a relief to have got the difficult part over with.

"Yes, I went to Cookington," she said in unfriendly

vein, "just to have a good look round at the church and the parish. I found the church open."

"Now there's a surprise in the dear old C of E, eh?" Alistair laughed, hoping to ease the tension and adding, "I gather from David and Bill that it's only locked for insurance purposes to keep the premium down."

It was extraordinary how humour always reduced tension, because Sheila laughed too, but it gradually changed from seeming genuineness into a rather unpleasant, insincere laugh.

"Well, anyway, I actually hadn't been there very long, just looking at the odd plaque, when Henrietta suddenly appeared from nowhere, and we fell talking and she started showing me round. She said she tried to leave the church open as much as possible, but there had been break-ins and also some bad types around - vandals and tramps actually asking for money. She made some joke about the difficulty of taking the teaching literally with these undesirables. Funnily enough, I recall ticking her off for using that phrase, and I remember she said, 'I'm not a saint.' Well, we had a really good look round; she showed me a lot. Of course, I never said who I was and in fact made myself out to be a kind of American research person, which wasn't difficult because I've picked up this transatlantic accent real bad, what with Rhys's business being over there right now. Anyway, I really did learn a lot from her about the parish. We popped into the vicarage before walking back to the station. She was going to some kind of Society of Mary meeting, and I was going back to our airport hotel.

"We walked down to the station together. We were going past the allotments when Henrietta suddenly said, 'Hey, look, there's Charles!' There was this big man lying on the other side of the fence between the street and the allotments. Henrietta was saying, 'goodness,

484

we can't just leave him there.' Now this time, by contrast, I was rather impressed, I didn't think Henrietta was that sort of priest, if you know what I mean. Charles turned out to be an allotment holder, and actually the one in charge of all the allotments, the guy who ran the organisation, if you know what I mean. I remember Henrietta said that was not the first time she had seen him drunk and tried to help him. Henrietta told me he had been really ashamed of his behaviour and never referred to it, apart from begging her to keep quiet about it. Well, somehow, by hook or by crook, we kind of managed to get him up on his feet and propped up on an old bench on his allotment. He was in a very bad way, all dishevelled and dirty, smelling badly, not least of alcohol. He kept telling us not to tell anyone how we had found him – almost pleading, he was. Said something about the allotments annual general meeting was coming up.

"Well, we set off back up the central path to the street, but I'm afraid to say made a very small diversion and, I have to admit, helped ourselves to a few raspberries on one of the allotments. I felt bad about it at the time, because I remember joking to Henrietta that it didn't make it any better her being a vicar. To be fair to her, she seemed a bit put out by that remark. Anyway, that's about all that happened; we pushed on to the station and I caught a westbound train back to the hotel near the airport, and she caught a train going the other way to the city. I never told the police about that; it didn't seem fair on Henrietta to report her helping herself to other people's raspberries, especially when she'd just been helping some drunkard. I just thought it would all be too awkward to report – really, it would have - and this drunk guy, Charles, that was his name, had just sworn us to secrecy. Yes, I never told the police all that."

Alistair gave her a penetrating but fearful look.

"Oh God, I wish I had," she added, not very convincingly.

Alistair decided he would bluff about a return to the allotment and keep his trump card - her visit to Greg - up his sleeve.

"No, fair enough, but why did you make a second visit?"

Sheila went white and appeared stunned. "I never made a second visit," she retorted sharply.

"What if I told you I had incontrovertible photographic evidence that you returned?" Alistair bluffed, aware that now he had gone as far as he could, and would back down like mad.

There was a silence.

"I don't see how you could."

"Oh, quite simple – our resident photographer in the house in Lime Grove overlooking the allotment," said Alistair, surprised by his own sarcasm.

"It can't be – this is mistaken identity or it's that day I've just told you about when I went with Henrietta," Sheila responded defensively.

"The problem is," said Alistair, "there's something else."

To be fair, he thought, this time she did not flinch.

"What?" she asked in a shrill voice.

"That," he said very deliberately, before continuing with the lie, "the police have asked me not to tell."

"I need to speak to my husband!" came her swift response.

Alistair took a doubtful decision, as he could imagine the police saying, "I must warn you that anything you say etc." But something made him blurt out, "Fair enough, it's always nice to see Rhys. Let's get him over here – I mean, all we're trying to do is clear up confusion and get to the truth so everybody's life can eventually get back to normal." Then he added, for a number of reasons, "including the perpetrator of the crime – whoever he or she may be."

"I want to see my husband alone," demanded Sheila rather suddenly.

"I'll give him a ring anyway," said Alistair, nicely but forcefully. His thoughts were racing.

This interminable mystery just possibly could be unravelling, he thought, as he turned to use the phone on the side of the desk.

Sheila put her hand into her cardigan and pulled out a gun.

She raised it very carefully and deliberately and pointed it towards the back of Alistair's head.

Emma Duncan had arrived at the French windows seconds earlier and, witnessing this horrifying scene, was momentarily paralysed; but then with remarkable presence of mind she picked up a large stone on the patio and threw it with lucky accuracy through the open French windows directly at the would-be assassin.

There was a loud report of a gun firing, and simultaneously Alistair fell back. Emma, seemingly indifferent to her own danger, rushed through the French windows and knelt over him as if to save his life. They both stared open-mouthed at the slumped body of Sheila. It was clear that the bullet which Sheila had fired had missed Alistair, ricocheted round the room and finally embedded itself in Sheila's head.

She appeared dead, though both of them thought she mumbled a few words asking forgiveness.

Alistair kicked the gun away, just in case. It was some time before he could bring himself to speak.

"Why – how were you here?" he mumbled, still shaking.

"I had a book for you but that can wait," gasped Emma, before turning aside to vomit.

487

"What can't wait is for us to contact the police immediately!" gasped Alistair. "Emma, you are the first to learn it, but I reckon we have solved the allotment murder mystery."

"We?" she queried with trembling voice.

"You, me and Zoe," he said, conscious that he was still shaking.

"You'd make a lovely couple … Goodness, I'm going funny in the head. I think I'm saying things in shock and speaking deliriously or something."

He crawled over to the telephone and rang the police.

"We've just got to wait for them now," he mumbled, sitting slumped by the telephone table and adding, "we should hear the siren any minute."

He started telling Emma bits of the thread that had led him to the situation in which they found themselves.

"I'm not sure I'm taking in what you're saying," she replied. "I'm in shock."

"What was the book, by the way, that you said you were bringing me?" he asked, attempting to laugh, but aware by his trembling that he was in shock.

"Oh, something like *First Steps in Belief*, or something like that, anyway," she began, "but I think that can all wait right now, because I'm in shock too. Look, I'm trembling like mad. God will understand the need for a little delay on that front, just now."

At that moment they both heard it: the siren of the approaching police car, distant but unmistakeable. Alistair slumped back, the persistent and ever louder police siren reminded him oddly of the ambulance he had called for Len Stephenson; but this should have a happier ending, as he was unhurt and would soon overcome the shock. Then he'd be well and his investigation would be concluded.

A lovely feeling of job done or, as Zoe would say, "Mission accomplished" came over him. Soon he would be able to give her all the attention a fiancée deserved.

He fainted, but knew he was in good hands, as Emma patted him on the cheek and said, "Here, you should be doing this to me!" Then she added with tongue in cheek, "But of course you haven't got that inner strength which we Christians have." He thought he heard her say something like "at least not yet" and then finally something like "sorry, I shouldn't have said that".

He was feeling better now. His feeling of faintness had quite subsided and he was trembling less. Nonetheless, the rest of that day was passed in a daze. He remembered the police arriving. He remembered the ambulance people assuring him that his only problem was shock. He remembered the good-looking ambulance girl saying, "Haven't I seen you before somewhere? He remembered mumbling something to her about that being when she came to help poor old Len Stephenson in Kingfisher Row, and her saying, "If we go on meeting like this, people will start talking." He remembered several photographs being taken. He remembered he and Emma seemingly answering more questions from the police than he had ever asked in the whole of his investigation. However, the questions were all asked in a friendly and polite manner.

It was eleven o'clock at night when a rather senior policeman said to him, "Right, Mr MacTavish, it seems all we have to do is to say thank you for your help and expertise in solving what has been such an incredible national mystery. We're also able to convey Dennis Carr's great gratitude to you for enabling him to get some kind of closure after all he has been through. We contacted him, and gather that he's actually due back here at the vicarage later tonight."

"What about Rhys?" asked Emma, genuinely concerned and sipping brandy in a big armchair, where she had been ensconced since the arrival of the ambulance men.

"Poor Rhys, the man's utterly devastated," replied the detective sergeant. "We are convinced of his non-involvement; he's been able to show his complete innocence about some nasty suspicions we began to have of his collusion."

"Poor fellow; we'll have to work on him – a bit of pastoral care needed there, I think," commented Emma, looking better and more like herself by the minute.

"You'll have a hard job there, Emma. The man swears like a trooper!" joked Alistair.

"Look at Len Stephenson. He was in the army during the war and ended up in our congregation, never saying a rude word," retorted Emma indignantly.

Alistair looked at her with amusement.

"Well, hardly ever," she added.

CHAPTER 39

(An official engagement seals two mysteries solved)

A few days later, Alistair sat philosophising with his fiancée, Zoe, in the car outside the allotment entrance. He turned to her, saying, "You know, it's a funny thing but while investigating this case I kept thinking of that line from Richard II. It goes something like, 'This land of such dear souls, this dear, dear land.'"

However, the phrase that really stuck in his head was the one used by Emma. Her last words to him had been, "You know, while you've been accusing me of murder, I've been praying that you find God."

"I mean, violence and murder," continued Alistair to Zoe, "they just highlight how wonderful a place England is, left to the good. They are good people – all these parishioners, sidesmen, churchwardens, PCC members, what have you."

Zoe remained quiet, sensing that he wanted to get his thoughts off his chest.

Eventually she said, "You liked all those people at St Peter's and in and around Cookington, didn't you?"

"Yes, I've met some really nice old beans," he agreed.

"A whole row of them," she laughed.

He changed tack, "Do you realise, Zoe, that by asking Emma to go to the vicarage to keep an eye on things, you were responsible for Emma saving my life? And Emma not only saved my life by coming through those French windows and intercepting Sheila but, it sounds an extraordinary thing to say, she's kind of saved my soul too, and brought me to a new understanding about life – a new faith, even."

Zoe now began to stroke his hand, whispering, "Listen, darling, I don't mind if you're a Buddhist or a Confucian or whatever, just as long as we get married and you can invite all these good people to the wedding, and it can even be in a church if you want it, even here in St Peter's, Cookington, if your Presbyterian instincts allow."

"And we had better let Emma do the flower arranging," he replied, throwing his head back and laughing.

Then, catching sight of Helen Archer coming along the road, he pulled down the car window a bit further to be able to speak to her.

"Hi there, Helen! Where are you going, I wonder?" he inquired jokingly, recalling how she had said she felt under suspicion every time she went to the allotment.

"I'm just off to pick some more beans," she beamed back at him and jokingly stuck her tongue out.

"More?" he shouted with a laugh in his voice.

"Oh yes – just look at my row of beans over there; they're more prolific than ever this year," she replied, looking up at the bright blue sky, stretching her arms above her head and clapping her hands.

The tears came to Alistair's eyes. He had solved a crime; but more than this, he had found both his faith in mankind restored, and his faith in God.

Lightning Source UK Ltd.
Milton Keynes UK
UKHW012007290722
406581UK00002B/554